MOONLIGHT AVENUE

GERRI HILL

BELLA
B O O K S
2019

Bella Books, Inc.
P.O. Box 10543
Tallahassee, FL 32302

Printed in the United States of America on acid-free paper.

First Bella Books Edition 2019

Editor: Medora MacDougall
Cover Designer: Sandy Knowles

ISBN: 978-1-64247-027-7

Other Bella Books by Gerri Hill

Angel Fire
Artist's Dream
At Seventeen
Behind the Pine Curtain
Chasing a Brighter Blue
The Cottage
Coyote Sky
Dawn of Change
Devil's Rock
Gulf Breeze
Hell's Highway
Hunter's Way
In the Name of the Father
Keepers of the Cave
The Killing Room
The Locket
Love Waits
The Midnight Moon
The Neighbor
No Strings
One Summer Night
Paradox Valley
Partners
Pelican's Landing
The Rainbow Cedar
The Roundabout
The Secret Pond
Sawmill Springs
The Scorpion
Sierra City
Snow Falls
Storms
The Target
Weeping Walls

About the Author

Gerri Hill has thirty-five published works, including the 2017 GCLS winner *Paradox Valley*, 2014 GCLS winner *The Midnight Moon*, 2011, 2012 and 2013 winners *Devil's Rock*, *Hell's Highway* and *Snow Falls*, and the 2009 GCLS winner *Partners*, the last book in the popular Hunter Series, as well as the 2013 Lambda finalist *At Seventeen*.

Gerri lives in south-central Texas, only a few hours from the Gulf Coast, a place that has inspired many of her books. With her partner, Diane, they share their life with two Australian shepherds—Casey and Cooper—and a couple of furry felines.

For more, visit her website at gerrihill.com.

CHAPTER ONE

The office was dark and shadowy. She shifted in her chair, only now noticing the blackness that surrounded her. Without much thought, she reached over and flicked on the lamp that sat on the corner of the desk. She looked away from the light for a moment, blinking several times before reaching for the whiskey glass. It had been her father's. There really wasn't anything unique about it, other than it was his. The single malt scotch inside, however, made it special.

She heard shuffling upstairs and she looked overhead, knowing that Sammy would be down in a few minutes. She let out a heavy breath, then finished off the scotch. She should have left hours ago, but the splatter of rain against the windows had lulled her into a sense of peacefulness that was rare. She hadn't wanted to disturb it.

A few moments later, the door to her office opened, and Sammy stared at her. His wrinkled black face was hidden by the shadows, but his snow-white hair seemed to glow around him.

"Why, Finn…you still here?" he asked in his gravelly voice.

She pushed the chair back from her desk and stood. "Just about to leave."

"That means you missed dinner again," he said disapprovingly. "I had me some fried flounder. You should have come on up."

"Fried food's gonna kill you, Sammy."

He laughed. "Oh, hell…I'm eighty-two. Been eatin' fried fish my whole damn life. And most of it, I caught right out there in the bay."

She went over to him and touched his shoulder. "I've been out most of the day. I don't think there's any need for you to clean up tonight."

"Oh, I'll check the trash and run a vacuum, like always. Mr. Simon gets a little irritated if I don't tidy up over there on his side," he said, referring to the accountant who rented the other office. He tilted his head, eyeing her. "You got anything interesting going on? I was sitting by my window before the rain came. You had some man in here for quite a while."

"The usual. The guy thinks his wife is having an affair."

"You hate those," he said with a nod of his head. "Bad memories."

"Yeah. But they pay the bills." He followed her out into the reception area, and he helped her slip on her coat. She smiled at him. "I'll see you tomorrow, Sammy."

"The good Lord willing," he murmured quietly on cue.

The rain wasn't much more than a light mist now and she stood beside her car, looking up into the sky. There was a half-moon peeking out from behind a cloud, then it disappeared again. It was a cool, chilly night by Corpus Christi standards, especially for November. She unlocked her car with the push of a button. When the interior light came on, out of habit, she glanced in the back. She wasn't sure why, but she wouldn't be surprised to find someone hiding back there one day. She'd pissed off enough people in her line of work.

She drove down the dark street, aptly named Moonlight Avenue. There were no streetlights near her office. It was a dead-end road, and yes, moonlight was the only thing illuminating it. It was only four blocks from the bay and from the small cottage she called home. The cottage her father had left her. The cottage her mother never even knew existed.

Maybe it was the new client she'd taken on, but memories of that time in her life had come flooding back with distinct clarity. Eighteen years ago—it could have been only yesterday instead.

She had just graduated from college and was about to start law school. To this day, she still didn't know if her father's murder was what caused her to change her mind or not. They had it all planned. Law school, then she'd join her father's firm. They'd work side-by-side. Knight and Knight. Her father had been so proud of her. But after…well, after his death, she decided law school wasn't for her.

She shook her head as she pulled into her driveway, stopping as she waited for the gate to open. No, not law school. Would her father have been proud that she'd become a cop?

CHAPTER TWO

Mrs. Frazier disappeared into Kathy's Hair Salon and Finn noted the time, scribbling notes on the legal pad she used. She'd tried working on her laptop in the car but found her attention wavered too much. She preferred to make notes and records this way and transcribe everything later.

She put her camera down and picked up the small binoculars instead. Posters in the windows—pretty smiling women with chic haircuts—blocked her view, however, and she tossed them down as well.

She'd been thirty when she quit the force...only two years after making detective. At the time, becoming a private investigator hadn't crossed her mind. At least not consciously. But six months after working as a security guard, she'd quit that job too.

She leaned her head back, letting in old memories. They were memories she'd just as soon stay buried, but at times like this, when she sat idly in her car—waiting for the cheating wife or husband to show their hand—they crept in anyway.

She remembered the call, her mother's voice sounding almost calm, businesslike. "Finley, your father's been shot. They found him in his car. It apparently happened last night."

It all came out into the open then. Suspecting an affair all along, her father had hired a private investigator. Finn had been shocked. An *affair*? Her *mother*?

"It was your fault! You left home. Your father worked all the time. I was alone...*all the time*!"

"So maybe you should have gotten a job instead of a lover!" she'd shot back at her.

She shook her head. A *job*? Her mother? No. A lover? Yes. A man stupid enough to fall in love with her...a man stupid enough to kill when she wouldn't file for divorce.

Her mother still lived in Corpus. Still lived in the same house Finn had grown up in. A new man shared it with her now. Finn couldn't remember the last time she'd seen her. Fifteen years or more, she supposed.

The door to the hair salon opened and Mrs. Frazier came out. The woman paused to run a hand over her slightly shorter hair and Finn snapped two photos, then quickly lowered the camera when Mrs. Frazier's gaze drifted out over the parking lot. She shielded her eyes from the sun, as if looking for someone. Instead of getting into her metallic gray SUV, Mrs. Frazier walked down the sidewalk of the strip center. Once again she paused to glance around the parking lot. Finn knew the woman hadn't seen her. She was parked far enough away and her tinted windows provided the necessary cover that she needed. No...Mrs. Frazier was looking for someone.

When she ducked into the Tropical Tan and Massage, Finn looked around the parking lot too. A man emerged from a red sports car. Mid-forties, perhaps. A handsome man with dark hair, cut neat and short. Professional. Suit and tie. Shiny black shoes. She was about to dismiss him. She'd worked enough of these that she knew he didn't fit the profile. Mrs. Frazier, while not totally unattractive, was over fifty and a little on the plump side. This man moved with an athletic grace. Tall, shoulders squared, fashionable sunglasses hiding his eyes. He walked confidently into the Tropical Tan and Massage.

She shrugged. It hardly implicated him, but she snapped five or six shots of him before he disappeared inside. She jotted down the time—3:12—and location on her notepad, then shifted in her seat, trying to stretch her legs.

She wondered if her mother had ever hooked up at a place like this. She couldn't picture it, but you never know. Her mother had never offered an explanation for anything, never delved into the gory details of the affair with her. Of course she hadn't exactly been on speaking terms with her mother after the murder.

Her mother's lover, Richard "Dick" Falwell, had slipped into the backseat of her father's car, hiding on the floor behind the passenger's seat. What her mother had said was true: her father worked insane hours and was rarely home. That particular night was no exception. Dick Falwell popped up from his hiding place and held a gun to her father's head, making him drive to a secluded spot…a spot where Dick had stashed his car. He shot her father right there and that's where he was found, slumped over the steering wheel, a bullet hole in his head.

Even if the private investigator her father had hired hadn't come forward—her father had instructed him to go to the police if anything happened to him—Dick Falwell would have still been caught. He'd been stupid enough to leave prints on the outside of the car as well as the door handle on the inside. He'd apparently tossed the gun into one of the channels leading to the bay. It had never been recovered, but no need. The stupid son of a bitch didn't know there were security cameras at her father's firm. He had practically posed for the camera when he'd broken into the car.

Still, the trial was ugly and the defense had tried to implicate her mother, saying she'd suggested the murder. Finn would be lying if she said the thought hadn't crossed her mind as well, but her mother's reaction convinced her that Dick Falwell had done it all on his own. The jury believed that too.

She reached for her bottle of water and took a sip, then leaned her head back against the seat. Sleep had eluded her last night and she was feeling the effects of it now. Her stomach rumbled, letting her know that the lone piece of toast she'd had with her coffee that morning was long gone. From the backseat, she pulled the goody bag she kept with her at all times. When she unzipped it, however, she remembered she hadn't restocked it. There were two protein bars, a bag of salted peanuts, three warm water bottles, and an orange that had moldy spots on it. She pushed the orange aside—as she'd been doing for the last two weeks—and took one of the protein bars.

She'd only taken two bites when Mrs. Frazier came out. She had a definite smile on her face and Finn captured the dreamy look not once but three times before the woman headed toward her car. She kept the camera trained on the front door to the tanning salon, taking another photo when the guy came out only seconds later. He was adjusting his tie as he hurried toward the red sports car.

Finn looked between the two cars, but the guy never once glanced toward Mrs. Frazier and she didn't look his way. As the sports car pulled away, Finn zoomed in on his license plate, snapping a clear picture. She then started up her car, waiting until Mrs. Frazier got ahead of her before following. Connie Frazier retraced the same route she'd taken that morning, back to her house. Finn drove past the street, slowing enough to verify that Mrs. Frazier had indeed pulled into the driveway. It was 3:51.

"That was a quickie," she murmured as she drove past.

Instead of heading back to her office, she turned toward the bay and home. She was tired and hungry. Her little cottage was at the end of Ocean Drive where Corpus Christi Bay swallowed it up. It wasn't really all that little—twenty-two hundred square feet—but compared to her neighbors' homes, it was tiny and dated. But it suited her fine.

She pushed the remote for the automatic gate—something she'd added about six years ago when she'd installed her security system—then drove up the short driveway to the garage, waiting patiently as the door opened. She disappeared inside and closed the door...hoping to shut out the world for the rest of the day...and night.

CHAPTER THREE

"Mr. Frazier, like I said, when I have something, you'll have something. I'm not going to update you on every little thing she does."

"But I want to know if—"

"I'll hand over my report at the end of the week like we agreed." She paused. "And I hope you complimented her on her haircut."

"What?"

"Never mind. I'll be in touch."

Was that how her mother had felt? Had she changed hairstyles, only to have her husband not notice? Had he come home after working fifteen or more hours to find dinner long cold and her mother already in bed? Had he gotten up early the next day to do it all over again while her mother slept in?

According to Mr. Frazier—owner of four pizza parlors in the city—his wife rarely got out of bed until after nine. It was a quarter of nine now and she'd have to hurry. She only hoped that it wasn't a repeat of yesterday. Finn was in no mood to stake out their house for half the day before there was any activity.

She pocketed her keys and was headed out when Simon opened the door that joined their two offices.

"You got a minute?"

She shook her head. "Not really. What's up?"

He looked around as if making sure they were alone, then came closer. "It's about Sammy."

"What about him? Is he okay?"

"No, no. He's fine. It's about his cleaning. Or lack thereof."

"Simon, come on, he's eighty-two years old. Cut him some slack."

"Yes, I know. But my wife came over yesterday and said the place was filthy. I meet clients here, Finn. I can't have them—"

"What do you want me to do?"

"Hire a real cleaning crew."

She shook her head. "Sammy does the cleaning."

"Look, you own the building. You're responsible for cleaning. Our agreement—"

"Simon, you've been here what? Five, six years? Sammy does the cleaning."

"But—"

"I gotta run." She paused at the front door. "Unless you want me to up your rent enough to cover a cleaning crew. That can be arranged."

She closed the door without waiting for an answer. They had this same discussion a couple of times a year. And it usually started with "my wife came over."

Simon was fifty-one or -two and looked the part of a stereotypical accountant—thinning hair, pale skin, thick, black-framed glasses, and a wardrobe that was decades out of style. And Karen, his nagging wife, ruled the house with an iron fist. Now that the kids were grown and had moved away, all her attention was directed at Simon. And poor Simon didn't have the balls to buck her.

"Not my problem," she muttered.

As she sat in her car—a charcoal gray luxury sedan that blended in—two blocks down from the Fraziers' house, she wondered if she needed to talk to Sammy. Maybe remind him to clean a little more thoroughly in Simon's office.

Sammy had been with her since she'd moved into the old building and converted it into two office suites. The apartment upstairs had already been there and she'd intended to rent it out. She figured a renter upstairs and a renter for the adjacent office would more than cover any expenses she had on the remodeling. But then Sammy had showed up on her doorstep one day, begging for a handout. Not exactly a handout. He'd offered to do light labor for either a meal or money.

His hair had been as snow white then as it was today. His face was wrinkled from hours and hours spent in the bay...fishing. But he'd fallen on hard times since his wife had died. He had three kids, he said, but she'd known him now nearly ten years and she'd never met a one of them. She wondered if they even knew where he was. He'd been homeless for two years when she'd met him. She'd taken an instant liking to the old man.

A week later she'd moved him into the apartment upstairs. As Simon had said, his cleaning skills could use some honing, but he kept the place tidy enough. And they shared meals from time to time. But mostly, they shared memories. She knew as much about his life as he knew about hers.

So, no, she wouldn't talk to him. He was a proud man, and she knew he would feel like he'd let her down if she said anything to him. No, she wouldn't worry him with something as trivial as that.

In fact, she might invite him over to her house for fishing soon. He still walked to the bay most days, but she knew he loved it when she asked him over. They had her long fishing pier all to themselves—providing her neighbor, Larry, didn't come over to join them—and they'd spend the afternoon drinking beer and telling fish tales. They hadn't done that in many months, she knew.

Without much thought, she picked up her camera when Mrs. Frazier's car backed out of her driveway. She snapped a couple of shots, then glanced at the clock. It was 10:12.

CHAPTER FOUR

"What have we here?"

After following Mrs. Frazier across the causeway and onto Mustang Island, she was actually surprised when she pulled into the parking lot of a Best Western. Mrs. Frazier drove past the office—as if she'd done this before—and parked opposite the swimming pool. Still, she wasn't hidden from the traffic on Park Road 22. Apparently she didn't fear her husband catching her here, despite one of his pizza joints—the original one—being just down the street.

Finn slowed, letting Mrs. Frazier get out before pulling into a spot only three cars from her own. The woman didn't bother to look around as she hurried to a door directly across from where she was parked. A quick knock and the door opened.

"Gotcha now," Finn murmured as her camera captured the smiling face of the man she'd seen yesterday. The door closed and she snapped a shot of the room number: 113.

Finn was smiling as she lowered the camera. She loved it when cases like this wrapped up in a couple of days. At two hundred dollars an hour, she figured she could bill him for two thousand, depending on how big Mrs. Frazier's smile was when she came out of the room.

She backed the car up, then parked across from the room, next to the pool. She still had a clear view of room 113 and she settled down to wait. She lowered both windows in front and stretched her legs out as far as they would go.

Her mother hadn't used a hotel. There had been no need to. Her father was never home. Dick came right to the house. According to the private investigator, he popped over four, sometimes five days a week.

Back then, her mother had been an attractive woman. Still was, she supposed. Long, flowing blond hair, she looked years younger than she was. When Finn was a teen, she'd often wished she looked more like her mother. She'd gotten her father's dark hair and on more occasions than she could recall, her mother often commented that she'd gotten his handsome face as well.

She looked in the mirror now, seeing the beginnings of laugh lines around her eyes. That was funny, wasn't it? She rarely laughed.

"Let's call them what they are, Finn," she murmured. Wrinkles. Yes, she was forty years old and sporting wrinkles now. And there were a few rogue gray hairs popping up too.

She fingered her hair. It was longer than she usually kept it. Long and a bit on the shaggy side now. Not intentional—her new hairstyle. She simply hadn't had the time—or inclination—to get it cut. Perhaps she should have joined Mrs. Frazier at Kathy's yesterday, she thought wryly.

She glanced at herself in the mirror again. No, she rarely laughed. What was there to laugh about? Her father was long gone. Her only friends consisted of Sammy, an eighty-two-year-old black man, and Larry, the nosy neighbor who she'd learned to tolerate over the years. Larry was older, too. In his seventies. His wife died the very year Finn had moved next door. Larry liked to fish and when Finn wasn't working, she'd either join him on his pier or he'd join her. Larry liked to drink rum and usually by three he was holding a cocktail in his hand. They'd sit out on the pier, him with his rum, she with her scotch, and fish until dark. She imagined he was as lonely as she was.

She'd quit the force at thirty because of the envelope. Well, that was what she'd told herself anyway. She'd made detective and thought she was happy. Happier than being in uniform, that's for sure. But...well, she had a hard time following rules...orders...protocol. She glanced in the mirror again, giving herself a smirk. Yeah. Undisciplined, her captain had called her on more than one occasion.

He came to the squad room one hot and humid day in August—the PI who her father had hired. He held a large manila envelope in his hands. Eight years after her father had been murdered...two days after her thirtieth birthday. She resigned from the Corpus Christi Police Department the very next day.

She blew out her breath. Ten years ago now. *Funny how life takes you places*, she thought. Places she never dreamed she'd go. Like sitting here now outside the Best Western, waiting on Mrs. Frazier to have sex so she could snap a picture of her coming out of the room with a smile on her face.

The envelope had her name scrawled across the front—her father's handwriting—and a date...the day that Mr. Granger showed up out of the blue. She hadn't seen him—or given him much thought—since the trial. She'd taken the envelope home with her, to her apartment. She remembered placing it on the table, almost afraid to open it. She'd drunk two beers before she felt calm enough to touch it.

The envelope was thick and heavy, taped shut, and it took her several seconds to tear into it. She dumped the contents out onto the table. A wad of cash—twenty thousand dollars—caught her attention first. Then the keys. Three of them, taped neatly to a piece of paper. She picked up a folded note, on stationery that she remembered from her father's office. Again, it was his handwriting and she simply stared at it for the longest time before reading what he had to say.

He'd suspected an affair for years. Richard Falwell probably wasn't the first one, he'd said. He wrote the note the day before he was killed. The next day, he'd planned to confront them. However, the next day—that fateful day—he never got the chance to do that. Dick Falwell confronted him first.

One of the keys was to the cottage on Ocean Drive. The cottage was in her name—had been all along—and a management company was taking care of it. She'd driven out there the next morning and had returned to give her apartment complex notice that she'd be moving out. She'd moved into the fully furnished house three days later. And a day after that, she'd gotten drunk on her ass, sitting down at the end of the pier. She shook her head now. It's a wonder she hadn't fallen into the bay and drowned. That would have been a fitting end, wouldn't it?

A slamming door brought her attention around and she reached for the camera even before she looked up. But it wasn't Mrs. Frazier and she relaxed again. It was now after eleven—11:06. At least this wasn't a quickie like yesterday's had been. Of course, the only evidence of sex yesterday was the dreamy smile Mrs. Frazier had sported as she'd left the tanning place.

The plates on the red sports car were registered to Michael R. Drake. Best she could tell, Michael R. Drake didn't have a job. In fact, she could find very little on him. It didn't take a rocket scientist to figure out that Michael R. Drake was using a fake identity. She'd run the VIN number on his car. It had been purchased two months prior, paid for in cash. No trail to follow there. She guessed the car—while not brand new—still set him back a good twenty or twenty-five grand.

She hadn't spent much time on him. Mr. Frazier was paying her to find out if his wife was having an affair and with whom. If he wanted detailed info on Drake, it would cost him more. She didn't care one way or the other. She wasn't getting paid to care.

She reached into the backseat and grabbed her goody bag. She'd remembered to add a few things to it that she'd had at the house. She forgot to take out the orange, though, and she moved the nearly spoiled fruit aside again as her fingers closed around a package of peanut butter crackers. She really needed to start eating better. Actually, she needed to just start eating. She was getting too old to exist on junk food and scotch...with the occasional fish dinner tossed in, either with Larry or Sammy.

Maybe she should find a friend to have dinner with. A friend. Nothing more. She didn't have the time or energy—or desire— to devote to anything else. It had been too many years since she'd actually dated anyone. Too many years for her to even remember how the process worked. When the image of a young blonde popped into her mind, she wasn't really surprised, though. How long ago was that? Summer? June? No, she was no longer surprised to find herself thinking of the woman. She'd drifted in and out of her mind often in the last six months...drifting by, sometimes just under the surface, sometimes out front. And sometimes the memory hung around for a day or two before sneaking away again.

She rarely went to bars. She certainly never picked up women at bars. She was far too careful for that. For some reason, that particular night, she hadn't been in the mood for only her own company. She'd gone to the bar intending to have a couple of drinks and be around people for a change. She'd been sitting on a barstool, sipping her drink, her foot tapping unconsciously to the music, when she looked up, locking eyes with a woman. It was as if—with just that one look— the woman had stolen her breath away. She remembered thinking how crazy that was for a woman her age...a woman about to turn forty. It wasn't even a conscious thought that had her up and moving, going to the younger woman. She asked her to dance, her voice nearly stuttering with nervousness. They didn't talk much at all; they didn't even exchange names. One dance led to two. She still wasn't sure who initiated the first kiss between them. She shook her head now. It had been a stupid thing to do. The woman was probably barely twenty-five and Finn knew she was too damn old to be acting like a hormone-crazed teen. Yet she found herself pressed against the wall, blatantly making out with the woman. Fevered kisses and bold touches finally caused someone to yell at them to "get a room." She had been shocked to realize that she wanted to do just that. But she came to her senses. She certainly wasn't going to take a stranger to her home.

The woman had looked at her, her blue eyes still dark and aroused. She looked almost embarrassed by their earlier actions, but her gaze never wavered.

"Yes…let's go somewhere. If you want."

Yes, Finn wanted. So they got a room. And what a night it had been. She didn't remember talking…at all. She glanced up to meet her eyes in the car mirror. One-night stands being what they were, the woman was gone the next morning when she woke up. She called a friend to pick her up, Finn supposed. Or maybe she called Uber. Regardless, Finn had been shocked by the whole encounter. It was something she never did. It took her a while to get over it and she'd been surprised at how often—especially at first—the young woman crossed her mind. She never went back to the bar, but that's not to say she didn't *consider* going back, perhaps hoping she'd spot the blonde again. But that wasn't her style. She gave a quick, humorless laugh now. Did she have a style?

She rolled her shoulders around, staring at the door to Room 113. Was Connie Frazier having a good time with the so-called Michael Drake? Was she screaming his name? Did she feel guilty? Or was she reveling in the thrill of it all? Did she have any idea that her husband was suspicious?

She took a bite of the cracker. She hoped Connie was enjoying herself. Finn suspected that by the weekend, the affair would be all over with. Or else Mr. Frazier would have started divorce proceedings.

She rested her head back against the seat, letting her mind drift away from the Fraziers. The second key in the envelope had been to a safe deposit box…a box secured in her name, not her father's. Inside were records of investments that he'd made—also in her name. Some more recent, others made when Finn had been a child. There was a sizeable life insurance policy, payable to Finn when she turned thirty. In there as well was yet another key, unmarked and untagged. She had no idea what it went to. She still didn't. She took it and everything else that was in the box. It was all hers, after all. There was no mention of her mother on any of the records.

Her father's note had been very businesslike and to the point, not emotional in the least. She assumed that at the time he had been writing it, he had no inkling that he would die the next day. Still, she wondered if he had some premonition. Something must have made him write the note and leave the envelope with Mr. Granger. Something must have made him transfer a lot of his assets into her name, unbeknownst to her mother.

She never mentioned the envelope—or the money or the investments—to her mother. Not that she had an opportunity to. It wasn't like they saw each other. Her mother called on occasion, she'd give her that. Despite Finn's cold reception to her calls, her mother ignored her tone and chatted away, filling Finn in on what was happening in her life.

Most of which Finn already knew. In spite of them being estranged, Finn still kept tabs on her. When she'd found out her mother was engaged to be married, Finn had done a thorough investigation of the guy. She couldn't find any dirt on him. She wondered if she had, would she have warned her mother?

Her camera was at her eye and she was snapping shots even before it registered that Mrs. Frazier had opened the door to Room 113. Smiling? Oh, yeah. Connie Frazier was practically floating to her car. She zoomed in to the open door, seeing Michael R. Drake with a smile on his face too. She frowned as that smile completely disappeared seconds before he closed the door.

She put the camera down. It was 11:46.

CHAPTER FIVE

Finn sloshed the amber liquid in her glass…her father's glass. She should go home. She had the report all ready for Mr. Frazier. After following Connie Frazier back to her house, Finn had called it good and had stopped for a burger, which she brought back to the office to eat. She'd brought one for Sammy, too, but he hadn't been upstairs. Two hours later, he'd come ambling in, dressed in his fishing garb. He had one nice-sized speckled trout in his bag, but he'd snatched up the burger all the same, grinning his thanks as he closed her office door.

Eighty-two years old and he still managed to make the trek to the bay, four blocks away. She doubted anyone would guess his age. He was still spry and walked with a youthful grace, his shoulders square, not hunched. She'd told him more than once that he was her inspiration for growing old. He'd then told her that she needed to start taking better care of herself. Then he'd smiled impishly. Or get some cute young woman to take care of her, he'd said. She'd been surprised. They'd never once discussed her personal life. She'd never mentioned to him that she was gay. Why would she? The last ten years, the few times she'd slept with someone…there was never any need to tell Sammy about it. Certainly not the last time—the woman from the bar.

She opened her desk drawer and pulled out the key. The key. The key that had been in the safe deposit box...the unmarked, unclaimed key. She twirled it around in her fingers, wondering how many hundreds—thousands—of times she'd done that in the last ten years. She'd racked her brain trying to think of things it might go to. There were no markings on it. It was a copy of a key. She assumed the original had either been in his office or home. Had her mother even bothered keeping his things?

Why had he left the key in the safe deposit box? Why had he left three keys in the envelope and not all four? Well, the likely reason was because this fourth key had been in the safe deposit box at the time of him writing the note and the other three keys had already been in his possession.

The final key in the envelope had been to the front door of this old building. She never knew why her father had bought it or why he'd purchased it in her name twenty-odd years ago when she'd first started college. It wasn't exactly in the part of town where a prestigious law firm would be located, so that wasn't it. And of course, at the time, she had no aspirations of having her own office. Three months after she'd received the envelope, she realized she was too young—and too bored—to not have a job. Law enforcement was her only skill, so she did the next best thing—she got a job as a security guard. That had lasted all of six months. Another four months went by before she decided to open her own agency. An agency with one private investigator—her—and no receptionist or assistant. Moonlight Avenue Investigations.

She'd almost taken her father's idea—Knight and Knight. Or simply Finley Knight Investigations. But in the end, she chose to keep it more ambiguous. Whether it was the prospect of her mother finding out or not, she wasn't sure. To this day, she still didn't know if her mother knew of her profession or not.

She downed the last of the scotch, pausing to savor it before swallowing. She'd already heard Sammy creeping down the stairs and she didn't want to put him behind on his cleaning. She opened her office door just as he pulled the vacuum out of the hall closet.

"That burger won't hold you all night," he said. "Best stop for something on your way home."

"What makes you think there's nothing at my house to eat?"

He laughed. "Oh, Finn, I've seen your fridge. You're getting too damn skinny." He shook his finger at her. "I told you, you need to start taking better care of yourself. You're not a spring chicken anymore, you know."

"Don't remind me." She touched his shoulder affectionately. "I'll see you tomorrow."

"Good Lord willing," he murmured with a smile.

The breeze off the bay made the air damp and cold. It wasn't unpleasant though. She paused at her car, looking up into the dark sky, seeing a few stars twinkling overhead. The feel of the breeze, the salty scent of the air…both familiar. She'd been born and raised in Corpus. After her father was killed, she'd thought about moving. College was over. She had her degree. She could go anywhere and start over. But this was home.

Out of habit, she glanced into the backseat of her car, then got inside. Was she sorry she hadn't moved? If she had to do it over again, would she? She started up the car. She had no friends. She had no lover. She had no family. She took a deep breath, then stared out onto the dark street of Moonlight Avenue. There was Sammy. He was her friend. He was her family. A ghost of a smile lit her face, then disappeared quickly.

With a sigh, she drove off. Sammy was right. There was nothing in her fridge except a few bottles of beer and perhaps a couple of bottles of water and a butter dish that was empty. Her freezer contained a handful of tasteless frozen dinners that had been in there for more months than she could recall. Grocery shopping—cooking—wasn't really her thing. Instead of taking Ocean Drive to her house, she headed into the city. It seemed like a nice night for seafood.

CHAPTER SIX

Mr. Frazier was a small man. She stood at five seven. He was at least two inches shorter than she was. He read through the report silently. Finn watched his expression, his brows drawing together occasionally, a quick nod here and there. Then he scratched the side of his head absently, his eyes no longer on the pages she'd given him.

"So it's true? She's having an affair? With *this* guy?"

"Appears that way. I wasn't actually in the room with them."

He looked her square in the eyes. "I'm paying you a handsome fee. Is she sleeping with this guy or not?"

She blew out a breath. Why did they always want *her* to confirm what the pictures showed? "I've been in the business long enough... yeah, she's having an affair. But then again, he could be teaching her to do the tango or something."

"Yeah, right. At a massage parlor? At a hotel?"

"Unless you put a camera in the room or catch them in the act, this is all I got. They're being careful, that's for sure. Maybe this is new. Maybe that's why they're being so cautious. A couple of weeks from now, maybe they'll slip up. Or maybe she'll invite him to your house, to your bed."

He stared at one of the photos she'd included, then held it up. "*This* guy?"

She motioned to the pages he held. "Drake. Michael R. Drake."

"Drake, huh?"

"That's all I got."

"That's it?"

"You didn't pay me to find out about him. You paid me to do surveillance on your wife."

"So I did."

He paced in front of her desk, an odd expression on his face. It wasn't anger, which is what she would have expected. And it wasn't shock. But why would it be? He'd already suspected an affair.

"So he hasn't been to my house yet?"

"No. At least not since I've been on the job. I would assume if he's been to your house, there'd be no need for the Best Western."

He folded up the pages that he held. "These are mine, right?"

"Yes. I also have an electronic copy for you."

"I don't need it. What do I owe you, Ms. Knight?"

"With the five hundred dollar retaining fee applied, fifteen hundred and ten."

He was muttering to himself as he signed his check. She remained silent. After all these years, she still didn't know how—or if—to console them.

He handed the check over and she took it from him. "Nice doing business with you, Mr. Frazier. May I offer some advice?"

He stared at her questioningly.

"Take a day or two to cool off. You might do something you're going to regret."

His smile was forced. "Oh, you have no idea."

He left quickly and she tried not to think about what lay in store for Connie Frazier. She always hated this part of the job...having to tell someone their spouse was cheating on them. When it was women, they'd sit across from her and cry and she'd have to offer meaningless soothing words to them as she handed over the box of tissue. Men? Quite the opposite. Never tears. Always anger, with revenge on the brain. She wasn't sure which she hated more.

But then again, it wasn't anger that she'd seen on Daniel Frazier's face.

CHAPTER SEVEN

Dee Woodard covered her mouth as she yawned, taking a quick glance up into the dreary gray sky. The breeze off the bay was cold and she barely resisted turning up the collar of her jacket to ward off the chill.

"Man, I hate these early morning calls," complained her partner, Joel Yearwood. "I didn't even get coffee."

"I did. And it's not that early." She looked at her watch. Seven thirty. She'd been up since five. Another sleepless night—she was actually thankful for the call.

"There won't be any evidence, you know. Even if the body wasn't washed up with the tide, it'll still be contaminated. On top of that, it's going to rain like any second now."

"Quit complaining," she said as they trudged through the sand toward the pier.

"It's just…Jordie was over. Still sleeping when I left."

"Oh, yeah? I thought she dumped your ass," she teased as she nudged his shoulder.

"So did I. She said she missed me. Go figure."

"She doesn't miss the hours you keep. Wasn't that the source of contention between you?"

"Yeah, she hates my job. Afraid I'm going to get shot."

The body was lying face down in the sand. Dark hair was matted with blood. Dee nodded at the two officers who stood watch.

"Detectives," one greeted. "Hard to tell if the tide washed him up or if he was dumped right here."

She squatted down beside the body, already putting on her gloves. "There's still blood. I don't imagine he was out in the gulf."

Joel put on gloves too and bent over, moving the hair aside. "Single shot looks like."

"Small caliber, not much damage," she murmured. She looked up at the officers. "Who found him?"

"An older couple doing a little shell hunting," one said. "Found him at first light. We got their information, then sent them on their way."

She nodded as she patted the tops of his pockets, looking for a wallet or a phone. His pockets appeared empty, but the jeans were soaked and the denim was heavy. She reached inside the front right pocket and pulled out a business card. She glanced at it, then handed it to Joel. "Nothing else."

"Moonlight Avenue Investigations," he read. "Private eye?"

She shrugged and took the card from him. "I'll check it out. You can wait for the ME."

"Oh, come on, Dee. I don't want to sit out here any more than you do."

She gave him a fake smile and touched his cheek, slapping it gently. "But you're the man. Isn't that what you always tell me? You're the man."

He grinned. "Yeah. When it suits me."

She nodded. "Yeah. Typical. I'll let you know what I turn up."

* * *

The buzzer rang, signaling that someone was at the front door. Finn pushed away from her desk and stood, wondering again why she'd never bothered to hire a receptionist. She walked out into the entryway, seeing the fuzzy shadow of a person through the tinted glass.

She opened the door, coming face-to-face with a woman perhaps a few years older than she was, light brown hair just brushing the top of her shoulders. Finn wouldn't swear on it, but the woman's demeanor screamed "cop" loud and clear.

"I'm Finley Knight. May I help you?"

The woman opened her jacket a little at the waist, showing Finn her shield and duty gun. It appeared to be a Glock, much like the one she carried. Finn nodded, flicking her gaze back to the woman's face.

"I'm Detective Woodard. Just need to ask you a few questions."

Finn raised her eyebrows. "About?"

Detective Woodard looked past her. "May we go inside?"

With a sigh, Finn stepped aside and let the detective in. She closed the door, then headed back to her office, Detective Woodard following close behind.

Finn motioned to one of the chairs, then sat down behind her desk. "What can I do for you?"

The detective placed an evidence bag on her desk. Inside the clear plastic was a business card. Her card. It was quite rumpled and appeared to be wet. She raised an eyebrow but said nothing.

"That's yours, I'm assuming?"

"Seeing as how the sign on my door says Moonlight Avenue Investigations…"

"I guess what I'm asking is, are there other investigators here beside yourself, Ms. Knight?"

She shook her head. "Just me." She glanced pointedly at the card. "Is it significant?"

"There was a body found under the Packery Channel Pier this morning. No ID. Nothing found except your business card."

"I see." Finn tried to keep her expression even as Detective Woodard stared at her. She gave her business card out all the time. It could be from anyone. Although she wouldn't be surprised to learn that Daniel Frazier actually killed Michael Drake. But why leave her card on the body? No. It made no sense.

"Do you have any idea whose this was?"

Finn shook her head. "It could be anyone. Do you have a description?"

"Dark hair, middle-aged man. Fifties. Five six or so."

Not Michael Drake, Finn thought. He was mid-forties, at least five ten, maybe closer to six-foot tall. The detective's cell phone rang and she pulled it off a clip that was attached to her belt.

"Excuse me."

Finn watched her as she listened, nodding slightly at whoever was talking in her ear.

"Got it. Thanks." She clipped the phone back without looking. "Do you know a Mr. Daniel Frazier?"

She nodded. "I do."

"He's a client? He hired you, I'm assuming."

"He did."

"In what capacity?"

Finn shook her head. "I'm sorry, Detective. That's private and confidential."

"He had a single gunshot wound to the head. Small caliber. Either killed right there at Packery Channel Pier or dumped there. A couple found him on the beach at daybreak."

At that, Finn was certain she did show surprise on her face. "Daniel Frazier was the body you found on the beach?" *Michael Drake, sure.* She even wouldn't have been shocked to learn that Connie Frazier was dead. But Daniel? "I'm sorry to hear that."

Detective Woodard raised her eyebrows. "That's it?"

She leaned forward slightly. "Look, we both know how this is going to play out. You're going to have to get a subpoena and then I'll have to hand over my file. No need to waste time arguing about it."

"Subpoenas take time, Ms. Knight. Murder cases grow cold very quickly." Detective Woodard gave her a flirty smile. "Just a little help is all I'm asking."

If there was one thing Finn prided herself on, it was sticking to her principles. Her clients expected privacy. That was something she never wavered on. She leaned back in her chair, meeting the light brown eyes of Detective Woodard. Yes, she was attractive. And there was no ring on her finger. But...

"I'm sorry, Detective. I have my reputation to think about."

The flirty smile disappeared quickly. "When did you last see him?"

"Yesterday morning. He left here a few minutes before eleven."

"How much contact had you had with him?"

"I met with him twice and spoke on the phone once."

"So he wasn't a regular client?"

"No."

"And what is it that you specialize in, Ms. Knight?"

Finn smiled at her attempt to garner information. "I specialize in a lot of things, Detective Woodard. Perhaps if we got to know each other better, I could show you."

The detective arched an eyebrow. "Perhaps if you played nice, that could be arranged."

Finn laughed. "Come back with a subpoena, Detective. I'll play nice then."

But when Detective Woodard left her office, Finn's smile faded. What in the world had Daniel Frazier done to get himself killed? Was she somehow to blame?

She shook her head. No. He hired her for a service. What he did with the information she gave him was not her concern. She assumed he would confront his wife, sure. But what if he confronted Michael Drake instead? Again, she shook her head. How would he even find Michael Drake? Unless he followed his wife yesterday and found them together, he would have no way of locating him. Finn hadn't given him Drake's address.

She stared at the wall, remembering the look on Michael Drake's face when Connie had left the motel room. A smile on his face that disappeared so quickly it was as if it was never there to begin with. What would a man like Michael Drake—a handsome, dashing man— be doing having an affair with the rather plain, somewhat plump, Connie Frazier?

CHAPTER EIGHT

Finn knew she should leave it alone. It wasn't her deal. And when Detective Woodard came around with the subpoena, it really would be out of her hands. But until then…she felt like she owed Daniel Frazier something. Surely it wasn't a coincidence that he was killed only hours after receiving her report on his cheating wife. She was, of course, already blaming Michael Drake. The similarities between this case and her father's murder were eerily alike…that wasn't lost on her. Perhaps that was why she felt compelled to delve into Michael Drake's business.

She was finding, however, that there wasn't much business to delve into. Besides the car purchase—the red sports car—the only other hits on his name were a few sporadic credit card charges, all within the last two months. Which made her think that Michael R. Drake was created for the sole purpose of buying a flashy car to help seduce Connie Frazier.

But why?

She leaned back in her chair, again seeing the smile disappearing from Drake's face when he closed the door to Room 113. So why an affair? What was Drake hoping to gain? Was the affair more about Daniel Frazier than it was his wife?

Her office phone rang and with those questions still bouncing around in her head, she answered offhandedly.

"Moonlight Avenue Investigations."

"Yes…Daniel Frazier…he was a client of yours?"

The male voice was deep with a slight accent. She frowned at his question.

"Excuse me?"

"Daniel Frazier," he said again.

"Who are you?"

The call ended and she stared at it for several seconds before hanging up. What the hell was that about? She leaned back in her chair, trying to memorize the voice. The accent was so slight, there almost was no accent…yet there was. She had a nagging suspicion the voice belonged to Michael Drake.

Whoever he was.

The buzzer on the front door sounded and with a sigh, she got up and went out into the reception area. She recognized the shape of Detective Woodard through the stained glass. She opened the door with a smile.

"That was quick, Detective. Less than twenty-four hours."

The smile Detective Woodard gave her appeared to be genuine. "I don't like to waste time."

Finn stepped back, letting the detective inside. "I guess that means I should stop snooping around then, huh?"

"Snooping around?"

She had already printed out copies of the file, assuming Detective Woodard would come around sooner rather than later. She handed the file over to her.

"Michael R. Drake is the man having an affair with Frazier's wife. As far as I can tell, he's only existed for two months. No history on him."

Detective Woodard was looking intently at one of the photos of Drake. "Good-looking guy."

"Well, if you like that sort of thing."

Woodard looked up and met her eyes. "There are some that do, I guess." She then picked up a photo of Connie Frazier. "I met with her yesterday, after I spoke with you. She was pretty distraught."

"Never mentioned an affair, huh?"

"No, that must have slipped her mind." She held the photo toward Finn. "What attracted him to her, you think?"

Finn was about to share her own theory on it but decided not to. The police could do their own digging, just as she had.

"Yes, I thought they made an odd pair."

The detective put the photos back in the file and stood. "Well, thank you, Ms. Knight."

"Finley," she corrected as she walked her out. "Or Finn. I haven't been called Finley since I was a kid."

Another genuine smile. "And when I'm not Detective Woodard, my friends call me Dee."

Finn nodded. "If you have any questions, I'll be happy to assist."

"Funny, you weren't this accommodating yesterday."

"Yesterday you didn't have a subpoena."

Dee Woodard paused at the outer door. "How long have you been in this profession?"

"Ten years, give or take."

She held up the file. "You do a lot of cases like this?"

"My share, yes."

The detective nodded. "Well, thank you again…Finn."

Finn also nodded. "My pleasure…Dee."

She closed the door as Dee Woodard walked away. Finn guessed her age to be forty-five or so. And she had a rather flirty smile. She wondered how long she'd been a detective. Even though it had been ten years since Finn was on the force, occasionally she still ran into officers who she'd worked with. Dee Woodard's name didn't ring a bell.

Didn't matter. She'd probably never see Detective Woodard again.

CHAPTER NINE

"There's nothing on him? *Nothing?*" Dee asked incredulously. The file that Finley Knight had turned over to her had been rather void of any information on Michael R. Drake. Of course, Finn had warned as much.

"Nothing much more than what the PI gave you. Got some credit card charges at a couple of local restaurants. Got a charge at the Best Western where these shots were taken," Joel said, pointing at the photos of Connie Frazier and Michael Drake.

"Well, I guess we need to pay Mrs. Frazier another visit then."

Unlike yesterday, though, there were four other cars in the driveway of the Fraziers' house. Family, no doubt. Or someone from the pizza chain. Daniel Frazier's Pizza Jamboree—with their all-you-can-eat lunches—had been a mainstay in Corpus for the last fifteen years. Or so she was told. She'd only moved to the area nine years ago. She and Joel had taken advantage of their lunch specials on more than a few occasions.

"You think we should wait? Maybe a couple of more days until after the funeral," Joel suggested.

Dee shook her head as she got out of the car. "Don't be ridiculous. We're investigating a murder. For all we know, the wife is involved."

"I don't think so, Dee. She was a wreck yesterday. She can't be that good of an actress."

Joel was young, barely thirty. When Captain Mabanks had partnered them, she'd balked initially. She was too old to be teaching some young gun the ropes. At first, Joel hadn't been receptive to her opinions and direction. And they'd clashed...big-time. But it didn't take long for him to realize that her experience far outweighed his exuberance. The fact he'd been shot after ignoring her command that he give up a chase hadn't hurt. After that—and after a firm lecture from Captain Mabanks—he'd settled down a bit. Now, a year later, he was almost too conservative.

"How about you let me do the talking?" she said as she rang the doorbell. She tucked the file she held under her arm and waited. But it wasn't Connie Frazier who opened the door. A young woman, mid-twenties, stood there, a questioning gaze leveled at them.

"Sorry to intrude," she said, holding her jacket to the side to reveal her gold shield. "I'm Detective Woodard, this is Detective Yearwood. We need a word with Mrs. Frazier."

The woman came out onto the front porch. "Now's not a good time. Her kids just got here. Aunt Connie's not...she's not handling this too well."

No, Dee imagined not. She was most likely eaten up with guilt. Well...too bad. She met the woman's gaze directly. "It'll just take a minute. It's very important. We have some new information we need to share with her."

The woman nodded. "Okay. I'll let her know. Please wait here."

"Of course."

As soon as the door was closed, Joel turned to her. "I told you we should have waited. If she's crying like she was yesterday, we'll get nothing out of her."

"Yes, we will."

A few minutes later, a teary and red-nosed Connie Frazier opened the door, a tissue clutched tightly in her hand.

"She said...she said you had some new information. Do you know who killed Dan?"

Dee met her eyes, refusing to be swayed by the tears. "Who is Michael Drake?"

Connie frowned and shook her head. "I...I don't know anyone by that name."

Dee took the manila folder from under her arm and pulled out one of the photos that Finley Knight had supplied. She held it up to

Connie Frazier. Connie gasped and covered her mouth with the hand that held the tissue. She turned wide eyes to Dee.

"How did you…how did you get this? I mean…" She shook her head. "I don't know who he is."

"Too late for that, Mrs. Frazier. Your husband suspected an affair. He hired a private investigator to follow you." She held up another photo, this one of Connie coming out of Room 113 of the Best Western. "Who is he?" she asked again.

Tears filled Connie Frazier's eyes and her shoulders began to shake. Joel shifted uneasily beside her. Dee blew out her breath.

"So you're having an affair with this guy. The plates on his red sports car come back to Michael Drake. Where can we find him?"

Connie Frazier shook her head. "No…no. He's…he's Mark Condra. I met him…" She paused to wipe her nose. "I met him a couple of months ago."

"So where can I find Mark Condra? Where does he live?"

"Live?"

"Yes. The address we found for him is fake."

Connie shook her head. "I don't…I don't know where he lived. We never went to his place."

"Where did you first meet him?" Joel asked.

Connie looked at him, her lower lip trembling. "At…at the grocery store. He was…he was so handsome and he was flirting with me." A ghost of a smile touched her face. "Me…he was flirting with *me*. Dan wasn't home much. He was always checking on the stores, always paranoid that someone was stealing from him. And Mark…well, one thing led to another."

"Do you have his phone number?"

"Yes. It's stored in my phone." She looked at Dee, her eyes again filling with tears. "You don't think…you don't think Mark had something to do with this, do you?"

Dee met her gaze. "Can you account for your whereabouts two nights ago, Mrs. Frazier? And early the next morning?"

Connie gave a startled gasp. "You don't think…surely to *God* you don't think I had something to do with Dan's murder, do you?"

Dee held her gaze. "Can you account for your whereabouts or not?"

Tears flowed again from Connie's eyes. "I was here. I got home about six. I made dinner, like always. Dan came home about eight. He was…he was different. He would hardly speak to me. He barely touched his dinner."

Yes, that would have been shortly after Finn had given him the bad news. Frankly, Dee was surprised that Daniel Frazier hadn't taken his anger out on his wife.

"Then what?" Joel asked.

"He…he left. Like I told you yesterday, he wouldn't tell me where he was going. He left about nine or a little after." Her lower lip trembled again. "And he never came home," she sobbed.

Dee wanted to tell her to spare the tears. They weren't tugging at her heart, if that was the intent. Or perhaps the tears were genuine. Maybe she did love her husband but—in his absence—she just couldn't resist the handsome Michael Drake. Or Mark Condra…whoever the hell he was.

"If you could get us his phone number, Mrs. Frazier, we'll be on our way."

CHAPTER TEN

Finn yawned and glanced at the clock. She hated all-night stakeouts. She still had four or five hours to go until dawn. It was only 2:13.

Mr. Honeywell—owner of the two Honeywell Furniture stores—was losing inventory at this particular location. Security cameras had revealed nothing. In-store receipts all checked out. Home deliveries matched receipts. It wasn't a case she was really interested in and she quoted him an outrageous price—four hundred an hour for an all-night stakeout. She assumed he would leave her office and head to one of her competitors. Hanson Investigations, perhaps. They were the largest in Corpus.

But no. He accepted without blinking an eye at her and here she sat, six hours into it and twenty-four hundred dollars richer.

She had his personal laptop in the car with her. He had a feed to the security cameras and when he'd offered to have "one of his guys" give her access, she thought it would only call attention to the fact that she was snooping around. Even though he swore they could trust them, she was adamant that no one know about her because *she* didn't trust them. He'd reluctantly given up his laptop. She didn't really blame him for his reluctance. There's no way she would hand her personal laptop over to someone, private investigator or not.

She glanced at it now, the feed alternating between the showroom and the warehouse's loading dock in back. There had been no movement at all...not even a mouse had streaked across the floor.

She should have said five hundred an hour, she thought, as another half hour ticked slowly by. She rolled her shoulders and stretched out her neck, trying to get comfortable. If someone was ripping him off, what were the chances they'd hit on her first night?

"Slim," she murmured sleepily. Which meant she'd be out again tomorrow night.

Yeah...she should have said five hundred an hour.

* * *

Finn rolled over and slammed her fist down on the alarm, silencing it. She'd fallen into bed at seven that morning, barely taking the time to shed her clothes. She was getting too old for all-nighters, she thought as she sat up and rubbed her eyes. It was two, but it was a dreary, overcast day. It could still be morning. She *wished* it was still morning. She stretched her arms out and yawned as she stood.

A quick shower—and a strong cup of coffee—helped revive her somewhat. But it was still after three before she got to her office. The uneventful night meant there'd be no notes to log, other than her time spent. A few hours at the office, then she'd grab dinner somewhere before her nightshift started all over again.

The car parked in front of her building looked like Dee Woodard's plain white Ford, the vehicle the Corpus Police Department used. Judging by the looks of it, it was a car that had been in service way back when Finn was on the force.

Detective Woodard was nowhere around, however, and she was surprised to find the front door unlocked. She was even more surprised to find Dee in her office, casually chatting with Sammy, who was sitting behind the desk. She raised her eyebrows questioningly and Sammy smiled at her.

"Found Ms. Woodard outside waiting on you. Didn't think you'd mind none if I brought her inside with me."

The look on the detective's face indicated that this was a business trip, not pleasure. Finn nodded.

"That's fine, Sammy. Looks like Detective Woodard may have some questions for me."

Sammy took the hint and got up, giving her a wink as he left the office. Finn put her keys and phone on the desk, then sat down, finally giving Dee Woodard all her attention.

"What brings you around, Detective?"

"You were right. Michael Drake doesn't exist," she said, getting right to the point.

"And the address?"

"It's a legitimate address in a residential area. It's the home of Rebecca and Tom Gipson." Dee smiled. "Lovely couple. Becky was quite friendly and no, they'd never heard of Michael Drake." She crossed her legs with a sigh, her khaki pants lined with wrinkles, indicating she'd already had a long day. "Connie Frazier was quite surprised when we showed her the photos you'd taken. She didn't know a Michael Drake either. Connie knew him as Mark Condra."

"Phone number?"

Dee nodded. "Yes, she gave us the number she had to contact him with. Came back to a prepaid burner phone."

"So Michael Drake has secrets." Finn leaned back in her chair. "So what's your theory?"

"What's yours?"

Finn smiled. "I'm just a lowly PI, remember. I don't have theories."

"A lowly PI who used to be a cop."

"Checked up on me, did you?"

Dee Woodard ignored her question. "So? Your theory?"

"We both questioned the attraction between Connie Frazier and Michael Drake. Obviously, then, he was using her to get closer to Daniel Frazier."

"How would sleeping with his wife get him closer to Daniel Frazier?"

"If they're sneaking around, they're going to do it when Daniel was otherwise occupied. Maybe he had a pattern. Maybe he was looking for information and Connie was a free talker. Could be anything."

Dee's next question surprised her. "So who is Sammy?"

"Sammy? He lives in the apartment upstairs. Why?"

"He was dressed for fishing. I was a little startled when he pulled out a key to your office."

"Sammy's like family. He takes care of things here."

"Why a private investigator?"

"Why not?"

"From what I understand, you were a good cop."

Finn laughed. "You obviously didn't talk to my captain."

"Why the change?"

"Why the questions? I thought you had a murder to solve."

Detective Woodard stood up. "You're right. I do." She paused at the door. "You're working on another case?"

Finn nodded. "Nothing as exciting as a cheating wife, however. Why?"

"You look exhausted."

"Yeah…was out all night. Fruitless. There'll be a repeat tonight. And probably tomorrow night."

"Well, if you ever have a free evening, perhaps we could get dinner." Dee smiled quickly. "If you're interested, that is."

Finn had years of practice in hiding her emotions, her thoughts, her feelings. Now, however, she wasn't sure she'd been able to keep the surprise from her face. Was Dee Woodard asking her out on a date? She stood up too, hoping she appeared as nonchalant as she was trying to be.

"Sure, Detective. Dinner would be nice. You can fill me in on all the latest gossip over at CCPD."

"I try my best to stay out of the gossip loop." She placed a card on Finn's desk. "My cell number is on there. Give me a call if you want to grab dinner."

"I will. Thanks."

CHAPTER ELEVEN

It was three a.m. and a light drizzle was falling. The fog off the bay was settling down around her and Finn could barely see the streetlight at the corner. She picked up her binoculars and scanned the loading dock once more, again seeing nothing out of the ordinary.

Mr. Honeywell had given her the names of all of his employees at this store. She'd spent the day running background checks on them. There was one in particular she was interested in—Jason Singleton. He was in charge of security for both stores. She ran his financials, but there wasn't an exuberant amount in any of his accounts. Possibly more than his salary warranted but perhaps he was a frugal guy. There was, however, the fact that he'd paid cash for a midnight black Toyota Camry. Again, maybe he'd saved for it.

According to Honeywell, in the last four months alone, he'd lost twenty thousand dollars. In the last year, nearly a hundred. Earlier that day, she'd pretended to be a customer and had strolled through the store. Judging by some of the prices, it wouldn't take a whole lot of pieces of furniture to hit that mark.

Which made her wonder if this might be a once-a-month type thing. Less chances of getting caught. It was obvious to her that the security guy had to be involved. Perhaps he doctored the security feed.

But would thieves be so bold as to bring a large truck right up here to the loading dock? Five or six guys could fill it in no time. And a large truck at a loading dock wasn't going to cause suspicion should someone see it.

She blew out her breath. She didn't think she had the stamina—or patience—to do this every night until someone made a move. Apparently money wasn't an issue with Honeywell. She doubted he would pull her, just because of the cost.

She rubbed her eyes. It was 3:24.

* * *

Dee punched her pillow for the fifth and final time, finally giving up on the sleep that eluded her. She sat up, rubbing her face with both hands. She couldn't get the mysterious Michael Drake out of her mind. Who was he? More importantly…*where* was he?

She yawned as she went into her kitchen and turned on the Keurig. She blinked several times to clear her blurry vision. Was it really only 4:15? She blew out a tired breath and ran a hand through her hair.

Who was Michael Drake? She tilted her head. And who was Finley Knight? She was hard to read. Did she have secrets or was she simply a private person? Finn was younger than she was, she guessed. Attractive in a dark, quiet sort of way. Her offer of having dinner was more out of curiosity than a desire to go out with the woman. For one thing, she assumed they were far too much alike to actually consider dating. And two…she didn't have the time or energy to devote to dating. Nor the inclination, really. She was nearly forty-six. Her job was her life… her life was her job. Sad but true. Of course, she knew if she met the right woman, that would change. It had been so long since she'd been in love with anyone, she no longer even thought about meeting the *right* one.

Her thoughts went to Angela. She'd been the right one. Dee still looked back on their relationship fondly, even though Angela had been the one to end things. Angela couldn't deal with her being a cop. Angela couldn't deal with the long hours, the long absences, the fear that Dee would end up dead.

Dee shook her head slowly. Ten years ago Angela had ended things. On December 24th, it would be ten years. She reached for her coffee cup, seeing the steam swirl above it. Hell of a Christmas present. Angela said she still loved her…but. Always a "but," wasn't there? Yeah, Dee had had her heart ripped out that night. After that,

Houston simply wasn't big enough for both of them. They had too many mutual friends, too many things in common. And Dee couldn't handle going out and seeing Angela with someone else.

She got hired on in Corpus Christi a year later. Her captain had made some calls, pulled a few strings, and now here she was, a detective, nine years on the force. She'd been born and raised in Houston, but she had to admit, Corpus felt like home now. She knew her way around the city like the back of her hand. She had good relationships with the guys, with her captain. And she went out sometimes. Sometimes they ended up in bed. Occasionally. She was happy. Happy enough. She didn't *need* to have someone in her life. It was so much less complicated.

She sipped her coffee, her gaze going to the dark window above the sink, absently noting the raindrops sliding down the pane.

Yeah…she was happy enough.

CHAPTER TWELVE

Finn wasn't in any hurry to get back out to the furniture store. She figured if anything went down, it would be after midnight, not at eight o'clock.

"We haven't been out fishing together in a while, Finn."

"I know, Sammy. We'll get to it. Soon."

Sammy reached out and took one of the packets of ketchup from the pile. "You look tired."

"I am."

"You're living off coffee and junk food. No wonder."

"I'm living off four hours' sleep," she countered as she bit into her hamburger.

He shook his head. "You're never going to make it to my age if you continue living like that. I keep telling you, you need to find you a nice young woman to take care of you."

"I know you do. But I'm used to being alone. What in the world would I do with some nice young woman in my life?"

He looked at her sadly. "When my Isobel died, I thought my chest would crack right open from the pain in my heart. I wanted it to, I tell you that."

She already knew the answer, but she asked the question anyway. "How long were you married?"

"Fifty-two wonderful years," he said wistfully. "Got hitched when we were eighteen. She wasn't sick a day in her life, I tell you. Why, I remember…"

Finn let him ramble on as she nibbled at her burger. She knew the story well. Seventy years old and dropped dead of a heart attack. The kids were already out of the picture by then. Sammy couldn't function on his own, and he lived on the streets for nearly two years. Then on that fateful day, ten years ago now, he showed up on her doorstep, willing to work for some food.

"You need to find you someone like that." He leaned forward. "Your eyes, Finn, they're almost lifeless. You need to find you someone to love. Bring some joy into your life." He paused. "Like that detective woman, maybe."

Finn smiled. "I thought you said I needed to find some young woman. Detective Woodard is older than me, I imagine."

"I think she fancies you."

No. While Dee had casually offered dinner, Finn didn't get the impression she "fancied" her in the least. The look in her eyes was nothing more than friendly. "She did ask me out to dinner. Well, she said I should call her if I wanted to grab a meal sometime."

Sammy's eyes crinkled up as he smiled. "See there! And here you sit with an old man like me. You should have called her up."

Finn glanced at her watch. It was 8:33. "I've got to work tonight, Sammy. Every night, it seems, until I can bust this." She looked up at him. "Remind me not to take a case like this again."

"You know what you need, don't you?"

"I do not need another investigator working here. I can handle things."

"You do need someone working here with you. I heard you on the phone turning down a job."

"Yeah, I have to turn some down, but not often."

"What was it?"

"Cheating husband. I sent her over to Hanson." She wiped her mouth with a napkin, then tossed it on top of the remaining burger. "I'm making enough on this case that I can afford to lose a client. Especially if this drags on much longer."

"If this drags on much longer, you'll be sleepwalking."

"Maybe it'll end tonight, Sammy. I got a good feeling."

CHAPTER THIRTEEN

"I've never been here before," Dee said. "And that's saying something. I like to find these hole-in-the-wall places. They're usually very good."

"This place has been here twenty years, at least," Finn said as she reached for her beer mug.

When her good feeling from last night turned out to be nothing, she'd taken Sammy's advice and had asked Dee out for an early dinner. Coming here to Paul's Bar and Grill was the first thing that popped into her mind. It was casual and usually crowded. It was so obviously not a romantic dinner.

"How are the steaks?" Dee asked as she looked over the menu.

"I normally stick to seafood, but I have had the chicken fried steak before. It was good. They say the chicken fried chicken is excellent although I've never had it."

Dee closed the menu with a nod. "I think I'll try that. You?"

"Seafood platter. There's always enough for leftovers. I'll take that with me tonight while I'm working."

"What kind of case this time?"

Finn hesitated. She wasn't used to sharing work details with anyone. "Nothing exciting," she said vaguely.

"What? Confidential?" Dee took a swallow of her beer. "Or is that your standard reply when people ask."

"People don't normally ask."

"I see. So what led you to become a private investigator?"

"I was bored being a security guard."

Dee laughed. "You left CCPD to become a security guard?"

"No. I left CCPD because I wasn't very good at following orders."

"Good enough that you made detective."

Finn leaned her elbows on the table. "Why were you checking on me?"

"I suppose because you're not very forthcoming with information."

Finn nodded. "So how's your case coming? Any luck finding Michael Drake?"

"I'm afraid not."

"And you're going with the assumption that he's your killer?"

Dee stared at her. "Now who's fishing for information?"

"Just curious, of course. I certainly don't miss doing police work that much that I want all the gory details," she said truthfully. "Daniel Frazier was a client. I'm naturally interested in there being closure in this case."

"Well, I'm not really able to discuss the case with you. I'm sorry."

"No problem. I know there are rules and protocol to follow. I was never very good at that, unlike you." She motioned to the waitress, indicating they were ready to order. She declined a second beer, opting for tea instead. She still had a long night ahead of her. And if Detective Woodard wouldn't answer questions about the case, Finn wondered if she'd be open to more personal questions instead. "How long have you been with CCPD? I left ten years ago. I'm assuming after that."

Dee nodded. "Nine, actually. I was in Houston before that."

"Detective there as well?"

"Yes." She paused only a moment, as if deciding whether she wanted to elaborate or not. "A bad breakup sent me running, I'm afraid. My captain was able to get me on here. He's good friends with Captain Mabanks."

"Ah, yes. Captain Mabanks. He wasn't my biggest fan," she said, remembering all the reprimands he'd given her.

"He's retiring soon, he claims. I can't say anything bad about him. He's always been very fair with me."

"Obviously you follow the rules and take orders well."

"Most of the time, yes. I'm pretty much a stickler." Dee folded her hands together. "What's the real reason you quit?"

"I…I didn't like the constraints of the job." That was mostly true. She certainly wasn't going to tell Dee Woodard that her father had come back from the grave, leaving her money and a house on the bay. And an old rundown building on Moonlight Avenue.

"I would imagine there were more constraints being a security guard."

Finn smiled. "Yes, well, that lasted all of six months."

"And being a private investigator, I suppose there are very few constraints."

"I have a lot more freedom on how I obtain the information I need, yes. No worries about a judge throwing out evidence. People pay me for information. They don't care how I get it. Unless, of course, my clients are attorneys. I have a few."

Dee nodded. "A lot of ex-cops get in the business, I understand."

"Yes. The largest agency in Corpus—Hanson Investigations—has several ex-cops working there. Most, in fact."

"You know them?"

"Yes. I've had my share of run-ins with them."

"I see. Competitors."

"Yes. But in my opinion, they're not very thorough. Like I said, they're the largest. They rush through jobs to get on to the next one. I've had quite a few clients come to me after not being satisfied with their work."

"If you don't mind me asking…how old are you, Finn?"

"I don't mind, no. I turned forty this past summer." She raised her eyebrows. "You?"

"Forty-five. It seems odd to say that out loud," Dee said with a quick smile. "I sometimes think I'm still thirty-five." The smile disappeared. "And then again, some mornings, I feel downright old."

"I know what you mean."

"Do you date?" Dee asked expectantly.

"Date?" Finn shook her head. "No. I keep crazy hours, as I'm sure you can relate." She glanced at her watch. It was nearly eight. "You?"

Dee shook her head. "Not really, no. I go out occasionally, but… no."

"You said a bad breakup. Did that turn you off to dating?"

"Oh, I don't know." Another quick smile from Dee. "Angela. Her name was Angela. She didn't like me being a cop. I had no intention of quitting, of course, so…she quit me instead."

Finn nodded. "That's often the case."

"Have you had a similar experience?"

"No." She left it at that, finding no need to tell Dee Woodard that, at age forty, she still hadn't met anyone she wanted to share her life with. There had been no relationships, no long-term dating, no girlfriends. She wasn't looking. Had she ever truly looked? After her father's death, her sole focus had been getting through the academy, being a good cop. She didn't worry about there being love in her life. And at age thirty, when the envelope was delivered, her world essentially changed. Still…there'd been no one. She'd spent the last ten years building up her agency, not taking the time for personal relationships. And the years had slipped away so fast, they were almost a blur.

"You're an attractive woman, Finn. Why don't you date?"

Instead of giving the excuse she used—late nights and crazy hours—she decided to be honest with Dee. "I guess I've found I function better without a partner."

"A loner then?"

She never really had put a label on it before, but… "I suppose that's a good word, if we're looking to define my status."

"There's nothing wrong with that. A lot of people prefer their own company to that of others."

"And you?"

Dee laughed. "No. I'm not a loner by nature and I enjoyed being in a relationship. I just don't take the time for it now." She paused. "An excuse, of course. If there was someone, then I'd make the time. Maybe I am still a little gun-shy because of Angela. Broken hearts at our age take longer to heal."

Their meal was served, sparing Finn from commenting. When she was younger, she did often wonder what being in a relationship would be like. Now? It never crossed her mind. Her opportunities to meet someone were few and far between. No. She didn't even think about it anymore. As she picked up a fried shrimp, her mind was already on the laborious night that was ahead of her. But then there was a flicker of memory, a vision of blond hair, a charming smile…soft lips that had nibbled their way across her body. The young woman from the bar seemed to be crossing her mind more often lately.

With a nearly silent sigh, she pushed the memories of that night away, biting into the jumbo shrimp instead.

CHAPTER FOURTEEN

Once again, Finn chose a different spot to park, two blocks from the loading dock. With the security lights shining directly on the dock, she had a perfect view with her binoculars. She set them on the seat beside her and rolled her shoulders. It was 11:17 on a Thursday night. The hours ahead of her loomed long.

The dinner with Dee Woodard had proved to be uneventful and rather stress-free. She wouldn't imagine they'd have a repeat even though when they parted company, Dee had said she'd enjoyed the meal and their conversation.

Finn hadn't been out to dinner with anyone—a woman—since way back in early spring when Catherine, an old acquaintance from her days on the force, had called her out of the blue. Catherine had just broken up with her girlfriend of six years. After their dinner, Catherine had wanted to have sex. Finn had gone through the motions, feeling almost dirty afterward and wishing she hadn't answered the call in the first place. That had been in March. The last time she'd slept with a woman was, of course, the young blonde she'd met at the bar. That night had been the complete opposite of how she'd felt with Catherine. She'd felt totally alive during the encounter. She'd wondered at the time—if the woman hadn't run out on her, would she have tried to see her again, maybe even date? But the woman *had* run out on her and she hadn't been to the bar since.

Dee gave no indication that she was interested in anything from Finn other than to share a meal. For that, she was thankful. While she'd had a handful of friends when she was still at CCPD, those had dwindled to none in the last ten years. Other than Sammy, her solitary life was just that. Did she even have the energy—or want to—to forge a friendship with Dee Woodard? She supposed having someone to grab a meal with occasionally would be nice.

She leaned her head back and sighed. Ten years had sure slipped away fast. Where had they gone? She made a good enough living. Having cases like this padded her bank account. Not that she had to worry about it much. Her father had left her enough to live comfortably without having to work.

Moonlight Avenue Investigations. She remembered the day she'd started. She'd gone two weeks before a client came calling. The woman had come to her because she was an unknown agency on a dead-end street. She didn't want her husband—or anyone else—to find out she was hiring an investigator.

Jessica Sanderson had had a baby while she was in high school. A girl. She'd given her up for adoption. Her husband had no idea. They had three kids of their own.

Finn had found the girl, then nineteen, in north Texas, attending a community college. She'd taken photos of the young woman, gotten all the information that Jessica had asked for. When Finn had presented it to her, a mere four days later, she'd broken down in tears. That had been Finn's first lesson. Women cried, men got angry.

She never knew what Jessica Sanderson had done with the information. Did she go to Denton and try to connect with her daughter? Did she share it with her husband? Or did she simply hold on to it, keeping it to herself? That had been her second lesson…what clients did with the information she gave them…wasn't any of her business—or her concern.

That was ten years ago. She didn't remember all of her clients, of course. Some stood out more than others. Some cases were more unique than others. Cheating spouses were her least favorite, however. She smiled wryly. Of course right now, while staring out at a furniture store's loading dock, she'd probably rather be spying on a cheating spouse.

It was 2:52 when a midnight black Toyota Camry pulled up beside the loading dock. Finn grabbed the binoculars before the car had even stopped.

"Well, well," she murmured. Her intuition was correct after all. Jason Singleton got out, glancing at his watch, then his gaze traveled down the street.

She looked quickly at the laptop, but the security feed she was getting showed the loading dock as it had looked earlier. There was no sign of the car or Jason, even though he was obviously in the view of the security camera. She glanced at the timestamp, but it was accurate.

A few minutes later, a large truck came down the street, turning into the lot and backing up expertly to the loading dock. Again, the security feed showed nothing.

"Has to be on a loop or something," she said out loud.

Her camera replaced the binoculars and she got shots of both license plates, the driver of the truck—a tall black man—and the two guys who got out with him, both muscular-looking, one black, one white. Jason Singleton was giving instructions, pointing, and she got several shots of him.

She jotted down the time—now 2:58—when the large freight doors were raised. All four men went inside and it was only ninety seconds later when they came back carrying a brown leather sofa. They took a furniture dolly out of the truck and used it to load two large recliners. Another smaller sofa—loveseat, perhaps?—was loaded last.

Sixteen minutes later, at 3:14, the freight doors closed and the truck pulled away. Jason Singleton got in his car and followed. He stopped on the street for a few seconds, then continued on. She watched the security feed, seeing just a flicker—a hiccup—as the empty bay and loading dock filled her screen.

"So he stops the cameras but keeps the timestamp running."

She imagined if they were to go over the security feed, frame by frame, they'd be able to see when it was stopped and restarted, especially now that she had the exact time.

She smiled, relieved that this particular case was over. So relieved, in fact, she planned to head to the office right then to write up her report and download the photos she'd taken. Mr. Honeywell would no doubt be surprised by her findings.

* * *

As soon as she pulled up to the old building that housed Moonlight Avenue Investigations, she knew something was wrong. She stood staring at the front, trying to figure out what was different. The door was closed, but she pulled her gun off her hip even before it registered that she was seeing the smear of blood on the handle.

Her heart pounded to life as she went closer. Definitely blood. She tugged her shirt out of her jeans and used it to turn the knob, not wanting to contaminate any evidence should she have to call the police out. As soon as she walked inside, even in the darkness, she could tell the place had been trashed. She ignored the tipped-over chair in the entryway and stepped over the fallen lamp as she headed to her office. The door was open. Sammy always closed and locked it when he finished cleaning.

Using her elbow, she flipped the switch by the door, blinking against the bright light. Her office was an unrecognizable mess. Everything was turned upside down and inside out. She walked around her desk, her heart stopping as she saw him, blood pooled around his head.

She fell to her knees. "Sammy? Oh, my God. *Sammy?*"

His skin was cold to the touch when she rolled him over. He'd taken two shots, it seemed. One to the chest…one to the head.

"Oh, Sammy…*no.*"

She stood up on shaky legs, stumbling back outside, barely making it out before she lost what was left of the dinner she'd shared with Dee Woodard some six hours earlier.

CHAPTER FIFTEEN

Dee had been shocked to get a phone call from Finley Knight at 3:45 in the morning. Even more shocked by her strangled words.

"Sammy's dead. He's been shot."

She looked at Finn now, the shadows on this dark street—Moonlight Avenue—broken only by the flashing lights of the police cars. Finn's face alternated between red and blue as she leaned against one of the patrol cars, the lights swirling around her head. She hadn't been able to console Finn earlier. The woman had been rocked by tears and was as grief-stricken as Dee had ever seen someone. They didn't know each other well enough for the informality that had sprung up between them, but she'd offered her arms to Finn and Finn had clung to her desperately.

Now, Finn stared at the building, her tears appearing to have been pushed away, her face nearly impassive. Dee walked over to her, wishing she had coffee or something to offer her.

"How you holding up?" she asked stupidly.

It took several seconds before Finn looked at her. "Thank you for coming. And…for earlier."

Dee nodded. "I spoke with Captain Mabanks. He's going to let me run with this one since I was already on the scene." She cleared her throat. "Are you up for some questions?"

Finn let out a heavy breath. "No, I don't know who could have done this. Yes, they were obviously looking for something. No, Sammy wasn't a target. Yes, you can take a look at some of my prior cases if you think that'll help."

Dee smiled slightly. "Forgot you used to do this for a living. You could humor me and let me at least ask the question before you answer."

Finn glanced toward the building and Dee saw the expression on her face change. Dee turned, too, watching as they brought the body out.

"Sammy lived upstairs." Finn cleared her throat before continuing. "He didn't have a car so whoever did this would have assumed the office was vacant. Sammy probably heard them, went down to investigate."

"I'll…I'll need to notify his family."

"There's none. I was his family."

"Is there anyone else? Next of kin?"

Finn shook her head. "His wife died before I met him. He had three kids, I think, but he hadn't been in contact with them in…I don't know, twenty years or so."

"I'll see if we can't locate them." She arched an eyebrow, knowing that Finn, in her profession, could have found them easily. "You never tried?"

"I offered. He didn't want to. He always said it was their choice to leave, their choice to abandon the family." Finn looked at her. "When his wife died, he was all alone. He buried her all alone." She wiped at a tear. "I was his family. He was mine."

"I'm sorry, Finn. I truly am."

Finn brushed at her tears again, then cleared her throat once more. "So…where do we start?"

"We? No, no. There'll be no 'we' in this one, Finn." She pointed her finger at her. "You stay out of this. I can handle it."

Finn stood up. "Right. Whatever you say."

"I mean it."

Finn squared her shoulders. "That man…that lovely, beautiful, innocent man," she said, her voice cracking with emotion, "gets all of my attention, Detective Woodard. I'll try to stay out of your way."

Dee knew she could demand all she wanted and it wouldn't make a bit of difference to Finn. Not now, anyway. Maybe in a few days, but not now. So she nodded.

"Go home, Finn. We'll wrap this up here in an hour or so. I'll call you. We'll have a little more formal question and answer session. Okay?"

Finn nodded and turned away, heading toward her car. Dee doubted she was going home. It was nearly five in the morning. She ran a hand through her hair, then went back inside.

She paused in the doorway to Finn's office. Yes, they were obviously looking for something. All of the drawers and filing cabinets had been emptied, their contents strewn about. Books had been shoved off the shelves. The small sofa's cushions had been ripped open as well as the chairs.

So what were they looking for?

"Detective...we're out of here."

She nodded. "You get some usable prints?"

"Ton of prints on the desk. I assume most belong to Ms. Knight."

She wondered if they'd find hers mixed in there as well. Had she touched Finn's desk on the occasions she'd sat across from her?"

"Got a blood print on a piece of paper. Well, a partial, but enough. I think that's our best bet."

"Good, Jim. Good. Let me know as soon as you get something."

He nodded. "You'll be the first one I call."

The forensic team was small compared to Houston's, but she'd found them to be very competent. She hoped like hell the print panned out.

CHAPTER SIXTEEN

The sky was beginning to show some color, reminding her that no matter what happened—no matter who died—the world kept turning, the sun kept coming around, day after day.

She'd been sitting out on her pier since Detective Woodard had sent her home. She'd actually tried to work. She had a report to give to Mr. Honeywell. Instead, she'd taken out a bottle of scotch and nearly filled a glass to the top, then had slowly made her way to the end of the pier, forgoing one of the colorful Adirondack chairs in favor of sitting on the very pier itself. She sat with her feet dangling over the bay, the glass of whiskey cradled in her hands.

She tried to remember her last conversation with Sammy. He'd been fussing at her about taking better care of herself, telling her she needed to find a young woman. He fussed over her all the time. Fussed over her like she was family…like she was his daughter.

She wiped at a tear, hating that she'd broken down in front of Dee Woodard. She simply couldn't hold on to her stoic expression a second longer. It was at that moment, when Dee had offered her a shoulder to cry on, that Finn realized how completely alone she was in this world. So alone that she took comfort from a virtual stranger, sobbing in her arms as her heart broke for Sammy.

"See you tomorrow, Sammy."

"Good Lord willing."

She shook her head. No. There would be no more tomorrows. Because someone had shot Sammy dead. Shot him in her office. They were looking for something. She could picture it now, could almost hear it as they tossed furniture and drawers around. Sammy had heard it all, no doubt. She could see him coming down the stairs, could see him pushing her office door open a little wider. If he'd startled them, they would have shot him there at the door. No, he saw them. He probably crept up behind them, forgetting that he was eighty-two years old. They were by the credenza, their back to the door. Had he grabbed one of them? Did he get a punch in?

She stared out at the bay, barely noticing the sun changing from red to yellow, not seeing the flock of white pelicans soaring by. What were they looking for? What could she possibly have in her possession that would warrant all of that? What did she have that someone would kill for?

Nothing. She had nothing. She frowned. Someone obviously *thought* she had something. She thought back over her last handful of clients. None of the cases were spectacular, nothing unusual.

Daniel Frazier. He was murdered. Connie Frazier's lover was nowhere to be found. Her office was trashed and Sammy was killed. Was it all by chance? No. In her line of work, nothing was a coincidence.

So what did they think Daniel Frazier had given her? *Why* would Daniel Frazier give her anything to begin with? He was a businessman with four pizza joints. According to him, he worked his ass off. And even though he hired her to follow his wife, she'd poked around enough to know his finances were in order, no evident debt to speak of. No red flags popped up. In fact, he was doing a bang-up business. They lived in a nice house in a nice neighborhood, but it was nothing extravagant, certainly not what his finances indicated he could afford. They appeared to be a normal family with two children—a son and a daughter—both in college. The only glaring oddity from the picture of the perfect family was that Connie was cheating on her husband with Michael Drake.

Dee had told her to stay out of it and she knew she should. If the roles were reversed, she knew she wouldn't want a private investigator poking around in her case. But the roles weren't reversed and Sammy was family. No way was she going to sit idly by while the police did their thing.

No way.

CHAPTER SEVENTEEN

"What time did you arrive?" Dee asked as she stirred sugar into her coffee.

Finn rolled her eyes. "How many times are we going to go over it?"

"Until something jumps out at me."

Finn leaned against the counter and refilled her own coffee cup. Dee thought it'd be better to question Finn here, at her house, rather than request they meet downtown at the station. It was obvious that Finn hadn't slept. What was it going on? Twenty-four hours? More? She looked exhausted—physically and emotionally. Still, she couldn't tell if Finn was being intentionally vague with her answers or if she was telling the truth.

"Dee, if you're trying to see if I'm going to slip up and change one of my answers, you're wasting your time. And mine. I'm not going to keep answering the same questions over and over." She took a sip of her coffee. "No offense."

Dee gave a rather sheepish smile. "Sorry. Again, I forgot you used to be a cop."

"A detective," Finn corrected.

"Of course." Dee closed up the notepad she always used and moved it to the side. "Okay, then let's just talk."

"Where's your partner?" Finn asked unexpectedly.

"My partner?"

"Each time I've seen you on official police business, you've been alone. Mabanks was always a stickler for traveling in pairs."

Dee nodded. "Yes, well, I sometimes leave him behind. He's young. Green. We have different methods."

"What? Thinks he's a big stud with a gun now that he's made detective?"

"At first, yes. We still clash some." She picked up her coffee cup. "Sammy has a son living in the Dallas area. He's the only one we've been able to locate." She met Finn's gaze. "He's been in and out of jail. In more than out the last ten years or so. Drugs, mostly."

"Did he even know who Sammy was?"

"Yes." She shook her head. "I'm sorry, but he didn't care. He doesn't want to claim the body." She watched as Finn's fists clenched into tight balls.

"His wife is buried here in Corpus. That's where he'd want to be."

"If no next of kin claims him, then he'll be cremated."

"I'll claim him. I'll pay for the burial. Please don't cremate him. Sammy was old-school. He wanted to be buried beside his wife."

Dee nodded. "Of course. I'll take care of it then."

Finn seemed to relax then and she moved back to the table. "Thank you."

Dee stared at her. "Who do you think did it?"

Their eyes held for a moment, and she wondered if Finn would offer a guess or not. She could almost see the indecision as Finn warred with herself.

"I imagine it was the same person who killed Daniel Frazier."

Dee wasn't surprised that's where Finn's guess took her. Michael Drake was at the top of Dee's list too.

"Did Mr. Frazier give you anything to keep for him?"

"Now don't you think I would have already told you if he had?"

Dee smiled. "I think no such thing."

Finn gave a small smile too. "You're probably right, but no, he didn't give me anything. He was here at the office twice, like I said. We discussed nothing other than his wife." Finn paused. "You think it was Michael Drake too?"

"Perhaps. But we can't get locked in on something without evidence. Let's see if the prints turn up anything. It could have absolutely nothing to do with Michael Drake or Daniel Frazier."

Finn pushed her coffee cup aside. "When can I get back in my office?"

"Give me the rest of the day, at least. And I couldn't help but notice that the building is large, yet your office area is small."

Finn nodded. "I rent out the other side."

"To?"

"Simon Dorsky. He's an accountant."

"Is it possible that he was the intended target? I mean, his office and not yours?"

"Doubtful. He's a one-man show. Does mostly individual tax returns with just a handful of business clients. Very tame."

"Still, I'll need to interview him. Can you give me his number?"

"Sure. I already called him and told him he couldn't get into his office today. He would probably jump at the chance to meet you there. The murder has apparently inconvenienced him."

Dee jotted down the number on her notepad then stood. "You should get some sleep, Finn. A few hours, at least."

"I know. I plan to."

Dee knew she was lying but didn't comment on it. "Thanks for the coffee."

"You'll keep me in the loop, right?"

"As much as I can, yes." She expected Finn to protest, but she simply nodded. "I can see myself out."

"I'm not that exhausted that I can't walk you to the door."

As they stood outside, Dee looked around, admiring the manicured lawn, the view of the bay, the two large palm trees swaying overhead.

"You've got a nice place here."

"Thanks. I hope to slow down one day long enough to enjoy it."

"Yes. The years get away, don't they?"

Finn nodded slowly. "They certainly do."

CHAPTER EIGHTEEN

Finn stood in her empty office. Empty, that is, except for her old desk. The transformation had taken only a couple of days. She looked around the bare walls, but her gaze inevitably drifted to the spot where Sammy had been. The office had been scrubbed clean, the hardwood floors redone, the walls painted. Everything had been thrown out, including all the paperwork that had been strewn across the floor. It was mostly for show anyway. She kept everything electronically.

She walked over to her desk, touching the surface, her fingers running over the many scratches…scratches that were already there when she bought the thing at a garage sale all those years ago. The prints the police had collected from the desk had proven to be useless. Most were hers, of course. The bloody fingerprint that had been on one of the papers on the floor had been Sammy's. The guys, whoever they were, were professional. Wearing gloves, most likely, not leaving any evidence behind.

It was too late now, but she was finally getting around to having a security camera installed. She hadn't seen the point before. Moonlight Avenue was a dead-end street. There was no traffic, no crime. It was an old office building with nothing valuable inside. But in her profession—where surveillance was key—she should have installed one the day she opened up the agency. At the very least, she should have installed one when she'd had her home security system set up.

She went around the desk, taking care not to walk where…where Sammy had been. Would she always do that? She opened up the bottom drawer of the desk. One of the few items left untouched was her father's scotch glass. She picked it up, running a finger along the rim, then put it back down. She opened up the middle drawer and moved some papers aside, revealing the mystery key. She picked it up and twisted it between her fingers. The unknown key. She folded it up in her palm, wondering why she hung on to the damn thing. Wondering why it was the first thing she'd looked for when Dee had let her back into her office.

She heard a door slam and she looked up, listening. Simon, no doubt. She'd given him the option of breaking his lease with her. He'd jumped on it and he and his wife had begun packing immediately. She had no clue where he would go and she didn't really care. His office space was much larger than hers. She would have it cleaned and painted, then most likely move over there.

Alone.

She'd never been here alone before. Sammy had shown up while she was still getting the office ready for her. She'd moved him upstairs before she'd even hung her sign out. She looked up at the ceiling, as if she could see into his apartment. She needed to go up there and get it cleaned out. There wasn't much, she knew. Sammy had very few possessions. When she'd met him, the only thing he had besides the clothes on his back was an old, dirty knapsack.

"Hello? Anyone here?"

Finn tilted her head. A female voice. Pleasant. Definitely not Karen Dorsky. Simon's wife had a rather shrill voice. Irritating. Yes, she'd be glad when they were gone.

She walked out, finding a young woman looking around the empty reception area. The woman turned to her and as their eyes met, Finn felt the breath being sucked out of her chest. At first, she felt disoriented. Was she seeing a ghost? Was there an appointment she'd forgotten? Should she acknowledge this woman as anything but a stranger? God, she hoped her expression was remaining as neutral as she willed it to be. She had lots of practice at keeping her expression even; she hoped it was working now.

The woman's smile faltered a bit—as recognition set in? In the light of day, she was more attractive than Finn remembered. Her blond hair not quite reaching her shoulders, parted on the side, the bangs sweeping across her forehead. Eyes that weren't quite blue—tinged with a trace of green. Eyes that she remembered being darker than they were. Eyes that had been haunting her for the last six months. What in the world was this woman doing here? As their gazes held, Finn wondered if perhaps the woman didn't recognize her after all. Maybe not. The bar had been dark. The dance floor had been dark. Had they even turned on any lights in the motel room? Yes. A lamp. It had been the first time she'd seen clearly into her eyes...eyes that were dark with arousal.

The woman finally cleared her throat and stepped forward, holding out her hand. "I'm...I'm Rylee Moore. Is...is the owner around?"

Ah. So she didn't recognize her after all. Or maybe she simply didn't remember the encounter. Finn squared her shoulders a bit before answering.

"Finley Knight. Finn. What can I do for you?" she answered rather curtly.

"Oh."

Finn raised her eyebrows. "Problem?"

"Sorry. It's just that all the other agencies I've been to, it's always men, other than the receptionist. It's actually refreshing to find a woman." Rylee Moore looked around. "Are you open for business?"

"Yes. Doing some...some remodeling is all."

"Oh, okay."

Finn crossed her arms, eyebrows raised. Did this woman...this Rylee Moore...*really* not recognize her? Well, it had been six months. Maybe she'd picked up numerous women at the bar since then. She probably couldn't possibly remember them all. Her impatience grew as she stared at her. "So...what can I do for you, Ms. Moore?" she asked once more.

"It's what I can do for you. I want to come work for you."

Finn's eyebrows shot up again. "Excuse me?"

"As an apprentice. I need the experience."

Finn shook her head quickly. "I'm sorry. I'm not hiring. You should try the Hanson Agency."

"I have. I didn't get a good vibe. He only met with me for a second, then pushed me off on one of his underlings."

"He's a jerk," Finn said without thinking.

"I was going to say an asshole, but we can go with jerk."

Finn tried, but she couldn't keep the smile from her face. Steve Hanson was indeed an asshole. But her smile faded.

"I take it they didn't want to hire you?"

"They pretty much only hire ex-cops, from what I learned. And they also pretty much only hire men."

"True on both accounts."

"I've been to all of the agencies," Rylee said. "No one will hire me. Everyone wants experience...or the cop thing." She threw up her hands. "I mean, how can you get experience if no one will hire you?"

Finn shrugged. She certainly wasn't going to hire her either. "What do you do now?" she asked, more out of curiosity than anything pertaining to the non-existent job opening.

"Oh. Nothing really. I moved here recently. Well, about six months ago." She cleared her throat a bit nervously. "Amarillo. But...well, I wanted something different."

"That's quite a change from Amarillo to Corpus."

"I know. My mother hasn't gotten over it yet."

Finn nodded and offered a small smile. "Well, I'm sorry, but I'm not hiring."

Rylee's confident smile faltered a bit. "Are you sure? I wouldn't expect much. I'm just trying to get my feet wet, so to speak."

"Want to open up your own agency?"

"Someday, yes."

"Good luck, then. But I'm a small shop. I do all the work." She motioned to the empty room. "I don't even have a receptionist."

"You don't have *anyone* working for you?"

"No. And I manage fine."

A disappointed face—eyes—looked back at her and Finn very nearly gave in to her. There was something haunting in those blue eyes. A desperation, perhaps. She hadn't noticed that before. Maybe six months of no employment would do that do you.

"Okay. Well, if you could at least think about it. Please?" From the purse that was hanging on her shoulder, she took out a piece of paper and handed it to Finn. "That's my number. If you change your mind."

Finn glanced at the paper where Rylee had previously written down her name and number. She wondered how many times she'd handed a paper like this out to someone who wasn't hiring.

"Nice to meet you, Ms. Knight. Thanks for your time."

"It's Finn. And good luck."

Finn stared at the door long after Rylee Moore had walked out of it, aware that her heart was beating just a little too fast in her chest.

Rylee Moore. The woman from the bar. She looked even younger than Finn remembered. Of course, it stung a bit that Rylee didn't remember her.

Okay…so it stung a lot. The woman had been drifting in and out of Finn's mind for months now. Apparently the blonde hadn't had the same problem.

CHAPTER NINETEEN

Rylee stood beside her Jeep, finally able to breathe normally. Was it *her*? Really? Was it? Most certainly it was. The hair was a little longer. But those dark eyes…she'd recognize them anywhere. Finley Knight. Finn. Either the woman had an extremely good poker face or she didn't remember that night. At all. And maybe she didn't. For all she knew, the woman picked up strangers at bars all the time. That was probably it. Why on earth would Finley Knight remember her?

She blew out a frustrated breath. God…what were the chances she'd run into her again? She hadn't even been back to the bar since that night. She'd been too embarrassed to go back. She never—ever— did anything like that. She'd only been in Corpus a few weeks. She was trying to meet people. That had been her first time to go to the bar. First and last.

Because she'd gone to a motel with a stranger. She'd had sex—a lot of sex—with a stranger. She closed her eyes briefly, her mind flashing back to that night. God…it had been…well, mind-blowing was an understatement. And as she'd untangled from the woman's arms early that morning, she'd freaked out. Totally. She'd snatched up her clothes and run.

And now here she was, begging for a job from that same woman, a woman who didn't remember having sex with her.

She finally opened the door to her Jeep and got inside. Now what? Now what should she do? How could it possibly be this hard to get a job? Oh, she could always find a job as a security guard. She had eight years' experience and surely her father would give her a recommendation. Surely he would. That would be a last resort, though. She had little desire to go back to patrolling empty businesses at night. And really, she had little desire to beg her father for a recommendation.

She'd moved to Corpus Christi in early June, planning on an extended vacation before trying to find work. After her encounter at the bar that night, she'd tried to do more *normal* things. She'd been practically a beach bum while she settled into her new city, draining her savings at a rather rapid—and alarming—pace. But she'd had a fun summer, although she'd spent most of it alone. She'd met a couple of people and had even gone on a date or two. Corpus was certainly different than Amarillo in that regard. Even though she'd not been closeted there, she'd still been rather quiet when it came to her sexuality. Of course, when she and Kat had broken up, it was all the talk in the office. Especially when Kat had refused to even speak to her for months afterward. The hardest part had been explaining the situation to her father. While he'd never been crazy about the gay thing—to put it mildly—he was quite fond of Kat. She'd be lying if she said it hadn't hurt when he'd obviously sided with Kat after the breakup.

That wasn't the sole reason she'd left Amarillo, but it was the deciding factor. She needed a change. She was *years* past needing a change. Working for her father had its perks—her salary and her option to veto jobs—but it couldn't make up for the chasm between them. She'd graduated from college with a criminal justice degree, intending to work as a game warden. She thought it would be perfect. She loved the outdoors, loved being in nature. It would be ideal. Only she couldn't find a job locally and she hadn't been prepared to leave Amarillo. At least not when she was twenty-one. So she went to work for her father's company—Amarillo Security and Patrol—intending to save a little money, then make her escape. But in the blink of an eye, eight years had passed. During those eight years, she'd come out to her parents, moved out of their house—been forced out was more like it—and drifted farther and farther away from them. Emotionally, at least. Her mother tried. She really did. But having a gay daughter…

well, that was never in the cards. One night, while nursing a pitcher of margaritas—alone—she had vowed she would *not* still be living in Amarillo and working for her father when she turned thirty.

She gave a weary sigh, then started the red Jeep, finally pulling out of the tiny parking lot. She'd purchased the vehicle only weeks before moving down here. She had envisioned herself driving on the beach, the Jeep open and topless. A smile lit her face as she remembered the first trip she'd taken from Mustang Island, following the forty-something miles of beach down to the Padre Island National Seashore. She'd been in heaven. She'd even bought a tent and camped out on the beach a few times. But summer had ended and fall had come and now November was quickly disappearing. She still had no job. Her savings were disappearing as well.

"You're coming home for Thanksgiving, aren't you?" Her mother's voice was still echoing in her ear from their conversation the day before.

Truth was, she'd been surprised by the adamant tone of her mother. She never once thought they'd actually miss her for the holidays. But no, she wasn't planning on making the trip to Amarillo next week. She was planning on getting a job. And if Finley Knight—Finn—didn't reconsider, then her chances of becoming a private investigator were slim to none. She'd gone back to her original plan—game warden. But she was twenty-nine years old competing with twenty-one-year-olds fresh out of college. So she changed directions. Private investigator. It was something she'd toyed with in Amarillo, although she'd done little more than research it. She'd already hit up every agency in the Corpus area, surprised that there were nearly twenty to choose from. Some specialized only in background checks. Some specialized in missing persons—that'd be kinda interesting. Some specialized in surveillance. Hanson didn't specialize. He took on any and every client, she'd learned. And judging by Moonlight Avenue Investigation's rather plain website, Finley Knight also was versatile. And she didn't have anybody working for her, not even a receptionist. Surely she could use some help.

Or maybe she didn't have enough business to warrant hiring another person. Maybe that's why she didn't bother with a receptionist; she didn't have enough clients.

"God, do I really want to work for a woman I slept with? A woman who doesn't even remember me?" Well, maybe that was a good thing. If she didn't remember her, then…

How could she not remember? That night was etched in her brain for eternity, it seemed. Images popped into her mind more often than not.

But if it was something Finn did a lot…then yes, maybe she really didn't remember that night. And maybe that was for the best.

So yeah. She'd give her a week. If Finn didn't call, then Rylee would simply pop back over and talk to her in person.

She might even resort to begging. Something told her this was going to be her one and only chance to land a job in this profession.

As she drove down the street, she wondered if Finley Knight had been watching her from a window as she'd sat there traipsing down memory lane. She'd been so lost in thought, she hadn't even considered that she might have been watched. She looked at the nearly deserted street. A couple of old, closed-up buildings were across from the agency and farther up the street were two houses, both of which looked lived in and both of which had seen better days. A handful of aging, ragged palm trees lined the street. She wondered why Finn had chosen this area for her agency. She imagined at night, the street—Moonlight Avenue—would be downright creepy.

CHAPTER TWENTY

Finn turned away from the window when the young woman finally drove off. She'd thought at first the woman was on her phone, taking her sweet time leaving. But no. She appeared to be lost in thought, almost unaware of her surroundings. Was she remembering that night? Going back in time? Or had she walked in, seen her, and had only a flicker of recognition…like Finn was someone she'd met before but she couldn't quite put her finger on it? She glanced at the paper in her hand one more time—*Rylee Moore…Rylee*—then wadded it up. It didn't matter. She wasn't going to hire her. But there was no trash can to drop it into; even that had been removed. Instead, she tossed it onto her desk, making a mental note to add a trash can to her list of things to buy.

She was about to go see how Simon was doing with his packing when her office phone rang. She very nearly ignored it but snatched it up at the last minute. Despite everything that had happened, she still had a business to run.

"Moonlight Avenue Investigations."

"Finley Knight?"

"Speaking," she said a bit impatiently. It was a man's voice with just a hint of an accent that she couldn't place. She frowned. The same voice she'd heard the other week when a caller had been looking for Daniel Frazier? A caller who had hung up on her.

"Give me what Frazier gave you."

"Excuse me?"

"I'm sure you don't want any more trouble there, Ms. Knight. Hand it over and I'll leave you alone."

She gripped the phone tighter. "I don't know what the hell you're talking about. But if it was you who killed Sammy, I'll put a bullet in you myself," she said between gritted teeth.

There was a long pause and she swore she heard him chuckle. "Was that the old man's name?"

"You son of a bitch," she snarled.

"I need you to hand over what Frazier gave you. I don't have a beef with you. Hand it over and we'll call it good."

"Go to hell!"

She had the pleasure of slamming the phone down. It was only then she realized that her hands were shaking. She stood up, going to the window, half expecting to see a car screeching to a halt outside and several men running toward her.

The sunshine from that morning had disappeared. The clouds were heavy now, threatening rain. Dusk was but an hour away.

She went down the hallway to the door that separated her office suite from Simon's. She opened the door, seeing boxes in various stages of packing. There was no sign of Simon or his wife. Perhaps they had already moved a load out. She would call him, tell him not to come back tonight, tell him not to come until morning—and daylight. But first, she needed to call Dee Woodard.

* * *

"I told you, Daniel Frazier didn't give me anything," she said again, her voice louder now. "Quit trying to turn this into something it's not."

"Finn, you called me, remember?"

"Look, I just wanted you to know about the phone call. That's all."

She heard Dee sigh. "I offered to put a trace on your phone. You refused."

"Because I don't want the police to monitor my every goddamn move." She ran a hand through her hair, regretting calling Dee in the first place.

"Do you want protection?"

Finn snorted. "From the CCPD? I think I can handle it."

"You're being difficult."

"We don't know each other well enough for you to call me difficult."

"You're right. I should treat you like any other citizen who may or may not be linked to two homicides. So you know what? I *am* going to have the guys come by your office and set up a trace on your phone. First thing in the morning. And whether you like it or not, I may get a unit assigned to you, maybe two. One at your house, one at your office. How's that?"

"Now who's being difficult? But no, I won't consent to having my damn phone tapped. Forget it." She heard another sigh from Dee.

"Where are you anyway?"

"At home. Outside, watching it rain." She paused. "Anything new on the case?"

"You know I can't discuss an open case with you, Finn. Especially one that you are involved in."

No, she didn't think Dee would divulge anything. And probably, there was nothing to divulge anyway. Michael Drake was a dead end. Well, she would do her own poking around.

And she would start with Connie Frazier.

CHAPTER TWENTY-ONE

Finn rang the doorbell, then knocked. After a few seconds, she rang the doorbell again. As Dee had threatened, there had been a patrol car parked on her street that morning when she got up. Another was outside of her office. Instead of going in, she simply turned around and took that opportunity to pay Connie Frazier a visit. Dee would be pissed, she knew, but she didn't care. Whoever killed Daniel Frazier had also killed Sammy. Dee had rules to follow. Finn did not. Well, she did…she simply chose to ignore them.

"Who is it?"

She stared at the door. "Finley Knight, Mrs. Frazier. Your husband was a client of mine." She paused. "I'm a private investigator." She held up her identification badge to the peephole. "I just need a few minutes of your time."

The door opened slowly and Connie stared back at her. She looked…worn out. Gone was the smiling face Finn had recorded when she'd seen Connie Frazier after an encounter with Michael Drake. Now…hollow eyes, tearful eyes.

"You're who again?"

"Finley Knight. Your husband hired me. I'm sorry. He suspected you were having an affair. He hired me to…well, to investigate it."

Connie didn't invite her inside. Instead, she stepped out onto the porch and closed the door. "What is it you want? Did he not pay you or something?"

"Whoever killed your husband, they broke into my office, looking for something. Something they think Daniel gave me. They killed... they killed a friend of mine." She swallowed. "Has anyone contacted you?"

"Just the police. They think Mark...Mark killed Dan." Connie took a deep breath. "So you were following me?"

"Yes."

"Taking pictures?"

"Yes. I'm sorry." Finn couldn't recall ever meeting face-to-face with someone she'd run surveillance on. She'd certainly never offered an apology for doing it.

"I loved my husband," Connie said almost defiantly. "But he wasn't home much. He was more concerned with the pizza parlors than he was me. And I got lonely. I never thought he'd even notice, much less hire a private investigator."

"If you don't mind me asking, did you only recently get lonely and seek out someone or..."

"Dan has been absent for years. The kids are both gone and...yes, I was lonely. But I didn't seek out Mark. It's not like I've ever done anything like that before."

"I know him as Michael Drake."

"Yes. That's what the police said. I can't believe it, really. He was so...so nice to me, so sweet. I can't believe they think he killed Dan." She shook her head. "For what reason?"

"Perhaps he was jealous," Finn offered, even though she thought no such thing. "Maybe he wanted you all to himself."

"No. He was married too." She met Finn's gaze. "I suppose that was a lie as well."

Finn shrugged. "He's not contacted you?"

"No. I thought he would. I mean, surely he heard about Dan's murder. It was on TV and in the newspaper. But our kids were here... for the funeral, you know. I've tried calling him but there's never an answer," she said sadly. "I thought maybe, well, when the doorbell rang, I thought maybe it was him. Maybe he was letting things settle down first." She smiled sadly. "Of course, I never told him where I lived. Why would it be him?"

"He never came to your house?"

"No. I mean, he wanted to—he asked all the time if he could—but I…well, I wouldn't disrespect Dan like that, bringing another man into our bedroom, no matter how much he begged." As if realizing how that sounded, she tried to wave her words away. "I loved my husband. I really did. Only, he loved his business more than me."

"Was your husband mixed up in anything? Drugs? Gambling?"

Connie gasped. "Of course not! All he was mixed up in was pizza. He lived and breathed it."

Finn shoved her hands into the pockets of her jeans, debating how much to tell Connie Frazier. Dee would probably be pissed but…

"Look, I don't mean to be so blunt, but didn't it strike you odd that Michael Drake—or Mark Condra—sought you out? He was a handsome man, almost striking. No offense, Mrs. Frazier."

Connie blushed. "I know what you're saying, of course. Why would someone like that be interested in someone like me?" She smiled wistfully. "When I was with him, I thought I was the luckiest woman in the world. He made me feel beautiful."

"They trashed my office, looking for something. Something they thought Daniel had given me. I got a phone call yesterday demanding I turn over what Daniel had left me. Do you have any idea what that could be?"

Connie shook her head slowly. "No. I have no idea. Dan's life was the pizza business. That's all he did. From five in the morning until nine or ten at night, it was pizza. On rare occasions, he would get home at eight, in time to share dinner with me." Her lips set into a firm line. "That last night…he came home early, just before eight. We had dinner together. He would hardly speak to me, hardly ate a bite. I knew something was wrong. Not that we talked much, you know. He was always full of pizza stories and I would listen. But that night, no. There was mostly silence."

"And he left again?"

"Yes. It was after nine, I think. He wouldn't tell me where he was going. Then…then he never came back. I called his cell several times the next morning. I called all four of the stores. Then…then the police came." Her lip quivered. "Now I'm all alone. Dan's gone. The kids are gone. Mark's gone."

"Mark…did he have an accent?"

"An accent?"

"When he spoke, was there an accent?"

Connie smiled. "He had the sexiest voice. Yes, his mother was from Brazil. Some words he said different than we do. It was really cute."

Finn wondered who Connie Frazier missed more—her husband or her lover? If she had to guess, she'd say the dashing lover was who Connie was longing for.

"I've taken up enough of your time, Mrs. Frazier. Thank you for speaking with me."

"I'm sorry about your friend. But I can't imagine Mark would do something like that. I just can't."

Finn smiled politely. "Thank you for your time."

CHAPTER TWENTY-TWO

As she did the first time she'd visited Finn's house, Dee stopped at the gate and reached out the window, hitting the button for the intercom. Since Finn wasn't at her office, she assumed she'd be here. It was another dark and drizzly day. Where else would Finn be?

"Yeah? Who is it?"

"It's me. Dee."

"Ah, Detective Woodard. Come in."

The gate opened and Dee drove up the driveway, parking behind the closed garage doors. She went around to the passenger's side and took out the three bags she'd brought along. Finn was standing at the door as she hurried through the rain. Finn raised her eyebrows questioningly as Dee brushed past her.

"You haven't eaten, I hope."

"Eaten?"

"Thanksgiving."

"Thanksgiving?"

Dee nearly rolled her eyes. "Today's Thanksgiving. Turkey. Football."

Finn looked embarrassed. "I'm sure I would have figured that out eventually." She sniffed the bags. "That does smell good."

Finn helped her unpack the food; turkey and dressing, mashed potatoes and a tub of gravy, green beans that appeared to be swimming in butter, and four very soft, very fresh dinner rolls.

"I was lucky to find a place that still had food. They were out of that sweet potato dish with the marshmallows. I don't care for it myself, but it is traditional." She pulled a bottle out from one of the other bags. "I didn't picture you as a wine drinker. Scotch?"

Finn looked at the bottle of Johnnie Walker Black, smiling as if looking at an old friend. "Perfect."

They made their plates in the kitchen then took them over to the dining table. Finn put the TV on but turned the sound on the football game low enough so that it was only a murmur. They touched glasses, both sipping from their scotch before picking up forks.

"I went by to see Connie Frazier yesterday," Dee said.

"Oh, yeah?"

"Imagine my surprise to learn that you had paid her a visit."

Finn shrugged but said nothing.

"You can't work the case, Finn. That's my job."

"Yeah, but I'm the one whose office got trashed. I'm the one who lost Sammy. And I'm the one who got the phone call."

"You can't work the case. You'll get in the way."

"Why did you go see Connie Frazier?"

"Why did you?" Dee countered.

"She was actually quite talkative. When I told her who I was, I thought she'd be pissed as hell, but she wasn't."

"Gonna share what you talked about?"

"There was no revelation, if that's what you're asking. She didn't have a clue as to what Daniel could have had that someone would kill for." Finn smiled. "And thank you for the police protection. How long do you plan to keep that up?"

"As long as Captain Mabanks will let me. I take it there's been no further contact?"

"No." Finn seemed to hesitate and she put her fork down. "I had a call before. I think it was the day you came by with the subpoena. It was the same voice. Just a hint of an accent. Connie Frazier said that Mark Condra's mother was from Brazil and that he had a slight accent." Finn smiled. "Sexy, she called it."

"You're saying you had a call right after Daniel Frazier was killed?"

"Yes. The caller asked if Daniel Frazier was a client. I asked who he was and he hung up. I had actually forgotten about that call. Then when he called back, it was the accent that I remembered. A slight accent, mind you. Very subtle."

"Connie had said that you'd insinuated Daniel was mixed up in something. Drugs? Gambling?"

"Something, obviously. It got him killed. I poked around in his finances. There wasn't anything—"

"You did *what*? I'm pretty sure there are limits as to what you can dig in, aren't there?"

"I may have crossed a few lines, yes."

"Again, this is my job. Not yours."

Finn ignored her. "As I was saying, there was nothing that jumped out at me. No red flags."

"I know. That was the first thing we looked at."

"So it's been two weeks. You have anything?"

"You know I can't discuss this case with you, Finn." Dee pointed her fork at her. "And you need to quit poking around in things." She wished she could discuss it, though. Daniel Frazier's pizza business was doing really well. All four stores were profitable. One store, in particular, moved a lot of money. That was the one they were interested in.

"I have time right now. I'm in between clients." Finn shrugged. "And Simon moved out."

"The accountant?"

"Yeah. The whole Sammy thing freaked him out. Can't say I blame him."

"And you? Will you be able to stay there?"

"I own the building." Finn finished the scotch in her glass. "I think I'll move to Simon's side, though. When I'm in my office..." she said, her voice trailing away.

"Yes, I imagine so."

Finn cleared her throat. "Thank you for bringing food. I think probably in the back of my mind I knew it was Thanksgiving. It's not a holiday I normally celebrate anyway."

"No family around?"

"No. Sammy. We would sometimes go out and get shrimp and fish, never turkey."

"I'm really sorry about Sammy, Finn."

Finn took a deep breath. "Yes. Thank you." She paused. "My mother lives in Corpus."

Dee wanted to ask all sorts of questions, but Finn got up and headed toward the kitchen, her nearly empty plate in her hand. She smiled as she watched Finn take second helpings of everything.

CHAPTER TWENTY-THREE

So she couldn't give it a week. She was still feeling guilty over missing Thanksgiving—her mother had made sure of that. Rylee didn't dare tell her mother that she celebrated with a large, loaded pizza and beer, compliments of Leena, one of the new friends she'd met. She also didn't tell her that Leena had supplied the pizza and beer, hoping she'd get lucky and Rylee would end up in her bed. She didn't.

It was Friday, the day after Thanksgiving—Black Friday. She didn't think Finley Knight was the type to fight crowds at the mall. But still, she wouldn't have been surprised to find Moonlight Avenue Investigations shuttered on this day after a holiday. She was surprised, however, to see a police car parked across the street from the agency.

The same car as the other day was parked out front of the office—a dark Buick LaCrosse. She didn't recall this being the car she'd ridden in when they went to the motel that night, but she hadn't really been concerned with the car, had she? Maybe Finley Knight *wasn't* the woman she'd slept with after all. She smirked and allowed herself a quick roll of the eyes.

She parked her Jeep next to Finn's car, feeling her heart flutter a little nervously in her chest. Her last chance, she reminded herself.

She needed to be ultra-charming, ultra-convincing to get Finn to hire her. She admitted, though, that her chances were probably slim. She looked down at her jeans, wondering if she should have dressed up. She'd taken her cue from Finn. She'd been dressed casually in jeans the other day when she'd met her. At the bar, too…Finn had been in jeans. Even though their encounter the other day had been brief, she didn't picture Finley Knight as the dressed-up type. She looked too comfortable, too at ease in her jeans. She paused for a moment, recalling how she'd slipped those jeans off Finn's hips.

God.

Rylee walked to the door and took a deep breath, then turned the knob. It was locked.

"Great," she murmured.

She was about to knock when she heard a scuffling noise, then a bang. Then cursing. She smiled, her tension easing for a second before she knocked loudly. A few moments later, the door was jerked open. Finn met her gaze.

"You again?"

"Rylee Moore," she said with—she hoped—a charming smile. "You sound like you could use some help."

Finn stepped back, letting her enter. "I'm still not hiring."

She spied the desk that was wedged in the doorway of Finn's office. "Moving?"

"To the offices on the other side of the building."

"Taking a wild guess here, but I don't think your desk is gonna fit through the door."

"It fit going in, obviously," Finn said dryly.

Rylee moved around her and inspected the wedged desk. "You should have taken the drawers out. That would give you an extra inch or so." She looked back at Finn. "It was probably moved in on its side, though."

Finn stared at her. "What are you doing here?"

"Looking for a job," she said truthfully. "Willing to *beg* for a job."

Finn met her gaze, as if trying to read her. "Why?"

Rylee felt her confidence waning. In fact, she was suddenly feeling very sorry for herself. "Because I moved here in June and haven't worked since. My savings are nearly drained. My apartment rent is due in a couple of days. My mother is mad at me for not being home for Thanksgiving and I didn't have the heart to tell her I couldn't afford the gas." She folded her hands together behind her back, hoping she wouldn't embarrass herself by crying. "So I need a job."

Finley Knight tilted her head, studying her. "What do you know about being a private investigator?"

"Nothing, really. I...I don't even *know* someone who is a private investigator. I was a security guard, though," she said, as if that made a difference.

"You're not doing a good job of selling yourself, kid."

Rylee met her gaze. "Please? Just give me a chance." To her surprise, Finley Knight seemed to actually be considering it.

"How are your vacuuming skills?"

"My what?"

Finn sat on the edge of her desk, dangling rather long legs—clad in familiar jeans—off the side. "I need someone to clean the office."

Rylee's eyes widened. "You want to hire me as a...a *housekeeper*? Seriously?"

"I'll hire you as a receptionist-slash-housekeeper."

"Slash-apprentice?" Rylee asked hopefully. She could tell Finn was struggling not to roll her eyes.

"There's an apartment upstairs. You can start there."

"Start there? Cleaning?"

"Yes. And boxing things up."

"I don't understand."

"Sammy...Sammy doesn't live there anymore."

"Sammy? He moved?"

"He died."

"Oh, I'm sorry," she said automatically.

Finn chewed on her lip, then motioned toward her office. "In there. He died in there."

Rylee swallowed. "Oh."

"He...he was killed, actually. Shot."

Rylee's eyes widened again. "Like...recently?"

"Yes. The place was ransacked. Sammy must have heard them, came downstairs to investigate...they killed him."

"Oh." She blinked several times. "In there?" She swallowed again. "Does this sort of thing happen a lot?"

A hint of a smile lit Finn's face before she arched an eyebrow. "Changing your mind?"

Rylee shook her head. "That's why the office was...cleaned out?"

"Yes."

"And that's why you're moving?"

"Yes."

Rylee took a deep breath. "Have they arrested somebody?"

"No."

Jesus…was she really considering the job offer? The job offer of receptionist and housekeeper? Working for a woman she had a one-night stand with? A woman who apparently didn't remember it? *Really?* With a murderer on the loose?

"So?" Finn asked.

She took another deep breath. "Why was the office ransacked?"

"They were looking for something."

"Did they find it?"

"No."

Rylee raised one eyebrow. "*Will* they find it?"

"Considering I don't know what they're looking for…I'd have to say no." Finn shoved off the desk. "So? Still want to work here?"

Rylee nodded. "I was a security guard. I saw my share of scary men." She smiled quickly. "And I carry a gun."

Finn seemed to consider her statement, then she nodded. "Okay, then. How about you help me move this desk?"

* * *

It took them the better part of a half hour to get the desk through the door and yes, on its side. Finn wasn't worried about scratch marks. As she told Rylee, the desk was old. She'd bought it secondhand when she'd started the business. However, as they rested against it, Rylee made a suggestion that made too much sense.

"If I'm going to be the receptionist—and I'd much rather have the title of assistant—then why don't we move this huge-ass desk over there and you get a new one for your new office?"

Finn's gaze followed where she pointed, the little nook in the entryway, a spot where she'd always envisioned a desk…and a receptionist. Before, she'd kept a small table there, a lamp, a couple of chairs. Now? There was nothing there except a phone, which was plopped on the floor.

She raised an eyebrow. "Assistant, huh?"

Rylee smiled and Finn noted her perfect teeth, the smooth skin that showed not even a hint of a wrinkle or laugh line around her blue-green eyes. Blue-green eyes that seemed to look right into her very soul. It couldn't possibly be, but that look seemed so familiar to her. It had been six months, yet…

"Assistant or…apprentice…whatever works best for you."

Finn smiled. "Receptionist works best, but I'll go with assistant, if that makes you feel better." She tried to guess her age. Was she even twenty-five? "How old are you?"

"I'm fairly certain you can't ask that question in a job interview."

"I wasn't aware this was a job interview."

Rylee blew out her breath. "I'm twenty-nine, at least for another few weeks. And yes, I realize that's a little old to be making a career change." She shrugged. "It's also a little old to quit a job without having another one. Quit a job and move across the state to a city where I don't know a soul. And a little old to be concerned with my parents being disappointed in my choice. Choices," she corrected.

"Well, first off, I would have pegged you at about twenty-five—"

"Oh…thank you very much! That's sweet!"

"And second, I was thirty when I made a career change. If you're not happy in your current job, you're never too old to make a change."

"Thirty? And what were you before?"

"I was a…a detective. Here in Corpus."

"Really? You were a cop?"

"I was."

"So you just quit one day and opened up this place?"

If only it was that simple, Finn thought. She shook her head. "No. It was a little more complicated than that." She walked over to the reception area, wondering why she'd let this young woman—this woman she'd slept with—talk her into hiring her. She didn't really need a receptionist or an assistant. She certainly did not need or want an apprentice. She had a sneaky suspicion that the very lovely Rylee Moore would talk her into that title before too long. She turned back to her, wondering if Rylee remembered that night or not. Yes, of course she did. She supposed Rylee was choosing to ignore it…much like she was. If she was going to work here, it was probably best that they ignore it.

"I guess you're right. We should move the desk over here. I happen to be on good terms with the owner of a furniture store," she said, thinking of Mr. Honeywell. He'd been both pleased and shocked when she'd given him her report. "I think I'll go see him today and get some office furniture delivered."

Rylee gave a huge smile and ran her hand across Finn's old desk. "Great! When should I start?"

Finn looked up to the ceiling out of habit. "I'd like to get the apartment cleaned up as soon as possible."

"Consider me on it."

Finn pointed to a door in the hallway. "The stairs are there. There's a closet inside the stairwell where Sammy kept all his cleaning supplies." She looked at Rylee thoughtfully. "I'll go up with you. There may be some things I'll want to keep."

"I'm assuming he was more than just a renter to you. I'm sorry."

Finn nodded. "Yes, he was." She didn't feel the need to elaborate.

CHAPTER TWENTY-FOUR

Finn stood in her new office, looking at the new desk, the credenza behind it, and the bottle of scotch and her father's glass, the only things sitting on it. All the important things, she thought wryly as she took the key from her pocket—the unknown key—and slipped it into the middle drawer of the desk. After helping her pick out furniture on Friday, Honeywell had it delivered before noon Monday— yesterday. His guys had also hauled off all the old furniture in Sammy's apartment. There had been an awkward moment when she'd had to approach the patrol car Dee had assigned to her. It was in the way of the delivery truck. She had taken that opportunity to ask them to park a little farther away from the office, telling them they were scaring off potential clients. They didn't seem to care. Apparently, Dee had instructed them to park directly across the street. She hadn't seen or spoken to Dee since their impromptu dinner on Thursday.

Which had been nice. It was thoughtful of Dee to pop over, somehow guessing that Finn would be alone on Thanksgiving. She wondered if Dee had done it because Finn was alone or because she was alone and wanted company on the holiday.

It didn't matter, really. They'd spent a pleasant afternoon together, even venturing out into the light mist to walk the pier. She hadn't seen Larry—her neighbor—since she'd told him about Sammy. He had spent Thanksgiving with his daughter in San Antonio. He'd left a message on her phone last night. He was back and wanted to get together. He wanted to know the details about Sammy. She wasn't in the mood to talk about it, so she ignored his call.

"Do you ever sleep? I left at nine last night and you were still here."

She turned, startled by the voice. It was barely daylight on another drizzly morning; she wasn't expecting Rylee this early. She realized she was holding a cup of coffee and she hadn't even taken a sip yet.

"I sleep...some," she offered. "You're here kinda early this morning."

Rylee shrugged. "Trying to make a good impression on my new boss."

Finn gave her a small smile. "Well, it's not like we're overrun with customers."

"Do you have any clients? I mean, ongoing."

Finn nodded. "A few businesses in town retain me for their new hires. And I have a few law offices that use me for divorce cases or custody battles, things like that."

"I see. But nothing right now?"

Finn took a sip of her coffee, grimacing when she discovered it wasn't even lukewarm any longer. Just how long had she been standing there, staring into space? Should she tell Rylee that she turned down a client who phoned yesterday simply because she couldn't seem to focus on anything other than the connection between Daniel Frazier and whoever killed Sammy? Should she tell her that despite Dee's assertion that she should leave it alone, she was still poking around in Frazier's business dealings?

"No," she said simply. "Why are you here so early?"

"I thought I'd finish cleaning the apartment upstairs. Baseboards and such. You said you had painters coming this afternoon."

"They'll be here at one."

"So then, I thought...you know, I'd be available to help you, if anything came up."

"Ah. The apprentice thing, huh?"

Rylee smiled. "Yes, the apprentice thing. Can't you give me *something* to do?"

"Look, kid, I told you, I don't—" Her cell phone interrupted her and she answered without looking. "Finn here."

"It's me. Are you at home or office?"

"Office. What's going on?"

Dee cleared her throat. "I've been processing a scene. Connie Frazier was murdered last night."

"Christ," she murmured. "Where?"

"Her home. Her housekeeper comes at five a.m. every Tuesday. She found her."

Finn glanced at the clock she'd hung on the wall just yesterday evening. It was 7:22. "What happened?"

"Whatever they couldn't find at your office, they apparently were searching for it here. She was tied up. Appears she was tortured." Dee paused. "This is totally unorthodox, but I'd like you to come to the scene. Take a walkthrough with me. Get your feel on it."

"Of course. I'll be right there." She turned to Rylee. "I've got to go. Lock the front door. Don't answer it for anyone. If the phone rings, don't answer it. Don't worry about the apartment. We'll clean it up after the painters leave. It'll be a couple of days before the new furniture comes anyway."

Rylee's brow furrowed. "What's going on?"

Finn ignored her question. "You said you carry a gun. Do you have it with you?"

"I do."

Finn was about to walk out, then stopped. "I mean, you *legally* carry a gun, right?"

Rylee nodded. "I have a license to carry a handgun, yes. A Beretta."

Finn met her gaze, again taken aback by the blueness of her eyes. The blue tinged with green. She almost forgot what she was going to say. "The guy...the guy who killed Sammy, it looks like he may have killed someone else last night. That was Detective Woodard. She wants me at the scene," she explained.

Again Rylee frowned. "A detective is requesting a private investigator at a murder scene? Is that normal?"

Finn shrugged. "What can I say? Just lock up after me. I shouldn't be more than an hour or two."

"Okay, I'll be fine. Don't worry about me."

CHAPTER TWENTY-FIVE

Police lights cut through the cloudy drizzle and Finn parked along the street, five or six cars back from the driveway to the Frazier residence. She was stopped as soon as she stepped onto the driveway by a uniformed officer.

"Detective Woodard called me," she explained. "I'm Finley Knight."

He nodded. "Yeah, okay. She's expecting you. She was in the kitchen."

Finn walked in through the front door, then stopped, taking in the total mess that was now Connie Frazier's home. Much like her office had been, everything was turned inside out. She skirted around an oversized chair that had been tipped on its side, the cushions ripped open. The leather sofa had suffered the same fate. Her gaze was fixed on the blood that stained the beige carpet.

She followed the sound of voices, finding herself standing in the entryway to the kitchen. Dee was speaking on the phone and two men were beside her, one in uniform, the other in a rumpled suit. Dee must have sensed her. She turned and waved her closer.

"Yes, I'll be in later. We can go over it then." Dee pocketed her phone, then turned to the uniformed officer. "Captain says for you to stay until everything is processed. Send Baxter and Jones back on patrol."

He nodded and left without a word. Finn arched an eyebrow as she stared at the other man. Dee motioned toward him.

"My partner, Joel Yearwood. Joel, this is Finley Knight. Her card was in Daniel Frazier's possession when we found him."

"Yes. And I understand your office got broken into." He held a hand out and Finn shook it. "What brings you around? This is a crime scene."

Finn stared at him for a long moment, then dismissed him, turning to Dee instead. "Find anything?"

"What you see is what you get. They've already taken the body. You'll be spared that, at least."

"Tortured?"

"Excuse me," Joel interrupted. "Detective, this is highly—"

"I asked her to come by, Joel. As you said, her office was ransacked much like this house. Another set of eyes."

"But—"

"I used to be a detective with CCPD," Finn offered. "I'm sure Captain Mabanks will vouch for me."

Dee smiled quickly. "Yes, I'm sure he will. Joel, why don't you go upstairs, see if they need any help."

"Yeah. Sure," he said rather unenthusiastically.

Dee sighed when he left. "He's not very seasoned or intuitive. He wants evidence handed to him nice and neat." She headed back into the living room and Finn followed. "Most of the destruction is down here. It doesn't look like anything was left untouched. Upstairs, it's more hit and miss, really."

Finn stared at a chair in the middle of the room and again at the bloodstains on the carpet around it. "Is that where you found her?"

"Yes."

"So they made her watch while they ransacked everything?"

"I suppose. And of course we have no way of knowing if they found what they were looking for. Maybe that's why the upstairs isn't quite as bad. She could have given up the location."

Finn shook her head. "Connie Frazier, to me, didn't seem like the type to be able to withstand torture. I'd guess if she knew what they were looking for, she would have handed it over immediately." She glanced again at the blood splatter on the beige carpet. "They cut off fingers?" she guessed.

"Yes. Six of them." Dee ran a hand through her hair. "I don't mind saying, it's probably one of the worst things I've seen. She was covered in blood, head to toe."

"Cause of death?"

"Gunshot to the head. It didn't appear to be postmortem."

Finn met her gaze. "Tortured. Organized crime? Mob?"

"In Corpus? Come on."

"Drug cartel?"

"We're quite a ways from the border, but they do have a long reach. It's premature, at this point."

Finn tilted her head. "As I said the other night, there were no red flags in his personal finances, but I did find a few things in his business affairs that looked off."

Dee shook her head. "Finn, I told you, stay out of it."

"Stay out of it? Then why did you ask me here?"

Dee blew out a breath. "Because I need someone to talk to about this besides Joel."

Finn supposed it went without saying that Dee didn't trust her partner, so she simply nodded.

"Okay. I'll play along. After all, you are guarding my home and office."

"Yes, I am." Dee glanced at her watch. "I've got to brief Captain Mabanks. Let's take a walk through the house. I'll let you form your own opinion on it." She paused. "If you're free, I can come by your house this evening. We can go over it then."

"I'm free. Want to do dinner too?"

Dee smiled. "I don't picture you the cooking type."

"I'm not. I'm the pick-up-and-take-home type."

"Can we do it early? Six?"

"Sure."

"Okay. Let's go upstairs. I'll show you the bedroom."

CHAPTER TWENTY-SIX

Rylee stood with her shoulder pressed against the doorjamb, her eyes roving around Finn's office. She was curious about the woman, to say the least, but she did resist going inside. She wouldn't resort to snooping in her desk drawers. She eyed the glass tumbler and a bottle of liquor on the credenza. Rum or bourbon? She shook her head. Not rum. No...that night, Finn had been drinking whiskey. She'd tasted it on her lips.

She closed her eyes at the memory, feeling a ripple travel down her body.

That night.

What were the chances? It was her one and only time to go to the bar. She certainly hadn't gone with the intention of sleeping with someone. She was new in town and thought maybe she might meet someone, a new friend, something. Nothing more than that. But... *damn*. She'd looked across the bar and there she sat, her dark eyes watching her. Rylee had been paralyzed. Never in her life had she had such an instant attraction to someone. It was as if Finn had been looking into her very soul that night.

The first dance, she remembered the way their bodies had touched, remembered how she trembled when Finn had pulled her close...far too close for a first dance. She remembered thinking at the time that it felt like they'd danced thousands of times before. Perhaps that's why it hadn't shocked her when Finn's lips had brushed her face, her ear... her mouth.

"*God...*"

Fate was a funny thing, wasn't it?

She closed her eyes, then spun on her heel, heading back out to her own desk. Now here she was, working for that very same woman. And neither of them had so much as even hinted they remembered that night. No doubt there'd been surprise on her face that first day. Finn's face had flashed only a glimmer of recognition, but that was it. No comment. No innuendo. No nothing.

Which suited her just fine. Perhaps Finn really didn't remember. That would be super, wouldn't it? Rylee wouldn't have to face the embarrassment then. Because meeting strangers at bars—sleeping with them—was something she never, ever did.

So why that night? Why was that night different? Was she lonely? Not particularly so. She was in a new city, sure. But even in Amarillo, she wasn't constantly surrounded by people...or friends. So why that night?

She had no idea. Couldn't resist? That seemed too easy of an excuse, even if it was the truth. To be honest, she was the one who suggested a motel, not Finn. They'd gotten carried away, kissing and...and touching. She felt her face turn red at the memory. Right there in a dark and shadowy bar—with a stranger—making out like a teenager in the backseat of a car, fogging windows. Making out? That was an understatement. Finn's hands had been...well, in places that they shouldn't have been.

She should have called it a night right then. She should have walked away. But Finn had hesitated and she'd hesitated and the next thing she knew, they were on their way to a motel. Fifteen minutes later, they were naked. She blushed again. She'd had her first orgasm within thirty seconds.

She whipped her head around at the sound of someone knocking on the front door. She'd locked it as Finn had instructed.

"Hello? Are you open?"

Oh, crap. It was a woman. Should she open it? *Finn said not to open it for anyone,* she reminded herself. In fact, she had been adamant about it.

"Hello?"

She moved closer to the door. This was just a woman, she reasoned. Probably a potential client. It wasn't a murderer. Surely, it wasn't.

"Who is it?" she called.

"Excuse me?"

Rylee bit her lip. This was no way to conduct business. No wonder Finn wasn't overrun with clients. She unlocked the door and opened it, finding a young woman about her own age staring back at her.

"Is this Moonlight Avenue Investigations?" She took a step back. "Or…I guess I'm at the wrong place, huh?"

"No, no. You're at the right place. I'm sorry, come in." Rylee held the door open wider. "We've been moving offices around so…"

"Oh. Well, the sign is kinda small and…the neighborhood…"

"Yeah…kinda scary," Rylee said with a smile. "Just kidding, of course. Come in. What can I help you with?" She spotted the police car across the street. Oh, Finn was going to kill her.

"Are you a private investigator?"

Rylee swallowed nervously. "I am," she said with as much confidence as she could muster.

"I…well, I've never done this before," the woman said. "In fact, I only chose you because of your location. I didn't dare go to one of the larger agencies. I would die of embarrassment if someone saw me."

Rylee nodded appropriately. "We get that a lot. What is it you're looking for?" Rylee sat down at her desk—the receptionist desk—and motioned to one of the visitor's chairs she'd placed there not thirty minutes ago. "I apologize, but the offices aren't really set up yet for clients. Will this do?"

"Oh, it's fine."

"Good. What's your name?"

"Carolyn. Carolyn Baxter."

Rylee held her hand out across the desk. "I'm Rylee Moore. What can I help you with today, Carolyn?"

"Well, this might sound strange, but…well, I have a new boyfriend," she said with a big smile.

Rylee grinned back at her. "Congratulations."

Carolyn blushed. "Yeah…he's a really nice guy."

"But?" she prompted.

"Well, I'd read somewhere that it was a good idea…um, to do this sort of thing, you know, before things got too serious."

"Oh, I see. You want to check him out first? See if he's been lying about his past? His employment? That sort of thing?"

"Yes. It's crazy, isn't it? I mean, I should trust him. Right?"

"You're absolutely doing the right thing," Rylee said. "You don't want to marry the guy and find out later that he spent time in prison for rape or murder or something, right?"

Carolyn's eyes widened.

"Not that I'm insinuating anything," Rylee said quickly, holding her hand up. "Women do this all the time." *Do they?* "Better to be safe than sorry," she added.

"Oh, good. So you get these kinds of requests a lot?"

"We do," Rylee said, not knowing if Finn did or not. She pulled out a pad. "So, what's his name?"

"It's Johnny Arnold."

"Is Johnny his real name? His legal name?"

"Oh." The woman gave her a tentative smile. "I don't know. It's just Johnny."

Rylee winked at her. "Well, we'll find out for you. Where does he work?"

Before Carolyn could answer, the door opened rather abruptly. Finn stood there with a panicked look on her face. That panicked look then turned into a scowl. *Oh, no.* Finn did *not* look happy with her.

"Lock it. Don't let *anyone* inside." Finn cocked an eyebrow. "Remember?"

Rylee felt a blush light her face as she stood up quickly. "Carolyn Baxter...this is Finley Knight, owner of Moonlight Avenue Investigations." She met Finn's gaze, trying to decide if the look in her eyes was really anger. "Carolyn would like us to...to do a background check on her new boyfriend. I was just getting the information."

"I see."

Finn smiled rather charmingly at Carolyn Baxter and Rylee noted how the smile transformed her face. While she considered Finn to be nice-looking—she'd practically devoured her that night, hadn't she?— it wasn't until that very moment that she realized just how attractive she really was. Only the charming smile wasn't directed at her. Not this time.

"If you'll allow me a minute or two to speak with...with my assistant here," Finn said, glancing back to Rylee. "Then she'll be right out to get all the information we need."

"Of course."

"Great. Can I offer you something to drink? A bottle of water? A soda?"

"Oh, I'm fine."

Finn nodded politely. "Okay. Thank you. She'll be back in a second."

Finn turned and headed down the hallway to her new office and Rylee smiled apologetically at Carolyn.

"Be right back."

She hurried after Finn, wondering if she was about to get fired from a job she'd had for less than a week. *Lock the door and don't let anyone in.* Okay, so she'd ignored that directive. But they had a client. And from what she could tell...clients were few and far between here on Moonlight Avenue.

Finn was leaning against her desk when Rylee went into her office. Finn glanced at the door and Rylee took that to mean she wanted it closed. She closed it and leaned back against it, much like Finn was doing at the desk. As she met her eyes, she realized it wasn't anger that she saw there. For that, she was relieved.

"So...you got a client, huh?"

"I guess."

"Did she break the door down? Pick the lock?"

Rylee chewed on her lower lip. "I...I opened it for her."

Finn pushed off the desk. "There's a killer out there. He thinks I have something. The woman he killed this morning—or last night—he thought she might have what he's looking for. He tortured her before killing her." Finn stood in front of her. "There's a reason the police have a car watching my house, watching the office. There's a reason I said to keep the door locked and not to let anyone inside."

Okay, so maybe Finn was a little angry. She chanced meeting her gaze, wanting to plead her case. "But she's a woman. I could tell that she wanted—"

"You assumed. But what if you were wrong? What if he was using her to get you to open the door?"

Rylee blew out her breath. "You're right. I'm sorry."

Finn took a step closer. "I'm always right. Always. Remember that."

"Of course."

Finn then smiled, relieving some of the tension in the room. "So what information are you getting from her?"

"Name, where he works, his address, that kind of thing."

Finn nodded. "Cell phone number. We can use that to access a lot of information."

"So you're not mad?"

Finn stared at her. "I'm a little mad, yeah."

Rylee swallowed nervously. "Please don't fire me."

"I'm not going to fire you." She paused. "Do you like cats?"

Rylee frowned. "Cats? I guess. Why?"

"Because I've got one out in my car."

"Whatever for?"

"It was at the Fraziers' house. The woman who was killed. The police were going to take it to the pound until someone claimed it."

Rylee smiled. "How sweet. I wouldn't have taken you to be such a softie."

"Oh, yeah? A softie? Why do you think I hired you?"

Rylee's smile broadened. "Thank you very much."

"So? You'll help with the cat?"

"Sure."

Finn nodded, then motioned to the door. "Good. Now go take care of your client."

* * *

As soon as Rylee fled the room, Finn allowed a quick smile to her face. So the kid had a client. And yeah, she'd been a little angry when she'd found the front door unlocked. Angry and worried. She admitted that for a second there, she was almost afraid to open the door...afraid of what she might find. It had been damn stupid of her to leave Rylee here alone in the first place. Whatever the hell it was that Michael Drake wanted, he wasn't afraid to kill for it. She doubted that the patrol car parked down the street would have stopped him.

She shook her head. She had a receptionist. An *assistant*, she corrected. And now she had a damn cat. What the hell was wrong with her?

A softie? She would have never used that word to describe herself, but yeah, the cat—a ball of gray fur—had looked so pitiful when they'd scared her out of her hiding spot in an upstairs closet. The cat ran from the two officers trying to catch her and had darted between Finn's legs. She'd scooped up the frightened little thing without giving it a thought. The next thing she knew, Dee had found the litter box and food and had loaded up her car. To her surprise, the cat had sat quietly in her lap on the drive over. Finn had expected it to yowl its head off. The only sign the cat was scared were the claws that were digging into Finn's leg. And right now, she wondered if those claws weren't digging into her leather seats.

With a sigh, she went around to her desk and opened her laptop. Despite Dee telling her to stay out of it, she had a few things she wanted to check out. Namely, why was one of the pizza places moving so much more cash than the others?

CHAPTER TWENTY-SEVEN

Instead of using the intercom at Finn's gate, Dee pushed in the four-digit security code Finn had given her. The gate swung open and she drove inside. In her mirror, she saw the gate close again behind her. She was later than she'd planned. The briefing with Mabanks had taken longer than she'd thought and she admitted that it hadn't gone well.

The three murders were obviously linked; he wanted more than only her and Joel on the case. She, on the other hand, didn't know what good it would do to have more hands in the pot. There were no witnesses. There were no prints. It was a professional job—all three had been. She already had four guys pulling up everything they could find on Daniel and Connie Frazier and the Pizza Jamboree. She paused as she got out of the car. Yes, Daniel and Connie Frazier.

And Finley Knight.

She knew she really didn't have a legitimate reason to investigate Finn. And if Finn found out, she'd be pissed as hell, no doubt. She told herself that she was simply covering all her bases. And even though she believed Finn, everyone else involved was either dead or—as in Michael Drake's case—nowhere to be found. It could be that Finn was a player in this game—linked somehow to the Fraziers—and she didn't even know it. So Dee wasn't going to feel guilty about investigating Finn and her past. It was her job.

Finn opened the door before she could knock.

"I was about to start without you."

"Sorry."

"It's okay. I remember being a detective," Finn said. "Hard to keep decent hours working a homicide."

Dee walked past her, taking the time to look around. She'd been to Finn's house twice before, once after Sammy died and then again at Thanksgiving. As it had been on those occasions, the house was impeccably neat and hardly looked lived in. She glanced over at Finn.

"Do you have a housekeeper?"

Finn looked surprised by her question. "Do I need one?"

"Everything is so neat. Nothing out of place."

Finn shrugged. "There's actually not a whole lot here that could get out of place." She paused, as if deciding on whether to explain or not. "It was furnished when I moved here. I've replaced most of the furniture over the years, but I don't have a lot of personal stuff."

Dee went into the kitchen and felt Finn following her. "Did you keep it at the office?"

"It what?"

Dee met her gaze. "Personal stuff."

Finn leaned against the counter. "What is it you're fishing for?"

Okay, so maybe she did feel guilty. She decided to come clean. "I'm investigating your background. Your past."

As expected, Finn's expression changed and Dee saw a flash of anger in her eyes.

"I'm sure there's a reason you're invading my privacy," Finn said, her words a little clipped.

"I'm not trying to invade your privacy, Finn. I want to make sure you're not unknowingly involved somehow."

"Unknowingly? Is that a nice way of saying you think I could be 'unknowingly' withholding information from you?" she asked, making quotations in the air.

"Finn, I don't want to get into an argument with you. I thought you had a right to know, that's all." She took a step closer. "We have no usable prints. We have no witnesses. Our only choice is to dig into the backgrounds of these people and poke around...you included."

"I never met Daniel Frazier until he came to my office that day. My only link to him was that I ate pizza occasionally. So no, I don't appreciate you poking around into my past."

"Are you saying you have something to hide?"

"I'm saying I'm a private person." Finn turned and opened the oven door. "But you're right. I don't want to argue."

Dee couldn't help but laugh as Finn pulled the pizza box from the oven, the Pizza Jamboree's familiar logo emblazoned across the top.

"I suppose that's appropriate," she conceded. "I'm surprised they're still open. I think after Daniel's death, Connie did little more than sign checks at the request of the managers. I'm not sure what'll happen now."

"I would assume the son will take over. He's been on the payroll for the last year or more so I imagine he's already dabbled in the business." She motioned to the fridge. "I've got beer, if you're off duty." She glanced at Dee. "He's due to graduate in early December, by the way."

"And how do you know all that?"

Finn shrugged. "I may have poked around and broken a few privacy rules. Smart kid. Business degree. Marketing. 3.58 grade point average."

"You're very bad."

"Uh-huh. I'm sure you already have that information too."

"We do."

The beer was poured into two frosty mugs Finn took from the freezer and they ate at the bar instead of the table. The tension that had sprung up between them still lingered and Dee wrestled to find something to talk about that didn't involve the case.

"So…where's the cat?"

Finn's expression softened. "At the office. The damn thing sat in my lap most of the afternoon."

"Well, she was probably traumatized by what happened. Caging her up at the pound didn't seem right."

"You notify their kids?"

Dee raised her eyebrows. "The Fraziers? Captain Mabanks actually took care of that for me." She put her pizza down and wiped her mouth with the paper napkin. "Speaking of Mabanks, he wants to bring in another team on this one."

"Three murders…I suppose so."

Dee picked up her mug of beer and took a swallow before speaking. "Obviously you're still snooping around. What else have you found?"

"Probably the same thing you have," Finn said evasively.

Dee sighed tiredly. "Are we going to play that game?"

Finn stared at her for a long moment, then took a swallow of her beer too. "I was surprised by how lucrative the pizza business is."

Dee nodded. So yes, they had found the same thing. "Especially at the one over past the Causeway. The one on the island. Jamboree Number One."

Finn smiled. "Yeah, particularly that one. Maybe because it's the original restaurant." She picked up the pizza again. "Where do you think the money's coming from?"

"Drugs, most likely."

"That would be logical, but I don't think it fits in this case," Finn said. "There's nothing in Daniel Frazier's background to indicate he's involved in the drug business."

"That could be hidden easily."

"My gut tells me it's something else."

"Such as?"

"If it's drugs, what could Daniel Frazier have had—that they're willing to kill for—that would implicate them?"

"Suppliers, dealers, the traffic routes of how they move it across the border. Anything."

Finn shook her head. "Unless Daniel Frazier was very high up in an organization, there's no way he would know those things. Being anonymous—secretive—is how they survive."

"So? What else?"

"Why just one store? Why not spread it out among all of them?"

"Maybe he did. As we said, the pizza business was very lucrative."

"You've got to check out all the vendors, everyone he pays money to. You'll find some bogus ones. There's your money trail."

"And that money trail will have changed hands so many times, it'll be a maze."

Finn nodded. "So you've already found it."

"We found three vendors that aren't legit. The money is long gone from those accounts as well."

"Any names?"

"About as useful as Michael Drake. But we're still digging around."

Finn stood up, pacing behind the bar. "Connie Frazier was tortured. Who has the stomach for that? Not an amateur, that's for sure."

"No. Professional all the way around. No prints left at any of the scenes. Nothing. Not even a stray fiber."

"Was the same gun used on Connie?"

"Don't have ballistics back yet on her. Same gun killed Daniel Frazier and Sammy, yes." She frowned. "I thought I'd told you that."

Finn shook her head. "No." Then she smiled a little. "You don't discuss open cases with me, remember?"

"I suppose I've broken that rule."

Finn sat down again. "So Joel…your partner, you're not close?"

"Not really, no. I haven't been able to connect with him. And I do try," she added, reaching for another slice of the loaded pizza. "We don't make a good team, but Mabanks refuses to see it."

"He likes the way you operate and wants you to teach young Joel, huh?"

"I am usually very much by the book, yes. Having you at the scene today notwithstanding. I'd do much better with a female partner."

Finn laughed. "Wouldn't we all?" She leaned her elbows on the bar. "Speaking of that, I've…I've hired someone."

"Huh?"

"At the office," she clarified. "A receptionist. Well, more like she hired me."

"What do you mean?"

Finn shrugged. "She showed up one day, looking for a job. Wouldn't take no for an answer. Showed back up…next thing I know, she's working for me."

"A receptionist? Well, I thought it was odd that you didn't have one."

"Yeah…she wants to be an apprentice, but no, a receptionist. She prefers I call her my assistant." Then Finn smiled. "Although she did catch a client today."

"Are you sure she's…you know, *real?*"

"Meaning?"

"Meaning, if she showed up like you said, out of the blue when all of this is happening—the Fraziers…Sammy—is she for real?"

Finn stared at her for a moment, then shook her head. "She's real. I mean, even though I practically hired her off the street…she's real."

It was Dee's turn to stare. "You did do a background check on her, right?"

Finn shook her head. "No. It never even crossed my mind, actually." Finn tilted her head thoughtfully. "I'm a private investigator and I didn't do a background check," she said almost to herself. "No…but she's legit. Hell, she's just a kid, innocent…looking for a job."

"A kid?"

Finn smiled wryly. "Well, now that I'm forty, twenty-nine seems like a kid to me."

Dee laughed. "When you said 'kid,' I thought you were talking eighteen, twenty." Her smile faded. "But seriously, you didn't check her out? At all?"

"No. I guess I was preoccupied." Finn stole a pepperoni from one of the remaining slices in the box. "But she's harmless. She came looking for a job. Said she'd hit up all the other agencies already. Then she came back...Friday, after Thanksgiving."

"Okay, not to be a paranoid old cop or anything, but you really do need to run a check on her. I mean, she could be involved. She could be over there right now—"

"Doing what? Looking for what? There's nothing left," Finn reminded her.

"What about upstairs?"

"What about it?"

"The apartment. Sammy's place."

"There's nothing up there. Besides, we cleaned it out. She helped me. Had it painted today. Getting new furniture. There's nothing up there."

"It still seems strange that she popped up while all of this is going on."

"Yeah, you're probably right. I should run a check on her," Finn conceded. "I've just been...I don't know, out of sorts."

"Where's she from?"

"Amarillo. She moved down here this...this summer."

Dee elbowed her. "Is she cute?" She was surprised by the blush on Finn's face.

"She's a kid."

"Is she cute?" Dee asked again with a smile.

Finn gave a quick laugh. "Yeah...she's pretty cute. Blond. Blue eyes." Finn surprised her by the lingering blush. "Young."

"Twenty-nine is no kid, Finn."

"She barely looks twenty-five."

Dee nudged her again with her elbow. "Well, lucky you. And I'm stuck with Joel."

"Well, maybe you'll get lucky. He might request a transfer."

"I'm pretty sure he already has. And I'm still stuck with him."

CHAPTER TWENTY-EIGHT

"How did you get down here?"

Rylee smiled as the kitten rubbed against her legs. She picked it up and held her to her chest, listening to the constant purring. Well, it was not so much a kitten, but she doubted she was much older than six months.

She held the cat in one arm as she added sugar to her coffee. She supposed they needed to come up with a name for her sooner or later. Finn had said they would keep her here at the office—upstairs—until someone came to claim her. Rylee hadn't said anything at the time, but from what she'd learned from Finn and the newspapers, she doubted the Fraziers' two college-age children would be clamoring to adopt the cat. Their parents had been murdered only a few weeks apart. This cat, most likely, had not even crossed their minds.

She took the coffee and the cat and went back into the hallway, finding the door to the upstairs apartment ajar. She flipped on the light with her elbow as she took the stairs up. The door up there was ajar too.

She paused before pushing it open, wondering if she should be concerned. When she heard movement inside, she immediately turned, intending to head back downstairs. A familiar voice, however, stopped her.

"It's just me."

She turned back around, finding Finn standing in the doorway. "You scared the crap out of me!"

"Good."

She put the cat down. "Good?"

"Yes. You need to learn not to be so trusting." Finn scooped up the cat. "I see you escaped, hmm. Did I leave the door open again?"

"Either that or she's gotten very clever at opening them." She leaned against the wall, sipping from her coffee. "What are you doing up here anyway?" Finn arched an eyebrow and Rylee quickly smiled. "Sorry. I don't suppose that's any of my business."

Finn stroked the cat's head a couple of more times, then gently tossed it into the apartment and closed the door.

"How long have you been here?"

"First cup," Rylee said, holding up her coffee. "You?"

Finn walked past her, heading down. "Hour or so." She looked back over her shoulder. "You coming? I thought we'd work on your client this morning."

Rylee's face broke out into a grin. "You're going to let me do it?"

"I suppose. You've got to learn some time."

* * *

"So how do you get access to these databases?"

"I pay for them," Finn said as she logged into one. "I subscribe."

"So anyone—"

"No. You have to have a license to get a subscription. Some have a monthly fee, some have a fee per search. So don't go crazy," she said as she turned her laptop to face Rylee, who was sitting beside her.

"This is TLO. This is the one you'll use most often for background checks. When we find out where all he's lived, then we'll check the courts, see if there's been any warrants, any arrests, any DWIs, that sort of thing."

"Social media?"

"Oh, yeah. That's always fun," Finn said dryly, causing Rylee to laugh.

"I take it that's not your favorite thing to do?"

"I hate it. People are mostly idiots and I have to sort through all the crap they put out there." She motioned to the laptop. "Search away."

"But I don't even know if Johnny is his real name."

"You've got his phone number. We'll do a skip-trace from there."

Finn sat back as Rylee typed in the info she had. Rylee hesitated only a second or two before hitting the "search" tab. Finn had hesitated herself not two hours earlier. She had put in Rylee Moore's information, deciding that she did indeed need to do a background check on her after all. However, at the last second, she changed her mind. She didn't want to invade Rylee's privacy, for some reason. She decided to go with her gut and her gut told her that Rylee Moore was as harmless as a child.

That wasn't the only reason she'd changed her mind. She didn't want to delve into her background because she didn't want to be disappointed. She didn't want to stumble across something that might suggest Rylee made a habit of picking up women in bars.

"Oh, my God! Look at all this stuff," Rylee said excitedly.

Finn glanced at the screen and nodded. "A lot of it will be duplicated, but yeah, you should get an idea of what kind of guy your Johnny is."

"Jonathan," Rylee corrected. "I can even check out his parents and siblings." She looked at Finn. "Should I do that?"

"Only if you get red flags somewhere else. If he appears to be a model citizen, then no. You give your client the basic information she asked for. If she wants us to go deeper, then that'll cost her more."

"Do you get these kinds of requests often?"

"What? Women checking up on potential husbands? I've had a few. Hanson probably gets many more. I think I even saw an ad of theirs one time that suggested this was the latest thing in dating."

"I'm not sure how I feel about it. I mean, that's part of dating, isn't it? Getting to know the other person." Rylee leaned back in her chair and their shoulders were nearly touching. "Can you imagine how it would go? The other person tells you something from their past and you're like, oh, yeah, I already knew that. I did a background check." She made a face. "That would kill any romance right there for me."

"I tend to agree," Finn admitted, suddenly feeling crowded by Rylee's presence.

"You do? As a private investigator, I would have thought you'd be all into that."

Finn shoved her chair away and stood up, putting some space between them. "I am not into it for personal affairs and apparently, I'm not into it professionally either. Which should probably concern me."

"What are you talking about?"

"You. I should have done a background check on you, but I didn't."

"Oh, my God! You *didn't*? I assumed you had."

Finn shrugged. "Dee told me I was crazy for not doing it. I'm usually a good judge of character. I hope I'm not wrong."

"Dee is your detective friend?" Rylee folded her hands together. "What do you want to know? I don't have anything to hide. Except maybe my grades from a couple of college courses."

Finn shook her head. "Whatever I want to know, I'm not going to ask *you*," she said pointedly.

"Look, I'm an open book. Ask me whatever you want to ask me."

Finn tilted her head, looking at her. "Why did you leave your previous position?"

"Oh, please. That's where you want to start? I was a security guard, as you know. It was my father's company."

"Falling out with him?"

Rylee paused. "Um, not really, no. It was time to move on. Past time."

Finn leaned against her desk, the search on Johnny Arnold forgotten for the moment. Rylee's hesitation had piqued her curiosity. "Threw a dart at a map and picked Corpus?"

"The beach. I picked the beach."

Finn eyed her suspiciously. "And?"

Rylee pushed her chair away from the desk a little and stretched her legs out, looking up at Finn. It took all of Finn's willpower not to run her gaze along Rylee's legs, covered in jeans now. It wouldn't take much for her mind's eye to picture them as she remembered...bare, wrapped tightly around her.

"I didn't grow up wanting to be a security guard. I actually didn't know what I wanted to do. I have a criminal justice degree, but I didn't really want to be a cop. While I was in college, I thought being a game warden sounded fun, so I focused on that. Only I couldn't find a job there."

"In Amarillo?"

"Right," she said with a nod. "And at the time, I wasn't ready to move away. So I thought I'd work for my father a year or two, then venture out."

"So you still lived at home?"

"I lived at home until I was twenty-two. Then I didn't."

Finn raised her eyebrows questioningly and Rylee sighed.

"My relationship with my father is kinda strained. I couldn't live at home anymore."

"But not so strained that you didn't have a job?"

"He couldn't very well fire his only daughter." Rylee gave a quick shake of her head. "Although I'm sure he considered it at the time."

Finn studied her, wondering what all she was leaving out. She tapped the top of her desk with her index finger.

"What is it you're not telling me?"

Rylee stared at her. "What? You want all the gory details?"

"Yes."

Rylee blew out her breath. "Okay. My relationship with my father deteriorated because, well…when I came out to them, he pretty much blew a gasket."

Finn wondered if she should feign surprise at the news. It's not like they'd talked about that night. It's not like she would assume Rylee was gay if she met her on the street. She let her eyes move over her… the blond hair that was tucked behind one ear, minimal makeup, no lipstick. No earrings, at least not in the ear that was visible to her. No rings. A watch…a black sports watch on her left wrist. One of those exercise things—a Fitbit?—on her right wrist. As she'd told Dee… Rylee was cute. Pretty. Lovely, in fact.

"And your mother? How did she take the news?"

"I'm their only child. While she wasn't crazy about having a gay daughter, she didn't shun me or anything." Rylee still held her gaze and Finn found she couldn't look away. "She's not really speaking to me right now."

"Oh, yeah?"

"Because I didn't go home for Thanksgiving, she's upset. She gets great joy from playing the guilt card."

"Well, at least she wanted you there," Finn said, thinking briefly about her own mother. Did Finn even cross her mind over the holiday?

"I suppose. What about you?"

"What about me?"

"Thanksgiving? Family?"

"No," she said abruptly. She pointed at the laptop. "Your session will time out if you're not careful."

Rylee turned back to it. "So what should I do?"

"Download your search results. Read through it. Pull out whatever you think is pertinent. Make me a report."

"What if I do it wrong?"

"I'm going to do one on him too. We'll compare."

"But…I've never seen one of these reports before. How do you want it?"

Finn shrugged. "Whatever. Spreadsheet. Bullet items on a document. Whatever you feel comfortable with. Don't make it wordy. You're not doing a book report."

"So…just the facts. Timeline?"

Finn nodded. "That's how I would start. How old is the guy?"

Rylee looked at his date of birth. "Twenty-four."

"Go back to high school, then work through college to present day."

"Okay. I'm on it." She paused. "Thank you, Finn. For letting me do this."

"Yeah, well, don't go changing your title just yet, kid."

CHAPTER TWENTY-NINE

Dee rubbed her tired eyes, then finally clicked out of the report she'd been reading. A report about nothing, basically. They'd identified six bogus vendors from the Pizza Jamboree's books. Five of the vendors did business with all four of the pizza joints. Only one did business exclusively with the pizza parlor across the Causeway—Jamboree Number One. So yes, Daniel Frazier was moving money through all of his restaurants. All of the vendors' accounts were so neat and tidy, though, they'd lost the money trail after three transactions.

"You still here?"

She turned, finding Captain Mabanks watching her. His shiny bald head was covered with the fedora he normally wore when he was going out. He had a long raincoat draped over his arm.

"Raining again?"

"Off and on all day. I guess you haven't been out." He walked closer and sat down in the visitor's chair that was shoved close to her desk. "Anything pop up?"

"No. Dead end," she said with a heavy breath. "Everything about these murders is a dead end."

"I could bring in—"

"A fresh set of eyes won't do any good. There's no evidence to look at. Nothing. We have three dead bodies. That's it."

"What about Finley Knight? She's linked somehow. Have you found it?"

She shook her head. "Nothing in her background suggests she had any dealings with Daniel Frazier, other than he hired her right before he was killed."

"I don't guess you've considered she might be the killer."

Dee's eyes widened. "Excuse me?"

He shrugged. "Don't arbitrarily dismiss anyone as a suspect, Detective. You know the old saying…when you have no suspects, everyone is a suspect."

"The man who was killed at her office, Sammy Walker, was like family to her. I was there. I saw it." She shook her head. "She's not the killer."

He studied her for a moment. "I understand you've become rather friendly with her."

Dee arched an eyebrow but said nothing.

"When you have a patrol unit watching her home and office, it's hard to sneak in unobserved."

"I wasn't aware I was sneaking in. We've become friends, I guess."

"Nothing more?"

"Meaning?"

"Meaning…nothing more than friends?"

She gave him a quick smile. "If you're insinuating that we're romantically involved, you're way off base."

He stood up again and slipped on his raincoat. "How long do you intend to have her guarded? I would think it's been long enough. There's been no further contact, right?"

"No more phone calls, correct. It's only been five days since Connie Frazier's murder. I'd like to—"

"Let's pull them off, Dee. We're wasting resources."

Yes, she supposed it was time. Finn had asked her about it just yesterday. "Yes, sir. I'll take care of it."

He looked around the empty room. "Where's your partner?"

"He had a hot date, from what I could tell."

"And you?"

"Me?"

"You've been here a long time, Dee. What? Eight? Nine years?"

"Nine, sir."

He nodded. "I don't recall there ever being a mention of you and… well, someone special."

"No."

He nodded again, then turned to leave. But he paused, looking back at her. "Finley Knight. I remember her, of course. Not nearly as dedicated to the job as you are, however. She had a little problem with authority and rules and such. Attractive, though, I suppose."

Dee smiled. "Are you trying to play matchmaker?"

"Going through life alone is not much fun."

"Well, I've had years of practice. It's not so bad."

And it wasn't, really. She was used to it. Even though Angela still crossed her mind from time to time, she had reconciled with the fact that she would live out her years alone. She simply didn't have the energy to devote to dating. And Finn? She smiled to herself. No, they were too much alike. The tiny steps they were taking with their friendship was about all she could handle anyway. Although it was nice to have someone to share dinner with occasionally. She wondered what Finn thought of their relationship.

CHAPTER THIRTY

As she'd been doing every day, Rylee took her lunch upstairs to the empty apartment. Well, not empty. There was the cat that she was becoming quite attached to. She sat down on the new sofa, wondering why Finn had gotten leather. The cat immediately jumped up to join her.

"You are such a cutie," she murmured as she stroked her head. "You probably shouldn't be on the sofa, though." She had named the cat Smokey, her dark gray—smoky—fur nearly begging for the name. Of course, she hadn't told Finn. Then again, Finn hadn't been around much this week.

And neither had potential clients. She wondered how Finn stayed in business. Other than Carolyn Baxter, there had been no other customers to come through their door.

She took a bite of her turkey sandwich, remembering how happy Carolyn had been. Johnny had proved to be a good guy. Nothing in his background suggested otherwise. She'd been so happy, in fact, she hadn't even wanted to see the report Rylee had compiled for her. A report Finn had tweaked only a little. Carolyn had said she felt guilty for running a check on Johnny and didn't want to know anything from his past. She preferred to find out the old-fashioned way. Rylee tended to agree with her.

She glanced around the apartment, which still smelled of fresh paint. She wondered what Finn would do with it. Rent it out again, she imagined, since she'd already gotten new furniture. Although Finn hadn't seemed to be in a hurry. Sammy had been there ten years, she'd said. Whoever she rented to, she would have to trust them, considering the entrance to the apartment was smack in the middle of the offices.

Would Finn consider renting it to her? she wondered. Would she even want to live *and* work here? She looked up at the ceiling and let out a frustrated breath. Was she even working? Did doing a background check on one person constitute working? Finn had given her access to one of the databases that didn't charge by the search. She'd been practicing. That was the only thing that was keeping boredom at bay. Was she working?

For that matter, was she even on the payroll? Even though she'd filled out some payroll forms, she and Finn hadn't discussed salary. Surely Finn was paying her. Right? She wanted to be an apprentice… not a volunteer. Yeah…she probably should have worked all of that out at the beginning. She'd been too excited at the time to have actually landed a job—housekeeper-slash-receptionist—to be concerned with salary. She'd been too excited and too bewildered by the fact that Finley Knight was her boss…and a woman whose body she'd had her hands and mouth on.

She pushed that memory away where it belonged…to the far recesses of her mind. She hadn't said anything. Finn hadn't said anything. They were going to leave that night buried, apparently. That meant she needed to forget about it.

"I suppose I need to vacuum the offices, huh?" she said to the purring cat. The cat's eyes were fixed on the door and Rylee followed her gaze, finding Finn standing there watching them.

"What are you doing up here?"

"Keeping Smokey company." She held up what was left of her sandwich. "And lunch."

"Smokey? You know, we're only babysitting until someone claims her."

"Do you really think someone will come for her? Who? That family is surely devastated by what's occurred. I doubt they're concerned with the fate of this little cat."

"Hoping they forget all about her?"

Rylee smiled as she stroked the cat's fur. "Yes. I kinda like her."

Finn surprised her by coming fully into the apartment and sitting down on the opposite end of the sofa. Smokey crawled into her lap immediately.

"Can I ask you something?"

Finn looked up and nodded.

"You are...you know, paying me to work here, right?"

Finn laughed, a quick laugh that caused Rylee to return it.

"I mean...you are, right?"

The smile stayed on Finn's face. "What do you think you're worth?"

Rylee met her gaze. "I'm not sure you could afford what I'm actually worth," she teased, enjoying the relaxed smile on Finn's face. It nearly transformed her. She looked youthful, carefree. Gone was the serious expression that she normally sported. Serious, businesslike.

"Probably not. But seeing as how I didn't want to hire you in the first place..."

Rylee's smile faltered a little. "Minimum wage then?"

"Oh, I suppose we can do a little better than that." Finn moved the cat aside and stood. "When you're finished with lunch, come to my office. I've got a job for you."

"Really? Something fun?"

"Background checks. One of the clients that I have a contract with...they have three new hires."

"Oh, good." She made a move to get up, but Finn stopped her.

"Finish your sandwich. No big hurry."

Finn hesitated at the doorway, and Rylee wondered what it was that she was debating whether to say or not. She finally closed the door without saying anything else and Rylee leaned back, still smiling. So...better than minimum wage. Well, no matter what it was, it was better than what she had been making...which was nothing. At least she had a job.

CHAPTER THIRTY-ONE

"You haven't been around much."

"You keeping tabs on me?"

Rylee shook her head. "Simply stating a fact. I could have been overrun with clients."

"Uh-huh." Finn sat down in one of the visitor's chair across from the receptionist's desk. She motioned to the laptop. "How's it going?"

Rylee shook her head. "Nothing exciting. I can't find any dirt on any of them."

Finn laughed. "Hoping one of them had a criminal record, were you?"

"Yes." Rylee leaned back in her chair. "So? Where have you been?"

It was Finn's turn to sigh. "Surveillance."

"We have a client?"

"Not really, no."

Rylee nodded. "It has something to do with the murders?"

"Yes."

Finn rolled her shoulders. She hadn't had much sleep in the last three days. She'd spent more damn time in her car than anywhere else. But Dee had called. They'd pulled the patrol units that had been watching her house and office. Not that she was worried about her house—she had a security system and a locked gate—but she didn't feel comfortable leaving Rylee alone at the office any longer.

Not that her surveillance was paying off. As she'd expected, the Fraziers' son, Duncan, was taking over the business. The funeral had been a private affair and Connie Frazier had been plopped down in the ground beside Daniel without much fanfare. Duncan and his sister apparently were having a squabble. Finn had seen them arguing out by the cars shortly after the service. The sister—Grace—had gotten into a car with two women and a man. Relatives, perhaps. Duncan had sped away in a maroon truck and that was who Finn had followed.

"Is there anything I can help with?"

Finn brought her attention back to Rylee. "I'm supposed to let this go. I'm supposed to let the police handle it."

"Oh."

"Only they don't have any suspects."

"Your friend Dee? Is she the lead detective?"

"She is."

"So…would I be out of line by asking what kind of surveillance?" Rylee leaned forward. "Because…you know, I could help."

"Doing surveillance is, by far, the worst part of this job."

"I could help," Rylee offered again.

Finn shook her head. "You're barely getting your feet wet. Surveillance isn't something you just jump into."

"So take me with you. I'll learn while watching."

No. It was crazy to even entertain the idea. Wasn't it? But if she took Rylee with her, that would solve the problem of leaving her here alone. Rylee was looking at her expectantly and Finn debated with herself. Did she want to be stuck in her car for possibly hours with a woman she hardly knew? No, the question really was—did she want to be stuck in close quarters with a woman she'd seen naked, a woman she'd made love to…a woman who, when she looked at her, sometimes caused her to stop breathing. But hell…

"I suppose that would keep me from worrying about you."

"Why worrying?"

"They pulled the patrol unit that was sitting across the street."

"Oh…so that's why you've been here today."

Finn stood up. "If you're finished with that, email the client your results. I attached an old report so you'll see the format I use."

"Okay." Rylee paused. "Does that mean I can go with you?"

"It does." Finn glanced at the clock on the wall. It was 10:36. The last two days, Duncan Frazier had been at the pizza location on the island...Jamboree Number One. The same location where most of the money had changed hands. "Let's try to leave by eleven."

* * *

"So who are we looking for?"

"Duncan Frazier. He drives a maroon truck. Dodge Ram. Four doors."

She drove slowly through the parking lot, finding the truck parked where it had been yesterday.

"That one?" Rylee pointed.

"Yes."

The lot wasn't quite filled with the lunch crowd yet and she drove on, intending to park next door, at the Mexican food place. Shrubs lined the area between the two restaurants and she pulled up close to one, giving them some privacy.

"Why not just park at the pizza place?"

"Security cameras."

"Oh. But don't they have them here?"

"We're not staking out this place so I don't really care if we're on camera here. It's over there that we don't want to cause any suspicions."

"Okay. Makes sense."

Finn reached into the backseat and grabbed the camera, handing it to Rylee. Then she found the binoculars she'd placed on the floor behind her seat. From her console, she took out her notepad. It was 11:17.

"So...can I ask questions or do you want me to sit over here and be quiet?"

Yes, Finn should have expected that Rylee would have a hundred questions. "Ask away."

Rylee removed her seat belt and shifted in the seat, the camera still in her lap. "What do you do if you have to go to the bathroom?"

Finn laughed. "That's your first question?"

"Well, I probably should have gone before we left the office."

"I'm sure you can slip inside the Eldorado Cantina here and use their restrooms."

"Okay, good. Now...a real question. Why are we watching Duncan Frazier? I mean, I know his parents were both killed. Do you think someone might be after him too?"

"Maybe."

"That's vague."

Finn turned to look at her. "Daniel Frazier was a client. He hired me to follow his wife. He suspected an affair. He was murdered right after I gave him my report. A few days later, my office was ransacked." She paused. "Sammy was killed. They were looking for something, something they assumed Daniel had given me."

"Which was right before I came by."

"Yes. Connie Frazier was tortured before she was killed. Place was also ransacked."

"And you don't think they've found what they were looking for?"

"No."

"If it wasn't at his home, doesn't it stand to reason it would be at one of his pizza places?"

"Possibly. But all four have security cameras in the parking lots and inside. They close at ten on weekdays, eleven on weekends. It's after midnight by the time the last employee leaves. Everything is locked up, alarm system, the works. Daniel, being the paranoid person that he was, also employed a security firm."

"Ah. So a security patrol at night?"

"Yes."

"You were here last night?"

"I was."

"Did you sleep?"

"A few hours this morning." She took the binoculars and scanned the outside of the building, making sure she had a view of the back door.

"You need more than a few hours, Finn," Rylee said disapprovingly. "Did you even have breakfast?"

Finn looked over at her. "I'm used to getting by on little sleep. And no, I didn't have breakfast."

Rylee shook her head. "I get really cranky if I don't get at least six hours sleep. Seven is best. And you should always eat breakfast."

"I'm cranky whether I get sleep or not."

Rylee laughed. "Yeah, I don't doubt that." She took a breath. "So what are your thoughts?"

Finn looked through the binoculars again. "If Daniel left whatever it is they're looking for at one of his pizza joints, then Duncan is their way inside."

"Like they might kidnap him or something? Force him to let them inside after hours?"

"Something like that. Or kidnap his sister and use her as leverage."

"What do the police think?"

"I don't know."

"Your detective friend—"

"Dee Woodard. She doesn't discuss the case with me. Much," she added. In fact, Dee had been pretty much noncommittal when they'd last spoken. They were still trying to chase the money trail. If these were indeed professionals they were dealing with, the money trail was most likely stone cold. And with Daniel Frazier out of the picture, there would be no more money trail to follow. Unless…

She frowned. Unless one of his managers was involved. Maybe more than one. The kind of money that was being deposited each week would have surely caused some questions. Of course, according to Connie, Daniel Frazier was a micromanager. Perhaps he handled all the deposits at all the restaurants. Perhaps he was the only one with his nose in the books.

"You're frowning."

Finn turned to her, wondering if Rylee was the right one to bounce ideas off of. No. Dee would be the right one. Dee, however, had instructed her to "stay out of it" on more than one occasion. If she knew that Finn was doing surveillance on Duncan Frazier…well, she assumed Dee would be plenty pissed.

"There's a lot of cash that goes through this restaurant. More than the other three."

Rylee blinked at her questioningly.

"Sorry. Forgot you're not from around here. The Pizza Jamboree. There are four locations. Kinda a mainstay in the city. All-you-can-eat lunches. They—"

"I had their pizza for Thanksgiving. It was really good."

"That's right. You didn't make it home."

"No. A…a friend invited me over…pizza and beer."

"Date?"

Rylee shook her head. "No. Well, at least in my mind, no, it wasn't a date."

"Ah. But she likes you." Finn was surprised by the twinge of jealously she felt.

Rylee shrugged. "Anyway, go on. Lots of cash."

"Yes. The restaurants are popular and he makes a lot of money but…he's moving a *lot* of money. An audit would most likely reveal that what goes in is a whole lot less than what's going out."

"Okay. Money laundering. College was a long time ago, but from what I remember from my classes, using restaurants is a classic way to move money."

Finn nodded. "It is. Back in the day, they would open up a new place, not caring whether there were customers or not. They'd move a massive amount of cash through the system, then close up shop and disappear into the wind before the Feds caught on. There are more checks now, more regulations."

"So you use an already popular place that's making money."

"Exactly. Especially a popular place with four locations."

Rylee tilted her head. "Is this just speculation or do you really have proof that Daniel Frazier was laundering money?"

"No proof. Not me. Dee may have found something but she's not shared. I know they found some bogus vendors but that money trail went cold."

"Okay, so back to your frowning. We're watching Duncan Frazier. But something you thought made you question it."

Finn arched an eyebrow at her. "Think you can read me already, huh?"

Rylee gave her a rather flirty smile. "Yes, you're easy to read." She waved her hand in the air. "So tell me."

"He's got managers at each place. Surely they should know how much money they're bringing in. How could he get that past them?" She leaned back in the seat. "Connie said he was very hands-on, involved in everything at every restaurant. So maybe the managers didn't know." She rolled her head to look at Rylee. "Or maybe the managers *were* involved. Maybe Daniel Frazier had nothing to do with it. Maybe he found out. Maybe that's what he had on them. Something got him killed. Maybe that's what they're looking for."

Rylee shook her head. "No. I don't buy it. You own a successful business. You're going to know how much money you're making. You'll know how much you're *supposed* to make. No way the managers could pull that off."

Finn let out her breath. "You're right. Daniel Frazier knew. That doesn't mean that one or more of his managers didn't also know what was going on."

"Where's the money coming from?"

"Good question. Drugs? That seems to be the direction that the police are taking."

"What do you think?"

"I'm not sure. Everything I could find on his background was squeaky clean. I don't buy the drug angle."

"How does this work? Someone with money approaches him, says we'll give you X amount of money if you'll wash the cash through the restaurant?"

"Something like that, yeah. Unless, of course, he's involved directly."

Rylee shifted in her seat. "Have the police questioned the children?"

"I don't know. Like I said, Dee isn't inclined to share a whole lot about the case with me."

"Why not? You're friends, aren't you? Or...or is she...your girlfriend?"

"Not my girlfriend, no. But it's an open case, ongoing investigation. Besides, she thinks I'm involved."

"*What*? How could you be involved?"

"Inadvertently involved," Finn clarified. "And we're new friends. We haven't shared deep, dark secrets with each other yet."

There was a pronounced pause before Rylee spoke. "Do you have deep, dark secrets?"

Finn picked up the binoculars, scanning the pizza joint, surprised that she spied Duncan Frazier through the windows. He was behind the counter, talking with one of the employees. She lowered the binoculars slowly. Did she have secrets? Not really, no. She had been a little angry that Dee did a background check on her, though. She wasn't sure why, really. She didn't have anything to hide. She wasn't an open book and had no desire to be one. But secrets? Or was Rylee referring to...that night? The night they'd spent together.

At her silence, Rylee must have assumed she'd asked the wrong question. She shifted again in the seat beside her.

"Do you mind if I run inside?"

Finn looked over at her then. "Restroom?"

Rylee almost blushed. "Yes."

"Sure. Go ahead."

Rylee opened the door, but before she got out, she paused. "You won't like...leave me here, right?"

"I won't leave you. Hurry up."

CHAPTER THIRTY-TWO

Rylee didn't realize how hungry she was until she walked into the cantina. The smell of fresh tortillas wafted in the air and made her stomach rumble. Instead of heading to the restroom, she went to the bar, which was mostly empty at this early hour.

"Can I get an order to go?"

"Yes, ma'am," the young man said, sliding a menu over to her.

She flipped it open. Finn hadn't had breakfast. If she had to guess, she'd say that Finn hadn't had dinner last night either. So something quick. Something easy to eat in the car. Tacos? Burritos? Was Finn a picky eater? No. She didn't seem the type, although she was rather thin. She looked up into the mirror behind the bar and smiled at herself. Yeah, she was thin because she didn't eat and didn't sleep.

"Two beef tacos and two grilled chicken burritos," she said, closing the menu and handing it over. "And…kinda in a hurry," she added with a smile.

"You want a margarita while you wait?"

"Oh, no. Thank you." Sure, if she were still a beach bum and it was still summer, a margarita sounded good. But she wasn't a beach bum any longer. She had a job now. She was doing surveillance.

And she supposed she could see why Finn said it was the worst part of the job. She imagined boredom would set in quickly. But to her, it was nice to be included, nice that Finn was sharing tidbits about the case with her.

She frowned. Case? Finn seemed to think of it as a case, as if she were still a detective. What was happening was obviously personal to her. As she headed to the restroom, she made a mental note to pry just a little. Maybe Finley Knight did have deep, dark secrets.

* * *

Not that she thought Finn would actually leave her, but she was relieved to find her car still parked in the lot. It took much longer than she thought, but the food smelled divine.

"Thought I was going to have to send out a search party," Finn drawled when she got back inside. "You fall in the toilet or something?"

"Funny. And thank you for not leaving me." She was smiling as she opened the bag. "I was hungry and I *did* have breakfast. You must be starving." She handed Finn one of the tacos. "I also got you a burrito."

"Thank you." She unwrapped the taco with a nod. "Yeah, starving. I missed dinner too."

"I suspected as much."

"It's good. What do I owe you?"

"You don't owe me anything. My treat."

But Finn shook her head. "You haven't had a job for months. You've drained your savings. I haven't paid you anything yet. So no, not your treat. How much?"

"I haven't totally drained my savings." The taco tasted as good as it smelled and she nearly moaned at the first bite. "This could be my new favorite place," she murmured with a mouth full.

"How much?"

"Oh, Finn…my treat. I'll let you get lunch next time."

Finn stared at her for a long moment then finally nodded, to Rylee's relief. The meal wasn't much more than twenty bucks and yes, her cash was dwindling fast but she would never tell Finn that. They ate silently and she was so absorbed in her taco that she nearly forgot why they were there. Finn, however, did not and she reached for her camera, snapping off a series of shots as two men walked toward the Dodge truck they were watching.

"The younger one is Duncan," Finn supplied. "Don't know the other."

"Manager?"

"Could be."

"Looks like they're arguing."

The binoculars replaced the camera and Finn kept her attention locked on the two men. Rylee wondered if perhaps Finn could read lips. It wasn't long before the other man went back into the Pizza Jamboree and Duncan Frazier got into the truck. He backed out without looking, nearly running into a car that was coming into the lot. He left with a squeal of his tires.

Before she could even register it, Finn had the car started and was dashing out into traffic, maybe four or five cars behind the maroon truck. She couldn't take the suspense any longer.

"Well?"

Finn glanced at her. "Well what?"

"What did they say?"

Finn only arched an eyebrow.

"You can read lips, right?"

At that, Finn laughed. "Sorry to disappoint you, kid, but no. Besides, they were talking too fast. More animated than arguing, I think."

"Oh. So where do you think he's going?"

"Don't know."

Rylee reached over and took the last of Finn's taco from her lap and wrapped it up for her, adding it to the bag with the two burritos.

"Why do you always call me 'kid'?"

"Because you're a kid."

"I'll be thirty next month. Not a kid, but thank you, I guess."

"When's your birthday?"

"Christmas Day."

"Really? That must have sucked."

Rylee laughed. "Yes, it did. I don't think I ever had a proper birthday party." She paused. "How old are you?"

Finn sighed but said nothing.

"What? You don't seem the type to really care about age. I didn't think you'd mind the question."

"How old do you think I am?"

"I'll guess—and don't get offended if I'm wrong—fortyish."

"Fortyish?"

She couldn't tell if Finn's tone was annoyed or not. "Well, you don't really look forty...I would even go as low as thirty-five. But you seem older. Like...your mannerisms and such. And your sometimes grumpy attitude." She waved a hand at her. "Of course, the way you dress—jeans and all casual and stuff—makes you look younger, I think."

Finn continued to stare at the road and there was only a slight shake of her head.

"You're really not going to tell me?"

"I'm older than you."

Rylee let the subject drop as she also focused on the road ahead of them. They were now three cars behind the truck, whose right blinker was flashing. Instead of turning when it did, Finn stayed on the main road and headed across the JFK Causeway and over the bay, back into the city. When Finn offered no explanation as to why, Rylee had to bite her lip to keep her questions from spilling out.

"You're about to explode," Finn murmured after a while.

"Are you testing me or what?"

"Meaning?"

"Meaning...you didn't follow him. Am I supposed to know why?"

Finn glanced over at her quickly. "Sorry. I'm used to doing this solo." She looked into the rearview mirror. "Detective Woodard was two cars behind us. I'd just as soon she not spy me out here. Besides, he's going back to his hotel. Same routine as the last few days."

"Oh. What about his sister?"

"She went back to college. Semester is over on the thirteenth."

Rylee nodded. "Why is Duncan staying at a hotel and not his parents' house?"

"It was trashed...bloody. I doubt anything's been done with it."

"That's so sad. The kids are young. Now both parents are gone. Must have turned their world upside down," she offered.

Finn nodded. "Yeah. The murder of a parent can be rough."

Rylee stared at her, seeing her tight grip on the steering wheel. The words were spoken with such conviction, such certainty, she wondered again what Finn's past held. Was that a part of the deep, dark secrets she kept hidden?

Considering that Finn wouldn't even tell her her age...she was fairly certain that revealing hidden secrets wasn't going to be on the agenda anytime soon.

CHAPTER THIRTY-THREE

Dee was surprised to find Finn's car at her office. It was after eight and long ago darkness had swallowed up the misty city. Moonlight Avenue was dark and a little eerie with the fog from the bay drifting inland. She could barely make out the tops of the palm trees. Her headlights splashed across the front door when she pulled up beside Finn's car. She left her lights on as she walked to the door, knocking loudly several times. She heard nothing from inside and couldn't tell if there were any lights on. Instead of knocking again, she called Finn's cell. When she thought it would go to voice mail, Finn finally answered.

"Detective Woodard…to what do I owe the pleasure?"

"Open your damn door."

"Is that you knocking?"

"Surely you were expecting me."

She heard Finn sigh. "I suppose."

The call ended and she slipped the phone into the pocket of her jacket. She turned her back to the door, looking up into the dark sky, wondering when they'd see the moon again. Or the sun, for that matter. It seemed like most of November had been cloudy and drizzly. She hoped December—which was only a day away—would offer more warmth and sunshine. With a sigh, she walked to her car and killed the lights.

She looked up when the door opened. Finn stood there in her normal attire—jeans and leather boots. She had a sweater pulled over a collared shirt today. She looked rather nice.

"You're mad, I suppose," Finn said, in lieu of a greeting.

"You think?"

Finn stepped back, letting her inside. She closed and locked the door, then walked down the hallway, bypassing her old office. Dee followed silently behind. Sitting on Finn's desk was a bottle of scotch and a glass, perhaps a swallow or two remaining. Finn grabbed another glass from the credenza and held it up.

"Are you off duty?"

Dee nodded. "Although plying me with scotch won't help your case."

Finn shrugged slightly as she added a generous amount to the glass, then added more to her own. She offered the glass to Dee, then sat down at the desk.

"I like your new office," Dee commented. "Quite a bit larger than your old one."

"Yes. I'm still getting used to it."

"Going to rent out the extra space again?"

Finn smiled. "I'm not sure Rylee would allow it. I think she's got her sights set on getting that office someday."

"Rylee? Your new receptionist?"

"She prefers assistant to receptionist."

"She was the one with you today in the car? More than a little cute. Quite attractive."

Finn ignored the question...and the statement. "Where were you?"

"In the same lot you were in."

Finn took a swallow of the scotch, then set the glass down. "What interest do you have in Duncan Frazier?"

"Shouldn't I be asking you that?"

"Perhaps I was simply out to lunch."

Dee leaned closer. "Let's cut the crap, Finn. You have no business doing surveillance on Duncan Frazier."

"Are you any closer to solving these murders?" She picked up her glass again. "Actually, Sammy's is the only one of concern to me."

"Are you just doing the legwork for me and then you're going to present me with the suspect or do you plan to take out the guy when you find him?"

"I haven't decided which."

Dee shook her head. "I would like to think you're joking, but I don't believe you are." She leaned back again. "I thought perhaps that whatever it is Michael Drake is looking for might very well be at one of the pizza places. What better way to get inside than by using Duncan."

Finn nodded. "Great minds think alike. I've also been wondering about the affair."

"What do you mean?"

"The purpose of the affair," Finn clarified. "Something Connie Frazier said to me that day I stopped by. She said Drake—Mark Condra—had never been to her house. She said he wanted to, but she wouldn't allow it. Said he asked—begged—to come over frequently, but she said no."

"So what are your thoughts?"

"The purpose of the affair…to get into the Fraziers' house. Whatever Daniel Frazier had, Drake obviously knew about it. I think the affair was a guise to get into the house."

"Then what?"

"I don't know. Drug Connie or something. She's unconscious. He's got time to look around."

"She comes to and thinks what? That it was really good sex?"

Finn gave a humorless laugh. "Considering the dreamy look she sported after being with him…yeah. But did Michael Drake know Daniel Frazier or did Drake work for someone else?"

"If he's our killer—which we both think is the case—then he works for someone. As I said before. Professional, all the way around. This isn't the first time he's killed."

"Connie didn't know what he was looking for. I would go so far as to say she was in love with this guy. If he came to her house that fateful night, she willingly let him in."

"No evidence of a break-in," she confirmed.

Finn tapped the rim of her glass with her index finger. "If she knew what he wanted, she would have handed it over. No way she takes torture, not from a guy she's been sleeping with."

"So maybe it wasn't Michael Drake."

Finn shook her head. "Michael Drake wasn't emotionally involved in any way. When I was watching the motel where they hooked up, when she left the room, the smile disappeared from his face as if someone had flipped a light switch. Whatever he was doing with Connie Frazier was strictly for show. Strictly business. Based on what I observed, I don't think he would have had a hard time killing her."

"Since we're going with the assumption that he never found what he was looking for—"

"You're at a dead end?" Finn guessed.

"Pretty much. The money trail was covered up so nice and tidy, there isn't even a trail to consider."

"Why haven't the Feds swooped in yet? Money laundering gets them all excited."

Dee shook her head. "Because we haven't reported it yet. Mabanks wants to keep it in-house for now. Once they're involved, they'll swoop in as you say, shut the business down, and conduct an audit that'll take months. Our murder investigation won't be their main concern."

"They might be able to find the money trail, get you some suspects."

"You don't really believe that, do you?"

"No, not with Daniel Frazier dead. The audit will tell them how much money got washed through, that's about it. Where it came from is anybody's guess."

"Unless, of course, one of the managers was involved."

Finn didn't seem surprised by the statement. "One or more, yes."

"The more people that are in the know, the harder it is to keep under wraps."

"If you're a manager, you're going to have your hand in the books. You're going to know how much money should be flowing through. From what I saw, this has been going on for five years or more."

"Five years, six months," Dee supplied automatically. "At first, it wasn't a huge bump. Nothing for the bank to question. Each month, a little more."

"Percentages."

Dee nodded. "Yes. He stayed within the allowed percentages, which might be why he started filtering some through the other restaurants." She finished her drink and slid the glass onto the desk. "Mabanks has another team involved now. They think the money is drug related. That's the angle they're pursuing."

"You thought that too."

"You didn't."

Finn shook her head. "Doesn't mean it's not true. I just didn't get that feeling." She rested her elbows on the desk. "Professional, though. Whatever it is, it must be big players involved. But Frazier? I only met with Daniel Frazier twice. He seemed to be just a normal guy, but there was something odd."

"What do you mean?"

"There wasn't any anger. Not really. I'd thought at first maybe it was because he'd already accepted the fact that she was cheating on him. It wasn't a surprise. But I think it was something else. It was the way he kept looking at Drake's picture. Like he knew him." Finn finished off her drink. "But anyway, back to my feelings about Daniel. Just a normal guy. There was nothing sophisticated about him. Whatever kind of activities are going on, I don't think he's the guy."

"He was obviously very business smart. He had four successful restaurants," Dee said, shaking her head when Finn offered more scotch.

"Smart in the pizza business or maybe they just make a hell of a good pizza," Finn countered. "Maybe his business smarts are suspect. Maybe that's why he could easily be coerced into moving cash for someone."

"Sure. And going on that assumption, he gets tired of being manipulated and threatened them with exposure. They kill him."

"Threatened them by letting them know he had documented evidence."

Dee motioned to her empty glass, deciding a little more wouldn't hurt. Finn added scotch to it and shoved it closer. It made sense. They had no evidence whatsoever, but it made sense. It also made sense that Daniel could have been directly involved too.

"He had documented something, that's for sure," Dee allowed. "I'm not yet convinced that he wasn't a major player, though."

Finn stared at her for a long moment, long enough for Dee to feel uncomfortable. She finally raised her eyebrows questioningly.

"Why are you here?"

It was Dee's turn to stare. "Excuse me?"

"You didn't come to discuss the case because you don't normally discuss the case with me," she said pointedly. "Certainly not this in-depth."

Dee let out a long breath. "I seem to be the odd man out on the case," she admitted. "As I said, the new team is focused on the money trail. Mabanks even hinted that I should consider you as a suspect."

"Me? What the hell for?"

"The link between you and Daniel Frazier. And Sammy."

Finn's eyes hardened. "The son of a bitch thinks I'd kill Sammy? Ransack my own damn office for show?"

"You're not a suspect, Finn. He was just tossing that out there."

"Well, that still pisses me off."

"Thought it would. I'm pretty pissed off too."

"So you're not the lead any longer?"

"No. Josh Davis is. He's younger than me. Mid-thirties, I guess. I get the impression they think I'm old-school and they want me out of the way. Joel has hooked up with them, following their every suggestion like a damn puppy dog after a bone. They're treating him like nothing more than a gopher."

"So you staking out the pizza place wasn't part of the agenda?"

"No. They're getting a warrant. We'll be able to get into their accounting system." She shrugged. "Well, the guys will. I'm not sure what my role is anymore."

"Wouldn't hurt to find out who actually made the deposits."

"If it was Daniel Frazier, how does that help? If it was a manager, that's a different story." She held her hand up. "But enough of that. I'm sick of thinking about it." She leaned back in the chair, trying to relax. "Tell me about the cute blonde."

"Rylee?"

"Yes."

"What about her?"

"Oh, Finn…humor me. I haven't been on a date in more months than I can remember. She's young and cute. Does she flirt with you?"

Finn shook her head. "She doesn't flirt with me, no."

"Do you flirt with her?"

"Of course not. I don't even know how to flirt."

"For some reason, that doesn't surprise me." She cupped her glass with both hands. "I had thought briefly of asking you out. You know, on a real date."

"Oh, yeah?"

"Uh-huh. But I decided we were too much alike. Besides, if we ended up sleeping together, it would only be like sex buddies or something." She shook her head. "I could get that anywhere if I really wanted it. Friends are harder to come by."

Finn smiled. "Thanks. I guess."

Dee returned her smile. "Sorry. I guess that was presumptuous of me to think you had even considered sleeping with me." She finished the last of her scotch and placed the glass on the desk. "Mabanks hinted that I needed a personal life, which is what got me thinking about this." She stood, noting the smile that was still on Finn's face. "I can see myself out."

Finn stood too. "No need. I'm heading out too."

CHAPTER THIRTY-FOUR

Finn walked into the room that had been converted into a kitchen many years ago. Well, not much more than a break room, really, but it did have a sink and running water. The fridge was ancient, but the microwave was new. It was where she found Rylee. Rylee and the cat—the cat she'd named Smokey.

"She escaped the apartment again, huh?"

Rylee laughed. "Yes, I told you, she's quite adept at opening doors. I think *you* taught her that."

Finn smiled back at her, unable not to. "So you've been here a while already?"

Rylee raised an eyebrow. "What makes you think so?"

"The hood of your Jeep was cold."

Rylee rolled her eyes. "You should have stayed a detective."

Finn didn't add that she got the security feed on her phone and had watched Rylee park in front of the building at 6:06, a good forty-five minutes before there was any light in the sky. She knew that because she'd been out on her pier, sipping a hot cup of coffee.

Finn grabbed her own coffee cup, realizing that she didn't find Rylee's presence disruptive. She was used to the early morning quiet, the solitude. When Simon rented the office, he rarely got in before eight. Most often, it was eight thirty or later. And Sammy? Sammy was a night owl. She usually didn't see him until noon or later, if at all. Rylee was apparently an early riser too. Surprisingly, Finn found she was glad to have Rylee there. She was curious, though.

"Why so early?"

"You mean here?" Rylee took a sip of her coffee before answering. She had an almost apologetic look on her face. "I was awake. Nothing better to do." Then she gave a quick glance at the cat. "Besides, I figured Smokey could use the company."

"And you could use the company?" she asked gently, surprising herself with the concern she felt.

Rylee nodded. "I've only made a handful of friends." She shrugged. "And I use the word 'friends' loosely."

"You had a Thanksgiving date with one," she reminded her.

"So I did. I only accepted because I didn't want to be alone on Thanksgiving."

"And she only asked because she wanted to sleep with you?" she guessed.

Rylee blushed profusely. "Yes. But I managed to escape her apartment without an incident." She set her cup down. "Leena is her name. She's a couple of years younger than me. I met her on the beach a month or so after I moved here." She blew out a long breath. "It's hard finding new friends. Everyone's already grouped up, you know. So…anytime I was asked to do something, it was always…well, they weren't asking as a friend."

Finn had a hundred questions all of a sudden and she reined them in before blurting out the first one. Was that why Rylee had gone to the bar? Because she was lonely? Because she wanted to meet a new friend? No. If that was the case, she wouldn't have dashed off before dawn…before Finn was even awake. Unless Finn wasn't the type of new friend she wanted to meet. She pushed those thoughts aside.

"So you're not interested in dating?" she asked as nonchalantly as she could.

"Oh, I'd be interested if I met the right woman. I actually went out on a couple of dates, but…"

"What?"

Rylee blushed again. "This is going to sound really…well, weird."

Finn raised her eyebrows. "What?"

"I don't get the concept of sex on the first date," Rylee said. "If you want to have sex, then go have sex. But if you want to go on a date, then expect a date, not sex."

Their eyes met and Finn was at a loss for words. Is this where they would finally talk about it? Yeah…they'd had sex. It wasn't a date. But God, she didn't want to talk about it. Not yet, at least. She wasn't prepared to talk about it.

So she looked away from Rylee, clearing her throat lightly before speaking. "There's nothing wrong with that. I wouldn't call that old-fashioned or weird, as you say. You have your…your principles. That's good."

"Too many people think of sex as a physical act only. And yes, I get that. I mean, I was young with raging hormones once. But now that I'm older, I need it to mean something. I want it to be emotional too, not just physical." Rylee met her eyes again. "If I just want an orgasm, I can take care of that myself. And usually it's a *lot* better."

Finn nearly spit out her coffee and ended up choking as she tried to swallow.

"I'm sorry," Rylee laughed as she handed her a napkin. "We probably…well, shouldn't be having this conversation, should we?"

Finn coughed a couple of times, trying to clear her throat…and her mind. She'd be lying if she said she hadn't gotten a visual from her statement. She shook her head finally.

"I'm not used to these types of conversations, no." She paused. "I don't really…have any friends, so conversations like this…no."

Rylee's expression softened. "You don't?" She reached out a hand and squeezed her arm. The touch was so familiar, as usual, Finn lost her breath. "I guess I can see that. You're not very…open."

Finn felt Rylee's hand slip away and she breathed again. No, she wasn't open, was she? Not with anyone. Not in a very long time.

"Tell me something."

Finn raised her eyebrows. "Tell you something what?"

"Tell me something about yourself. Open up a little."

"Why?"

"Because that's what friends do."

"Friends?"

Rylee smiled. "Yes. I need a friend. *You* need a friend. Tell me something. Anything."

Finn thought for a moment, wondering what tidbit she could throw out that would appease Rylee. Wondering if what Rylee really wanted was to talk about…that night. Hell, she wondered why she didn't walk away and end the conversation so they *wouldn't* have to talk about that night. They weren't friends. They hardly knew each other. A handful of weeks working together hadn't changed that, despite…

that night. But Rylee was looking at her, her stare unwavering. Finn blew out a breath. *Oh, hell.*

"I'm estranged from my mother." Rylee met her gaze, her eyes telling Finn she expected more. Finn shook her head. "It's a long story."

"Tell me."

Finn blew out another breath. "My mother was having an affair. My father hired a private eye when he suspected. My father was murdered by her lover." Rylee's eyes widened but she said nothing. "I was in college when it happened. When I turned thirty, that same PI showed up...my life changed then."

"It changed because he showed up? Or—"

"Long story," she said abruptly, finally turning away and heading to her office. She heard Rylee following.

"You can't just tell me all that and walk away."

"Sure I can."

"No, you can't."

She sat down behind her desk, only to have Rylee plop down in a visitor's chair. The cat—Smokey—hopped up on the credenza behind the desk.

"Your life changed," Rylee prompted.

"It's not all that interesting."

"Your father was murdured? What happened?"

Finn opened up her laptop and logged into her email. "The guy my mother was sleeping with...he wanted her to divorce my father."

"And she wouldn't?"

"My father was an attorney, quite successful. I was about to start law school. I was going to join his firm. My mother was lonely, but she had no intention of leaving my father." She glanced at the three new emails she'd gotten since she'd left the house an hour ago.

"So this guy killed your father?"

"Yes."

"Then...then the Fraziers...I guess that kinda opened old wounds."

"Very similar, yes."

"So you didn't go to law school?"

"No. A cop. Then a detective." She smiled. "Then a security guard. Then this place."

"You're leaving out all the juicy details."

"Yes. Like I said, it's a long story." When Rylee would have spoken, Finn held up her hand. "I'm forwarding you an email. Same as before. Job applicant."

"Same company?"

"Different company."

Rylee stood up. "I'm on it."

"Thank you."

"And after I'm done, are we doing anything fun today?"

"Fun?"

"Like yesterday."

"You thought that was fun?"

"I did."

Finn hated to admit it, but Dee was probably right. She should let the police handle the case. No sense in her and Dee both following young Duncan Frazier around. Since Connie's murder, things had seemed to come to a standstill. She looked over at Rylee, who had scooped up the cat.

"Nothing fun, I'm afraid. Detective Woodard is doing surveillance on Duncan."

Rylee's smile disappeared. "Oh. So she saw us yesterday?"

"She did."

Rylee tilted her head. "When did you see her?"

"She came by here last night."

"Oh? Is she cute?"

Finn stared at her, wondering at the question. Was Rylee jealous? "She's cute, I guess. Too old for you."

Rylee laughed. "Is there an age limit? Or are you saying that because you're interested in her?"

Finn shook her head. "I'm not. We're friends."

Rylee held her gaze. "See? And you said you didn't have any friends."

CHAPTER THIRTY-FIVE

Rylee didn't really have a picture of Dee Woodard in her mind so when a woman walked into the office two days later, it didn't occur to her that it was the detective. That is, not until she spotted the detective's shield clipped to her belt and the gun at her waist. She had light brown hair that was barely collar length, some of it sticking inside the jacket she wore, other strands hanging free. In the few seconds it took to acknowledge her, Rylee knew without a doubt that there was nothing romantic between Finn and the detective. Unless she was totally wrong, this woman wasn't anywhere near Finn's type. Not that it was any of her business, she silently admonished herself. She certainly had no say in the matter.

"Hi. You must be Detective Woodard," she said with a smile. She stood and held her hand out. "I'm Rylee Moore."

Yes, Dee Woodard was attractive. Cute, Finn had called her. She was older than Finn, though. Rylee could tell that. Mid, maybe even late forties.

"Hello, Rylee. Pleased to meet you." Dee shook her hand firmly, then looked past her down the hallway. "The boss in?"

"She is." Which Rylee assumed she already knew. There were only the two vehicles out front. Her Jeep and Finn's Buick. She was about to pick up the phone to let Finn know she had a visitor, but Dee was already walking back, indicating she was quite familiar with the office layout.

She sat back down with a shrug. Maybe the detective had some news about the case. Or maybe she was coming by for lunch. A quick glance at the clock told her it was already past noon. She closed her laptop, then went back to the breakroom to get her sandwich from the fridge and a bottle of water. Finn's office door was ajar and she paused, trying to listen to the conversation between the two women. She finally gave up and—after telling herself once again it wasn't any of her business—she took her lunch upstairs to the apartment.

She found Smokey curled in the middle of the oversized chair beside the sofa. The cat lifted her head and yawned when Rylee went inside.

"Hi, sweetie," she murmured, taking the time to rub the cat's head a few times before taking her normal spot on the sofa. She glanced at the small kitchen table. She should probably eat there, but this was so much more comfortable.

Turkey again. This was the last of it. She still had two pieces of bread remaining. She supposed she would now be able to make a grocery store run. Finn had surprised her with a paycheck that morning. She still wasn't sure what her salary was, but the check had been for more than she was expecting. Even after she'd filled out her W-2 information, Finn had been mum on her salary. She knew Finn had seen the surprise on her face, but she hadn't commented.

In fact, the last couple of days, Finn had been extremely quiet... distant. They'd had a run on new hires—first of the year coming up, she supposed. Finn had forwarded her several emails from some of her recurring clients and Rylee had stayed busy doing background checks. She had no idea what Finn was doing. No matter how early Rylee got to the office, Finn was already there. And no matter how late she stayed, Finn was still in her office behind closed doors.

She chewed her sandwich absently, wondering at Finn's silence. Was she working the case? Snooping around in records pertaining to the Fraziers? Still trying to find the mysterious Michael Drake? Or was she perhaps avoiding her? Avoiding her and her personal questions.

"Hey."

She jumped at the sound of Finn's voice, finding her leaning in the doorway. Neither she nor Smokey had heard her come up the stairs.

"Hey," she replied.

Finn's gaze went to her sandwich. "Don't you get tired of eating the same thing every day?"

Rylee shrugged. "It's all I have at my apartment." Then she smiled. "But I got paid. Now I can afford to go to the grocery store. Thank you."

Finn frowned. "Are you saying you didn't have enough money to buy food?"

"I…I could have dipped into my savings again, but…well, I didn't know when—if—you were going to pay me and my rent…"

"How much is your rent?"

Rylee blew out a breath. "A hair over a thousand."

"I didn't realize rents were that high now in Corpus. It's been ten years since I lived in an apartment."

"Well, there are some that are cheaper, but I didn't feel safe at any of those. My apartment has a security gate." She bit her lower lip. "I may move, though. My lease is up at the end of the month. I think I need to change to something a little cheaper."

Finn glanced around the apartment, her gaze landing on the tiny kitchen before looking back at Rylee.

"You could move in here," Finn said, surprising her with her words. As soon as she spoke them, Finn seemed to reconsider. "But I don't know if *I'd* feel safe with you living here alone. At least not until they catch this guy."

"I…I was actually going to ask you about this place," Rylee admitted. "But I didn't know what you charged. I mean—"

"I don't charge anything." Finn came into the room and sat down at the opposite end of the sofa. Smokey got out of the chair and moved into Finn's lap. "You should have told me."

"Told you what?"

"That you needed money. We can do a twice a month paycheck. Hell, once a week. It doesn't matter to me."

"Oh, Finn…I've been managing. It's not like I'm down to my last penny."

"Well, don't renew your lease. We'll work something out."

Rylee met her eyes for a moment, giving Finn an almost embarrassed smile. "You don't have to feel responsible for me. I barged into your life as it is."

Finn's gaze had a faraway look to it, and Rylee wondered where her thoughts had taken her. Back to that night, maybe? Finn finally blinked as if chasing away whatever had popped into her mind. She cleared her throat before speaking.

"Since Sammy's been gone…well, I don't have anyone." Finn offered her a smile. She couldn't tell if it was regret that she saw or apology. "There's no one in my life to be responsible for. So…sorry, but you're it now."

Rylee should simply accept her statement for what it was. Finn had no close friends, no involvements. It made her feel terribly sad to think she had no one in her life. Not that Rylee did either, but at least she had her parents.

"You told me about your father," she said gently. "And you're estranged from your mother. What about siblings?"

Finn took a deep breath and tilted her head back, staring at the ceiling. "No siblings. And my mother still lives here in Corpus. She'll call every once in a while, but we don't speak."

"Meaning *you* don't speak," she guessed.

Finn turned to look at her and there was a hint of a smile on her face. "Correct. I don't speak. She wants me to forgive her."

"You blame her for your father's death," she said unnecessarily.

"If you're going to tell me there are two sides to every story, save your breath," Finn said. "Their marriage wasn't ideal, I know. My father worked insane hours, and yes, he was absent a lot and she was alone. That doesn't mean she has to go out and have an affair. If she was unhappy, she should have divorced him."

"Maybe she truly still loved him, but her loneliness overrode that." She shifted on the sofa, turning to face Finn. "She's alone, day after day, night after night. I'm sure it took its toll on her. She may have even been depressed. Having an affair may have brought some life into her world."

"You say that as if you have experience."

Rylee shook her head. "Not me, no. My mother. When my father was first getting his business started, he was rarely home. Some nights he didn't even bother coming home at all."

"She had an affair?"

"No. At least I don't think so. But they had an argument one night. I was in my room and I opened the door so I could hear. She gave him an ultimatum. I remember being afraid that he would walk out…that they would get divorced."

"How old were you?"

"I was eleven or twelve, I guess."

"And you said you were an only child, right?"

"Yes. They gave up after two miscarriages." She tilted her head. "Why are you an only child? Did they not want more?"

Finn's expression turned thoughtful again. "I don't suppose my father was around enough for them to conceive." She met Rylee's gaze.

"I guess maybe you're right. She was lonely." Then her face hardened again. "That doesn't justify an affair. She should have done like your mother."

"How do you know she didn't?"

"Because my mother would never chance losing what she had—a padded bank account and no budget to follow, a nice house with a swimming pool, a cleaning service that came not once, but twice a week, and a closet that was full of designer clothes."

Rylee wondered if Finn truly believed that or if that was the perception she carried with her. But it wasn't her place to argue with Finn over it and it certainly wasn't any of her business. She reached over and squeezed Finn's arm quickly, then decided to change the subject.

"So…I met Dee. She is kinda cute."

Finn shook her head. "I told you, she's too old for you."

"So you say. Is there any news on the case?"

"Not really, no."

"What does that mean? They're giving up?"

"No. They got a warrant to go on the premises of all four pizza places." Finn shrugged. "I think they're hoping they'll stumble upon whatever it was Daniel Frazier supposedly had."

"Why did they wait so long?"

"They were trying to do everything behind the scenes without calling attention to it. That's failed, so…"

"And what about Duncan?"

"Dee doesn't think he's involved in any way. There's been nothing suspicious about his activity. By all appearances, he's simply taking over the family business."

Rylee frowned, watching Finn's expression. She found her very easy to read. "You don't believe that, do you?"

"Just a gut feeling, that's all. He seems too…I don't know, there's something not right about the whole thing."

"What does Dee think?"

"Dee thinks I should stay out of it and ignore my gut feelings," she said as she stood up. "We've got a client, by the way."

Rylee's eyes widened. "We do?" she asked excitedly. "Something fun?"

"Depends if you consider a cheating spouse fun or not."

"Spying on people while they're sneaking around…yeah, that'd be kinda fun."

Finn laughed. "Thought you'd say that. This one's a little different though. He says the marriage has gone south. He wants to divorce her and needs a reason."

"Why does he need a reason?"

"Three kids. Future custody battle, I assume."

"Oh. So when did you meet with him?"

"I didn't. He called this morning. He's coming by this afternoon to meet with me. We'll start surveillance tonight or tomorrow, depending on the particulars."

"Can I sit in on the interview?"

"I don't think so. He's high profile. Professional. Concerned with his privacy."

"I see." Then she smiled. "Some bigwig in town?"

"The bigwigs in town go to Hanson. Unless they want to be discreet and private, that is."

"Ah. Discreet…like coming to Moonlight Avenue instead of going downtown."

"Exactly."

Rylee stood up too. "Is that why you located your office here? So people could be discreet?"

"No. My father bought this building when I was still in college." Finn held up her hand, effectively cutting off Rylee's next question. "And that, too, is a long story."

"Well, while we're doing surveillance you can tell me all about it."

CHAPTER THIRTY-SIX

Finn waited until the silver Mercedes turned the corner before following. She glanced at the clock on her dash: 2:37 p.m.

"Write it down," Finn instructed. "The time."

"Oh." Rylee scribbled on the notepad Finn had given her.

"Write down anything else you observe."

"Like what?"

Finn lowered the sunglasses that were perched on top of her head. "Like it's a bright, sunny day for once."

"It's beautiful today, isn't it? It feels like spring." Rylee pulled out her phone and swiped through some apps. "I checked the weather for Amarillo earlier. Can you believe it's in the 20s? I so do not miss that."

"You get snow up there?"

"Yes. Some years just dustings, more or less. And some years, blowing blizzards that cut right through you. I think I could get used to this," she said with a grin. "Seventy-two degrees in December. How glorious."

Finn smiled. "How quickly you forget the damp, cool weather we had in November."

"Cool, not cold. Big difference." She adjusted her seat belt and faced her. "So? What kinds of observations besides the weather?"

"The car she's driving. The route we're taking. How fast she goes. Is she on her phone or not."

"How does that help you?"

"Establishes a pattern, that's all."

Rylee scribbled a few notes, then put the pen down. "Why does he want to divorce her?"

Finn shook her head. "That's not any of our business, kid. That's the first thing you've got to learn. Clients hire us for a service. We provide the information they ask for, nothing more, nothing less."

"Okay. But what do you think? Is he having his own affair? You said they had children and he needed some dirt for a possible custody battle."

Rylee blinked at her expectantly, and Finn finally turned her gaze back to the road. Mrs. Peterson appeared to be heading out of the city as she drove across Harbor Bridge.

"I love this bridge, by the way," Rylee said as she sat up high in the seat, looking out over the bay and the port. "What's that ship again?"

"USS Lexington."

"That's right. I wanted to tour it, but I was alone. I did go to the aquarium, though. That was fun." Rylee turned to her. "You've been on the ship before?"

"Many times. Field trips in school. A couple of times with my father. Why? You want to go sometime?"

"It would be fun, yes. Different. We don't have ships in Amarillo." Then Rylee laughed. "We don't have water in Amarillo. I don't think I would ever tire of this," she said, motioning to the bay as they crossed to the other side.

"I've lived here my whole life. I hardly pay it any mind anymore."

"So…back to the case. What's he up to?"

"Are you wanting me to speculate or what?"

"Aren't you curious? I mean, don't you want to follow him around too and see what he's doing?"

Finn laughed. "It doesn't work that way, Rylee. For one, I don't *care* what he's doing. He's not paying me to care."

"Okay, so he *thinks* she's having an affair or he's *hoping* she's having an affair?"

"He suspects."

"What's her name?"

"Lori Peterson. The husband is Brett. Brett recently had his name added to his father's prestigious law firm—Peterson, Barnes, Wilcox and Peterson."

"Ah."

"Ah?"

"Spoiled rich kid. Which then leads me to ask, why would he hire you?" Rylee laughed sheepishly. "Sorry. That didn't come out right."

"You mean, why didn't he hire one of the larger agencies in town instead of little Moonlight Avenue?"

"Yes. Not that I don't think you're good at what you do. But you have an outdated website. You don't advertise—that I can tell. Your sign is barely big enough for people to see from the road, and the office is in a rundown building on a dead-end street."

"Wow. All of that?"

"Yes. So what gives?"

Finn shrugged. "What do you think gives?"

"I think you operate undercover."

"Excuse me?"

"Word of mouth. You don't advertise because you don't have to. My guess is Mr. Peterson—the father—has either hired you before or he knows someone who did and they gave you a good reference. There's little to no publicity when they come to you."

Finn nodded, surprised Rylee had figured all of that out this quickly. No, she didn't advertise, other than a listing in the Yellow Pages. And the website? God, she hadn't looked at that thing in years. She was frankly surprised it was still up and running.

"Am I right?"

"I'm very discreet, yes. My clients know their privacy will be protected. There's little fanfare where I'm concerned. And yes, word of mouth."

"Almost like working undercover in the dark of night. And because you mind your business, they trust you." Rylee leaned back in the seat, her gaze on the Mercedes that was two cars ahead of them. "I don't think I'm going to make it in this profession."

"Oh?"

Rylee turned to look at her. "I want to know the *why* of things."

"When you start knowing the why of things, then it gets personal. Take the Fraziers. Daniel thought his wife was having an affair. I verified that. I could speculate as to the why of it, but I didn't really know for sure. Not until I spoke with Connie Frazier that day at her house. Then I knew the why. Her kids were gone, her husband was rarely home, and she was lonely."

"So once you knew the why, you felt sympathy for Connie Frazier."

"Yes."

"And had you known the why beforehand, you might have ignored some of her actions. Maybe you're really a softie and you would have told Daniel that no, his wife *wasn't* cheating on him."

Finn laughed. "And then very quickly I'd be out of business."

"So the rule is, you remain detached from the subjects and the situations."

"Exactly. Back to Rule One. They're paying you for a service. You give them what they ask for. Nothing more, nothing less."

Rylee rested her chin in her palm for a few seconds, obviously chewing over the rule in her mind. When she spoke, however, it wasn't about the rules of the game.

"What do you do at night?"

Finn raised her eyebrows. "What?"

"At night. No matter how late I stay at the office, you're still there. And usually, you're already there in the mornings when I get in."

"Are you asking if I work all night?"

"No. I mean, as far as I can tell, we aren't overrun with clients. Unless you're keeping them all to yourself and not sharing with me," she said with a grin. "Do you have...you know, a...a secret lover or something? Or do you...go out...to a bar?"

Finn didn't dare look at her. Did she go out to the bar? Yeah...one time. Was Rylee fishing? Did she assume Finn did that often? Best to ignore that question and focus on the first one. Because right now wasn't the time to talk about that night.

"Secret lover?"

"Well, you said you and Dee weren't involved and you never indicated there was someone in your life. In fact, the opposite. You know, no friends and all that."

"I see." She tapped the steering wheel, wondering at Rylee's curiosity. Did Rylee want to know if she dated? Did she want to know if she made a habit of hitting on women at the bar? Yeah, that's probably what Rylee really wanted to know. She stared at her for a second, thinking she looked ten years younger with her hair pulled back into a ponytail. Young and fresh and oh so attractive. "I don't really do anything at night. I..."

What? *I sit at my desk and sip on a glass—or two—of scotch. Sit and fiddle with a key that I have no clue what lock it opens. Stare at the empty walls and wonder where the last ten years disappeared to. Sit and listen to the silence, made even more hushed now that Sammy is gone.* Yes...what did she do?

"You what?" Rylee asked, her voice quiet in the car.

"I…I go home. My house is only four blocks from the office. On the bay."

"Do you cook?"

"Cook?"

"Yeah. You know…cook and then eat."

"No."

"No to cook or no to eat?"

Finn slowed as Lori Peterson exited, taking the shortcut into Aransas Pass. She followed, staying a little farther behind as there was no car between them now.

"Why all the questions today?"

"I worry about you."

Finn shook her head. "You don't need to worry about me, kid. I've been alone for a very long time."

Rylee stared at her for a long moment, but she didn't say anything else. Finn didn't either. The only person who'd ever worried about her was Sammy. Why would this woman—who she'd known less than a month—be worried about her? Well, maybe because in reality, it wasn't just a month, was it? Maybe Rylee worried about her for the same reason Finn worried about Rylee. They'd slept together. They'd been intimate. They'd shared their bodies. Sometimes, when she thought back to that night, she'd swear they'd shared much more than only their bodies. At least in her mind. Rylee? Maybe not. She had been the one to flee, after all.

When the silver Mercedes turned into an apartment complex, Finn drove past the entrance, keeping an eye on Lori Peterson's car. She took the block around, watching as the Mercedes parked next to an older model truck with a dented front fender.

"Note the time," she said to Rylee as she circled back around.

Lori Peterson looked completely out of place in this rather rundown complex. Her blond hair flowed past her shoulders and designer sunglasses shielded her eyes. Even from here, Finn could see the sparkling of diamonds on her well-manicured hands. Pressed slacks, a fashionable sweater…dark, leather boots with a three-inch heel. Whatever in the world was she doing at a dump like this?

"I hope he's good in bed," Rylee murmured.

Finn smiled. "How so?"

"Because if he lives here, he doesn't have much else going for him."

Finn pulled into an empty parking spot and reached for her camera. Lori Peterson disappeared inside Apartment 19 just as Finn snapped off two shots. She'd only barely gotten a glimpse of someone inside. She hoped the camera saw more than she did.

"So now we find out who lives here?" Rylee asked.

"When we get back to the office, yeah. Now, we sit and wait."

"Okay, so I'm not saying that she doesn't look the type to be having an affair…but I will say, she doesn't look like the type to have an affair *here*."

Finn nodded. "I tend to agree. But maybe she's a spoiled rich girl married to a spoiled rich guy. Maybe whoever she's seeing is the complete opposite. Maybe he's a badass. The kind of guy she secretly wished she could have been with in high school. The dangerous, rowdy guy who could have kicked Brett's ass if he wanted to."

"Do you do that often?"

"What?"

"Try to reason it out."

"Sometimes. Like Connie Frazier. She was a little frumpy, a little plump. Plain Jane, really. And Michael Drake…handsome, dashing. Ten years younger than she was. Made no sense." She shrugged. "But…not my business. I follow, I take pictures, I give a report."

Rylee leaned back in the seat. "Tell me about your father. You said he bought the office building when you were in college."

"Not much to tell, really. The PI showed up a few days after I'd turned thirty. He had a large envelope. My name was on the front— my father's handwriting."

"Why did he wait so long to give it to you? I mean, you were in college when your father died, right?"

"My father's instructions were to give it to me after I turned thirty. I guess he wanted to make sure I had my life in order."

"So you were a cop," Rylee prompted.

"Yes. And I quit the next day."

"So what was in the envelope?"

"There was a note from him. Very businesslike. Some cash, a key to the office building. A key to the house where I'm living now. And a key to a safe deposit box."

"That's kinda neat."

"There was another key. In the safe deposit box." She turned to Rylee. "That's the key that haunts me."

"Why?"

"Because I don't know what it's for."

CHAPTER THIRTY-SEVEN

Dee still wasn't used to the reception area being occupied and she stopped up short when Rylee smiled at her.

"Hi, Dee." Then her smile faltered. "Or should I call you Detective Woodard?"

"Dee's fine," she said. There were papers spread out across the desk. "Busy day?"

Rylee nodded. "Fun day. Now I'm doing research."

Dee nodded. "Finn in her office?"

"She is."

Dee headed in that direction, then stopped. "How's the cat?"

"Smokey? Oh, she's adorable." Rylee's eyes widened. "Oh, my God...you're not here to get her, are you?"

"No, no. I'm pretty sure everyone's forgotten about the cat by now."

"Good. Because she's kinda got the run of the office."

"Oh? I thought Finn kept her upstairs."

"Only at night. In fact, the last I checked, she was in Finn's lap."

Dee laughed. "This I gotta see."

The door to Finn's office was wide open and Dee stood there, smiling as Finn swatted away the cat's tail from her laptop.

"Got a helper there, huh?"

Finn looked up. "Hey. Yeah, she's being a pest." Finn picked her up and deposited her on the floor, only to have the cat jump back up onto her desk again. With a sigh, Finn stood and picked her up once more, tossing her out into the hallway and closing the door. "Should have done that an hour ago."

"Rylee panicked when I asked about the cat. She thought I was here to take her away."

"Yeah, I think you'd have a custody battle if that was the case." She sat down again. "What brings you around?"

Dee sat down across from Finn and crossed her legs, wondering why she continued to come by here and discuss the case with her. There was nothing in Finn's background—however interesting that background was—that indicated she was involved in any way.

"The Fraziers...and your parents," she said, wondering if she should even go there. "So many similarities, it's...well, it's—"

"What? Bizarre? Odd? Ironic? What?"

"It must have brought back unpleasant memories."

Finn waved her hand dismissively. "That was nearly twenty years ago. And I've done my share of surveillance on cheating spouses. The only odd thing in this case is that Daniel Frazier ended up dead and we assume the killer was his wife's lover. The facts may be similar to my parents' situation, but the circumstances are completely different. My mother's lover killed because he was in love."

She nodded. "I'm assuming you don't have a relationship with your mother?"

Finn raised her eyebrows.

"You said at Thanksgiving—I think it was—that you had no family, yet your mother still lives here in Corpus."

"I'm guessing you didn't find anything in my background check that links me to the Fraziers. Is there another reason you're curious about my past?"

She leaned forward. "Why so secretive?"

"Just because I like to keep my private life private doesn't necessarily mean I'm being secretive, Dee."

"Not secretive, I guess. Guarded," she clarified. "And I suppose that goes for me too." She leaned back in her chair, relaxing again. "I've been in Corpus for nine years. Nine years, Finn. And I've never told a soul about Angela or anything about my past. Except for you." She crossed her arms, wondering at the turn their conversation had taken. "They know I'm gay, of course, but not because I came out to them. Someone tried to set me up on a date the first summer I was here."

"Date with a guy?"

"Yes. But other than them knowing I'm gay, they know little else." She shrugged. "I'm not close with anyone here." She met Finn's gaze. "I've known you for such a short period of time—less than two months—and yet you know more about me than anyone else here. How sad is that?"

"So does that mean you're guarded too or that there's not anyone to share the details of your life with?"

Dee smiled. "Both, actually."

Finn nodded. "Yes. Me too." Then she sighed. "Sad. Yes, we're both pretty sad."

Dee laughed lightly. "We're both pretty pathetic."

"I'll say."

"So…Rylee's really cute," she said, the smile still on her face.

"She's too young for you," Finn said sharply.

Dee raised an eyebrow. "Oh?"

Finn cleared her throat. "I mean…well, she's young. Innocent."

"Cute, though. Thirty? I suppose that is a little young for me, considering I feel like I'm in my fifties most days." She wiggled her eyebrows teasingly. "Not too young for you."

She was surprised by the quick blush that lit Finn's face. A blush and…something else. Relief? Was Finn relieved that she didn't have designs on the very lovely—yet young—Rylee?

"Any news on the case?" Finn asked, abruptly changing the subject.

Dee let out a breath. "Oh, yes…the case. I was allowed to accompany the new team—which includes Joel and not me—when they showed up with the warrant."

"The restaurant by the JFK? Jamboree Number One?"

"Yes, although they'll hit all four of them."

"Anything odd?"

"Not at first glance. The manager was very helpful. Of course, they're going over all the books now in fine detail, which I'm not a part of."

"Mabanks pushed you out?"

"Yes, surprisingly, because he's always been very fair to me. In so many words, he said I was old-school and he felt like this particular case needed young blood."

"What the hell does that mean?"

"I think that everyone feels like we'll solve this case using computers and banking records and the like."

"Not beating the streets?"

"As you know, there aren't any streets to beat. There's not one shred of evidence to go on and our only suspect might as well go by the name of John Doe."

"What about Duncan Frazier?"

"Yes, that's an angle I'd like to pursue, but no one else thinks it's viable." She leaned forward again. "He was there. It was as if he was expecting us. He's so young, yet he was very composed."

"Twenty-one still, I think," Finn said.

"Yes, I believe so. But he was very poised, very sure of himself. I would think someone his age, just out of college, taking over a successful family business—especially when both parents were brutally murdered—would have had some jitters when the police showed up in force. With a warrant, no less. But no. And I hate to use this word, but he was almost smug about the whole thing."

"You still following him around?"

"That's about all I've been doing in regard to this case. Nothing out of the ordinary. He goes between the restaurants and his hotel, that's about it."

"What about the sister?"

"Back at college, I assume."

"Wonder what the story is there? They were in quite an argument at the burial."

Dee raised her eyebrows. "You went to the burial?"

"Of course." Then Finn smiled. "Hidden, but I was there."

"So what kind of an argument?"

Finn shrugged. "Hard to say. Raised voices, lots of pointing. He took off in his truck and she went with, I assume, relatives. I followed Duncan. He went to the pizza place—Jamboree Number One—but was only there for a minute or two, then off to the hotel where he was staying."

"Interesting."

"So what about the house? Did they do anything with it?"

"I'm assuming not since he's still living at the hotel. I would think they'd get it cleaned out and put it on the market. Hard to imagine he or the sister would want to live there after what happened to their mother."

"Just taking a guess here, but judging by how little fanfare there was at the funeral, I don't think they were extremely close to their mother. I don't know what their relationship was to Daniel, though. It could have been one of indifference as well."

"Maybe they were still in shock. I mean, their parents were killed, what? Two weeks apart?" She stood up quickly. "I've taken up enough of your time. I'm sure you're busy."

Finn eyed her suspiciously. "So you only came by to visit?"

"Oh, hell, I don't know why I came by. Restless, I guess."

Finn stood up too. "You want to get dinner tonight? Or come over and we'll drink scotch?"

Dee sighed. "I feel like I'm at a crossroads with the job," she admitted. "I'm used to getting the good cases. I'm used to Mabanks trusting me. I mean, hell, he forced Joel on me because he wanted him to learn from me. Now? Now Joel is hanging with the new team and I'm on the outside. When did it change that I'm no longer trusted?"

Finn lifted one corner of her mouth. "So no on dinner?"

Dee smiled too. "Rain check." She walked over to the door and opened it, then paused. "Thanks for listening."

"Anytime."

She went out, then stopped again, sticking her head back inside Finn's office. "You should ask her out."

Finn's eyebrows shot up. "Her who?"

Dee rolled her eyes. "She's cute. And nice. Ask her out. Or I will."

"What makes you think she's gay?"

"Oh, please."

Finn motioned her away. "Goodbye, Dee."

Dee was smiling as she walked down the long hallway into the front part of the office. She was smiling and she was conscious of her smile. Stopping by to chat with Finn had been good for her. What a surprise it was to find that she'd made a new friend.

Rylee appeared to be deep in concentration as she stared at the laptop on her desk, but Dee noticed the lazy hand that was rubbing the cat—Smokey—that sat in her lap.

"She appears to like it here."

Rylee looked up and smiled. "She likes it much better now that we don't confine her to the apartment upstairs."

"I'm sure."

"You really don't think someone will come for her?"

"I doubt it. She's a young cat. They probably hadn't even had her but a handful of months."

"I hope that's the case. I love her, but I think she's done wonders for Finn."

"What? She's not as grumpy now?"

Rylee laughed, a laugh that brightened her eyes. "You said that, not me!"

The smile Dee had still been sporting faded as she stood beside her car. She looked up into the late afternoon sky, watching the clouds building to the north. A front was coming in that evening, bringing rain and cooler temperatures. She opened the door, pausing only a second before getting inside the car.

Dinner and scotch with Finn sounded good, but something was nagging at her. Not that she wanted to spend the evening following Duncan Frazier around, but something wasn't right with him.

CHAPTER THIRTY-EIGHT

"Something's not right."

Finn raised her eyebrows as Rylee paced in front of her desk.

"The Petersons have three young children. The youngest is only four. The oldest is eight."

"You know this how?"

Rylee grinned. "Well, I did a search, of course."

"So you've forgotten Rule Number One already."

"No. Not at first." Rylee sat down across from her. "The guy in the apartment is Carlos Hernandez. He rented that apartment exactly twenty-one days ago. He's also exactly twenty-one years old."

"And?"

"And Lori Peterson is thirty-six."

"So you're saying she's too old?"

"I'm saying he's too young. Too...*wrong*. She's high society. Always has been. Like her husband's family, hers is wealthy too. I'm talking Junior League, old money. In fact, Lori's mother is the current president."

Finn wasn't sure where this was going, but Rylee appeared to be on a roll. Rylee stood up again and resumed her pacing.

"So I'm thinking, where could they have possibly met? Maybe he worked on a crew that did their yard maintenance." Rylee shook her head. "No, that's not it. But maybe he cleans their pool." Again a shake of the head. "Nope. Doesn't do pools."

Finn struggled to keep a smile from her face as Rylee sat down once again. She was animated and…well, quite attractive.

"Guess where he works?"

"I have no idea. Please tell me."

"His uncle owns an office cleaning business. Carlos works for him."

"And?"

"And one of the contracts they have is for none other than Peterson, Barnes, Wilcox and Peterson."

"Okay. So he cleans her husband's office. They could have met there."

Rylee shook her head. "Not unless the wife is there at midnight. They clean that particular office building midnight to three a.m."

Finn nodded. "Okay. So what's your theory?"

"Well, I'm not sure I have one. But I'm pretty confident in saying that Lori Peterson and Carlos Hernandez are *not* having an affair."

"She was in the apartment over an hour," Finn reminded her.

"And I'm guessing she didn't even sit down, much less take her clothes off. You saw the look on her face. It wasn't ecstasy after having sex. It was relief to get the hell out of there."

Finn did agree with that. There was no dreamy look on her face like Connie Frazier had sported. There was no afterglow. Relief. Yes, that's how she would describe it too.

"So what's your next plan of action then?"

Rylee's eyes widened. "Me?"

"Yes, you. Brett Peterson asked us to follow his wife. If she's not having an affair, what's she doing there?"

"Can we tap her phone?"

"No, we cannot tap her phone!"

"What about a listening device?"

Finn shook her head. "You've watched too many movies. We stay the course."

"What does that mean?"

"That means, tomorrow morning, we stake out their house again and follow her if she goes out. And we also dig a little deeper into Carlos Hernandez."

"But what about Rule Number One?"

Finn smiled. "You've already broken it. Might as well do a thorough breakdown on Carlos."

CHAPTER THIRTY-NINE

It was getting dark outside and she should have already headed out, but she wanted to check on Smokey. Rylee shook her head as she lifted the cover on the litter box. Even though she and Finn were supposed to take turns scooping out the litter, she'd found it was hit and miss as to whether Finn remembered or not.

"She forgot again, huh," she said to Smokey. Smokey didn't seem to care. She was hunched over her food bowl, crunching away.

After scooping the clumps into a plastic bag, she was about to add more fresh litter to the box when something inside the lid caught her eye. She lifted the lid off the floor, frowning as gray duct tape hung from the top.

"What the heck?" she murmured.

She pulled the duct tape off, her eyes glued to the object stuck on the tape. She pulled it off, frowning as she fingered the flash drive. Then...

"Oh, my God...oh my freaking *God*!"

She dropped the lid on the floor as her hand closed around the flash drive. Her eyes darted to Smokey, then back to the litter box.

"Oh, shit," she whispered. When they trashed the Fraziers' house, they didn't find it. And unknowingly, Finn brought it here. That's what it was, right? It had to be.

She turned, dashing to the door. As she jerked it open, she collided with a sturdy body and she let out a scream. Strong arms held her in place when she would have fallen.

"Whoa, there," Finn said, still holding her. "What's your hurry?"

Rylee held a hand to her chest. "You scared the crap out of me." She pointed into the apartment. "I was cleaning the litter. I found—"

"I didn't forget," Finn said quickly. "Honest. I was coming up now to clean it."

"Yeah, right. But look what I found." She opened up her closed fist, revealing the flash drive. "This is it, right?"

"It?"

"It. The thing they were looking for. The thing they killed for."

Finn frowned. "What are you talking about?"

Rylee made a fist again around the flash drive and slugged Finn on her shoulder. "The *thing*! They tore your office apart, remember? They ransacked the Fraziers' house. The *thing*," she said again, her words coming faster and faster. "It was in the litter box. Well, taped to the top. Genius, really. I mean, who would ever look in a litter box?"

"Rylee, you're making no sense."

Rylee let out a frustrated breath. "For a private investigator, you're being a little dense right now." She opened her hand again. "It's a flash drive. Taped inside the lid of the litter box." She tilted her head. "You *did* get the litter box from the Fraziers' house, right?"

Finn took the flash drive and held it up, inspecting it. "Jesus Christ," she whispered. "Yeah…yeah, I did." It was Finn's turn to fold the flash drive up in her palm. "You found this in the litter box?"

"Yes. Taped to the lid. Duct tape. It had come loose."

"Wow."

"That's all you have to say? Wow?" Rylee tugged on her arm, pulling her down the stairs. "Come on! Let's see what's on it."

* * *

Finn stood with her back to her desk, staring out of the lone window in her office, looking out into the fast dwindling twilight, absently noting that the wind had picked up and rain was beginning to splatter the glass. The window looked out onto the backside of the property, essentially a vacant lot. A lot that was part of her property where the old office building sat. She hadn't done anything with it. During the summer, it was overgrown with coastal grass. There were no trees at all, unless you counted the three palm trees, one of which was partially uprooted from a past storm.

She closed her eyes to the view, wondering what it all meant. The flash drive contained three files. One was a spreadsheet—a ledger—with a list of names. Members, it was titled. In the column next to some of the names...most of the names...was a monetary amount. The column was titled simply "debt." The second file was also a spreadsheet. It contained one column titled "account numbers" and there were five accounts, ranging from twelve numbers to twenty-one. The third file was perhaps the most disturbing. It contained photos. Still shots captured from a video feed, most likely. Shots of men—presumably the men from the list—having sex. With prostitutes, she assumed. And judging by the high profiles of some of those men—high-dollar prostitutes to match those high profiles.

"Okay, this is pretty much disgusting."

Finn turned at the sound of Rylee's voice, nodding in agreement.

"What does it all mean, Finn?"

"I guess this is some sort of documentation for blackmail or leverage of some sort. I'm assuming the men aren't aware there's a camera in the room with them."

"So this debt is for sex? Good Lord! This one guy owes close to half a million. For *sex*?"

"That's Roger King. Largest car dealership in the city. I think he's got four dealerships up and down the coast. Sleazy guy."

"Oh, yeah. I've seen his commercials. Gravelly voice, kinda yells at the camera." Rylee pointed to another name. "So I haven't been in town long enough to recognize these names, but Nathan O'Leary? Is that *the* Nathan O'Leary?"

Finn nodded. "Yes. Mayor O'Leary."

Rylee met her gaze. "Wow. And the others?"

"High profile." Finn moved back around her desk, leaning over Rylee's shoulder. She pointed to one. "That's the county judge."

"Jesus. A who's who of Corpus? What about this guy? He owes six hundred thousand."

Finn stared at the name again. She still couldn't believe it. She let out a long breath. "That's John Mabanks. My old boss."

Rylee whipped her head around. "*What?*"

"Dee's current boss, actually."

"Oh, my God! A cop?"

"Captain."

"How in the world can a captain in the police force be mixed up in this? And for that kind of money?"

"Easy. Whoever's running the show—whatever kind of show it is—they let the debt pile up. Then they own him. Same with the mayor and the judge. They own them now."

"We should do a background check on all of them," Rylee said excitedly as she rubbed her hands together. "Find out what's going on."

"You do realize that three people have been killed for this information, right?"

"Oh, yeah." Rylee went back to the list, silently reading through the names. "Finn?" She ran her finger along the screen, pointing. "Fredrick Peterson? Any relation to Brett? They're both on the list."

"Yeah. That's his father. I've done work for him before. You suggested that he referred his son to me and that's most likely the case."

Rylee's eyes flew to hers. "But I thought we were in agreement that the deal with his wife was fake."

Finn smiled quickly. "*You* were in agreement with yourself, just because it didn't add up. And yes, I tend to see it your way too, but there's no proof one way or the other yet."

"So what are we going to do? About this, I mean. Not the Petersons."

Finn ran a hand through her hair. Yes, what were they going to do? "I've got to let Dee know."

"But if you let Dee know, then your Captain Mabanks will find out."

And that couldn't happen. Not yet, anyway. She pointed to the laptop. "Close it down. We need to get out of here."

"But—"

"Rylee, it's only a matter of time before they realize that we've got this, whatever *this* is—whoever *they* are. When they didn't find it at the Fraziers' house and if they don't find it at any of the pizza places, they'll turn their focus back to me. I was the last person Daniel Frazier saw before he went home to his wife." She paused. "Before he was killed. Peterson hiring me can't be a coincidence. The timing's too perfect."

Rylee closed the laptop and pulled the flash drive out. "Why do you think they haven't been to your house yet? I mean, break in and search it."

"Locked gate, security cameras, alarm system. Plus, I had a patrol unit parked out front, remember?" She held her hand out and Rylee handed over the drive.

"Yeah, but that's been gone for a while now."

"My guess is when they didn't find it here—which is where I met with Daniel—and they didn't find it at the Fraziers' house, then they began focusing on the pizza places. When they don't find it there, then..." She slipped the flash drive into her jeans pocket. "Come on, we need to get out of here. Let's go."

Rylee stopped her with a hand on her arm. "Finn...wait. What about Smokey?"

Finn blew out her breath. The cat. "Okay. Go get her things. We'll take her to my house with us."

She went back over to her desk and opened the middle drawer. She picked up the key and fingered it for a second, then slipped it into her pocket.

She put the laptop under her arm and turned out the light, only to put it back on again. She walked over to the credenza and picked up her father's scotch glass. They'd ransacked the place once already. Surely they wouldn't do it again. But still...she didn't want to take a chance that the glass could survive a second break-in.

Rylee had Smokey's litter box and food by the front door. Smokey was sitting on top of Rylee's desk, cleaning herself, seemingly unconcerned with the happenings around her.

"Take your laptop too," she instructed.

"Where are we going?"

"We'll go by your apartment and get you some clothes, enough for several days. We'll leave your Jeep, then go to my house."

"Your...your house?"

Their gazes locked together and in that moment, Finn could see all the memories from that night swirling around in Rylee's blue eyes. Was she afraid? Afraid Finn would assume they were going to have a repeat? Rylee's mouth parted, as if to say something else. Surely she didn't want to finally talk about it, did she? *Now?*

But no. Rylee closed her mouth and nodded. "Okay. Your house."

"I'll call Dee, have her meet us there," Finn said, hoping that might ease whatever fears Rylee was feeling.

Rylee surprised her by taking a step closer. She surprised her further by squeezing her arm rather tightly. "You're...you're really worried, aren't you?"

"Yes, I am. There are a lot of powerful men on that list. I would think most of them would do anything in their power to keep that list a secret."

"Like kill," Rylee stated quietly.

"Yes. I may be overreacting but I'd rather let my paranoia take over than ignore it."

Rylee held her gaze again. "I trust your intuition. Let's get the hell out of here."

CHAPTER FORTY

Finn watched as Rylee and Smokey took a walk through her house. Rylee's gaze didn't linger on anything too long, looking over the furniture in the living room, then out the large windows that framed the bay. She spun around in a circle, finally turning to face her.

"Either you have a housekeeper or you're very, very meticulous about cleaning."

"No housekeeper."

A quick smile. "Neat freak then, huh? I wouldn't have guessed that."

"Why? My office is tidy, isn't it?"

"That's only because there's nothing in it," Rylee teased. "Where's all your stuff?"

Finn looked around the familiar room...the tidy, very neat, very sterile room. She looked back at Rylee. "I don't guess I have any stuff."

Rylee came closer, brushing her fingers—causing Finn to tremble at the simple touch—as she took the glass from her hand. It was her father's glass, of course. The one she'd forgotten she was still holding.

"What's this? You took it from your office."

"It...it was my father's." She gave a quick smile. "His scotch glass."

Rylee nodded. "Which is what you use it for." She held it up, inspecting it, her eyes on the large K etched on one side. "You treasure it, I suppose."

"I do." She took the glass from Rylee. "There's nothing spectacular about it, really."

"Of course there is. It was your father's."

Finn shrugged. "I don't really have anything. When he died... well, my mother and I...well, I didn't want anything to do with her. Then the trial, all that." She shrugged again. "I never went back to the house."

"How did you get this?"

"I stole it from his office." She smiled, remembering how she'd slipped it under her shirt when his secretary wasn't watching.

"Of all the things you could have swiped, you chose the glass?"

Finn went over and set it down on the bar, next to the other glasses there. "At the end of a long day, he loved to have a splash of scotch," she said, thinking of how many times she'd sat across from his desk as he sipped on his drink. When she got older, he would let her indulge too. "This was the glass he used. Always." She cleared her throat. "Anyway, Dee's going to come by. I've asked her to pick up dinner. Do you have a preference?"

Rylee stared at her a long time, as if she had more questions, but she finally shook her head. "Not choosy, no."

"Seafood okay? There's a place I use for takeout."

Again, Rylee hesitated. "Is that what you exist on? Takeout?" She tilted her head. "Or nothing at all?"

"Yes."

"You're probably one of those people who forget to eat." Rylee laughed and shook her head. "And that's just crazy. I *never* forget to eat." Rylee surprised her by walking closer and touching her stomach. "That's why you're so thin. *Too* thin, in my opinion."

Finn didn't realize she was holding her breath. The light pressure from Rylee's hand disappeared and Finn sucked in air, trying to appear nonchalant as she took a step away.

"As a matter of fact, I was quite chunky when I was a kid."

"Chunky, huh?" Rylee shook her head. "I can't picture it. I was thin as a rail growing up, but I like to eat. If I'm not careful, five or even ten pounds will sneak up on me in no time."

Finn couldn't stop herself from doing a quick inspection of Rylee's body. She wasn't surprised that she could picture every inch of it...

naked. Rylee wasn't rail thin, no. She looked healthy…nice curves. Not rail thin, but certainly not fat. She brought her eyes back up, meeting Rylee's, seeing the questions there. She felt a blush light her face and she was embarrassed for that.

"I don't think you have anything to worry about," she managed with a quick clearing of her throat. "So? Seafood?"

Again Rylee had that look in her eyes like they needed to talk. Talk about that night. Which she imagined they'd have to do sooner or later. But apparently not now.

"Sounds good. Do I pay Detective Woodard when she gets here or—"

"It's already taken care of. I have an account with them." When she would have protested, Finn held up her hand. "I owe you, remember. Don't argue. You won't win this one."

"Okay." Rylee pointed at the litter box that they'd left near the entryway. "Where would you like me to put that?"

"I guess in my bathroom. The spare bath is fairly small. There's room in mine."

Rylee raised an eyebrow questioningly.

"In the back," she motioned with her head. "First door there is the spare bedroom. You can put your bag in there. Mine's in the back."

* * *

Rylee stood in Finn's bedroom, slowly shaking her head. Nothing. Not one personal item could be found. A dresser with a large mirror was against one wall. There was nothing on it, not even dust. A chest of drawers was along another wall. An end table beside the bed held a lamp and a digital alarm clock, nothing else. Like the rest of the house, it was almost too tidy, too clean.

The bathroom—at least—looked lived in. A neatly folded hand towel lay on the counter and a soap dispenser was beside the sink. The toilet was in a separate space, the door ajar. She opened that, finding enough room inside for Smokey's litter box.

She paused to glance around the bathroom. The glass shower door was clear and she spied the few personal toiletries inside—shampoo, a razor and cream, a squirt bottle of liquid soap. As she stared through the glass, an image of Finn popped into her mind. An image of Finn— naked—showering. She could see her clearly. Her dark hair wet and slicked back from her face. Her small breasts glistening, her nipples erect…her hands lathering soap across her body.

She turned away from the image and closed her eyes for a moment. How long were they going to pretend that neither of them remembered that night? Finn had given no indication she wanted to talk about it. And at first, Rylee thought that was probably best. But they were working closely together now. She was staying at her house, for God's sake. Surely they should talk about it. Surely Finn could feel the energy between them.

She blew out her breath. Well, if Finn wanted to keep it buried, then maybe that's what they should do. It would come up eventually. It had to.

She found Finn and Smokey in the kitchen. Smokey was on the counter, eating. Rylee shook her head disapprovingly.

"No wonder she jumps on the counter in our little breakroom. *You* let her!"

"I've never had a pet before."

Rylee leaned her hip against the counter beside Smokey. "No?"

"You?"

"Yes. We had two outdoor cats and my mother had a dog— Princess—who was queen of the house. She died when I was in college. She has another one now, but since I don't live there, I'm not really attached to it."

"I don't remember ever asking for one," Finn volunteered. "I guess I knew my mother would have said no." She moved back into the living room and went to the small bar. "You want something to drink?"

Rylee shrugged. "What will you have?"

"Scotch."

Rylee shook her head. "I don't think so, but thanks."

"Beer, then?"

The look in Finn's eyes was familiar. Yes…she'd been drinking a beer that night. Finn had walked over…asked her to dance. She didn't remember touching the beer again. No, she'd been touching Finn instead.

"I'm sorry I don't have any wine. I do have a really nice cognac, though. You'd probably like that."

"Okay. I'll try it. My dad is a beer drinker. Nothing else. Ever. My mother only drinks wine and only on special occasions." She smiled. "Her taste in wine is cheap and sweet. I'm not much for wine, myself. I normally stick with beer or a cocktail, if I'm out." She watched as Finn slid her father's glass over and poured from a decanter. The decanter was square, with etched glass and a round glass ball on top. By the way Finn held it, it appeared to be heavy. Lead crystal, she guessed. Nice.

And expensive. She then opened the cabinet and took out a tulip-shaped wineglass.

"If you're out?" Finn asked as she poured a little cognac into the glass. "Where do you go?"

The question was asked innocently enough, but yet there was an awkward pause before she answered.

"I...I don't go out much. Ever, really." She took the glass from Finn, daring to meet her eyes for a moment. They were alone. Should she bring up that night? Should they talk about it finally?

But Finn didn't give her a chance. She lightly touched Rylee's glass. "Cheers."

Rylee gave her a quick, relieved smile. "Cheers," she returned before taking a sip. It was unexpectedly smooth. She nodded. "I like it." She cleared her throat. "So, what did you tell Dee?"

Finn took a sip of her own drink, then shook her head. "Not much. I didn't want to cause alarm."

"You're going to show her the files?"

"Yes."

Rylee wasn't sure why, but she moved closer to her. "Have you thought any more about it? The Petersons, I mean."

"I think you're right. There is no affair. His reason for hiring me was a ruse. I'm not sure the reason, though." Finn met her gaze. "I wouldn't have come to that conclusion without you, you know."

"What do you mean?"

"I'm not curious like you are. I don't need to know the why of things. If you weren't here, I would have followed Lori Peterson, I would have taken pictures, I would have done a little background on Carlos Hernandez but not much. Mr. Peterson didn't ask for detailed info on the guy. Just like Daniel Frazier didn't ask. They only wanted to know if their wife was having an affair and with whom."

"When you researched Carlos Hernandez, you would have realized it didn't make sense."

"Make sense to who, though? Michael Drake threw up all sorts of red flags. But I didn't care. Daniel Frazier wasn't—"

"—paying you to care," Rylee finished for her.

"Exactly." Finn set her glass on the table. "I have a theory, some guesses as to what's going on...and a whole lot of questions. But we'll wait and talk about it when Dee gets here." She looked at the watch on her wrist. "Which I hope is soon. It's getting late."

She'd no longer said the words when a beeping sounded in the kitchen. Rylee raised her eyebrows.

"Alarm. The gate opened. Dee has the code."

"What other security features do you have?"

"Outside cameras. And I have a home security service that monitors the house. The same thing I had installed at the office last month. Why? Are you worried?"

Rylee shook her head. "If you're not worried, I'm not."

"Having a system like this sometimes gives one a false sense of security. So yeah, I'm still a little worried."

CHAPTER FORTY-ONE

Dee hadn't known what to make of Finn's request. Not really a request, she noted. Finn needed to see her. It was urgent. And oh, can you pick up the dinner I've already ordered? There'd been no mention of Rylee joining them, so she was quite surprised when the young blonde was the one to open the door to Finn's house. If Rylee noticed the startled look on her face, she didn't show it. Instead, Dee was greeted with a genuine smile, a smile that made her again take note of Rylee's attractiveness. Damn…if Finn didn't hurry up and ask her out, she had half a mind to.

"Detective Woodard—Dee—please come in," Rylee offered as she held the door open. Her smile faded, though, as she looked past Dee. She then quickly closed and locked the door. "Here, let me help," she said, taking one of the bags from Dee.

"Thanks."

She followed Rylee, pausing in the living room as she spotted the cat sitting on the sill of one of the large windows facing the bay. The lights were on along the pier and there was a swirling fog over the water. The cat seemed fascinated by it. Why was Smokey here? For that matter, why was Rylee here?

She looked over toward the kitchen, past the bar separating it from the living room. Finn was there, watching her. She walked over, placing the bag she still held on the counter.

"What's going on?"

"What makes you think something's going on?"

"Because I'm a detective and I notice things."

"Yeah. Well, we've got—"

"Let's eat first," Rylee interrupted.

Finn shook her head. "Rylee, we need—"

"—to eat. We didn't have lunch and if I had to guess, you didn't have breakfast either." When Finn would have protested, Rylee held a hand up. "Don't argue. If we talk first, we'll never eat. Now…where are the plates?"

Finn sighed, then motioned with her head. "The cabinet there, closest to the fridge."

To say that she was perplexed by their interaction was an understatement. The Finn she knew was too…too obstinate to take an order from someone. Too self-controlling, if that was even a word. She did what she wanted, when she wanted. To see her acquiesce now… well, what was going on?

"You want a drink?"

Dee turned to Finn and nodded. "I think I better."

She followed Finn out to the living room and to the small bar, watching as she poured them each a scotch. She also noticed the glass Finn normally used at her office was now here.

"You move out of your office?" Finn looked at her quizzically and Dee motioned to the glass. "That…and the cat is here, not there."

"This was my father's," she explained. "I…"

Finn looked past her to the kitchen. Dee turned too, seeing Rylee watching them as she brought plates out to the table. She took a sip of her scotch, noting that Finn's eyes never left Rylee. Indeed…what was going on?

* * *

Conversation over dinner was either nonexistent or forced and Rylee finally threw up her hands…literally.

"Fine," she said to Finn. "Tell her already."

Dee looked up and Finn had just shoved a jumbo shrimp into her mouth. "Tell me what?" she asked, her curiosity having gotten the better of her.

Finn said nothing as she chewed. Rylee leaned her elbows on the table, moving a bit closer to Dee.

"We found it," she said quietly.

Dee raised her eyebrows. "It?"

"Yes. *It*. The thing they were looking for."

Dee's eyes flew to Finn, who had finally swallowed and was taking a drink of water. "You found what they were looking for?"

Finn nodded. "Yes. Rylee found it. It was in the damn litter box, taped inside on the lid. A flash drive."

Dee put her fork down, the fried snapper forgotten. "What the hell was it?"

"A list of names," Rylee supplied. "And a debt ledger of some sort. And some account numbers. And photos. Sex photos. Disgusting, really." She pointed at Dee's plate. "Finish your fish first." She looked over at Finn. "I knew this would happen."

"Yes. Sorry."

Dee ignored her plea to finish eating, shoving the plate away from her instead. "Names? Who?"

Finn, too, moved her plate to the middle of the table. "I think we're in trouble, Dee. Powerful men. The mayor is on the list. The county judge. Businessmen. Councilmen Stevens is on there too. Ten total."

"Rumor has it that Mayor O'Leary is going to run for state senate. Stevens is running for mayor."

"They're not the ones I'm worried about."

"Who then?"

"John Mabanks."

Dee couldn't stop the startled gasp. "Oh, my God! *Captain* Mabanks?"

"Show her the files," Rylee suggested. "I'll clean up."

Finn nodded and stood, motioning for Dee to follow. "Don't put it in the fridge yet," Finn told Rylee. "I'll have some later. You were right. No breakfast or lunch."

"I know. What am I going to do with you?"

The look they exchanged was…what? Intimate? Dee stood quietly, watching them, wondering if Finn had forgotten she was even there. It was almost as if Finn had to physically pull herself away from Rylee.

"We'll…we'll be in my office. It's—"

"I'll find you. Go on."

CHAPTER FORTY-TWO

Finn stood behind her, watching as she scrolled through the photos one-by-one. They both gasped when the one of Captain Mabanks appeared. Dee quickly went on to the next one.

"I didn't need to see that," she murmured.

"What do you make of it?"

She clicked out of the file with the photos, pulling up the list of names again. "I agree with you. The photos are for leverage... blackmail, if need be. In each still, the face is clearly visible."

"To what end, though?" Finn motioned to the laptop. "If we take this at face value, these guys pay for sex. Some obviously don't pay and they have a debt. But as Rylee said, that's a lot of money for sex. It has to be something else."

"It could be a combination of things. Sex, drugs...what else?"

"Big debts like that? Gambling. It's got to be."

She nodded. "You suggested that at the beginning. The men on this list could certainly afford to be in a high-stakes game. All but Mabanks. How the hell did he get involved?"

"Someone he knew had to have recruited him. Judge Santos, maybe?"

"He lunches sometimes with O'Leary. I always assumed it was a business lunch. Maybe not. Only one way to find out, though. Ask him."

"Oh, hell no," Finn said quickly, holding up her hand. "You can't let him know we have this."

"I've got to. This is major evidence, Finn. These account numbers are probably where the money trail leads. The trail we've lost. He's—"

"He's involved, Dee. Until we find out what the hell is going on—and who's behind it—we tell no one. Three people are dead, remember?"

Dee blew out a breath. This was evidence, sure. But evidence of what? Daniel Frazier wasn't listed here. Neither was Michael Drake. On the surface, there was nothing about this flash drive that linked to the murders. On the surface. But Daniel Frazier had obviously hidden it. This was the thing the killers had been looking for. The debt, the photos…that was for leverage. The account numbers? That's probably what was most important to them. The account numbers would lead to the money. And the money would lead to whoever was running this little operation. She took another deep breath. Finn was right, though. She couldn't go waltzing into Captain Mabanks's office with this. It would be too easy for him to bury it.

"Okay, Finn. It's against my better judgment, but you're right. But how do we find out what's going on?"

Finn let out a relieved breath. "My specialty. Surveillance."

"But Finn…there are ten names on this list."

"And there are two of us. Three, counting Rylee." Finn looked up, finding Rylee standing in the doorway. She motioned her inside. "Come in." She turned back to Dee. "We start by doing background checks on everyone. We pick someone to start with and do surveillance. Where do they go? If it's a brothel of some sort, where is it? A hotel? That's unlikely."

"Apartment complex," Rylee suggested. "I'm talking your smaller, mom-and-pop type places. One with only a handful of rooms. Eight to ten."

Dee nodded. "Makes sense. But most of these small complexes are rather rundown and are located, well, shall we say in the shady side of town." She motioned to the list on the screen. "These guys, I can't see them going to a place like that."

"No. Especially the public figures. O'Leary? Judge Santos? They'd be recognized," Finn said as she paced in front of the desk. "Where else?"

"How many women do you think there are? Two? Three? More?" Rylee asked as she sat down in the lone guest chair.

"Hard to say," Dee said. "If these are the only clients—ten—then two, maybe three. The fewer women they have, the smaller place they'd need to operate."

"The camera was pretty much focused on the men, but I'm sure we could determine a roundabout count," Finn offered. "If it even matters."

"True. If the gambling angle is correct, then *that's* where they're making the money, not sex for hire."

"What kind of gambling?" Rylee asked. "Poker? Sports betting? What?"

"I'm picturing a high-stakes poker game," Finn said, glancing at Dee. "I can see these guys sitting around a table, smoking cigars and slapping down poker chips."

"For high-stakes poker, you'd need a secure place, certainly nothing public."

"Someone's home?"

Finn shook her head. "These guys are the players. Whoever started this, it's not one of the names on this list."

"Members," Rylee corrected. "Not clients, not customers, but members. That suggests some sort of a club or something."

"A secret club by invitation only?" Finn nodded. "I can see that. But who started it? And where do the girls come from? Who do they work for?"

Dee was surprised by Rylee's astuteness. Perhaps because like Finn had said—she looked much younger than thirty—Dee hadn't expected her to contribute.

"You're good at this. Ex-cop?" she guessed, addressing Rylee.

"Who? Me?" Rylee smiled and shook her head. "No, sorry. Not a cop."

Rylee didn't elaborate and neither did Finn.

"How the hell did Daniel Frazier get mixed up in it? He's not listed as one of the members," Finn continued.

"Maybe he organized it from the beginning," Dee offered. "After all, it's his restaurants that are moving the money. This could very well be his gig."

Finn leaned against the wall, her brow furrowed. "Then who killed him? If he started it and he's making the money, who killed him?" Finn shook her head. "I know we've talked about it before, but I don't see Daniel Frazier in this role. The whole setup seems too…

too organized. You've got your fake vendors where you're washing the money through…you've got prostitutes. There's got to be a secure location for these members to meet. All of the logistics of this thing leads me to believe this is a professional operation. Not just a bunch of local guys getting together for a good time."

Dee nodded. "I suppose. There's also the question of where does Michael Drake fit in. Who hired him? If they knew Daniel Frazier had this information—and perhaps threatened to disclose it—why kill him without securing it first?"

"Maybe he didn't give them a chance," Rylee said. "He found out that Drake was sleeping with his wife. He confronts Drake. He may have even had a gun. Perhaps they didn't intend to kill him, but Drake had no choice."

"So with Frazier out of the way, the race was on to find this drive and the account numbers," Dee agreed. "Whoever is in charge, I doubt they'd be concerned with this list of names getting out. I assume they're only interested in the account numbers."

"I agree." Finn pushed off the wall. "A lot of these scenarios that we're tossing out here make sense. Doesn't make any of them true, though." She pointed to the laptop. "We divide the names and do surveillance. We find a pattern, a common denominator, something."

"Or their secret hideout," Rylee said with a confident smile.

Dee nodded. "Divide it three ways?"

"No," Finn said quickly. "Two."

Dee glanced at Rylee. "But—"

"No. She's inexperienced. She'll ride with me." Finn looked at Rylee. "Or she'll stay here and do background checks."

"I'd rather ride with you."

Dee didn't miss the look that passed between the two of them. What in the world was going on? "So you're ditching the office?" she asked Finn.

"I think so. It's safer here. Locked gate. No side streets. Nowhere for anyone to hide a vehicle and walk to the house."

Dee had to agree. Moonlight Avenue was downright creepy. Dead-end street, no lights, no traffic. Creepy at night, anyway. She turned her attention back to the list of names. Finn was right. The only way they would know what was going on would be to follow these men. The fact that some were high profile—county judge, the mayor, her own damn captain—was her only hesitation.

Well, that and the fact that she was withholding evidence in a murder investigation. She reminded herself that she was the one who followed the rules, followed protocol. Always. Finn? No. She was the rulebreaker. She'd admitted that herself. Dee hadn't needed Captain Mabanks to reinforce that. Nonetheless, she was following Finn's lead in this case. It was the only way.

If they uncovered something, though, where would she take it? Captain Mabanks was out of the question. Did she go over his head? Did she trust the young detectives he'd assigned to the case?

It was starting to make sense now. Was that why he'd pushed her aside? He didn't *want* these murders solved?

"He wanted me out of the way," she murmured. She looked up, meeting Finn's gaze. "Mabanks. He wanted me off the case."

"And now you know why."

CHAPTER FORTY-THREE

Rylee sat at the table, across from Finn, watching as Finn nibbled on a cold piece of fish, her eyes fixed on the paper in her hand...the list of names Dee had printed out, their five highlighted in yellow. Smokey was perched on the counter, eyeing the fish. Finn had already tossed her off the table twice.

Dee had left a half hour ago after they'd finalized a plan. Rylee and Finn would run background checks on everyone on the list and provide addresses—both work and home—and photos. They'd agreed to focus their surveillance to after working hours, hoping to follow one of their targets to the "clubhouse"—her words, not Finn's or Dee's—before he went home to his wife and family. Dee was also going to keep an eye out on Mabanks, stating that he frequently took long lunch hours. By looking through the pictures, they'd determined there were at least three different women. It wouldn't be shocking to find that some of the men used their lunch time for a quick hookup.

"I think we should start with Peterson. The father, not the son," Finn said, breaking the silence.

"Okay. You have a feeling?"

Finn shrugged. "It's not a coincidence Brett hired us. I've worked for the old man before. He sent the son to us." She tapped the paper. "The old man has no debt, the son does."

"Did you tell Dee about Peterson hiring you?"

"No. I didn't get around to it." Finn tossed the paper down. "A lot of trails to follow here. I doubt there'll be a quick resolution."

"You never know. Peterson might lead us right to the place."

"It's one thing knowing where they go. What they do *inside* is going to be hard to determine from the outside."

Rylee leaned forward, resting her elbows on the table. "Did you and Dee ever consider that maybe you should get the FBI involved? I mean, the money laundering thing, prostitution, gambling…it screams organized crime."

"Yes, it does. And no, we didn't discuss the FBI." Finn pushed the fish platter away and picked up her father's glass, twirling it slowly on top of the table in a circle. "It's probably what we *should* do, yes. Dee, especially. She's the cop. I'm just a lowly PI." She took a sip of her scotch. "They should have already alerted the FBI to the money laundering, but they haven't. If the Feds come in, they're going to pounce on the gambling, the prostitution, the money trail. Three murders will fall through the cracks. And if they come in with guns blazing, then Michael Drake will disappear into the wind. He and whoever he works for."

"Maybe he's the boss. Of course I know you said Michael Drake wasn't his real identity."

"He could be, but I doubt it. Bosses don't do their own dirty work." Finn sighed heavily. "It's late. I'm ready to call it a night. We'll start early on these background checks. I want to get the profiles on Dee's five sent to her before noon."

"Okay." Rylee looked over at Smokey, who was now sprawled out along the counter. "She's made herself right at home, hasn't she?"

Finn smiled as she looked at the cat. "She's kinda cute. I can't believe I've gotten attached to a damn cat."

"Well, believe it. She's sleeping with you."

"Why me?"

"Because you have the litter box," she reminded her. "Or do you sleep with your door open?"

"Open. You?"

"Closed. And I know, false sense of security like you said earlier."

"We'll be okay here. If anyone tries to break in, the alarms will go off."

"They could still break in. How many minutes before the police come around?"

"Don't worry. You have a gun. I have a gun." Finn surprised her by reaching across the table and squeezing her arm. "But you are worried, huh?"

"A little. Obviously I feel safer here with you than I would alone at my apartment. Of course, I'm just your lowly assistant," she said, using the word Finn had used to describe her. "I doubt they even know I exist or where I live."

Finn leaned back again, her hand sliding off Rylee's arm slowly. It was the first time Finn had touched her like that. She was surprised at how familiar it felt.

"Whether they know about you or not doesn't matter. There's no sense in taking a chance when you can stay here."

Rylee met her gaze, then smiled. "Thank you for worrying about me, by the way."

Finn returned her smile. "Not worrying really...I just don't want to take chances."

"You're lying but thank you all the same."

Finn laughed lightly. "Yeah...so I am."

Rylee got up and placed the fish platter by the sink. She turned, leaning her hip against the counter.

"Why do you trust me?"

Finn's eyebrows shot up. "Should I not?"

"You gave me a job when you didn't want to hire me. You've let me tag along with you. You've brought me into your home. You've included me. Why?" Was it only because of that night? Was it because Rylee was somewhat familiar to her?

Finn shrugged but said nothing.

"You don't have people in your life, Finn. You've said so and...well, it's obvious. Yet you let me in."

"I like to think I'm a good judge of character. Sammy, for instance. He was homeless. He showed up on my doorstep when I was just getting the building set up for an office. He was dirty and raggedy and I should have sent him on his way. Instead, I moved him upstairs a few days later." Finn met her gaze, holding it. "I *am* a good judge of character. I felt so sure about you, I didn't even do a background check." She cupped the glass again, unconsciously perhaps. "There aren't many people I trust. And no, there aren't many—any—in my life, really. Dee...Dee and I met by chance and just clicked. And then you..."

Rylee felt mesmerized as their eyes held. "Me, what?" she asked quietly, hoping Finn might bring up that night. Hoping they could finally talk about it.

Finn twirled the empty glass around in her hand, a smile playing on her lips. "You...you barged in and demanded a job. Twice." Finn's eyes were fixed on the glass now, her thumb moving lightly across the etched K. She looked back up, once again capturing her eyes. "I found I couldn't say no to you. I *can't* say no to you."

Rylee didn't know what to say to that. Finn seemed so serious all of a sudden. She took a deep breath, smiling slightly as she shoved off the counter.

"Well, you know, you *did* say no," she reminded Finn. "I was just... persistent."

"Is that what you're calling it?"

"Yes, persistent. You know, like...housekeeper-slash-receptionist."

"Slash-assistant."

Rylee grinned. "Slash-apprentice. See?"

"Oh, kid," Finn said, with a shake of her head. "Why do you want in this line of work?"

"Why not?"

"Because it's not exciting. It's not glamorous."

"Who said I needed excitement and glamor? It's been rather interesting so far, you have to admit."

"You call this interesting? Hiding away like this? Hiding from someone? Someone we don't know? Someone who would kill for this information that we now have?"

Rylee walked over to her, seeing genuine concern in her eyes. She reached out with one hand, hesitating only a second before cupping her cheek.

"Stop calling me a kid," she whispered. "You, of all people, should know I'm not one."

CHAPTER FORTY-FOUR

Finn couldn't seem to concentrate on her portion of the list. Her gaze—her attention—was drawn to Rylee, who was sitting across from her at the table. They each had their laptops open, cups of coffee sitting beside them. Finn had her notebook where she scribbled down information. She would use it later to compile a report on each of her five people, which was her normal routine. Rylee was working on her report as she went, foregoing the notepad.

Rylee glanced up and once again caught Finn staring. Finn looked away quickly, turning her attention back to Eric Lawrence. Perhaps she should have stayed in her office and worked. It would have been less distracting.

Distracting? Why was she letting Rylee distract her?

She'd never heard of Eric Lawrence before. Eric was in real estate. Apparently Eric didn't bother with listings that were less than half a million. Eric was married with two young daughters. Eric owed a measly twenty grand for sex and/or gambling, according to this ledger. Judging by his assets, that was only a drop in the bucket. Why hadn't he paid up?

She looked at Rylee over the top of her laptop. Rylee was distracting her because she was young and cute and…and, well, because memories of that night were fresh in her mind. Fresh, because she'd gone over them in very fine detail while she'd waited on sleep to come last night. Rylee had gotten into her personal space. Rylee apparently was *comfortable* being in her personal space. Maybe that's what had her reeling a bit. *She* was comfortable with Rylee being there.

"Stop calling me a kid. You, of all people, should know I'm not one."

No, Rylee was certainly no kid. And yes, Finn knew that as well as anyone. And then Rylee had cupped her cheek. Rylee had been leaning closer when she whispered those words last night. And for one crazy moment, Finn had thought Rylee was going to kiss her. She couldn't breathe. She couldn't speak. Right then…in that moment…with the air charged around them…she couldn't take a breath.

But no, there was no kiss. Perhaps *she* was the only one feeling the charged air. Rylee had pulled away, taking her touch with her, and Finn wasn't sure whether she was relieved or disappointed. She should have been relieved. She had no room—or time—in her life for a romantic twist with her new receptionist-slash-assistant. Yet the truth was, she was more disappointed than relieved.

But it was out in the open now, wasn't it? *You, of all people, should know I'm not one.* Yes, it didn't take a genius to know what Rylee was referring to. And that night, no, Rylee had been anything but a kid. So were they going to talk about it? Finally? No. Not yet, apparently.

Rylee had bid her a goodnight and gone into the guest bedroom, closing the door behind her. Finn had let Smokey climb into her lap and they'd sat there a while longer, her hand brushing through the cat's fur time and again…her thoughts still on the woman who was sharing her house. She had no idea how long she'd sat there, how long visions of Rylee had tumbled around in her mind.

Rylee caught her staring once again, and this time Finn didn't pull away. No, she looked into the blue eyes that were becoming so familiar to her, eyes that *were* familiar to her…blue eyes that held a hint of a question in them. Like why was Finn staring at her, maybe?

Finn cleared her throat before speaking. "How's…how's the list coming?"

"Just starting the last one."

Finn nodded. She was only on her fourth one—Eric Lawrence. She looked at the time on her laptop. It was 10:36. "Are you getting hungry?"

"Past that. Can't you hear my stomach rumbling?"

"I'm sorry I don't have anything for breakfast here."

"I snooped around this morning. You don't have *anything* here except moldy bread that should have been thrown out weeks ago."

"I don't really ever think about going to the grocery store," she apologized. "It's easy to grab something while I'm out."

"Easier than cooking for one?"

When was the last time she'd cooked something? she wondered. When she was living at the apartment—still a cop—she would attempt breakfast sometimes. Can't really screw up scrambled eggs and toast. But since she'd been living here by the bay? Ten years now? Had she *ever* cooked a meal?

"Yeah…easier than cooking for one."

Rylee smiled at her. "You don't know how to cook, do you?"

Finn laughed. "No. You?"

"Yes. But since I've been in Corpus, very small scale. When I moved, I brought the bare minimum with me, thinking I could restock my kitchen after…well, after I had a job." She leaned back and stretched her arms out behind her head with a smile. "Maybe I should stock *your* kitchen instead!"

"Yeah. Maybe when we're out today, we could stop by a grocery store. Surprise Dee when she comes over tonight."

"What are we going to do about Peterson? We're supposed to be doing surveillance on his wife, aren't we?"

"I know. I can't decide what to do."

"The wife didn't leave her house until after two. We could still do a lunchtime stakeout first."

Finn held up the list. "And who would be your first one?"

"I thought you wanted to start with the older Peterson."

"But who would *you* start with?"

Rylee put her elbows on the table and folded her hands together. "Is this a test…or—"

"I want your opinion. You seem to have a knack for this." Finn smiled at her. "Maybe you've found your calling." Rylee seemed pleased with her statement, judging by the quick grin that lit her face.

"Oh. Well, in that case…" She rested her chin on her folded hands, her brow furrowed a bit. "I would start with Brett Peterson."

"The man who hired us? Why?"

Rylee lifted her chin, her index fingers tapping against each other quickly. "Why did he hire us? What purpose could it serve him? I mean, assuming it's a ruse, as you said. What is the purpose?"

"To get inside the office? Look around? Get a feel if I'm suspicious of him or not."

"Right. If you'd already seen this list," she said, motioning to the laptop, "then you would have reacted differently when you saw him. So if his reason for hiring you was bogus, why have his wife go through the motions of meeting up with Carlos Hernandez? At a sleazy apartment complex, no less."

"So *we* wouldn't know it was bogus," Finn supplied.

"Right. But it didn't have to happen. She could have stayed home or gone on about her normal routine. We would watch her for a week, report back to him that she never met up with anyone, and call it a wrap."

Finn leaned her elbows on the table, mimicking Rylee. "Okay. I can practically see the wheels turning in your mind. What are your thoughts?"

"That Carlos is involved somehow…just not with the wife." She waved a hand in the air. "But back to Peterson. He's only a person on this list. Did he know that Daniel Frazier had this information? Do they *all* know? Or is Peterson involved higher up? Is he one of the founding members of this little club? Or his father, perhaps?"

"So you're suggesting that this list of members was compiled by Daniel Frazier?"

"Yes."

"For him to know who all was involved and how much debt they each had, then he had to be connected somehow. For him to know the account numbers, he had to be connected. Maybe *he's* a founding member. Maybe he started the whole thing and that's why the money moved through his restaurants."

"Moved where, though? Moved to whom?" She leaned forward. "Who's getting rich off of this little scheme, Finn? And from what you told me, he moved a *lot* more money through his restaurants than what these few guys would generate. And we now have the account numbers of where we assume the money went. If he was the one who started it, why would he need to hide this information? Why would someone kill for it?"

"Go back to what you said earlier. That Carlos was involved."

"Oh, just a hunch. The likelihood that Lori Peterson ever heard of Carlos Hernandez before is slim to none. And what are the chances that Brett Peterson knows him simply from the cleaning crew? The cleaning crew that comes at midnight?"

"So you're thinking Carlos is involved in this whole operation somehow?"

"Yes."

"If that's the case, then why would Brett Peterson lead us to him?"

Rylee frowned. "Oh. I didn't think of that."

"Carlos works for his uncle? He has a cleaning business?"

"Yes."

"A lot of these guys are businessmen, professionals. With offices."

Rylee's eyes widened. "Who cleans their offices?"

Finn smiled and nodded. "Let's see if we can't find a common link with some of these members."

Rylee rubbed her hands together. "Oh, this is fun!"

"We'll need to wrap it up in about a half hour if we're going to do a lunch stakeout."

"Okay. But you have got to feed me something or I'll be so cranky this afternoon that you won't be able to stand me."

"Duly noted."

CHAPTER FORTY-FIVE

Rylee put the binoculars down. "So Brett's having lunch with Oliver Judge. That's a great name for a prosecutor, isn't it?"

"It'd be an even better name for a judge," Finn said dryly.

"Well, perhaps he has aspirations." She motioned to the deli shop they were watching. "I wouldn't think that two bigwig attorneys would lunch at a place like this."

"If they had lunch at a fancy restaurant where other professionals went, they'd be easily recognized. Here? There's probably not a soul in there who knows them."

"I could go in, try to eavesdrop on their conversation," she suggested, an idea which Finn immediately shot down.

"Absolutely not. I'd just as soon no one even knew you existed."

Rylee wasn't offended. She knew Finn was only trying to protect her. "Gonna hide me away, are you?"

Finn took a deep breath. "We don't know who we're dealing with. Professional killers, that's for sure. If I feel like the situation is too dangerous, then yes, I'll hide you away."

"Surveillance is safe, then?"

Finn turned in her seat, looking at her. "You want to get thrown into the fire, is that it?"

Rylee met her gaze. "I don't want you to baby me, Finn. I'm not a kid, even though you seem to think so. I worked in a man's world for a long time. I know how to use a gun. I'm not a helpless kid," she said again.

"This is different."

"Why?"

"You don't have experience in this."

"That's a lame excuse."

Finn stared at her again. "Why are we arguing?"

"Are we arguing? I thought we were discussing."

Finn smiled quickly. "Why do I feel like I'm no longer the boss around you?"

Rylee laughed. "I'm sorry. Yes, you are the boss. I'm only your trusty sidekick. I should be thankful you're trying to keep me out of harm's way."

"Yes, you should."

Rylee tucked her hair behind her ears. "Once we find out what is going on, we're going to turn that information over to someone, right? The FBI? I mean, you and Dee aren't going to try to do something stupid and confront them, right?"

"Dee's a cop. She'll only break the rules so far. The fact that we have these files in our possession and she hasn't alerted someone is probably driving her crazy."

"Dee is what? Mid to late forties?"

"Something like that, yes."

"I like her."

Finn looked at her quickly. "She's a little too old for you, kid." Then she held up her hand. "Sorry. Didn't mean to call you a kid."

"I like her. She's nice. I didn't mean I was attracted to her. I'm not."

Finn wouldn't meet her gaze. She picked up the binoculars instead and pointed them at the deli shop.

"You're not, huh?"

"No, I'm not. Would it bother you if I was?"

Finn put the binoculars down, but she didn't pull her gaze from the shop. "It's not really my business."

Rylee laughed. "Yet you are quick to tell me she's too old for me. Which she's not. Age isn't a factor. I'm simply not attracted to her."

Finn smiled then and turned in the seat to face her. Rylee was surprised by the relief she saw there. Was Finn jealous?

"Who did you leave behind in Amarillo?"

"You mean...a girlfriend?"

"Yeah."

Rylee shook her head. "No, no one. Kat was my only long-term relationship."

"Kat?"

"Kathryn. She worked for my father too. When we broke up, it was a little uncomfortable there, to say the least. My father…well, he liked Kat."

"Is that why you moved?"

"Because of the breakup? No. Our relationship wasn't ever *real*, if you know what I mean. She wasn't the one, I knew that. But it was comfortable and easy…until it wasn't. She wasn't in love with me any more than I was in love with her. Yet when I ended things, she acted like I'd torn her world apart." She sighed, remembering the very public scene they'd had in the breakroom at work, tears and all. "Everyone kinda took her side, including my father." She waved a hand in the air. "Anyway, I'd been thinking about moving away from Amarillo for at least a year before that happened. So the breakup wasn't the *reason* I moved, but it—and the aftermath—made the decision much easier."

"Why was she your only relationship?"

"I don't know. We were together three years. Before that, I dated some. Not a lot." She shrugged. "I…I don't know. When I was younger, college, relationships seemed so superficial…friendship and the romantic kind, both. So many little games. I had no patience for it."

"No close friends?"

"Oh, I had friends. And we had a group that hung together. Only…" She paused. That had always been a question she'd harbored in her own mind. Why didn't she have close friends? A *best* friend? Why?

She never really connected that way with anyone. It was her fault, of course. She seemed to keep people at arm's length—whether consciously or not, that seemed to be the case. If she was being honest with herself, that was one reason she wanted to move. Amarillo held nothing for her. No lover. No friends. A broken relationship with her father. And a mother who relished heaping guilt on her for whatever reason. She often wondered if it lessened her mother's own guilt for something.

While she wouldn't say that her mother was unhappy in her marriage, there was something missing. More kids? Is that where her guilt came from? The two miscarriages? She felt like she was to blame, Rylee supposed. Did shifting that blame—and guilt—to Rylee help ease her own?

"Only what?" Finn asked quietly.

Rylee looked at her apologetically. "Sorry...lost in thought."

"You want to talk?" Finn offered.

"Oh, no...it's just..." She paused. "I don't miss Amarillo. I don't miss my parents. I don't miss my job or my friends...I don't miss all the things that were so familiar to me for the past thirty years."

"And that's got you thinking what?"

"I don't know. It doesn't matter." She turned to face Finn. Was now the time to talk about it? To have a heart-to-heart? Is now the time to tell Finn that she never—ever—did what she did that night? No. Probably not. So instead, she thought she'd pry. "What about you? When's the last time you've been in a relationship?"

"Never," Finn said easily.

"Never? Surely, at some point in your life—college, perhaps—there was someone."

"No. College was only a means to get into law school. Then the thing with my father, my estrangement from my mother, the academy, being a cop, then a detective...the years slipped away so fast."

"You didn't nurture any relationships, friend or lover," Rylee said, more a statement than a question. It went without saying, of course. Finn had already told her that she had no friends...no lover. "You're very attractive." Those words caused Finn to blush and Rylee thought she looked even more attractive at that moment. "Women didn't throw themselves at you?"

"I pretty much kept to myself. There's no glowing personality under this," Finn said, motioning to herself. "I've been called standoffish more times than I can recall."

Rylee nodded. "Yes, I can see that about you. Yet you seem to have let Dee into your life. You've let me in, haven't you?"

Their eyes met and there was something in Finn's that she couldn't quite read.

"I suppose I have. As I said, I can't seem to say no to you."

Rylee tilted her head. "Do you find me attractive?" Finn's face turned red and she seemed to have choked on the breath she'd sucked in. Rylee reached over and squeezed her arm. "It's okay. Just breathe."

Finn cleared her throat. "Why...why would you ask?"

"Because..." Rylee glanced out the window, then squeezed Finn's arm harder. "They're coming out."

Oliver Judge and Brett Peterson stood five or six steps from the door, still talking. Discussing. There were no smiles, no hand gestures...just talking. They parted with a firm handshake, then turned in opposite directions.

"What do you think? Who should we follow?"

"Let's go with Peterson," Finn said.

But Brett Peterson stood outside his car, now talking animatedly on his phone. Rylee glanced at her watch. It was already after one. They would have to head over to the Petersons' house soon. He finally got inside, pausing again as he continued talking. Then the phone was slipped inside his jacket pocket and he put his seat belt on. He sat there for a few moments, both hands resting on the steering wheel, before backing out of his parking spot. Finn let him pull out into traffic before following.

"Make notes," Finn instructed. "Time, especially. How long they were in there."

"Wonder what they ate?"

"You had two tacos…you can't possibly still be hungry."

"They were so small. Let's don't ever go to that place again." She scribbled down the time. "He's heading back to his office?"

"Looks that way."

"Well, that was uneventful."

"I warned you it could take a while to find their clubhouse."

"Thanks for humoring me by using the word 'clubhouse' like you do."

"What should we call it? A lair?"

"That might be more appropriate."

She leaned back against the seat, absently watching Brett Peterson's black BMW that was two cars ahead of them. Yes…why had she asked Finn that question? They'd slept together. Obviously, there had been an attraction. God, that night, it was as if she'd been on fire. But Finn was her boss now. She was attractive and she was her boss. Regardless, there was some mystique about her that Rylee found alluring and… well, a bit fascinating. Finn was self-confident, she was strong and decisive, she was attractive…yet she was perpetually single, having never been in a relationship. Why? Her reasoning that time got away from her didn't seem plausible. Did no one ever measure up to her standards? Or did she do what she did that night…pick up women at bars? Or would she rather keep her own company than someone else's? Or maybe there was some hidden flaw that Rylee hadn't found, some imperfection that turned people off. True, Finn was a little short sometimes, a little abrupt. Personal things, she kept private, only divulging what she wanted and even then, it took prodding on Rylee's part. She still didn't know how old she was.

The BMW turned into the small parking lot of the one-story office building that housed Peterson, Barnes, Wilcox and Peterson. Finn kept going.

"Note the time."

Rylee did. It was 1:26. She put the notepad in her lap, then turned to Finn.

"How old are you?"

Finn arched an eyebrow but said nothing.

"Are you going to make me do a background check on you to find out?"

At that, Finn turned to look at her. "You wouldn't dare."

"Try me."

Finn gave the tiniest of sighs as she turned left on Chaparral Street and headed out of the business district. "I'm forty."

Rylee smiled. "See? That wasn't so hard." Then she playfully slapped at Finn's shoulder. "You're only ten years older than me yet you call me a *kid*?"

"I sometimes feel like I'm much older than forty."

"Why?"

"I don't know. I guess I've always felt older than my years." Finn glanced at her quickly. "So is your curiosity satisfied?"

"I suppose for now it is."

"Good. Then let's go see what Lori Peterson's up to this afternoon."

CHAPTER FORTY-SIX

"Push the back arrow," Finn said as she handed Rylee the camera. "What's your impression?"

She hadn't given much thought to the pictures she'd snapped yesterday of Lori Peterson. She hadn't even bothered to download them. But now that she'd reviewed them, Lori's facial expression was odd, to say the least.

"Well, with the sunglasses covering her eyes, it's hard to tell, really. But these first ones where she's walking up to his apartment, I'd say the look on her face is…scared. In fact, this second one, I'd almost say terrified."

"My thoughts exactly. Now look at when she comes out."

"She's more relaxed. Definitely relief on her face, like what we thought yesterday." Rylee turned to her. "Relief that the encounter is over with? Relief that she's intact? Not injured? What?"

"You're very good at reading people."

"You think so?"

"Yesterday, you were spot-on when you said there was no affair. I do this thing for a living and I…well, I think I don't look beneath the surface enough. Or perhaps I've been doing this so long, I take everything at face value."

"When a husband comes to you and says his wife is having an affair and he needs you to get him proof...then you already have a preconceived idea of what is going on. So she goes to an apartment—out of town—and stays inside for over an hour. Your preconceived notion rings true—she's having an affair."

"But?"

Rylee smiled. "But...he could be giving her Spanish lessons, for all we know."

Finn tapped the steering wheel as they watched the Peterson house. It was 2:41 and the cloudy day was darkening right before their eyes. She had looked at radar earlier on her phone—rain was imminent. Would Lori Peterson venture out in that case?

"So she's not having an affair, yet she went to this guy's apartment. By the look on her face, it wasn't something she did willingly. It had to have been initiated by her husband. Let's forget about the purpose of it for a minute, because we have no idea. But for whatever the reason is that he wanted us to follow her, how—and why—did he get her involved?"

"I'm not following your line of thought here."

"What did he tell her to make her go there? Not just go there, but hang out for an hour. Did he tell her the truth? That he owes a gambling debt? That he's been banging a prostitute?"

Rylee shook her head. "Why on earth would he tell her that?"

"Maybe he's being blackmailed."

"But Daniel Frazier is dead. Who's going to blackmail him?"

"Look at the photos of the wife again. She's being *forced* to go to Carlos Hernandez. Why? For show? For us? What if she's being forced there for some other reason and Brett Peterson hired us to really do surveillance?"

"Like he's afraid of what might happen to her and wants us here as a witness? But Finn, if something happens to her in that apartment, we're not going to know."

"You think I'm grasping at straws?"

"A little. And like you said last night, we can throw out assumptions and scenarios all day long, but that doesn't make them true."

"I don't like being played," she admitted. "And I don't like not knowing what's going on."

"Ah. Control freak," Rylee teased. "In that case, continue to guess away."

Finn started the car. "Garage door just opened."

They were parked two blocks from the Petersons' home, on the opposite side of the street than yesterday. Lori Peterson backed out of the driveway but instead of going north, she turned, heading right toward them.

"Duck down," she said quickly.

"What?"

Finn grabbed her shoulder and pushed her forward. "Duck down. I don't want her to see us."

Finn was lying across the console, trying to keep her head below window level. Rylee was bent down, her nose practically on top of the gearshift. Their eyes met and Rylee smiled.

"So this is kinda fun," she whispered.

Fun? Their heads were almost touching and they were much, much too close. So close that Finn noticed a tiny scar on Rylee's forehead she'd not seen before. So close she saw the faintest of laugh lines at the corners of Rylee's blue eyes. And so close she could see the steady pulse in Rylee's neck, just above her collarbone. She closed her eyes. So close she could imagine moving Rylee's sweater aside and trailing her lips there...lower, until she—

"Finn...I think that was her that passed by."

Damn.

Finn sat up, glancing in the rearview mirror to see the silver Mercedes already turning at the corner. *Keep your head in the damn game*, she chided herself as she made a U-turn on the street and sped after Lori Peterson.

* * *

Like yesterday, Lori Peterson led them to the same apartment complex. Unlike yesterday, she didn't take Harbor Bridge. She took the long route to get there, going to Mustang Island and Port Aransas, then taking the ferry across to Aransas Pass.

"Why do you think she came this way?"

"I don't know. Maybe she's afraid someone is following her."

As before, Lori parked across the lot from the apartment's door. She seemed to sit in her car a bit longer today. Perhaps it was because of the rain. However, when she got out, she did not hurry. Finn snapped several shots of her, frowning as she zoomed in.

"What do you see?" she asked Rylee.

"It's raining...not a downpour, but still a good rain, yet no umbrella."

"What else?"

"She's wearing sunglasses. That's odd."

"Uh-huh." Finn replaced the camera with her binoculars and she only got a quick close-up of Lori Peterson before the door to Apartment 19 was opened. She saw nothing but the shadowy figure of a man as the door closed quickly behind Lori as she went inside.

"Note the time," she murmured automatically, her binoculars trained on the window beside the door. Cheap mini blinds covered the glass and she saw them part for a second, before closing again.

"I got a bad feeling."

Finn looked over at her. "What do you mean?"

"What do you think he's doing to her?"

Finn shook her head. "Don't do that. You'll drive yourself crazy if you do."

"But what if—"

"Rylee...we watch. When she leaves we follow. Nothing more."

Rylee sat back in her seat. "I'll never get used to this."

"Ready to change career paths?"

Rylee smiled at her. "I think I'd miss you."

Finn's breath caught and she cleared her throat. "Oh, yeah?"

"And you'd miss me. If I'm not around, who's going to make sure you eat?"

Finn couldn't help but think of Sammy in that moment. "Think I need taking care of, do you?"

Their eyes met and again, a smile—a sweet smile—played around Rylee's lips. "I do," she said quietly. Rylee leaned closer. "Everyone needs someone, Finn."

"I've managed," she countered, pulling her eyes away from the smile on Rylee's lips. Lips that were far, far too familiar. Damn, what was wrong with her today?

Rylee leaned back again, her attention now on the apartment. "You think Dee had any luck on her lunch stakeout?"

Finn wondered at Rylee's abrupt change of subject, although she was thankful for it. She, too, gazed at Apartment 19.

"I suppose she would have called if there was any news."

"How long do we continue to watch Lori Peterson? I mean, if this was a real cheating spouse case, how long?"

"Depends. With Connie Frazier, it took a week before I caught them at the Best Western. And as I told Daniel Frazier, I wasn't actually in the room with them."

"So the cheating spouse thing, that's an easy case, right?"

"Most of the time. The spouse in question is usually only worried about getting caught by their husband or wife. The idea that a private investigator is following them around probably doesn't ever cross their mind."

"Do you have a lot of cases like this?"

"Not too many. Ten or twelve a year, maybe. Fifteen at the most."

"That's not many, no." Rylee shifted in her seat. "What do you do mostly? Who are your clients?"

"Background checks. Custody battles. Missing persons."

"Missing persons? Isn't that a police function?"

"If they file with the police department, sure. But after a couple of days, the police officer is going to move on to other things if there's no foul play involved."

"What do you mean?"

"Say it's your brother. You haven't talked to him in a couple of days. You call his work. They haven't seen him. You call his friends. They haven't seen him. You call the police. What do they do? They contact his work, they contact his friends. They run a trace on credit cards. They try to map his last whereabouts. People disappear all the time. If there are no hits on credit cards and no evidence of foul play, then there's not much else to do. The police simply don't have the manpower to continue to follow up on cases like that. There are hundreds of them."

"So what do you do differently?"

"Delve into their background. Interview coworkers and friends. Was he mixed up in drugs? Did he have enemies?"

"Aren't those all things the police should do?"

"Oh, don't get me wrong. They do those things, only on a smaller scale. That missing persons case is but one of many cases they're juggling. Whereas the family hires a private investigator, I can devote all of my time to it."

"Do you find them?"

"Sometimes. A lot of times."

"Alive?"

"Mostly."

"So you find them? Then what? Do you notify the police?"

"The police didn't hire me. The family did. So no, I don't. Whether the family does or not, that's not my concern."

"I guess a lot of them don't want to be found so they're not real happy with you, huh?"

"Some, yes."

The rain had turned into a downpour and she could barely see the apartment door. Rylee pulled her jacket tighter around her.

"Are you cold?"

"A little. It's the rain."

"Yeah. This kind of weather will last through January. By February, spring is in the air and you kinda forget about these months."

Rylee turned to look at her. "What do you do for fun?"

"For fun?"

Rylee shook her head. "You don't do anything, do you?"

"I...when Sammy was here, we'd go fishing some." Of course, that was a lie, wasn't it? She hadn't made time for fishing in a very long time. "And my neighbor, Larry. He's a widower. We'll grill a steak every once in a while." Again...a lie. She hadn't even seen Larry since Sammy's death.

"The first sunny, warm day...you know what we're going to do?"

"Tell me."

"Take the top off my Jeep and drive the beach all the way to Padre Island. The wind in your hair, the sun on your skin...there's no better therapy."

"So you're saying I need therapy?"

Rylee rolled her head against the seat, meeting her gaze. "I'm saying you need some fun."

Finn nodded. "I can't remember the last time I was out on the beach."

"You're kidding? You live like...right *here*."

"I know. Sammy was always going to teach me how to fish off the island...in the surf. I just...well, never got around to it."

"I'll go with you."

Finn raised her eyebrows. "Do you like to fish?"

"I don't know."

Finn laughed. "So you've not been before, huh?"

"Fishing opportunities in Amarillo are kinda limited. So no."

"Yeah, then we'll—"

Her reply was cut short when the door to Apartment 19 opened. A man came out, not Lori Peterson. He looked around suspiciously, and she froze, even though she doubted he could see them from this distance. Her side windows were tinted and it was still raining, although the downpour had eased up. Rylee, too, sat still, watching him.

"That's not Carlos Hernandez," Rylee murmured.

"Didn't think so. This guy's too old, for one thing."

"Hair's too short too."

He went back inside but didn't close the door. Finn slowly put the binoculars up to her eyes, but she couldn't make out anything. It appeared to be dark inside the apartment.

"Nothing," she murmured.

A few moments later, Lori Peterson appeared in the doorway. Her sunglasses were on top of her head and she stepped out, slipping on her jacket. A man's hand reached out to help her and she jerked away from it. She stood outside the door, looking in both directions, as if waiting for someone. A few seconds later, an older model black Cadillac pulled up next to her. Lori Peterson took a step away from the car, then froze in place. Finn felt her adrenaline build, felt her heart begin to race. Something was going to happen. Was Lori about to be abducted or something? But she didn't try to flee when the door opened. A small child got out and Lori dropped to her knees, arms open. The kid ran to her, nearly flinging herself into her arms. The black Cadillac sped away and Lori picked up the child, nearly running across the parking lot to her car.

"What the hell just happened?"

"DWQ1473." She lowered the binoculars. "Write it down."

"License plate?"

"Yeah. And I think I know why she was wearing sunglasses earlier." She started up the car and drove slowly through the lot. "She had a hell of a black eye."

"Oh, no. From Carlos, you think?"

"Hard to tell how fresh the bruising was. A couple of days, maybe."

"Now what do we do?"

"Let's follow her."

"You think that was her kid?"

"Looked like it."

"Are you thinking what I'm thinking?"

"If you're thinking someone snatched the kid, then yeah."

CHAPTER FORTY-SEVEN

Rylee listened to Finn's conversation with Dee. From what she'd gathered, Dee was at King Chevrolet, waiting on Roger King to leave for the day. She glanced at the clock. It was almost four-thirty. They were parked across the street from Peterson's office. They were still debating whether to tail Brett Peterson or his father.

"We'll meet at the house. With this weather, I'm not too confident we're going to hit on anything today." Finn nodded at something Dee said. "Let me know." She put the phone on the console, then glanced over at her. "You hungry?"

"I'm always hungry."

"I'm sorry we didn't have time for any shopping. Looks like it'll be takeout again tonight."

"If we could at least stop somewhere so I could pick up some things for breakfast, that'd be great. If we're going to be finishing up on these profiles tomorrow morning, I'll need more than coffee." Her stomach rumbled as she imagined a big breakfast—eggs, bacon, hash browns, buttered toast.

"I guess we can manage a quick stop." Finn motioned to the backseat. "In my bag there, I have some stuff. Snacks."

"And you're just now telling me this?" She twisted in the seat, reaching for the bag. When she opened it, something slimy touched her hand. "Oh, my God. What is *this*?"

"Oh, yeah. Forgot to throw that out. That's an orange."

"This is like way past being an orange." She used a bag of peanuts to shove the offending orange aside and then picked up a package of peanut butter crackers. "You want something?"

"I think there's a protein bar in there."

Rylee found it and took it out. "So this is how you survive, huh?"

Finn stretched her legs with a loud sigh, then took the protein bar Rylee held out to her.

"I feel like we've been in the car all damn day."

"That's because we have." Rylee opened her crackers and took one. "At least the rain has almost stopped." She turned in her seat to face Finn. "So what's new with Dee?"

"Her lunch was about as productive as ours. She's hoping Roger King will lead her somewhere."

"You didn't mention Peterson to her. Or the kid."

"I thought it would be better to talk in person. The fact that it looks like the wife has been punched in the face doesn't help us much. We can't lay that blame on Carlos Hernandez. Peterson could have done that himself."

"You know what I think?"

"No. Tell me."

"I think we should ask her."

Finn shook her head. "Rylee, we're supposed to be secretly following her at the request of her husband who thinks she's having an affair. You can't walk up to her and ask her."

"Then Dee can do it."

"And say what? Heard a rumor you're having an affair? That's not against the law, you know."

"Punching a woman in the face is, though. Abducting a child certainly is."

"I know you think she needs help but we can't do it. There's too much at stake."

Rylee leaned her head back. Of course she knew that. "Then let's call his hand."

"Who? Her husband?"

"Yes. Let's give him a report. Pictures. Carlos Hernandez's name. Tell him this is who she's meeting. Let him decide if it's an affair or not."

"We can do that. But chances are, he's going to want more information. More proof. And frankly, we can't spare the time to follow her. We have five members of this little club to monitor."

"What if he does want us to continue?"

"I'll tell him I have another client. I'll give him a report based on what we have. I'm interested to see his reaction to Carlos Hernandez."

"Will you tell him that you know Carlos cleans his office?"

"No. He didn't ask for anything on Hernandez."

"We don't have any photos of her with Carlos, though."

"Right. Apartment 19 is being rented by Carlos Hernandez. Lori Peterson has gone there twice and stayed for over an hour each time. We have no usable photos from today, not with the rain. I especially wish we'd gotten one of the kid."

"And we can't access phone records?"

"Not legally, no."

"Meaning there is a way to?"

"There are services that offer that information. It's a questionable practice and I don't use them often."

"Questionable because it's illegal?"

"That. And often not accurate. And it's not anything that would ever hold up in court." Finn pointed out the window. "There's the old man." She tapped the steering wheel. "I think we should follow him. After what happened today, I'd guess that Brett Peterson will rush home to his wife and kid."

"Okay. And what if the older Peterson goes home too?"

"Then we'll go grocery shopping."

* * *

Fredrick Peterson did not go home, however. He headed south and hopped on the Crosstown Expressway. Five o'clock traffic didn't leave her many options and Finn ended up six cars behind him. The rain had ended, but a foggy mist remained and her wipers cleared the windshield intermittently.

"He's changing lanes," Rylee said.

"Going to get on the SPID, most likely. Maybe he's taking the JFK over to the island."

"What's SPID?"

"South Padre Island Drive." She changed lanes too. Peterson was now at least seven cars ahead of her. In the waning light—dusk brought on sooner by the fog—she was having a hard time seeing him.

He put his blinker on to exit and she did as well. Five cars behind now, they made the curve to the left, merging into traffic.

"I'm glad I don't have to drive in traffic every day," Rylee said. "This would make me nuts."

"You didn't renew your lease, did you?"

"No. It's up at the end of the month." Rylee looked at her expectantly. "Why? Do I have an option?"

"The apartment at the office is the logical solution, but until this is over with, no. I wouldn't let you stay there alone."

"As it is, I'm not at my apartment either."

"True." Finn glanced at her quickly. "You can stay with me until this is wrapped up." Actually, she would insist on it. They didn't know who they were dealing with here. Well, they were dealing with killers, that much they knew. So no, Rylee wouldn't be going back to her apartment. Not alone. Still, she expected Rylee to protest, and she did. A little.

"Are you sure? I mean…well, that's a lot of togetherness. You'll be sick of me."

Too much togetherness? Too close? Too familiar? Too…intimate a setting? No. Only if they let it. So she smiled, trying to keep things light between them. "Maybe you'll be sick of me."

"Yeah. Maybe."

Instead of taking the JFK Causeway across the bay and onto the island, Peterson exited, taking the frontage road that ran parallel to the highway. There was only one car between his car and theirs now. A turn to the left took them into a residential neighborhood with large, expensive homes.

"Do you know where we are?"

"South Bay Park," Finn said, slowing down as there were no longer any cars between them and Fredrick Peterson. "It dead ends up here, I think."

He turned on Seashore Drive and she pulled to the side of the road, letting him get ahead of them. She killed her lights, then drove on, slowly.

"This is a cul-de-sac," Rylee said quietly.

"Use the binoculars."

"It's hard to see anything. He's stopped at a gate. Looks like he's punching in a code."

Finn stared through the fog and the fading twilight, trying to make out Peterson's car.

"Okay. He went inside. The gate closed behind him."

Finn let out a deep breath, becoming aware of how tense she'd been. "It'll be full dark soon. We wait, then drive close enough to get the address."

"Locked gate. Fence all the way around. Are you thinking what I'm thinking?"

"Kind of a fancy place for a clubhouse. Expensive. Huge house."

"Judging by the names on the list and the amount of debt that's been racked up, this place isn't out of the question."

"Let's see who owns it. We'll go from there."

Finn was about to drive on when she saw headlights behind them. She put her hand behind Rylee's neck, pushing her down. She did the same, ducking her head low as the car passed by them. Their heads bumped as they both sat up at the same time.

"Sorry," she murmured.

The red taillights brightened as the car stopped at the gate. She grabbed the binoculars from Rylee's lap, focusing them on the license plate.

"BXQ1872."

Using her phone for light, Rylee scanned the spreadsheet they'd made with pertinent information on all the members.

"Yes! It's on here. It's O'Leary," Rylee said excitedly. "This has got to be the place, Finn."

"Or maybe it's someone's house and these guys are visiting. Or it's a dinner party or something. Let's don't jump to conclusions." She looked in the mirror, seeing no headlights coming from behind them. She crept closer to the gate, still leaving her lights off. "Write the address down. We'll research it when we get home."

CHAPTER FORTY-EIGHT

"I'm only familiar with South Bay Park because I know I could never afford to live there," Dee said as she bit into an eggroll. "I love these. Great choice for dinner."

"Chinese food was Rylee's suggestion," Finn said before shoving a forkful of rice and shrimp into her mouth. "She says we need more vegetables."

Dee smiled at that, noting the quick glance shared by the other two women. "So the house is owned by Jose Hernandez? He's not on the list. Is he significant?"

"Actually, yes," Rylee said. "He's Carlos Hernandez's uncle."

Dee raised her eyebrows. "Should that name mean something to me?"

"Oh, I forgot. Finn hasn't told you yet."

Dee turned to Finn. "Told me what?"

"A couple of days before Rylee found the flash drive, Brett Peterson hired me. Surveillance on his wife. Suspected an affair."

"Really? Coincidence he hired you or what?"

"Unlikely, but then again, who knows? We followed Lori Peterson—the wife—to a rather rundown apartment complex in Aransas Pass. She went inside one of the units for about an hour. Then back home. The renter of that particular unit is Carlos Hernandez."

"And she's having an affair with him?"

"No, we don't think so," Rylee said. "Lori Peterson is high society. Carlos…not so much. He's also twenty-one. She's thirty-six. Nothing about it adds up. So I did a background check on young Carlos. He works for his uncle—Jose Hernandez— who owns a cleaning service. That cleaning service has a contract with Peterson's father to clean their office."

Dee put her fork down, her mind racing. She looked at Finn. "What's going on? What does this have to do with our case?"

"At first, we thought maybe he hired me to see my reaction."

"I don't understand."

"If we'd seen the list—the members—and he's on it, then my reaction to him showing up in my office may have given that away."

"That would mean he's involved, if he knew that Daniel Frazier had this information to begin with."

"Right. It could also mean that *all* of the members knew Frazier had the info and was going to expose them."

"There's also the possibility that he wanted us to follow his wife for another reason," Rylee added. "From her reaction to being at the apartment, she didn't go willingly. And today, after she came out of the apartment, a black Cadillac drove up and a young child—most likely the Petersons' youngest—got out and ran to Lori. She scooped the kid up and took off. We followed her home."

"Lori'd also been punched," Finn added. "She had a black eye."

"What the hell's going on? You think the kid was snatched?"

Finn nodded. "That's what it looked like to us."

Dee ran a hand through her hair. "So the Petersons' kid is abducted and they don't call the police. They call you."

"On the pretense that he suspected an affair. Now, did he hire me specifically because of Daniel Frazier and all this mess? Or did he hire me because his father recommended me and he was genuinely worried about his wife's safety? For all we know, he may not be aware that Daniel Frazier hired me. None of them may know."

"Why the father?"

"I've done work for him in the past. But the thing is, it's over with now. Brett Peterson called me earlier this evening. Said he and his wife had worked things out and my service was no longer needed."

"So if you've been doing surveillance, he has to know that you saw what went down today, right?"

"I would think so, yes."

"You didn't confront him?"

Finn shook her head. "It's not any of my business, Dee."

"Of course it is! Somebody had his child! You saw the exchange!"

"I'm not a cop. Brett Peterson hired me to follow his wife. I did. End of story."

"You're unbelievable!" she said, pointing at Finn. "It's all related to our case. It has to be."

"I agree. The plates on the black Cadillac came back to Jose Hernandez."

"The guy who owns the house? Why didn't you tell me all of this earlier? I could have tried to—"

"Dee, this is my job. This is what I do. Again, I'm not a cop nor do I want to be."

"Finn, I swear. Sometimes you—"

"Hey, guys…yelling won't solve anything," Rylee said, holding her hands up. "The Peterson thing is over with. Let's talk about the house."

Dee blew out her breath. She wasn't cut out for this, apparently. There were rules that she didn't break. There were orders that she followed without question. Well, usually. But now? Now she was hooked up with an ex-cop who admittedly didn't follow rules or orders and a young woman whom she knew nothing about. It'd be a miracle if she didn't lose her job over this. But what else could she do? She was already in too far.

"Okay." She took a deep breath, trying to put the image of an abducted child aside and focus on the possible clubhouse. "So two of these so-called members went to this house owned by Jose Hernandez. Peterson and O'Leary. They knew the gate code." She folded her hands together. "Tell me about the house."

"It's at the peak of a cul-de-sac, only one close neighbor. The other side is vacant. Ten-foot privacy fence, gated entrance. The house sits off the road. Bay front. Judging by the size, I'd guess at least four or five bedrooms."

"So you think this could be their clubhouse? Where the girls are?"

"At this point, it's only a guess. We'd need more of the names on the list to show up there to be sure." Finn stood up. "You want a drink?"

"Definitely. Make it a double."

Finn smiled slightly, then looked at Rylee, who nodded. "I'll have a splash of that cognac."

"Tell me about the wife," Dee asked her when Finn walked away. "Are you certain it wasn't an affair?"

"Where would they have met? Their social circles are so far apart he may as well be in China. But it was her demeanor, the look on her face that was the most telling. It was fear on her face, not ecstasy."

"What do you think went on?"

Rylee leaned back in her chair. "You want my opinion?"

"What's your gut feeling?"

"Well, what it looked like, after we saw the kid, was that Lori Peterson was exchanging sex for her child. Which I can't quite wrap my mind around it, it sounds so crazy."

"Yeah, well, in my line of work, there's crazy...and then there's *crazy*. Nothing would shock me."

Finn came back in and set a glass down beside her, then handed Rylee one. "The way this house is situated, it'll be hard to do surveillance on it. I would need to go there in the daylight and see if a side street might have a view, but that's unlikely. I'm thinking our best bet is to watch South Bay Drive. That's not the only street they could take to get back there, but it's the main one. We could also park on Sealane, I think it was."

"Have you linked Jose Hernandez to any of the others?"

"We haven't had a chance to research it. I thought we'd tackle that in the morning," Finn said as she sat down again. "I'll also do a thorough workup on Jose and his business."

Dee cupped her glass, her eyes going to Finn before she even took a sip. "What the hell are we going to do with this information, Finn?"

"Are you afraid of going rogue?"

"I'm a cop and a damn good one," she said, tapping her chest. "What we're doing goes against all of my principles."

"So what do you want to do?"

"I've got a friend with the FBI. I could—"

"Dee...please, not yet. I know we're sitting on something here that's way out of our league...my league, especially. I shouldn't be this involved. I know that. *You* know that. But whoever killed the Fraziers, whoever killed Sammy...the FBI's not going to be concerned with that." Finn stood up, leaving her drink on the table. Dee glanced at Rylee, whose eyes were fixed on Finn. "Once we know who's the organizer of this little club, once we know who all the players are, then you bring in the FBI. We'll serve up this information on a silver platter. But if you contact them now, then it's game over." Finn stared at her. "Game over for you too, I imagine. You're going over Mabanks' head. Hell, you're going over everyone's head by reporting this to the FBI first."

"Before I got taken off this case, Mabanks was already hedging on the money laundering. He said there wasn't enough evidence to support it. That's the reason the FBI was not notified."

"You found phony vendors. You've got Frazier's accounting records. How can he say there's no evidence?"

"The detectives on the case, they know the real deal. They're not that stupid. They're young and they're following orders. If they knew everything that we know, it might be different. But still, I don't think they'd question his order, even if we supplied them with these account numbers we have." Dee shook her head. "I can't figure out how the captain plans to make this case disappear."

"Easy. There are no suspects. Wrap up the money laundering angle as not enough evidence—he's already essentially done that—and let the murder cases go cold. Hell, they're already cold."

Dee turned to Rylee. "You're awfully quiet. What are your thoughts?"

Rylee looked first at Finn, then brought her attention back to Dee. "Blackmail him."

Dee's eyebrows shot up. "Who?"

"Your Captain Mabanks. Blackmail him. That's the reason he's trying to cover up these murders, isn't it? Because someone owns him now? Because of the debt? Because of the pictures?" She leaned her elbows on the table, her gaze now on Finn. "We've got the information that they're all afraid will get out."

"But what do we have exactly? A spreadsheet with members' names and their debt. Account numbers. Pictures of these men having sex. That's not against the law. There's no proof these women are prostitutes. There's no proof as to what this debt is for." Finn picked up her drink and stood, walking a few steps away. "We've been guessing and assuming, but there's no proof of anything."

Dee took a swallow of her own drink. "I think we should stick to the original plan. Follow these guys, find out where they meet. Maybe this house you found is the place. If so, then Rylee has a point. Mabanks keeps talking about retiring. He's been married forty-something years, he's got grandkids he dotes on. We may not have proof of what's going on, but if he knows we've got this information and we threaten to turn it over to the FBI, I think we can use that against him. Hell, we threaten to turn it over to his wife."

Finn sat down again. "Why would he spill his guts to us? If he's worried about the FBI, it's still going to get out. It'll get out to everyone. But if he plays dumb when we tell him…if he keeps quiet, then our little secret is out. We've got the information that three people were killed for. All he has to do is make a call. Then the three of us will have targets on our backs."

"I would like to think the man I've worked for for nearly ten years would do the right thing. If he's offered immunity, then that would be a way out for him."

"We're not in a position to offer immunity, Dee. Remember? We're not even supposed to be working this case."

"After all of this, I still trust the man. He's not going to 'make a call' as you put it."

"It's very risky for us. The man's career is on the line, his legacy, his whole damn life. Maybe they all feel that way. Maybe that's why this little club setting has worked for whoever started it. They're all in now and there's no way out. Maybe that's the whole point of it. Once they're in, they can't ever get back out."

"Because they now know too much," Rylee interjected. "They don't have a choice any longer."

"So you're suggesting they're all being blackmailed already?" Dee shook her head. "I find that hard to believe. A few people, maybe. But ten? That would be hard to pull off."

"Think about it," Finn said. "These guys aren't your run-of-the-mill Joes. They're politicians. They're judges. They're businessmen. Hell, they're law enforcement. These are all guys who have a *lot* to lose if this gets out."

"They're also powerful men who I would think would be smarter than to let themselves be blackmailed," Dee said with a shake of her head. "I'm thinking some of these guys are involved in the running of this little scheme. They've got to be."

Rylee got up to clear the table but Finn stopped her with a hand on her arm.

"You don't have to do that."

"I don't mind. I'm not contributing much anyway," she said as she stacked Finn's plate on top of hers.

"I don't know if any of us are contributing anything worthwhile," Dee said. "We simply don't have enough information." She stood up, taking her own plate with her. "And I'm beat. Gonna call it a night." She turned back to Finn. "You'll see what you can dig up on Jose Hernandez?"

"First thing in the morning."

"Good. The guys are supposed to brief Mabanks tomorrow at ten. I didn't get an invite to the meeting, but Detective Davis has been keeping me in the loop. Without Mabanks knowing it, I imagine." She shrugged. "They have nothing new, really. The books had been doctored, but we already knew that. The account numbers on the ledger? Still haven't nailed them down. Offshore, obviously. Next step is one-on-one interviews with the managers, see what they knew."

"What about Duncan?"

"Yeah, get this. Mabanks wants to sit in on that interview. My guess is, take over that interview."

"For what reason?"

"What's your guess?"

Finn smiled slightly. "That our intuition was right after all. It suggests that Duncan Frazier is involved and Mabanks knows it."

"It suggests that on the surface, yes. Or maybe Mabanks is trying to be respectful to a young man whose parents were murdered." She put her plate in the sink where Rylee was rinsing the others. "There's no evidence whatsoever linking Duncan to anything. By all accounts, he was a normal college kid. We both followed him around, thinking there was a link. And yes, he was a cocky ass when I met him, but that's not a crime."

"Maybe we should focus on him again. Now that we've got a list of names, maybe he meets with them."

"I think we've got our hands full."

"There is another way," Finn said. "We get tracking devices."

Dee shook her head. "That's illegal."

"Yes, I know that. We could leave them on for a few days, then remove them."

"Tracking devices that dot a map cost a hell of a lot more than cheap devices that you follow. But more importantly, anything we find will not be admissible in court."

"Jesus, Dee…worrying about what's admissible in court? Who the hell cares? We're just trying to find some links with these guys. Quit thinking like a cop!"

"I am a cop!" she shot back.

"Hey…" Rylee said as she came back to the table, standing between them. "We're all tired. How about we discuss tracking devices tomorrow?"

Dee blew out her breath. "Yeah, okay." She pointed her finger at Finn. "I'm breaking all sorts of rules as it is. I'd just as soon not lose my job over this."

Finn stood up. "Yeah. Sorry. But there's something else. Have you considered that they know you've been coming here?"

"What do you mean?"

"Well, if we assume they think I have this flash drive, they may be watching the house."

"Do you think someone's been following us?" Rylee asked.

Finn shook her head. "No. I can spot a tail. But maybe they watch the house, try to see what pattern I have."

"If they knew I was seeing you as often as I am—if Mabanks knew—he would have brought it up, I think. But for your safety, with your alarm and security cameras, do you think they'd try to break in?" she asked.

"Not unless they disabled the system. If the alarm goes off, it'd still take a few minutes before a patrol car came by to check it out. But not so long that they'd have time to get inside, search the place, and get back out. I don't think they'd take that chance."

"What other option would they have?" Rylee asked.

"Snatch me up, hope I've got the drive on me. Kill me."

Rylee squared her shoulders. "Well, I guess we need to be careful then, don't we?" Then she smiled. "I'd hate to have to look for another job."

Finn laughed lightly. "And here I thought you were worried about me."

"I am. I'd miss your witty charm."

At that, Dee laughed. "Yeah, right. Grumpy charm is more like it."

CHAPTER FORTY-NINE

Rylee leaned against the counter with her hip, following Finn's movements as she tidied the already clean kitchen.

"Is this how your house stays so clean?"

Finn paused and tilted her head, as if only then realizing that she'd been wiping the countertop repeatedly.

"Lost in thought," she said as she put the dishcloth down.

Rylee moved closer to her. "Thoughts about the case...or..."

Finn hesitated in meeting her eyes, but it was just the two of them in the room. She had nowhere to escape to. When she did look at her, Rylee realized where her thoughts had been. She wondered if this would be the time they finally talked about that night.

"About the case, yeah," Finn said.

But no. Finn apparently still wasn't ready. Rylee took another step closer. She never thought she'd have to be the one to bring it up. But enough already. Finn might not be ready, but she was.

"There's no need to lie, Finn."

Finn raised her eyebrows. "What makes you think I'm lying?"

Rylee tried to hold her gaze. "Let's talk about it." But still, Finn feigned ignorance as she turned away from her.

"Talk about what?"

"God, I had no idea you'd be this stubborn," she said as she grabbed Finn's arm and spun her around to face her again. "This is ridiculous, Finn. I don't want to pretend anymore." She shook her head. "I don't like this game we're playing with each other." Her hand was still touching Finn's arm and she swore she felt her tremble. She squeezed a little tighter. "Finn...we've seen each other naked. Let's stop pretending that we haven't."

Finn moved away from her touch, going to the other side of the sink. "What...what is there to talk about?"

"Well, for one thing, I need you to know that I don't do things like that. I...well, obviously I did, *that* night. But...never before and certainly never since."

"Is that why you left?"

"I panicked. I woke up...I had no idea what time it was. I was in bed with a stranger. A stranger whom I had been incredibly intimate with." She met Finn's gaze. "I panicked and I ran."

Finn nodded. "You would have been what? Embarrassed?"

"Yes. Embarrassed. Ashamed."

Finn nodded again. "So what time was it that you ran away?"

Rylee smiled slightly. She knew exactly what time it had been. She remembered looking at her phone, the large numerals staring back at her, permanently imprinting on her brain. "It was 4:47."

Once again, Finn gave a subtle nod, then she cleared her throat. "I don't..." She cleared her throat again. "I don't do things like that either. In fact, I hadn't been out to a bar in years, I guess. So...if I had woken up first, I might have been the one to run."

"Wow. And all these months I imagined you did that sort of thing a lot."

Finn smiled. "Yes. I thought the same of you."

Rylee's eyes widened. "You did? Oh, my God! See? That's why I left. I was embarrassed."

"If you'd stayed, you could have explained."

"If I'd stayed, we wouldn't have gotten out of bed." She was surprised by the blush that lit Finn's face. "So *you're* embarrassed."

"Like I said, I don't...don't do things like that."

"So neither of us do, yet we met at a bar that night. A simple case of coincidence? Or...fate?"

"Aren't they the same thing?"

Rylee smiled at her. "I never thought I'd see you again in a million years. I almost fainted when I came to your office and...and there you were."

"You hid it well. I thought at first that you didn't recognize me."

"Not recognize you?" God, they'd spent hours in bed. Her mouth had been on every inch of Finn's body. Of course she would recognize her. She felt a slow roll begin in her stomach as she remembered Finn's mouth on every inch of her body as well. *Every* inch. She swallowed as images raced through her mind...naked skin, soft, wet...hot. Their eyes held and yes...she felt hot. And she needed to get away. "I...I should..." She turned away from Finn quickly. "I...I think I should...I mean...I'm tired." She nodded curtly. "Goodnight." She turned, not looking back.

"Rylee?"

She paused at the door but kept her back to Finn. She felt Finn walk closer to her. "Yes?" she managed with a shaky voice.

"I'm glad we talked about it. But you don't have to be afraid of me. I would never presume there'd be a repeat of that night. That was out of character for both of us, apparently. So don't worry. I'm not interested in a repeat."

Rylee turned slowly to face Finn, trying to decide if what she felt was relief or disappointment. She should be relieved, yes. She *wanted* to be relieved. There didn't have to be a repeat of that night. Finn, obviously, didn't want one. So, yes...what she was feeling was relief.

Involuntarily, her gaze dropped to Finn's lips. She remembered how they tasted, of course. She also remembered all the delicious things those lips had done to her. Now, with her pulse pounding in her ears, she turned away without commenting on Finn's statement, heading purposefully to the spare bedroom without looking back.

She hated lying to herself. It did no good whatsoever. So no, it wasn't relief that she was feeling. She felt crushed with disappointment...and perhaps regret.

But when she closed the door to the bedroom and leaned back against it, she allowed herself to see the truth. The words that came from Finn's mouth may have said one thing, but her eyes said something else entirely. Finn wanted to forget that night. Finn wanted to pretend she wasn't interested. Rylee found herself believing Finn's eyes...not her words.

Because her eyes didn't lie.

* * *

Finn added a splash of the amber liquid to her glass and sat down in her chair. The lights were still on at the pier and she could see the water lapping along the retaining wall. High tide. Smokey jumped in her lap and Finn shifted a little, giving the cat more room. Her gaze went to the hallway. It was dark. Was Rylee already in bed? She closed her eyes, trying to imagine what Rylee would sleep in. Completely naked? A T-shirt and undies? Or no shirt? She smiled and let her hand drift across Smokey's fur. Yes…a T-shirt.

Of course, it didn't take much for her to imagine pulling that T-shirt off Rylee, exposing her breasts. She remembered cupping them in the motel room when they'd been standing beside the bed. They'd filled her hands, the nipples becoming rigid as soon as she touched them. Rylee had guided her mouth, urging her to taste them. She remembered the moan Rylee uttered when her tongue had…

"*God*," she murmured, chasing the image out of her mind. "What are we going to do now?" she whispered to the cat.

She liked it better when they were pretending not to recall that night. Because the look in Rylee's eyes earlier told her she was remembering every detail. It also told her something else. The attraction she felt for Rylee definitely wasn't one-sided. But there was nothing to worry about. Right? They'd slept together. There was no reason to do it again.

With a quiet sigh, she leaned her head back and closed her eyes, letting the images move slowly through her mind, one by one…over and over and over again.

CHAPTER FIFTY

"Okay, so get this," Rylee said. "King Chevrolet has two cleaning services. Hernandez's crew—Bayside Janitorial—and another one, Mitchell Commercial Cleaners. Why would they have two?"

"I think I know why. Come take a look at this."

Rylee got up and walked around the table to Finn's side, leaning over her shoulder. "What is all that?"

"I thought the easiest way to find out who his clients are was to look at his financials."

"Is that legal?"

"Not really, no. As a private investigator, there are boundaries. Snooping in someone's financial records requires a subpoena or search warrant. Privacy rights, you know."

"But?"

"Well, I can access some of the information, but if I was doing it for a client, nothing would be admissible since it was obtained illegally. And I could lose my license."

Rylee put her hand on Finn's shoulder. "So why are you doing it?"

Finn felt her pulse race at Rylee's touch. It was a familiar touch. Too familiar. She tried to ignore the hand resting on her, ignore the body that was nearly leaning against her. "Because I'm counting on you not reporting me."

Rylee smiled at her. "I see. Trusting, aren't you?"

"Apparently." She pointed at the screen. "Here. All of our guys are on here. Even Mabanks. These are deposits."

"Wow. He charges a lot for cleaning."

"Right. But you said you found that King Chevrolet has another cleaning service." Finn turned her head to look at her. "Why would they pay two?"

Rylee took a step away. "Is this a test?"

"Yes. A test."

"Okay. Then I'm guessing that Bayside Janitorial is a fake service. They don't really clean offices. These aren't really payments."

Finn smiled. "Good. That's my guess too. But it's made to look real. He's got clients, they make monthly deposits." She brought up another screen. "He's got payroll. Employees. Sends out W2s. I'm sure—on the surface—it's all legit. No red flags."

"But if he's got all of this, why did he need Daniel Frazier's pizza places?"

"I have no idea." Finn shrugged. "Unless…well, he's got more money coming in than Frazier could handle. Then that means drugs."

"Drug cartel? Mexico?"

"Speculating…but yeah."

"So maybe we should be focusing on Jose Hernandez. See where he lives, what he does. Follow him around."

"The only property in his name is the house out at South Bay Park," Finn said. "He may own others under different names. Maybe even the business name. We'll need to check that."

"Do you think he lives out there? At their clubhouse? Where God knows what goes on?"

"If he's the guy running the show, then I'd say no. It would be too risky."

"Do you think all these guys know what's really going on?"

"It's hard to say. Something is obviously going on with Peterson."

Rylee went back to her own laptop. "So what's the plan? Tracking devices? Dee wasn't crazy about that idea."

"It probably wasn't a good idea to begin with. Let me download all of this so I can show it to her. Then we'll head out to South Bay."

"You are going to feed me, right?"

Finn looked at her over the top of her laptop. "Don't I always?"

Rylee rolled her eyes. "I've lost like five pounds since I've been working for you."

"Really? I guess I do need to feed you more then. Because from what I remember, you really didn't need to lose five pounds." The words were out before she could stop them and Rylee arched an eyebrow.

"Are you saying you're picturing me naked?"

Finn pulled her eyes away, feeling a bright blush cross her face. Rylee's smile turned into laugh.

"Oh, my God! You are too cute when you blush." Rylee's smile still lingered on her face. "If it makes you feel better...I can picture you naked too." The smile left her face as their eyes held. "And from what I remember...you were just about perfect."

Finn felt her heart lodge in her throat and she tried to swallow, tried to find her breath. "We should...we should go." She closed her laptop. "We should stop talking...and go."

But Rylee didn't move. She continued to hold her gaze.

"Now who's running?"

Finn pushed away from the table. Yes. Now who was running?

I am.

CHAPTER FIFTY-ONE

The last thing Finn wanted to do was to be stuck in a car all day with Rylee. Because yes, she could still picture her as she'd been that night. Passionate. Demanding. Relentless, really. And yes…naked. Finn couldn't resist her at the bar. She couldn't resist her on the dance floor. She certainly couldn't resist her in bed. How in the hell did she think she could resist her now? Because if Rylee wanted a repeat of that night, Finn knew without a doubt that she'd go willingly. And really, what would it hurt? They'd done it before.

It would make things awkward, that's what it would do. Awkward? She mentally smiled at that. Could things get any more awkward?

So here they were, parked under a cluster of trees where Sealane became Seashore Drive, a long block from South Bay, the main street into the neighborhood and the street most likely to be taken by the so-called members.

"If you're not going to finish your fries, I'll take them off your hands for you."

Finn looked over at Rylee, who was still eating her burger. "Trying to gain back those five pounds all at once?"

Rylee grinned. "This may be our only meal today."

Finn handed over the rest of her fries but not before shoving one into her mouth. "Dee's turn for dinner."

"We have *got* to start cooking. Eating like we do is not healthy. We need some veggies. And I don't mean like the few included in our Chinese food last night."

"So you say, but you know, *we* don't cook."

Rylee nibbled on a fry thoughtfully. "Did your mother cook?"

"God, no. She didn't do anything except shop and do brunch with her high society friends."

"Oh, no. Snooty rich?"

"She came from money, yes. And my father was very successful, so..."

"You seem perfectly normal. Take after your father?"

Finn shrugged. "He worked all the time. Family definitely came second. If I wanted to see him, I went to his office. And as you know, my mother found another way to pass her time."

"Yet you wanted to be an attorney like him? Is that why you don't take time for yourself? You learned from him?"

Finn took a deep breath. "I don't know. Maybe subconsciously, I didn't want to be in the same rut that my parents were in. Easier to be alone."

"Then why me? Why that night?"

Finn looked into the blue-green eyes...eyes that were questioning. What should she tell her? That she'd planned to have a drink or two, then leave? Should she tell her that one look into her eyes had stolen her breath away? Should she tell her the truth? Should she tell her that she was lonely? Yes, she'd been lonely. She pulled her eyes away from Rylee, staring out at the empty street instead.

"I...I'm usually content with my own company. That night, I wanted to be around people. I was...I was lonely." She let out a breath. "I...I don't sleep with strangers, Rylee." She turned to look at her, wondering what it was she was seeing there in those blue eyes. Compassion? Sympathy? Something else? "I was going to have a couple of drinks and relax a bit. That's all."

Rylee's head tilted, her gaze still locked with Finn's. "But?" she whispered.

Finn could feel her heart beating a little too fast, could feel some of the same sensations she'd felt when she first saw Rylee that night. "When I saw you, when I looked into your eyes...I couldn't breathe." She swallowed. "The rest is all kind of a blur."

She felt Rylee's hand squeeze her arm. "It's not a blur, Finn. I remember every detail, from the first dance to the last kiss." She squeezed her arm tighter. "I think you do too."

Yes, she did, didn't she? The way she trembled when they danced, the way her knees had nearly buckled when Rylee slipped her tongue into her mouth. The fevered kisses, the bold touches...all of that while still at the bar. Then the quiet of the motel room. The muted lighting. The crisp sheets against their naked skin. How aroused they'd both been. How Rylee had pulled her down, opening for her. How it felt to slide her fingers into her wetness. The way Rylee had screamed when she climaxed. And how loud she'd moaned when Rylee's mouth had claimed her. Not just claimed her...devoured her until Finn exploded. Yes...she remembered it all.

Finn looked at her now, feeling Rylee's hand still touching her. She said the first thing that came to her mind.

"I lied."

Rylee's eyebrows rose, disappearing into her bangs.

"I...I lied when I said that I...that I didn't..."

"Said what? That you had no desire to...to be with me again? To make love with me?"

"Yes." Finn swallowed. "I lied."

A hint of a smile touched Rylee's lips. "I know."

Finn swallowed down her nervousness as Rylee's fingers tightened their hold on her.

"And for the record...when you looked at me across the bar, I couldn't breathe either. I've never been so instantly attracted to someone before. And now that we've gotten to know each other a little...I'm still very attracted to you, Finn," she finished in a whisper.

God...how in the world had they gotten this far, this fast? She had no idea how to respond, she only knew she wished they weren't here, stuck in a car. No. She wished they were at home...alone. In bed. Naked. With lots of time on their hands. Did Rylee want that too? Or were they rushing things? Maybe they should start slower. No need to jump into bed right away. Maybe just kiss, get reacquainted with each other again. Yes. Because Rylee liked to kiss. Rylee liked slow, soft, sensual kisses. She also liked fierce, wet, hot kisses. She also liked—

She pulled her eyes away. Her world was about to change, wasn't it? She could feel it. Tonight. Tonight, her world was going to change. Rylee. Not some stranger she'd met at a bar...a stranger who she started out having sex with and ended up making love to. A stranger whose image had danced around in her mind often during the last six months. A stranger she never thought she'd see in the flesh again.

Was it fate that their paths had crossed once more? Blind luck? Or just a stupid coincidence?

"Finn?"

She turned, loving the sound of her name on Rylee's lips. Finn met her eyes, wondering how it would be to make love with her again. Wondering if there'd be any hesitation, any uncertainty. Wondering if Rylee wanted it as much as she did.

"Hmm?"

Rylee smiled, a slow, sweet smile. "Everything's going to be okay."

CHAPTER FIFTY-TWO

"Where are you?"

"South Bay Park. What's going on?"

Dee stared at the body, her eyes on the bullet hole in his head. She turned away, moving past the officers who were still on the scene.

"I caught a case," she told Finn. "Single GSW to the head."

"One of our guys?"

"No. Hispanic male, late teens, early twenties." She tucked a strand of hair behind one ear, but the wind whipped it around again. "I don't know how much help I'm going to be to you now. I've got to focus on this."

"Well, you are a cop after all."

Dee could hear the smile in Finn's voice and she gave a quick laugh. "Yeah, glad you remembered that."

"It's okay. We're hanging out here. Brian Hodge—he's on your half of the list—showed up about forty minutes ago." A pause. "Are you going to be able to make it tonight?"

"I would think so. I'll let you know." An officer approached and she nodded at him. "Hang on a second," she told Finn. "What'd you get, Sanchez?"

"Found a wallet over in the water."

"Our vic?"

"Photo matches. They're running prints. There's cash in here, cards too."

"So not a robbery. What? They tossed it in the channel?"

"Apparently not far enough." He held up the driver's license. "Carlos Hernandez. Twenty-one. Not a local. The address is Brownsville."

She stared at the picture on the license and at the name. God… things were unraveling, weren't they? "Thank you, Sanchez."

"Yes, ma'am."

She took a deep breath before putting the phone up to her face again. "Finn…the body…it's Carlos Hernandez."

"You're serious? *Our* Carlos Hernandez?"

"It's not been verified with prints. Brownsville address on his license."

"Christ, you don't think Brett Peterson killed him, do you?"

"God, I hope not." She squeezed the bridge of her nose. "We need to talk, Finn. I'm not used to this. I don't know what to do."

"What do you mean?"

"I mean I know Brett Peterson hired you, but I'm not supposed to know that. I mean I know his child was possibly abducted, but I'm not supposed to know that either. And I know that his wife was at Carlos Hernandez's apartment, probably having sex, and I'm certainly not supposed to know that."

"Dee…I'm a private investigator. All of that is confidential. My clients have an expectation of privacy and I provide that to them. If I didn't, I couldn't stay in business. Now you have to *forget* that you know those things."

"This is ridiculous! How can I—"

"Look, it may not matter anyway. When Mabanks finds out who the vic is, he may pull you from the case."

"If he does that, then we'll know he's beyond saving. We need to go to the FBI."

"Not yet, Dee."

"Finn—"

"Listen, I'll call Peterson. I'll tell him that Carlos was killed. I'll play dumb. I'll tell him I was concerned, that's all."

"What? Do you think he'll confess? Then what?"

"Let's worry about that later. Work the case like any other. I'll be in touch."

The call ended before she could protest further and she let out a heavy sigh. Now what? Go along with Finn? Did she have a choice?

Finn would kill her—absolutely kill her—if she brought up Brett Peterson's name. And for that matter, Finn might be right. Mabanks might very well pull her.

She took a deep breath, then walked back over to where the body was.

"Looks like he was shot right here." She turned in a circle, looking around. They were near one of the many channels that had been cut into the shallow waters of the bay. This time of year, it wasn't filled with fishermen. She saw only one boat out in the open water. "I don't suppose there are any surveillance cameras around?"

"No, ma'am."

"Who found him?"

"A couple of guys came out at daybreak to fish. They damn near drove over him."

"They still around?"

"Yes, ma'am. I told them to wait."

"If you got their statement, cut them loose. Make sure you get their contact info."

"Already have."

She smiled at him. "Good job, Dustin. You still dreaming of being a detective when you grow up?"

He laughed. "I have a baby face, I know, but I'm twenty-six already."

"Yeah, and in the blink of an eye you'll be thirty. Don't rush things."

She should know. She busted her ass to make detective by thirty. And what did she have to show for it?

CHAPTER FIFTY-THREE

Rylee looked at Finn with raised eyebrows. "Really? Carlos is dead?"

"It appears so."

"And you think Brett Peterson may have done it?" Rylee nodded at her own question. "I can see that. I mean, they had your kid and Carlos did God's knows what to your wife…yeah, I can see him going over the edge."

"So can Dee." She flipped through her contacts, finding Brett Peterson. "I'm going to call him. Try to get a feel for what happened." Peterson had given her both his office number and his cell. She had never contacted him before and thought his cell would be the best choice. He answered on the second ring.

"Ms. Knight, as I told you yesterday, I'm not in need of your service any longer. I've already sent a check out to you for the agreed-upon amount."

"You paid me to follow your wife and hired me for a service. Yet you don't want a report from me and you don't want to know who she was meeting."

"Frankly, that's none of your business, is it? I should have never hired you. My mistake. My wife and I are—"

"Carlos Hernandez is dead." Her statement was met with silence. "He's the one your wife was meeting, Mr. Peterson. Yesterday, in fact. When she picked up your daughter at his apartment complex."

"Surely you don't...you don't think that *I* killed him."

"Was your child abducted, Mr. Peterson?"

He gave a nervous laugh. "Don't you think I would have called the police if that was the case?" He cleared this throat. "I have never met Carlos Hernandez nor did I kill him. Now, I trust that—as one of your clients—that my privacy is still protected."

"Of course. I was simply concerned, that's all."

"Thank you. I appreciate that. I'll be in touch if I'm ever in need of your services again. Goodbye, Ms. Knight. Please don't call me again."

She lowered her phone with a sigh. "Hard to get a read on him one way or the other. He sounded nervous. But..."

"But?"

"I don't know. Nervous...or scared." She shrugged. "Hard to tell which."

"So what do we do? And don't tell me it's not any of our business."

"Rylee, technically it's not. I just don't know if Dee is going to be able to sit on what she knows." She pointed down the street where a silver SUV was heading their way. "Here comes Hodge." She looked at her watch. "About fifty-six minutes. Quite a long time to be with a hooker, don't you think?"

"I have no idea. What? You think he'd be in and out, then gone?"

Finn laughed as she picked up her binoculars. "Yeah, in and out. Something like that." Her smile faded, though. "That's not Hodge driving. Some young guy." She felt Rylee's hand on her arm.

"Check the gate. That's the black Cadillac from yesterday."

The silver SUV turned onto South Bay and she panned the binoculars toward the gate as the black Cadillac pulled out.

"Two inside the Caddy. Looks like Brian Hodge is riding shotgun. Older guy driving."

"Jose Hernandez? We never found a picture of him."

"Caucasian, not Hispanic. And I say older compared to the young guy driving the SUV. This guy's probably fortyish."

Rylee laughed quickly. "I see. Older as in forty then."

Finn smiled but kept the glasses up, watching until the Cadillac turned onto South Bay too. She lowered the binoculars and nodded. "Yeah...old, like forty," she said as she started her car. "Let's follow them."

Rylee nodded. "Do you think you're old or do you feel old?"

"Both."

Rylee leaned back in her seat with a quick shake of her head. "There's nothing old about you, Finn. It's mental, not physical."

"Says the woman who's still in her twenties."

"For a few more weeks, yes." Rylee turned to look at her and Finn took her eyes off the road long enough meet her gaze. "Is that it? *My* age? Is that what bothers you?"

"You look younger than your age. I feel older than mine. So..."

Rylee reached across the console and Finn felt the now familiar touch on her arm. "You know what? That night...I never once even considered your age. Not at the bar, not when we were dancing...not when we kissed. And not even when we were in bed. Not once."

Finn felt her stomach roll over, something else that was becoming familiar when Rylee was close, when Rylee touched her. Did Rylee's age bother her? Their ten-year age gap sometimes felt like twenty. Unlike Rylee, she *had* considered age that night. She had assumed Rylee was early twenties—twenty-three, twenty-four. It hadn't mattered, however. Like she'd told Rylee...she'd looked at her and couldn't breathe.

She glanced at her now. Her blond hair was hanging loose today, not in a ponytail. She had a sweatshirt on rather than a sweater, a T-shirt underneath that was peeking out at the neckline. The usual jeans and comfortable sneakers.

She said the words she was thinking. "You're very beautiful."

Rylee smiled and squeezed her arm before pulling away. "I'm not beautiful, Finn, but thank you for saying so."

"Oh, kid, you have no idea, do you?"

"About what?"

"About...about what you do to me."

"Do I make you have butterflies in your stomach?"

"Yes."

"Good. Because I have them too."

CHAPTER FIFTY-FOUR

Rylee held Smokey in her arms, listening to the loud purring in her ear. She was tired and really wished Dee wasn't coming over for dinner. Of course, Dee wasn't really coming over for dinner, she was coming over to talk. The few times Dee had been over to share a meal, she noticed that she was like Finn...eating wasn't something that really mattered to them.

"Unlike me," she murmured to Smokey.

She put the cat down, then went into the kitchen. She was tired, yes. But she was hungry, and she already knew there was nothing in the house. She leaned against the counter, contemplating going out to Finn's car and raiding her snack bag. But Dee would be here soon enough, she supposed.

She'd already showered and changed. Finn was in the shower now. She smiled as she chased images of Finn from her mind. They would get to that soon enough, she imagined. How could they not?

It seemed a little surreal. They'd gone from ignoring it and pretending it didn't happen to finally talking about it. Her doing. If it had been left up to Finn, they'd still be in that state. Now? Now they were doing more than talking about it. Each glance, each look...it was there, out in the open now. In fact, she still got goose bumps thinking about it...thinking about that night. Thinking about everything they'd done...every touch, every kiss. It had been a magical night. But that hadn't stopped her from panicking when she woke up. She'd actually been terrified Finn might wake before she could sneak from the room.

What if she hadn't run? What if Finn *had* woken? Would they have talked? Or would they have fallen back into bed? Knowing Finn as she did now, it would be the latter. Finn wasn't much for talking.

It didn't really matter anymore, did it? They were here now. She only wished things could be normal and not involve a murder case they had no business being in. Her, especially. And she admitted she had been a little scared today. They'd followed the Cadillac and SUV to what Finn said wasn't the greatest part of town. They had turned south, off the JFK Causeway, just before the highway crossed the bay to the island. There was a smattering of abandoned buildings and warehouses, vacant and unkempt lots, and rusted boats and vessels. There were no houses, no trees, and little to no traffic. Finn hadn't felt comfortable following too closely, and she'd pulled over, using the binoculars to spy on them.

The SUV had stopped at a gate and the driver got out, unlocking and opening it. Both vehicles went through, then the gate was closed and locked again. Behind the wire fence was a large metal building. Once the vehicles had disappeared behind it, Finn drove them closer. The lot around the building was littered with old boat trailers, suggesting it used to be a repair shop or perhaps they built the trailers there onsite. Finn had snapped a few pictures, then went back toward the highway where they could blend in better.

A short ten minutes later, the SUV and Cadillac had returned, minus one passenger. There was no sign of Brian Hodge. When they got to the highway, the SUV went east, toward the island, and the Cadillac went west, back toward the city. They had chosen to follow the black Cadillac. Unfortunately, traffic and a rain shower made that difficult and they'd lost sight of it.

"Are you hoping somehow my fridge got stocked today?"

Rylee smiled, not realizing she'd been staring at the stainless steel appliance that held only a few water bottles, an empty butter dish, and absolutely nothing else. She turned to Finn, noting the damp hair. She'd put on clean jeans and a T-shirt. Despite the cool, damp weather outside, it was quite warm in the house.

"We have *got* to go grocery shopping." She moved closer to Finn, holding her gaze. "How long before Dee gets here?" Her question was met with a blush and she laughed lightly. "God, you are too cute. But no. Not for that. For *that*, we need hours of free time."

Finn took a step away, a blush still lingering on her face. "I'm sorry. I'm not used to this."

"This what?"

Finn motioned between them. "This. You."

Rylee frowned. "Me?"

"It's been forever since someone has been...teasing, playful with me."

"Oh, sweetie...I'm sorry. I—"

Finn held her hand up. "No. It's not you. It's me. I'm...I—"

"Finn, do I make you nervous?"

"Yes," she said quickly.

Rylee tilted her head. "Do you want to sleep with me?"

"God, yes."

"Good. Because I want to sleep with you." She moved closer, close enough to see Finn's pulse throbbing in her neck. "Consider being playful and teasing as foreplay then." Her gaze dropped to Finn's lips. "Actually, a kiss would be considered better foreplay," she whispered as she looked back into Finn's eyes, seeing them darken. It was the same look she'd seen at the bar that night and like then, she couldn't resist it. She moved closer, their bodies nearly touching. The sound of the gate alarm stopped her from moving completely into Finn's arms, however. It was a good thing, she supposed. Because one kiss would never be enough. "Saved by the bell," she murmured.

Or were they? Finn never looked away and even though they weren't quite touching, Rylee could *feel* Finn's hands on her, could taste her kiss. Instead of moving away, she moved closer, wanting— needing—some contact...*any* contact. Their thighs brushed and it was apparently more than Finn could stand. Before another thought could enter her muddled brain, Finn's lips were on hers.

The room started spinning and she closed her eyes, holding on to Finn much like she'd done at the bar. Hands were everywhere— hers and Finn's both—and she moaned into Finn's mouth as fingers circled around her nipples, making them rock hard. Her hips jerked involuntarily, pressing close to Finn. She moved closer still, opening her thighs, feeling Finn's hands slide down her back, cupping her, pulling her even tighter against her. Finn's tongue was in her mouth and Rylee's own wrapped around it as they battled for control. She gave up the fight as Finn's thigh pressed against her clit.

Rylee rocked against her, not caring that Dee was on her way, not caring that she was seconds away from an orgasm, right there in Finn's kitchen. She pulled her mouth from Finn's, gasping for breath as her hips moved wildly, bucking hard against Finn's thigh.

Then Finn's mouth covered hers again, catching her scream, strong arms holding her upright as her legs gave way.

"Oh, my God," she whispered as she buried her face against Finn's neck. Should she be embarrassed? Ashamed? No. She knew it would be like that if they kissed. That's how it had been at the bar too, only they'd stopped before things got totally out of hand. "So…that had to be the best kiss ever."

"I'll say."

The sound of the doorbell chiming pulled her out of Finn's arms. Finn was obviously aroused and Rylee couldn't help herself as she slipped a hand between her thighs, pressing hard against her, feeling her wetness through her jeans. Finn jerked against her hand, her eyes closed tightly.

"I'm sorry," Rylee whispered.

"I'm not." Finn took a step away as the doorbell chimed again. "Foreplay," she said with a wink.

Rylee smiled at Finn's attempt at being playful. "Definitely."

Then Finn cleared her throat. "So…Dee's here."

"Yes, she is." Rylee blew out a breath when Finn left. Yes. Dee was here now. So maybe she was a little embarrassed. She hurried down the hallway and into the bathroom, not wanting to be caught looking all disheveled when Dee walked in. She stared at herself in the mirror, noting her tousled hair—had Finn's hands been there too?—her flushed face, her well-kissed lips. She looked into her own eyes, seeing the wonder there. They'd been kissing for thirty, maybe forty seconds. How could she possibly have had an orgasm in that short amount of time?

Because Finn did that to her.

She smiled at herself. Yes…it had been a great kiss. She was glad they'd broken the ice between them. Because tonight—as soon as Dee was gone—she planned to have her way with Finley Knight.

And from what she remembered, Finn would have her way with Rylee…all night long.

She could hardly wait.

CHAPTER FIFTY-FIVE

Dee was about to ring the doorbell a third time when she heard the lock turn. Finn opened the door, then reached out and grabbed one of the bags she was holding.

"Sorry. Was…was in the back. You're here earlier than I expected."

Finn's face was flushed and her voice sounded a bit odd, but she didn't comment on it. She had more pressing things on her mind. "You were right. Mabanks yanked me from the case."

"Man…he's in deep, I guess."

Dee followed Finn through the house. "He gave me some lame-ass excuse about letting Fender take a shot at it. Matt Fender," she explained. "He's been a detective for all of six months."

Rylee came in from the back of the house and Dee noted the look that passed between her and Finn. Rylee then turned to her and smiled in greeting. "I'll set the table."

"Nothing fancy, I'm afraid. I got a couple of pizzas."

"That's okay. I love pizza." Then Rylee laughed when she saw the Pizza Jamboree logo on the box. "Appropriate, I suppose."

Dee pulled out a chair and sat down at the kitchen table. "Productive day?"

"A rather odd day, but I guess productive, yes," Rylee said. "I'll let Finn give you the rundown."

Finn set a drink down beside her and handed a cognac glass to Rylee. "What do you know about Brian Hodge?"

Dee shrugged. "Nothing more than what you gave me on the profile."

"We did a little more digging. On the surface, his real estate firm is rather small, dealing with mid-range prices. Eric Lawrence, now he only deals in your higher priced homes, mostly multimillion, beach- and bay-front homes. The smallest we found for him was half a mil," Finn said.

"What's this got to do with Hodge?"

"The house Jose Hernandez owns was listed by Bay Shore Realty. That house has been the *only* listing for them in three years of their existence. The owners of Bay Shore Realty? Eric Lawrence and Brian Hodge."

"Okay. I'm sure you're going somewhere with this."

"When Hodge left the house today, someone else was driving his SUV. Hodge was riding in the black Cadillac."

"The black Cadillac that Lori Peterson's child was in," Rylee clarified.

"We followed them. They went down south in the old warehouse district. Locked gate. Abandoned site and buildings. They stayed in about ten minutes, then the SUV and Cadillac came out. No sign of Brian Hodge."

Dee picked up her drink, looking at Finn across the rim. "Are you suggesting they're holding Hodge hostage?"

"Or worse."

"Thanks," Dee said to Rylee as she slid a plate with two pieces of pizza toward her. "I found the apartment that Carlos Hernandez was renting. I requested a warrant. That's when Mabanks pulled me."

"How's he been acting toward you?"

"Distant. Very. Goes out of his way to avoid me."

"What about the warrant?"

Dee nodded. "Yeah. Fender is probably on his way there now. If Lori Peterson was inside, surely her prints will be there. If that's the case, then Mabanks can't stop this train any longer."

Finn took a bite of her pizza, her brow furrowed. "What do you think Brett Peterson did? What did he do that justified his child being abducted and his wife used as payment?"

"I don't know. He doesn't owe a lot of money."

"A sizable amount but not as much as some of the others."

"I think he wanted out," Rylee said. "Daniel Frazier gets murdered. Connie Frazier gets murdered. I think he wanted out."

"So they snatch the kid? Threaten him? His wife?" Dee shook her head. "Why not call the police?"

"They threaten him with exposure. He might lose his family, his career. If he goes to the police, same thing. But he would be exposing everyone, not just him. He's a dead man then."

"I don't know, Rylee."

"She might have a point," Finn said. "Maybe he did get freaked out with the murders. So he wants to pay his debt off and get out. What do they do? They lose their clients, they lose money. Or more importantly, they lose leverage. The debts here, that's chump change compared to the money that's being moved. These clients—or members—were picked for this little club for a reason. And it may not be only that. All of these guys probably know too much, whether they think they do or not. If you're Jose Hernandez—or whoever the boss is—are you willing to chance that one of these ten men won't go to the cops? Or the FBI?"

"So you start killing them? Remember, Daniel Frazier wasn't listed as one of the members."

"He could have removed his own name to save face. Daniel wants out, threatens exposure…they kill him. Maybe Brett Peterson wanted out too. Maybe Brian Hodge wanted out."

"What do you think I should do? Send a unit out to check on Brian Hodge?" She shook her head. "Locked gate, you said. We'd have to have probable cause to go in."

"What if you say you got an anonymous tip?" Rylee said.

"I could fabricate a tip, yes. It would still have to go through Mabanks to get a warrant."

The subtle tone on her phone letting her know she'd received a text sounded, but she ignored it. When she got a second text, she pulled her phone from the clip on her belt.

"Oh, my God." She looked at Finn, eyes wide in disbelief.

"What is it?"

"O'Leary's body was found out in the gulf, picked up by Coast Guard. Single GSW to the head."

Finn pushed her plate away. "Okay, that's it then. Game over. We go to Mabanks. We lay it all out in the open. Better yet, we bring him here."

"He's not going to tell us anything, Finn. But Christ, what's this guy doing? Trying to eliminate all of these guys?"

"He *will* tell us what's going on. His buddies are getting murdered. He's scared for his life now. He could be next. He's not worried about exposure any longer," Finn countered.

"You want me to call him?"

"No. Pick him up. Bring him here."

"Pick him up? Finn, he's my captain. I can't order him to come with me."

Finn stood up. "Fine. Then I'll do it. Rylee? Find his picture on that file. Print it out. Print out the list of members and their debt too."

"What are you going to do?" Rylee said as she stood up too.

"I'm going to go get him."

"Alone? But—"

"I'll be fine, Rylee. I can handle him."

"But—"

"It'll be okay."

Rylee shook her head. "You should take Dee. You should—"

"No. Dee stays with you. You're safer here."

Dee could tell Rylee wanted to say more. Instead, she nodded a bit curtly. Finn smiled at her.

"Nothing's going to happen to me. We have some…unfinished business."

Rylee smiled at that and as Dee watched the exchange, she wondered what was going on with them. She also wondered if it was any of her business.

Finn turned to her then, the look on her face all business now.

"Dee, see if you can get the particulars on O'Leary."

Dee nodded. "I should be able to. I've got a few buddies at the Coast Guard."

"And maybe it's time you called your friend at the FBI. It appears this is going to get out of hand very quickly."

"I will. I hope she's not on assignment."

"Someone you trust?"

"Yes. We were at HPD together years ago. CJ Johnston."

"Okay. Good. And Rylee? Do a search on the others, see if anything odd pops up. Check cell phone activity and credit cards. And I know I told you cell phone data was off limits but do it anyway. Some of them may have left Corpus."

Rylee was already at her laptop and she nodded at Finn's directive.

"I'll be back as quick as I can. Don't eat all the pizza."

* * *

"There are two laptops. If you can spare the time, I could use some help. I'm still learning my way around all these databases."

"Of course," Dee said, sitting opposite Rylee at the larger dining room table where the laptops were set up. "Let me call in first. Mabanks may still be there. If it's true and Jose Hernandez is trying to eliminate these guys, then Mabanks would surely feel safer there than at home."

"Unless he feels like his wife is threatened." Rylee's fingers were tapping on the keys, then she paused, glancing up at her. "This has gotten out of control, hasn't it?"

"Yes. Coast Guard is involved now. Getting CJ to come down here is one thing, but I'm not in a position to ask the FBI for assistance. Not formally. Someone higher up on the food chain would have to do that." But Rylee was frowning, not appearing to be listening to her. "What is it?"

"I think it's true. He's trying to eliminate everyone. I think he is trying to dissolve all of this," she said, motioning to the screen.

"What are you talking about?"

"Come look. We had alerts set up on Hernandez's accounts." She pointed at the screen. "The accounts are all closed. Zero balances."

"Transferred where?"

"I don't know. Maybe into the accounts that were on the flash drive."

"Can you find it?"

"No. Finn's the expert on that."

"Offshore accounts, most likely. That's been the assumption, anyway."

"As I understand it, we're not even supposed to look at financials without a warrant."

"Why doesn't that surprise me?" she murmured as she put a call in to Mabanks. It went unanswered. She blew out her breath, trying to decide what to do. "Call Finn," she said to Rylee. "Tell her about the accounts. I'm calling CJ."

"Okay, good. Because this is way over our heads. I think we should have involved the FBI days ago."

"You do? I thought you were in agreement with Finn about keeping the FBI out as long as we could."

"I think we've reached that point, don't you?"

CHAPTER FIFTY-SIX

Finn slowed, driving past the Mabanks' residence, then stopped about a half a block down. When she didn't find him at the station, she had little hope of finding him at home. If this thing was escalating, if he was scared for his life, surely he wouldn't be foolish enough to go to his house unprotected. But apparently he was. The plates on the car parked in his driveway matched. It was a quiet, residential street. Quiet and dark. There were lights on inside, though. He was inside. Maybe his wife too.

She clipped her gun into the holster at her hip and got out, taking a precautionary look around before heading up the sidewalk to his front door. The papers Rylee had printed out were clutched in her hand. She rang the doorbell twice in succession, then knocked loudly several times.

"Captain Mabanks? It's Finley Knight. Open up." She listened, hearing nothing from inside. She knocked again. "Mabanks? Open up."

The silence was finally broken by a shuffling sound at the door. "Who is it?"

"It's Finley Knight. I need to talk to you."

There was a long hesitation before he spoke. "Are you...are you alone?"

"Yes, sir. Open up."

She heard the deadbolt disengage, then the lock on the doorknob turn. Finally the door opened a crack and Mabanks peeked out. He looked at her quickly, then glanced behind her.

"What are you doing here?"

"It's time to talk, Captain. Enough games."

He opened the door fully but did not step aside. "What could a private investigator possibly want with me, a police captain?"

She smiled briefly, then held up the copy of the photo with him and the woman with jet-black hair. His eyes widened and he took a step back.

"Where did you…where did you get that?"

"I think you know where." She looked behind him into the house. "Where's your wife?"

"She's not here. Please…Finn, you can't—"

"Did you send her somewhere safe?"

He nodded. "How much do you know?"

"Enough. It looks like Hernandez is cutting and running. He's transferred money out of all of his accounts. Looks like he's trying to clean up his mess here. Take care of loose ends." She held up the ledger with the list of names. "You and your friends here are the loose ends. O'Leary is dead. I'd bet Brian Hodge is too."

"Brian Hodge?" He shook his head. "Look, you—"

"No, you look. You're coming with me. You're going to tell Dee everything you know. She's already put a call in to the FBI. She's—"

"What the hell? She can't do that!" he said loudly. "She has no authority to—"

Finn slammed her fist against the door, making him jump. "You're covering up three goddamn murders! You're hiding money laundering. You're protecting the guy who did it." She waved the list at him again. "He's killing the guys on this list, Captain. *You're* on this list. So whatever the hell you're mixed up in…too damn bad! And yeah, Dee went over your head. Somebody had to."

"You have no idea what's going on. You have no idea how powerful this man is."

"That's why you're going to tell us all about it. Now come on."

He shook his head. "No. I'm getting out of here, but it's not with you."

"John…these are professionals. You can't run. They'll find you. They'll find your wife. Your only option is to come with me."

"And you think *you* can protect me?" He laughed. "No offense, Finn, but I remember you as a cop. I ain't that trusting."

She pulled her gun out and pointed it at him. "You don't have a choice. You're coming with me."

"You're pulling a gun on a police captain? You've lost your goddamn mind!"

She grabbed him at the collar of his shirt, yanking him out of the door. "I swear, you haven't changed a bit. And you used to call me obstinate."

He jerked away from her. "You're not going to shoot me, Finn."

Before she could answer, they heard the squeal of tires as a car rounded the corner at far too fast of a speed. She took his arm and pulled him into the shadows of the overgrown shrubs at the side of his house. The black Cadillac pulled into the driveway, blocking Mabanks' car. Two men got out. She recognized Michael Drake as the passenger. The driver was the same man who'd been driving the Cadillac with Brian Hodge. He was a large man, almost lumbering in his walk. Drake was nearly six feet tall. This man seemed to tower over him.

She could feel the tension in the captain, hear his ragged breathing. She squeezed his arm but said nothing. They could hear the men searching inside the house…doors slamming shut, rustling footsteps running through hallways. The backyard light came on and they heard them on the patio, talking in hushed tones.

"Come on," she whispered, pulling him along with her.

They squeezed between the two cars and ran into the neighbor's yard, taking cover behind a bush near the privacy fence. They didn't have a good view of the house from here, but by the sounds she could hear, the men were now back out front. Finally she heard car doors open and close, the car start up and back into the street. She got down as low as she could, knowing if they turned this way, their headlights would hit them. But they didn't, they went back in the direction they'd come from, and only when the car turned the corner did she allow herself to breathe again.

"Looks like you were next on their hit list," she murmured as she stood, pulling him up with her. "Let's get out of here."

He didn't protest this time.

CHAPTER FIFTY-SEVEN

Dee was on the phone when Finn led John Mabanks into the house. Rylee was at the table, her nose stuck in the laptop, her fingers drumming across the keys as she read.

"Who's that?" he asked with a jerk of his head.

"My assistant," she said with a quick smile at Rylee. "This is Captain Mabanks." She motioned to a chair. "Have a seat."

Dee clipped her phone to her side, her face grim. "I sent a unit to the warehouse. They found Brian Hodge's body. Hands were tied. Shot execution style."

"The building is owned by Bayside Janitorial, which is owned by Jose Hernandez," Rylee said. "He's owned the building about three years. It appears that it's been vacant the whole time. It's also the only property Bayside Janitorial still owns. Everything else has been sold."

Finn turned to Mabanks. "Tell us what you know. Start at the beginning."

Mabanks looked at Dee. "You really called in the FBI?"

"I have a friend." She glanced at her watch. "She's supposed to get back with me within the hour. You'll need to put in a formal request."

"Normally, those sorts of things have to go through the chief."

"Yeah, well this isn't a normal case, is it? Or do you want to fill the chief in right now?" Dee pulled out a chair across from Mabanks. "And

I'm sorry to be so blunt with you, Captain, but what the hell have you gotten yourself involved with?"

Finn noticed that his hand was shaking and she went to the bar and poured a shot of whiskey for him. He nodded his thanks and knocked it back in one swallow.

"Judge Santos came to me," he said, looking at his empty glass instead of them. "Said they were forming a group. For some fun." He looked up then. "Gambling and girls. I said no, of course. Then O'Leary met with me. Said they needed a police presence. For protection."

Dee actually rolled her eyes. "Seriously? That's what lured you in?"

"They were going to pay me. Five hundred bucks a night to basically do nothing. Yeah, I took it."

"At the house in South Bay?"

Mabanks looked sharply at her. "How do you know about that?"

Finn shrugged. "It wasn't hard to find." She sat down at the table, joining the others. "When did this start?"

"I don't know. Four years, I guess. Maybe more."

"There are ten members. Who recruited them?" Dee asked.

"They call him Lobo. The White Wolf. He works for Jose Hernandez. He recruited them. They all serve a purpose."

"Who is Hernandez?" Finn asked.

Mabanks rubbed his bald head nervously. "I never met the guy. He's American, but he lives in Mexico from what I've heard…connected to some drug cartel there. He started paying off O'Leary and Santos, mostly for favorable zoning laws. He started buying up property, then selling for a huge profit after he got the zoning changed. He used Lawrence. They all got kickbacks. That's how it started. Peterson does legal work for him."

"What's his business?"

Mabanks shrugged. "Other than janitorial? Drugs, I guess. It's not like I'm in the loop, but I hear things."

"If he's moving drugs, why gambling and girls?" Rylee asked.

"It started with Santos and O'Leary. They wanted a little fun on the side. Hernandez gave it to them. Bought the house, brought in some girls from Mexico."

"And supplied cash when the stakes got too high?" Finn guessed.

"We were hooked by then. Got three girls living there. At first, it was all a big party. You only needed money for gambling, nothing for the girls. After about five months or so, things changed. You visited the girls, you got a bill. You went over on poker, he covered you…with interest. It added up quickly."

"He, meaning Hernandez?"

"Yeah, but Lobo does his bidding."

"So O'Leary and Santos knew the most. O'Leary has been eliminated. What about Santos?"

Mabanks shook his head. "O'Leary called me yesterday. Said Judge Santos missed a meeting with him, wanted to know if I'd heard from him. Now that Nathan is dead, I'm assuming the worst for Santos."

"What about Brett Peterson?"

Mabanks pushed his glass toward her. "I could use another shot of that."

Finn ignored his request. "What about Peterson?"

"He wanted out. After the thing with Frazier, he wanted out."

"Why was Daniel Frazier killed?"

"Because the stupid son of a bitch threatened to blow the whistle. Hernandez was moving all this cash through his restaurants, but he wouldn't pay what Frazier wanted. I don't know how the hell Frazier got access to the pictures or to anything else. One day, he sent us all an email saying he had the files. Sent us each a picture too. Said he was going to go public with it. Wanted a million dollars to start with."

Finn shook her head. "So extortion? And now everyone knew that Hernandez had these files on you all along. For blackmail? For leverage? I guess Peterson wasn't the only one who wanted out. Daniel Frazier did too."

"Who ordered him killed?" Dee asked.

"O'Leary and Santos let Lobo know. Wasn't two weeks later, Frazier is dead. Now the hunt was on for the files." Mabanks looked over at her. "Starting with you."

"They killed Sammy."

"They figured Frazier had left the files with you. When they didn't find it—"

"They tortured his wife," Dee finished.

"Why the affair with the wife?" Finn asked.

"O'Leary said they were trying to find the files before eliminating Frazier."

"My God. You knew they planned to kill him?" Dee shook her head. "You're a goddamn cop!"

"What was I supposed to do?"

"Your job! But I guess you work for the boss, don't you? And your *job* was to let the cases go cold, so you yanked me."

"I had no choice, Dee."

"Bullshit! Three people murdered. Now two more. Maybe three, with Santos. Does he plan to kill all ten of you?"

"The two men at your house...was the driver this Lobo guy?" Finn asked.

"Yeah. The other is who you know as Michael Drake. He has several aliases from what I hear."

"Why not kill Brett Peterson? Why take his kid, use his wife? To what end?" Dee asked.

"From what O'Leary told me, they were trying to send a message to the others. Then they found out he'd hired you...well, I think they thought he might have...you know, told you about what was going on."

"So Hernandez thought it best to cut and run before it blew up in his face."

Mabanks shoved the empty glass a little closer toward her. "Another shot, Finn. Please."

"Yeah, I suppose this is stressful for you. Five murders on your conscience. Six, I guess. There's Carlos Hernandez too. I guess he knew too much too...what with the Lori Peterson affair and all."

"I couldn't do anything, I swear. I was in too deep. I'd lose everything, including my family. Hell, they'd kill me like that," he said, snapping his fingers together. "I couldn't—"

"And what the hell do you think is going to happen now, John?"

CHAPTER FIFTY-EIGHT

"You stay here. Both of you," Dee said, pointing at Finn. "This is a police matter now."

"I could help."

"You're not a cop anymore, Finn." She pulled her jacket on, glancing toward Mabanks as he stood quietly by the door. "We've dispatched units to all of these guys' houses. Those that are left, anyway. We're about to raid the house on South Bay. It should all be over with tonight." She lowered her voice. "I'm worried about him. I've never seen him like this. So…so despondent."

"I guess he figures life as he knew it is over with. He's going to lose his job, that's a given. He'll be damn lucky if they let him retire with his pension intact."

Dee nodded. "Yeah, but at this point, I think he's probably more worried about his wife and family."

"Family can be forgiving."

Dee met her eyes. "Can they?"

Finn looked away. "Sometimes."

Dee touched her shoulder affectionately, then looked at Rylee. "Make sure she stays put."

"I will."

"Oh, and I'm leaving a unit out front," she said to Finn. "In case you're still a target."

"Thanks."

She stepped away, then looked at Mabanks. "Come on, Captain. We don't want them starting the raid without us."

* * *

South Bay Park was alive with police cars and lights. Apparently they did miss the raid after all. The house had already been secured.

"Captain Mabanks? I'm Sparks, the SWAT team commander."

Mabanks did little more than blink at him and Dee stepped forward. "I'm Detective Woodard. This is my case." She shook his hand firmly. "No problems?"

"No problems, no. But the house wasn't empty. Three women, chained to beds. Scared. Looks like they've been confined there without food or water for a couple of days. They're not saying much."

Dee glanced at Mabanks, seeing his ashen face even in the darkness. "They're probably terrified. Do they speak English?"

"Spanish, but they're not responding to us. I need a female officer to talk to them, calm them down a bit. You speak Spanish?"

"Not enough for an interrogation, no."

"That's okay, ma'am. I've got someone on the way. She'll be here soon enough." He motioned with his head. "Come on. You want to take a look?"

"Captain?" Dee asked with raised eyebrows.

"You can handle it," he said abruptly, turning away from her.

She looked at Sparks. "Give me a second." She hurried after the captain, stopping him with a light touch on his arm. "Everything's going to be okay."

The look in his eyes could only be described as haunted, but he nodded at her. "Yes. I believe it will."

She hesitated a moment, then turned. But he called her back.

"Dee...you're a good cop. That's why I took you off the case. But you figured it out anyway, didn't you?"

"Finn did. Not me."

He nodded slowly. "Yeah...figures. I never really did like her."

Dee smiled at that. "She kinda grows on you."

He waved her away. "I'll wait in the car."

* * *

"My God," she murmured.

The girls—women—were huddled together in one of the upstairs bedrooms.

The outside of the house belied the inside. It was sparsely furnished. The great room had been transformed into a game room. Two large tables—presumably for poker—were in the middle. Against the walls were gaming machines—slots. Six total. There was a bar. A quick glance told her every imaginable liquor was available. Two dart boards. Yeah…a clubhouse, complete with three young women for their sexual pleasure.

By the looks of them, they were here against their will. They were scared, malnourished…dirty. Of course, she'd seen the pictures. The state they were in now must be recent. Maybe things started spiraling downhill when Daniel Frazier was killed.

"Undocumented?"

"Most likely. We see stuff like this a lot. Girls brought over, told they'll be given a new life here and this is what they get. Some know coming in. Some do it to pay off their debt from being smuggled into the country. Some are forced to do it to pay off a family debt."

She nodded. "I'm going to take a look around. Let me know when your officer gets here. I've got plenty of questions for them myself."

"Of course."

CHAPTER FIFTY-NINE

"Did you hear that?"

Finn jumped up. Two shots in quick succession. Instinctively, she knew the shots hadn't come from the two police officers sitting out front by her gate. Most likely, they'd been eliminated. She turned, seeing movement outside the bay windows.

"Rylee! Get down!"

The bay window was shattered by gunfire and she dove behind the sofa. She reached to her side, grabbing the gun from her holster. She heard Rylee scream and she rolled to her back, finding a man—Michael Drake—standing over her, pointing an automatic rifle at her face.

"Well, well, Ms. Knight...we finally meet in person. Get up! Toss the gun!"

Finn stood, hesitating only a second before dropping her gun to the floor. Her gaze darted across the room, seeing Rylee being held by another man—the one Mabanks had called Lobo. Rylee struggled to break free of the hand clamped across her mouth. A quick elbow to his midsection loosened the grip, but Finn watched in horror as he slammed his gun into Rylee's head. Rylee crumpled onto the floor in a motionless heap. Finn moved to go to her, but the cold metal of the rifle touching her cheek caused her to stop.

"We must hurry. Where is it?"

She didn't pretend not to know what he was talking about. "It's too late. The police already have it."

Drake gave her only the slightest of smiles. "I'm not scared of the police. Besides, the money's been moved from the accounts. Those numbers are useless now." His gaze moved to the laptops. "Gather them," he said to her. "You're coming with me."

"Where to?"

This time his smile was much broader. "Your final destination, I would assume."

"What about her?" Lobo asked.

"Leave her. She is of no use."

Lobo pointed his rifle at Rylee, and Finn sprang forward.

"No!"

"Shut up!"

"Leave her," Drake said again. "She's nothing. Come on."

"No loose ends, remember?"

"No…no," Finn said quickly, holding out her hands. "She's…she's nobody. Just my receptionist. She knows nothing of this. Absolutely nothing."

Lobo still hesitated, his gun pointing at Rylee's head. Finn heard police sirens in the distance and they all looked up at the same time.

"The laptops are more important. Now come on. Let's go!"

Finn found herself being gripped by the arm, the rifle shoved against her side. Lobo ran to the table, scooping up their laptops. She glanced over at Rylee, watching as her eyelids fluttered. In that quick glance, she could see the nervous pounding of the pulse in Rylee's neck. *Good. Stay down. Don't move.* Then Drake jerked her with him, pulling her along as they walked across the shattered glass. It crunched under their feet as she was led out to the back. They hurried along the pier, their footsteps muted on the damp wood, the foggy mist circling around them. She could hear the water crashing against the pylons. High tide.

As they reached the end of the pier, a boat materialized out of the darkness.

Finn heard Spanish voices call to them and Drake answered in kind. The grip on her arm tightened and she was afraid Drake's words were true; she *was* going to her final destination.

She turned back once, looking to the house. Was Rylee okay? Was she sitting up now? Could she see them?

"Let's go!"

She tensed. The police sirens were loud…the flashing lights bouncing between houses now. They were close, almost there. Dare she make a run for it? Dare she dive into the cold, black water of the bay?

"Now! Move!"

CHAPTER SIXTY

Dee wouldn't have been surprised to find her car empty. She had suspected that Mabanks would flee the first chance he got. But no. She could see his silhouette in the front. The flashing lights of police and emergency vehicles lit up the night and as she walked in front of the car, he looked up, their eyes meeting. Then he looked away quickly and she moved on around the car, opening the door.

"Three girls," she said. "Is that how many?"

As soon as she closed the door, plunging the interior into darkness again, she felt the pressure of a gun being held to her side. She jerked her head around and he pressed it harder against her.

"Drive."

"What the hell are you doing?"

"They've got my wife."

"Captain, no. This isn't—"

"I swear to God, Dee…drive or I'll shoot you right here. They're going to kill her if this doesn't stop."

"It can't stop, Captain. It's too far along. You know that. I've already reported what I know to the FBI."

"But they don't know that, Dee. I don't care what happens to me. I just want to get Barbara out safe." He pressed the gun harder against her ribs. "Now drive. Nice and slow."

She was about to do his bidding when Sparks came hurrying over toward the car. Mabanks tensed, but his gun never left her side. If anything, it seemed to be digging in harder.

"Not one word, Dee."

She rolled the window down about halfway. "Something else?" she asked as casually as she could.

"Yeah, just got a call. Didn't know if you'd heard or not. Finley Knight's house was hit. You assigned a protection detail there earlier, I hear."

Her eyes widened. "Yes, I did. Hit? What happened?"

"Both officers are down, Detective. Looks like they were ambushed."

He'd no sooner said the words when her phone started dinging with alerts. She felt her heart jump into her throat and she swallowed down her fear. "And Finn? Rylee? The two women in the house?"

He nodded. "No sign of Finley Knight. Assumed abducted. Rylee Moore was the only one inside. She's okay. Blow to the head. They're interviewing her now."

She stared at him. "No sign of Finn?"

"No. But from what I remember, I think she can take care of herself."

"You know her?"

"Yeah. We came up at the same time. Worked together a couple of years too. I think she can handle herself."

Dee wasn't so sure. "She's gotten old and grumpy."

He smiled at that. "I haven't seen her in years, I'll admit. Kinda lost touch when she left the force."

Dee nodded slowly. "Yeah, we tend to do that, don't we? And the officers?"

He shook his head. "No. They didn't make it."

"Damn," she whispered.

She closed her eyes, trying to remember the two men who were positioned by the gate at Finn's house. She had been in such a hurry, she'd barely glanced their way when she and the captain had left. She looked back at him, nodding quickly.

"Thank you, Sparks. We'll head that way."

"Yeah, I think pretty much the entire police force is at that house right now."

As soon as he left, she turned to Captain Mabanks. "Two officers killed. They've got Finn. There's no goddamn way we're—"

"They've got Barbara. I don't care about Finn. I don't care about anything else right now. So drive!"

She gripped the steering wheel hard. "Captain…you've got to tell me where they are," she said calmly. "We can send in SWAT. We can—"

"No!" He shoved the gun harder into her side, making her flinch. "They want *me*. Because like the others, I know too much. If I come in, they let Barbara go."

"You surely don't believe that. No one is leaving there alive. Not Barbara. Not you. Not me. Not Finn. No one."

"He promised me Barbara. If I bring you in, if I come in…he'll let Barbara go." He leaned closer to her. "We're both already dead, Dee. Finn too. You should have left well enough alone."

"Well enough? We're cops! We don't turn a blind eye to this, Captain!"

"We do. *I* do. Like the saying goes, I'm a dead man walking. So I'm not afraid to shoot you right now. I have nothing to lose. My life is already over. Now drive."

* * *

Rylee clutched Smokey to her, shaking her head once again. "No. I don't need a doctor."

"Ma'am…"

"I'm fine."

And really, she felt okay, despite the throbbing in her face and the ringing in her left ear. The house had been a whirlwind of activity. She had been sitting up against the wall, trying to get her wits about her when officers had burst inside. She'd heard the boat, knew they'd taken Finn. She'd pointed the officers in that direction.

Actually, she'd heard everything. She'd braced herself, expecting a spray of bullets. She'd heard Finn plead with them to spare her. She was ashamed that she'd pretended to still be knocked out. It was cowardly of her to let Finn face them alone, but she had been paralyzed with fear. Had they known she was faking, she might have indeed gotten a bullet. She doubted they would have bothered taking her. As Finn had said, she was a nobody.

As ruthless as they'd been in everything else, she wondered why she was spared. It would have only taken a few seconds of their time to end her life.

"No loose ends."

Apparently she wasn't a loose end. But Finn definitely was.

"Have you been able to contact Detective Woodard?" she asked again.

The officer shook his head. "I'm sorry, no. She still must not be available. We can't get her."

"What does that mean? She's unavailable...like busy? Or...?" Her question was met with a curious stare. Should she explain? Dare she tell this officer how much she knew? "Dee is a personal friend," she said instead. "I know that she...she had a call earlier. I mean...a raid or something."

He nodded. "Yes, but they've left the scene. Said they were coming here." He shrugged. "Maybe the captain's got her doing something else. I'm sorry. I'll keep trying."

"Thank you."

As soon as he turned away, she glanced out toward the bay, looking through the opening where the large window had been. The fog seemed to be drifting inside now; it was so thick.

Where had they taken Finn? Did they have Dee too? Captain Mabanks?

She held Smokey tighter, feeling so very alone, so very helpless.

And so damn afraid she'd never see Finn again.

She hung her head, nestling against Smokey's fur. She should have done something. Not simply lain there like a helpless woman, afraid to move...afraid to breathe lest they shoot her. She should have done something to help Finn.

Yes, she should have. But a part of her knew—believed—that had she moved, had she opened her eyes, he would have shot her. She had no doubt. That wouldn't have exactly been helping Finn. Finn would have reacted then...and they would have probably shot Finn too.

Maybe playing dead as she did *had* been the best thing to do.

But now they had Finn.

CHAPTER SIXTY-ONE

Finn held her breath, diving down deeper, swearing she felt a bullet whiz by her head. She could hear the roar of the boat's engine as it circled back around. A spray of bullets from an automatic rifle pierced the water around her. She felt a sting and knew she'd been hit.

With her lungs threatening to explode, she swam farther away, finally shooting to the surface for air, then diving back down again into the cold water of the bay. In the brief seconds she was above water, she saw the beam of a strong flashlight scanning the water. Drake was looking for her. But the fog was thick, causing the water to appear as black as the night itself. There was another spray of bullets, then they took off, the sound of the engine fading as they sped away.

She floated on top of the water, breathing deeply. The waves from the boat washed over her and she spit saltwater out of her mouth, coughing several times as she turned her head. She felt disoriented as the foggy mist engulfed her. How far out had they gone before she'd jumped? A hundred yards? Two? More?

As panic was about to set in, she made herself relax. Sure, she hadn't been swimming in more years than she could recall. And yeah, she was out of breath and out of shape. And judging by the sting in her leg, she'd been hit by a bullet. And the cold water looked black and threatening…

But it was just the bay, nothing else. She saw it every single day. She loved the bay. The bay had kept her company on many a lonely night, many an early morning. The bay was like an old friend…one of her only friends.

So she floated again on her back, being still…listening. Through the fog, she heard a sound. Water lapping against wood. A pier. Might not be her pier, but a pier. She turned, swimming toward it. She stopped several times, pausing to float and catch her breath. As she got closer, she could see the hazy glow of lights through the low clouds. At the end of the pier was a bright red chair.

She hated that chair. She leaned her head back and looked up into the foggy sky and smiled. Her neighbor's pier with the godawful red chair that stuck out like a sore thumb. She swam toward that ugly chair now, feeling relief flood her when she finally reached the pylon. She rested again, getting her bearings. Her own pier was another fifty feet away.

With a push off, she swam on, feeling stronger now as the lights of her own pier came into view. She grasped the end of the wood decking, holding herself up and out of the water. However, she knew she couldn't pull up there—it was too high—so she moved around the deck that jutted out at the end, holding on to pylons as the waves of high tide tried to push her under the pier itself. She lost her grip on a slippery post and went under. She came up spitting water and she grabbed the edge of the pier again, pausing to rest. She could hear voices now and see the flashing of police lights at her gate, the misty fog making them appear distorted.

Lots of lights. A break-in at her house wouldn't warrant all of that. No. But the killing of two cops would.

She was tired and cold and she pushed on, moving to where the boat slip was. There was no boat there. She'd never gotten around to getting one. But there was a ladder. She recognized the sense of relief she felt when she grabbed it. It was only as she tried to pull herself out that she realized how heavy her wet jeans were, how chunky her wet sneakers felt…and how cold it truly was.

She was chilled to the bone—it had been warm in the house and she'd been wearing only a T-shirt on top. She wrapped her arms around her torso and headed toward the lights of her house, dripping on the already soggy pier and making a squishing noise as she stumbled onward. It was only then that she felt the ache in her left leg. She looked down, seeing her torn jeans. She'd almost forgotten she'd been hit. Judging by the feel of it, she'd only been grazed by the bullet. For that, she was damn lucky.

She saw Rylee standing at the broken bay window, staring out into the darkness. Rylee's head tilted...as if she wasn't quite sure of what she was seeing...as if she was seeing a ghost, perhaps.

Finn moved closer, out of the shadows. She could see the wonder on Rylee's face, the disbelief. Then Rylee was running and Finn stopped, bracing herself as Rylee sailed into her arms—unmindful of Finn's wet clothing—nearly tipping Finn over backward from her force.

"Oh, my God!" Rylee pulled away enough to cup her face, to run her hands along her shoulders. "Are you okay? Are you hurt?"

"I'm fine. Are you okay?" Finn inspected her cheek, seeing the beginnings of a bruise.

"Yes." Rylee touched the spot. "Tender. A little ringing in my ear, but fine." Rylee pulled her into another tight hug. "I'm so sorry. I thought the worst and I was so scared for you. God...I'm sorry, Finn. I should have done something. I was—"

"No. You did the right thing. You did everything right." Finn wrapped her arms around her and held her. "I was afraid they were going to shoot you. I didn't know what to do."

"I thought they were going to shoot me too," Rylee mumbled against her neck. "God...what happened? Did they push you out of the boat? You're shivering."

Finn pulled away from Rylee but took her hand, leading her back to the house. "I jumped overboard. It seemed like the lesser of two evils."

"You jumped out of the boat? Into the bay? At night?"

"I know...crazy." She motioned to the front. "The two cops...they make it?"

"No. They...they killed them. But this place is crawling with police. I peeked out the front door and there's like twenty or thirty cars, all with their lights on."

"Kill two cops. That makes for one hell of a distraction." She went inside. "I need to get into some dry clothes." She pulled her phone out of her pocket. "I guess we'll see if my phone lives up to the waterproof status. Need to check in with Dee. Or is she here already?"

Rylee shook her head. "No. They can't find her. They won't tell me much. Said she must be unavailable or maybe Captain Mabanks has her on something else." Rylee squeezed her hand tightly. "I think...I think they have her. She would have come here."

Rylee was right, of course. If Dee had heard about the shooting here, she would have come immediately.

"Who's in charge? Do you know?"

"There's so many people here, I have no clue. There are some detectives, though, I know that. I've been questioned several times."

"Okay. Let me change. Then we need to find out what's going on." She headed to the back, then stopped. "For everything's that happened tonight...that moment in the kitchen...with you...is the only thing keeping me sane right now."

Rylee came closer, leaning over to kiss her cheek lightly. "I had almost convinced myself that was all a dream."

Finn gave her a tired smile. "When this is over with, I'll show you that it wasn't a dream. A nice hotel maybe...one with a Jacuzzi."

"And room service."

Finn laughed quietly. "Trust you to be more interested in food than a naked dip in a Jacuzzi."

Both their smiles faded, though. Rylee gave her a gentle push. "Go get changed. I have a feeling it's a long way from over with."

CHAPTER SIXTY-TWO

Dee twisted her hands, feeling the rope cut into her wrists. Mabanks was on the floor beside her. Next to him was Barbara, his wife. She was crying quietly, her head buried against his shoulder. Like everyone else, she had her hands tied behind her back. She wasn't sure who was sitting next to Barbara. One of their ten, but who? By process of elimination, she determined it must be Oliver Judge. He wasn't on her list. She knew what Brett Peterson looked like, only because she'd made a point to look him up after Carlos Hernandez had been killed. And the man was too young to be Peterson's father. Had to be Judge.

It was the same warehouse where Brian Hodge had been found shot dead. Dee thought it ironic that the crime scene tape was still up. Drake and the others—there were five of them— had no fear of being here, though. The scene had already been processed. No one was coming back anytime soon. Besides, every cop in the city had descended upon Ocean Drive and Finley Knight's house. There probably wasn't a police officer within miles of this location.

She moved her hands again, feeling no give in the rope. She couldn't believe she'd gotten herself into this situation. Sure…Mabanks had his weapon pressed against her ribs on the entire drive out here. Would he have really shot her? She'd like to think no, but at the time, she couldn't be sure. Did it matter? Was her fate here going to be any different? Who would find her here, at this warehouse? Her phone—like all the others—had been confiscated and smashed to bits. There would be no tracing it. Would anyone even consider they'd use this warehouse a second time?

She glanced to her left. Roger King was beside her. For all of his loud, boisterous commercials, he had not uttered a sound. He was staring straight ahead, his eyes glazed. Next to him was Eric Lawrence, the real estate agent. She'd never met him before, but she recognized him from the profile pictures Rylee had assembled. Councilman Stevens was next to him.

She wasn't really surprised to see Duncan Frazier there, although he wasn't tied up like they all were. He was standing off by himself, away from the others. However, the cockiness she'd seen on his face before was absent. Apparently, this was more than he'd bargained for...whatever his role was in all of this. She was surprised, however, that Finn wasn't here. She didn't want to speculate or assume, but if she'd been taken from her house...and wasn't here now...well...she didn't want to guess what that meant. She couldn't.

A phone rang and Drake snatched it up. He began speaking rapid Spanish and Dee couldn't follow along. She heard the Petersons' names and from Drake's reaction, assumed they hadn't been able to locate them. Then he handed the phone to the one Mabanks had called Lobo. She could see why they'd given him that name; he was a hulk of a man. His Spanish was broken, however, and he reverted to English several times, enough for her to learn that Finn had apparently jumped from a boat out into the bay. They'd "sprayed the goddamn water with bullets" and assumed she was dead. Dee stopped listening then.

She turned her head toward Mabanks, finding him watching her. He'd heard too, yet there was no reaction. He was too far gone. They were all too far gone, apparently.

"Lobo, is that Hernandez? You can't keep us here like this! Do you know who I am? You tell him he can't keep us here like this!"

"Shut up!"

"I demand that you untie me! Right now! We can work this out. Let me talk to him!"

Demand? Didn't Stevens know who he was dealing with? They didn't care who he was. They didn't care that he was running for mayor in the next election.

Drake looked over at him. "Be quiet."

"I will not be quiet! Untie me!"

Lobo handed the phone back to Drake, then walked in front of Stevens. "I never did like you. Stop talking."

"Untie me. I can make this go away. I can make the police go away. We can work this out. Let me talk to Jose. I can work magic. He knows that. Let me talk to him!"

"Somebody shut him up," Drake shouted.

"Gladly."

Councilman Stevens was shot six times. Blood splattered against the wall behind him and he fell to his side, against Eric Lawrence. Eric Lawrence practically jumped into Roger King's lap. King never moved a muscle. Barbara Mabanks screamed, her cries turning into hysterical wails that echoed inside the empty metal building. Lobo turned his rifle in her direction.

"*No!*"

Captain Mabanks tried to shield her, but it was too late. The wailing stopped immediately as she fell backward, blood oozing from her head. For a few seconds, there was absolute silence in the warehouse. Then John Mabanks was the one to wail, his cries deep and wrought with emotion. He lunged at Lobo and Dee watched in horror as his body was riddled with bullets, his blood spraying against her cheek as she turned away from the sight.

"Anybody else got something to say?"

No one did.

CHAPTER SIXTY-THREE

Finn found Joel Yearwood and two other detectives in her front yard. She assumed they were the two who had taken over Dee's investigation. She walked up to them, interrupting their conversation.

"Excuse me. I'm Finley Knight. Don't know if you remember me. I—"

"Wait a minute. What are you doing here? We were told—"

"Yeah…they took me on a boat. I jumped. Where's Dee?"

One of other two stepped forward. "Ms. Knight, I'm Detective Davis. You've got to be interviewed. We've got two officers down. Our priority right now—"

"Where's Detective Woodard? Captain Mabanks?"

"Look, we've got to take you in. You're our only link—"

She took a step back and held up her hands. "I know the drill, but it ain't happening right now."

"You don't have a choice," Joel said.

"The hell I don't. Find me Detective Woodard and Captain Mabanks. I'll talk to them."

Detective Davis looked at the others, then let out a frustrated breath. "We can't locate them. Neither of them is answering."

"Trace their phones?" she asked quickly.

"It's in the works, yes. Now…how many men were involved?"

"Two. And I'm sure my assistant has already told you this when you interviewed her. We heard two shots. Then they came to the back, blew out the bay window. Took me."

"Why did they take you?"

Finn hesitated. "I have no idea."

Joel looked at her skeptically. "You're saying it doesn't have anything to do with the murder investigation?"

She met his gaze. "What murder investigation?"

"Come on. Dee was still working it, even if Mabanks told her to back off. And she was here quite a bit."

She took another step away. "Call me when you find them. I'll be happy to sit for an interrogation then."

"What are you going to do?"

"I'm going to my office." She pointed to her driveway. "And move some of these cars out of the way. They're blocking my garage."

Everything had gone down pretty much as she'd expected. Rylee was already in the car, waiting. Smokey had been secured in her bedroom. She hadn't bothered with the lights or locking the front door. She figured the cops would be there for several more hours, futilely looking for evidence that didn't exist.

But she wasn't going to her office. She had a hunch and she hoped it was the right one.

Only she needed help.

CHAPTER SIXTY-FOUR

"Sorry, kid. It's not going to work out after all."

Dee watched as Duncan Frazier was spun around, his hands jerked up behind him while one of Lobo's goons tied him up.

"Wait! He said—"

"Orders from the top."

"Orders? From Jose? But he said—"

"Shut up already," Drake said, pointing his gun at Duncan's face. "Join the others on the floor."

Duncan's lower lip trembled. "What…what are you going to do?"

"I'm waiting on a phone call. Then we'll know."

Duncan was shoved down next to Dee, his feet sliding through the drying blood of John Mabanks. The bodies of the captain and his wife, along with that of Councilman Stevens, had been dumped in a heap against the opposite wall. The rest of them had been quiet, no one even making eye contact with each other or their captives. Roger King was still in his catatonic state, barely breathing. Eric Lawrence's knee was twitching nervously. Oliver Judge was clenching and unclenching his jaw, his eyes darting around the room, never landing on anything. Beside her, Duncan Frazier was beginning to cry, a quiet sound that—despite his obvious involvement—tugged at her heart. He was just a young kid mixed up in something that was way over his head. She wondered if he'd had a role in his parents' deaths. Even that thought did little to harden her heart toward him. His fate—like theirs—seemed to be sealed.

She didn't know what the delay was or why Drake needed a phone call to tell him to pull the trigger. Unless Hernandez had some other unfinished business to take care of. Like maybe finding the Petersons. Brett and his father were the last. Everyone else involved was dead. Daniel Frazier, Carlos Hernandez, Mayor O'Leary, Judge Santos, Brian Hodge...now Mabanks and Stevens. The only others who knew anything about the goings-on of Jose Hernandez's business were Finn and the Petersons. Was Finn dead like they believed? Did that leave only the Petersons as the loose ends? Did he have another team out hunting for them?

Yes...her fate seemed to be sealed. Her only hope would be if she and Captain Mabanks were missed. They could put a trace on their phones, but she doubted the SIM cards were of any use any longer. She glanced at the pile of rubble that used to be their cells. No. A trace would probably do no good. The GPS tracking device on her car was of no use either. As far as she knew, her car was still parked at the Whataburger where they'd met up with three of Drake's men. By the time they pulled security images, this would be long over with.

She leaned her head back against the wall and stared at the ceiling. She no longer felt the cold concrete she was sitting on. Her body seemed to be going numb...accepting its fate. Duncan's quiet sniffling was almost comforting to her now.

Because her fate was sealed.

All they were waiting on was a phone call. She almost wished it would ring so they could get it over with.

Almost.

CHAPTER SIXTY-FIVE

"Do you think he believed you?"

Finn was speeding along the foggy JFK Causeway, not worried about being stopped. Every cop on the force had seemed to be parked near her house. Two cops dead? No...no one would be out patrolling, looking for speeders. Not tonight.

"I hope so. It's our only chance."

"But what if he didn't?"

"Then we'll go in alone." She glanced at Rylee. "*I'll* go in alone," she corrected.

"The hell you will. Quit trying to protect me. I...I folded earlier. That won't happen again."

"Rylee—"

"No! And maybe it's this gun on my hip that's got me feeling brave...but you will *not* go in alone."

Finn didn't argue, but she had no intention of letting Rylee get involved. Yeah, she'd folded, as she called it, but Finn was glad she had. Rylee had no police training...but she did. She just hoped her hunch didn't prove to be a dead end.

"A la bodega. Rapido!"

Or at least that's what she thought she heard Drake yell to the guy on the boat. Her Spanish wasn't great, but she remembered when she'd had the office building remodeled, the guys kept calling it "bodega."

Store. Warehouse.

According to Rylee, from the research of Jose Hernandez's business and property, the old boat trailer facility—warehouse—was the only thing still owned by Bayside Janitorial. Brian Hodge had been killed there. The police had it secured. Would Drake and Lobo be crazy enough to use it again?

But why not? If the police were going to revisit the scene, they wouldn't do it in the middle of the night.

"A la bodega. Rapido!"

They had been intending to take her there. If Dee and the captain had been abducted as well, it stood to reason they'd take them there too. And the others? What better place to tie up loose ends? Take care of business, then disappear. Jose Hernandez was already in Mexico. In a few hours, these guys could be in Brownsville and then cross over into Matamoros with ease.

Game over.

Of course, if they weren't at the warehouse…if there was some other property Drake was referring to…then it was game over for sure. She tightened her grip on the steering wheel, trying not to think about Dee and Mabanks being at the mercy of Drake and Lobo. They were obviously trying to eliminate all the players. She remembered what they'd done to Connie Frazier. Dee wasn't a player in this game, but she knew too much. And Finn knew part of that was because of her.

She nearly jumped when Rylee touched her arm.

"If you don't slow down, you're going to fly right by our exit," Rylee said, squeezing her arm.

"Sorry. I just…I have this nagging feeling that we're too late. That we're going to find…well…"

"I know. But slow down. I'm not sure the tires are even touching the pavement right now. And it's so foggy…"

Finn changed lanes, cutting off a truck. A loud horn blared behind them, and Finn moved into the far right lane, tires squealing as she skidded into the exit. Rylee was holding on to the dash now.

"You didn't see that truck, did you?"

"No."

"I'm driving on the way back," Rylee murmured.

* * *

It was dark...the fog thick. Finn slowed as they approached the gate. She killed her lights but doubted anyone could have seen them from the warehouse. They were enveloped in the swirling mist, as was the warehouse itself. Even through the binoculars she could barely make out the shape of the building. No vehicles were in front, but that wasn't to say they weren't hidden in the back. Of course, with the boat, they wouldn't need a vehicle.

"It's kinda creepy," Rylee said quietly. "The old boat trailers...they look like giant skeletons."

"I always liked foggy nights when I'd sit on the pier," she said as she lowered the glasses. "But yeah, it's a little creepy out here."

"How long do we wait for him?"

"We don't. You stay here. I'll—"

"Finn—"

"The gate's locked. I'll have to climb the fence."

"Are you suggesting that I can't?"

"Rylee—"

Rylee opened the door and got out before Finn could stop her. Finn got out too, looking at Rylee across the top of her car.

"Don't be stupid."

"Don't piss me off!"

"God...I had no idea you were so stubborn!" Finn said as she pounded the top of the car.

"Yeah? Look in the mirror!"

Finn hurried around the car and grabbed Rylee's arm as she was about to climb the fence. "I don't want anything to happen to you. Stay here!"

"That makes no sense. I don't want anything to happen to *you*! *You* stay here!"

Finn threw her hands up. They had no time for this. "Fine! Get yourself killed!"

Before either of them could attempt to scale the fence, lights appeared out of the fog. Rylee tensed, but Finn let out a relieved breath.

"It's okay. It's him."

"Thank God," Rylee whispered. "Because I'm not sure I could have climbed the fence."

Finn pulled her into a sudden hug, then released her just as quickly. "Please stay here, Rylee. Wait for me in the car. Please? Do it for me. Please?"

She could hear Rylee's breathing, feel her indecision, feel her hands tightening around her. "Okay. Go get Dee. But you better come back in one piece."

"I promise."

The large armored truck stopped next to her car and unlike her, they didn't kill the lights. She walked over to it, seeing Elliott Sparks hop out.

"About damn time."

They shook hands quickly.

"Going to get my ass into all kinds of trouble, Finn."

"I thought trouble was your middle name."

"When we came up together, trouble was *your* middle name, if I remember." Sparks turned to one of the three officers he'd brought with him. "Check it out," he told one of them. He walked with Finn over to the gate. "Damn glad you're okay. Heard you jumped off a boat."

"I felt like it was safer than wherever they were taking me. Which I assume was here."

"You think this is the place then? It's already a crime scene, according to the detectives I spoke with." He peered through the fence at the warehouse. "Nobody seemed to think they'd come back here. Not unless they were crazy."

"Yet you came anyway."

"I trust your gut, what can I say?"

"Commander…we got people inside. Looks like at least ten."

Finn looked at the monitor for thermal imaging he held, seeing the distorted images moving inside the warehouse. There were what looked like five stationary figures. Mabanks and Dee were two of them, she hoped.

"Cut the lock on the gate. Let's roll." He turned to Finn. "I'm calling for backup, then we'll go in. You stay here."

"No, way. I'm going with you."

"You're a goddamn civilian, Finn. I can't let you—"

"You can't stop me," she said, meeting his gaze in the fuzzy lights of the truck. "Got a friend in there. And in case you don't remember…I never had many friends."

He shook his head, then pointed to the truck. "Get in the back with Thompson. And put a goddamn vest on."

CHAPTER SIXTY-SIX

Dee felt her heart jump into her throat at the sound of Drake's phone ringing. Was their time up? From what she'd gathered from the little conversation she'd been able to decipher, they were most likely going to be eliminated right here and now...unless Hernandez ordered them moved somewhere else. She wondered how much Spanish the rest of them knew. There had been no reaction to the conversation so she assumed none.

Drake was speaking quietly now and she couldn't hear him. She watched Lobo's reaction instead. He was nodding at whatever Drake said. She saw the other three starting to fiddle with their guns.

Her throat was dry and she could barely swallow. She glanced over at Duncan. His tears had stopped, but their stains still marred his young, handsome face. He turned to look at her and she saw the fear in his eyes. Could he see the same in hers?

To her left, she felt Roger King shift—the first movement he'd made since she'd gotten there. She turned to look at him, but as before, he was staring straight ahead, unblinking. What was he thinking? For that matter, what were they all thinking? What was *she* thinking?

Nothing. Even her mind seemed paralyzed with fear. Should she be reliving the good times in her life? Should she be thinking of her parents, her younger sister…or thinking of Angela, the only woman she'd ever been in love with?

Drake pocketed his phone, then moved toward them. Duncan was shivering beside her, his lower lip trembling. If she had had a free hand, she would have offered him some comfort. All she could do was press her shoulder closer to his, giving him some human contact.

Eric Lawrence was the first to speak. He directed his question at Lobo, not Drake.

"What have we done to deserve all of this, Lobo? We did everything Jose asked of us."

"And you were paid well," he shot back.

"So why all of this? What did we do?"

"It's not what we did…it's what we know."

Dee's gaze went to Oliver Judge. At least he recognized the truth. The tone of his voice indicated that he knew—and accepted—the fate that was coming. He seemed calm now, his eyes no longer darting around the room, his jaw no longer clenching tightly.

"Jose is in Mexico," Eric continued. "It doesn't matter what we know. They can't touch him there."

Perhaps Eric Lawrence didn't know that Jose Hernandez was an American citizen. If he was linked to the deaths of this many people—a mayor, a councilman, a judge, a police captain—he would be a hunted man. If he wasn't extradited back to the US, if he was protected by a drug cartel, he would eventually be assassinated…somehow, someway. At least, that's what she wanted to believe.

Drake stepped forward. "For one of you…it's your lucky day. I've been told to keep a hostage…just in case." He looked at all of them, a smug smile on his face. His gaze returned to her. "A police detective will do nicely."

Lobo walked up to Duncan, jerking him to his feet. "Everyone. Get up."

"What…what are you going to do?"

"What do you think they're going to do? They're going to kill us."

Roger King didn't move. Dee was on her knees, struggling to stand without the aid of her hands—old and out of shape, she chastised herself. She leaned toward Roger.

"Get up," she whispered.

But why? For what reason? Were the five of them going to charge… hands tied behind their backs? Were they going to fling themselves at Drake and the others? Five men with guns? No. It would be over in a matter of seconds.

If they did nothing, it would still be over in a matter of seconds. For the rest of them. For her? Apparently, she was being spared for a little while longer.

Yeah…it was her lucky day.

CHAPTER SIXTY-SEVEN

Finn could feel the rapid pounding of her heart in her chest and she took a deep breath. It had been ten years since she'd been on the force. More years than that since she'd been in a situation like this… if ever. She tugged at the vest around her neck, pulling it lower. She didn't miss wearing that damn thing.

"There's movement, sir. Something's happening"

Finn looked over at the monitor. Everyone was moving at once. Yeah, something was happening all right.

"Ram the door!" Sparks instructed urgently. "Be ready. Remember…we got civilians in there."

Finn braced herself as the armored truck smashed into the dual metal doors on the side of the warehouse. Gunfire erupted immediately. Both doors of the truck were flung open and she was left alone in the back. She looked around the room, trying to find Dee and Mabanks among the chaos.

* * *

Roger King was seconds away from a bullet to the head when all hell broke loose. Dee was as shocked as anyone to see a SWAT truck crash through the doors. Lobo's automatic rifle began firing and Dee flung herself in front of Duncan Frazier, feeling a bullet rip through her. She collapsed on top of him, squeezing her eyes against the pain.

"Get down! As low as possible," she hissed at him.

* * *

Finn ducked down below the seat and crawled out the back side, ignoring Sparks's directive to "stay the hell down" as bullets bounced off the wall behind her. She saw Drake creeping along the side, trying to slither away. She ran after him, jumping over two bodies...realizing as she did that one of them was John Mabanks.

A bullet whizzed by her head and she instinctively ducked, then continued running. She heard the banging of a door and ran to it. She pushed it open, but stayed inside. Three shots rang out, ripping into the door.

She dove out the door, gun ready as she landed. Drake was running away and she fired twice, but he never broke stride.

"I'm too damn old for this," she muttered as she got up and ran after him.

* * *

Rylee chewed on her lower lip, wondering how long she should wait. The gunfire had stopped, but no one had come out. Should she stay put? Should she wait for Finn? Or should she go in?

She opened the door on Finn's car and got out, trying to see through the fog. She took a couple of steps through the gate, then stopped. She heard footsteps.

Someone was running.

She turned, seeing the shadowy figure of a man running along the fence toward her. Her chest tightened in fear.

It was Drake.

CHAPTER SIXTY-EIGHT

"I'm okay," she managed.

"You lost a lot of blood, Detective. Sparks says paramedics will be here in about a minute."

She looked at the tourniquet he'd applied, then saw the blood. "God…just my arm?"

"You're damn lucky the bone's not shattered."

"Where else? My ass hurts."

He smiled. "Yeah."

"Oh, God…I got shot in the ass?"

"Afraid so."

"I'll never hear the end of that. Where's Finn?"

"She's here somewhere," the officer said. "Now be still."

Dee winced as she shifted back against the wall, watching as Sparks shoved Lobo—hands cuffed—roughly against the truck. Only then did she look around her.

"My God," she murmured.

Bodies and blood littered the warehouse floor. Roger King was covered in red. His face nearly unrecognizable. Next to him was Eric Lawrence, his midsection riddled with bullet holes. Oliver Judge was on the floor, propped up against the wall much like she was. His eyes were open…lifeless eyes. He had a bullet hole in his forehead.

She swallowed, turning away from the sight. Duncan Frazier was sitting next to her, his hands twisting together nervously. She looked at him, seeing fresh tears on his face.

"You okay?"

He nodded slowly, then turned to meet her gaze.

"Why did you do that?"

"Because you're just a kid and you've got your whole damn life ahead of you."

"I'm...I'm not a kid."

"Yeah, you are. You're a kid who just lost both parents." She leaned her head back against the wall, wondering why her arm didn't hurt more than it did. "I don't know how you got involved in all of this or what they promised you...but you're damn lucky to be alive. Don't waste this second chance you're getting."

"They...they came to me at my dad's funeral. They made it seem like I didn't have a choice."

"There's always a choice, Duncan."

"I'm...I'm sorry you got shot. He meant to kill me, not you."

"He meant to kill all of us." She turned to look at him again. "Your father worked hard...had a successful business. But he got greedy."

"I knew what was going on. I'm friends with one of the managers. There was too much money. My dad got mad when I asked him about it."

"Yeah, there was a lot of money. He was making a good living without getting mixed up with Jose Hernandez. Now look what happened."

"Am I...am I going to go to jail?"

"Best I recall, you were tied up like the rest of us. But I tell you what...if you ever pull any shit like this, I'll be all over your ass."

"Yes, ma'am. I won't."

"Good. Because you've got some pizza joints to run, I guess. By the way, my favorite is the Bayside Bomber."

"With the jalapenos?"

"Yeah. In case you want to bring me one at the hospital," she murmured as her eyes closed. "Tell them to hurry, would you? I'm feeling...really faint."

* * *

For several seconds, Rylee stood still, unmoving as Drake came toward her. Then, instead of going back to Finn's car, she ran through the gate toward the warehouse. Barely ten steps into her run, however, she was taken crudely to the ground.

She was surprised that she didn't scream. Perhaps because she knew it was coming. With as much force as she could muster, she rolled them over, kicking him hard with her heels.

"Goddamn you!" he spat as he grabbed her shoulders, forcing her back.

Then he was flung off her; Finn had materialized out of nowhere, tackling him from behind. Rylee scooted out of the way as Finn wrestled with him on the ground. Her heart was pounding so loudly she could hear nothing else. She stood up, her hand shaking as she pulled her gun from its holster.

Drake tossed Finn off him, then scrambled to his feet, but Finn was too quick. She grabbed his ankle, tripping him, making him stumble. Rylee pointed her gun at him, but her hand was trembling too much to pull the trigger. Then Finn jumped on his back, knocking him to the ground once again. In the dark, foggy mist, she could barely make out their shapes.

She heard rather than saw Drake's fist connect with Finn's face. Finn lay still on the ground as Drake stumbled away from her. He turned then, coming toward her.

"Should have let Lobo kill you," he said as he wiped at the blood oozing from his lip. It was only then that he saw the gun she held. He laughed. "Really? I don't think so."

She took a deep breath and squared her shoulders. "Really," she said, her voice shaky, belying the confidence she suddenly felt.

"You're not going to shoot me. You're going to get in the car. We're going to drive off." Behind his back, he produced a gun. "See…I have a gun too. And unlike you, I'm not afraid to use it." He took a step closer, only six feet away now. "Get in the car."

She fired without thinking, hitting him in the shoulder. The gun fell from his hand. He stared at her in disbelief.

"On your knees," she said loudly.

He growled as he charged her, six feet turning to four, three. She fired again, twice, three times. He was upon her, taking her backward to the ground, landing squarely on top of her, nearly knocking the breath from her.

"Rylee!"

By the weight of him, she knew he was dead. Dead weight. His head was against her shoulder and she shoved hard, unable to move him. She heard running…voices. Then he was pulled away and Finn was there, scooping her up in one motion.

"Are you okay?"

Was she? Her body seemed to be shaking, head to toe. "I...I think so," she managed. "You?"

"I think he broke my damn nose."

CHAPTER SIXTY-NINE

"Lobo was the only survivor? Why the hell didn't you shoot him too?"

Sparks shook his head as he walked with her down the hallway. "It's probably a good thing you quit the force, Finn." Then he grinned. "Your nose is quite attractive, by the way."

"It must be. You're like the fourth person to say that."

He laughed. "I'm surprised they kept you, though. Something serious?"

"No. It wouldn't stop bleeding, that's all."

"Hurt?"

"Hurt like hell when they straightened it," she said, touching the bandage.

He nodded. "So where's your girlfriend?"

She frowned. "Girlfriend?"

"Rylee."

"She's not my girlfriend."

"Oh, come on. I saw that hug last night." He leaned closer. "I saw the kiss too."

She felt her face blush and she turned away from him. Yeah... there'd been a hug. And a kiss. That had been when she and Dee were being hauled away in an ambulance. Rylee had to stay behind. Because Rylee had shot a man.

"Has she been by yet?"

"Yeah. She came by last night. Or early this morning, I guess."

Rylee had come to her room, closed the door and—without a word—had crawled into bed with her. And cried. And cried some more. Finn had held her tightly, letting Rylee cry on her shoulder. She was obviously exhausted, both mentally and physically. It was two in the morning and when her tears finally dried up, she'd fallen into a deep sleep. Finn had simply held her, letting her mind go blank, pushing out all thoughts as her eyes closed, letting Rylee's even breathing lull her to sleep as well.

When a nurse woke her at six, though, Rylee was gone.

"Is she going to pick you up?"

Was she? Finn hadn't called her. For that matter, she didn't even know where she was. Did she go to her apartment? Or did she go by the house to check on Smokey?

"I don't know," she answered honestly. "I want to check on Dee. I'll worry about a ride later."

He nodded, then handed her a card. "That's my cell. Call me if you need a ride. Better yet, call me anyway. We'll grab a beer sometime, catch up."

"Yeah...we kinda lost touch, huh." She smiled at him. "Have I thanked you for...well, for everything? Last night was all kind of a blur."

"Just doing my job, Finn. We didn't exactly save the day, though."

"We were late to the party, yeah. At least it wasn't your guys who killed those hostages."

"It makes no sense. Why kill them?"

"It'll all come out, I suppose."

"You know, don't you?"

"Yes. I imagine Dee and I will be meeting with the FBI soon. It's a damn mess, I'll tell you that."

"It's maybe better I don't know." He touched her shoulder. "You call me."

"I will. Thanks, Sparks."

She watched him walk away, then took a deep breath before pocketing his card. Yeah, she'd probably call him, catch up, like he said.

She walked on, finding Dee's room. She knocked lightly, then pushed the door open. Dee was awake and she turned her head, smiling as she motioned for her to enter.

"About damn time you came by," she said, her voice raspy. Then she saw the bandage across her nose. "Yeah…looks good, Finn. He got a good punch in."

"That bastard," she murmured. "I just got sprung. How long you in for?"

Dee closed her eyes and smiled. "I hope a really long time. You should see my nurse."

Finn laughed. "Got a cutie, huh? I wasn't so lucky."

"Not only cute, but she's flirting with me. A lot."

"Yeah, right. You look a hot mess."

Dee groaned. "God…don't say that." She leaned her head back against the pillow. "My hair's all over the place, right? I suppose surgery will do that."

She pulled a chair closer and sat down. "How do you feel? Sparks said your arm was tore up pretty good."

"Yeah, but the doc said it looked worse than it was. He said I should recover, but at my age," she said, pausing to roll her eyes, "I'll lose some strength. Good news, the bone was only nicked. No bone graft, no additional surgeries."

"Good." Then Finn grinned. "And the other injury?"

"What about it? I got shot in the ass. It hurts worse than my arm."

Finn's smile faded. "Mabanks?"

Dee met her gaze. "It was pretty awful. I…I felt like…well, like when you hear about terrorists kidnapping someone, then holding them to be executed." She looked away, staring at the wall instead. "They shot Stevens. He was trying to negotiate with them. Then Barbara— Mabanks' wife—kinda went hysterical. They shot her. Then…well, the captain…" She looked back at her. "I had resolved… well, I knew what the end would be for all of us. I was…numb, I think." She swallowed. "How did you know where we were?"

"Something I heard Drake say when we were on the boat."

"Oh, that's right. You took a swim in the bay. How was it?"

"Cold."

"Rylee?"

Finn shrugged. "She's okay, I guess."

"You guess? She killed a man. She's probably going through all sorts of hell."

"Yeah…I'm about to call her."

Dee leaned back against the pillow and let out a weary breath. "She'll be good for you, Finn. Don't run her off."

"Not going to run her off." She paused. "We...we kinda have a history. I didn't tell you, but...well, early summer, we kinda..."

"You kinda what?"

"We met at a bar."

Dee smiled. "You *slept* with her? You old dog. I thought there was something too familiar between the two of you."

"I think...I think it could be special." She met Dee's gaze. "I've never had that before, you know. And she's young. But..."

"She's thirty, you're forty...that's nothing. And from what I remember, it's really nice to have someone, Finn." She flipped her hand over, and Finn took it, feeling Dee squeeze her fingers. "Thanks for coming by. Now get the hell out of here and go find her. It's time for me to buzz my cute nurse."

Finn smiled at her. "Tell her your ass hurts. Maybe you'll get a massage or something."

"Good idea. I'll try it."

Finn squeezed her hand before standing. "I'm really glad you're okay, Dee. As you know...me and friends..."

"Yeah. Soon as I get sprung from here, we'll do dinner. I'm not going to disappear, Finn. And I won't let you disappear either."

Finn nodded. "Thanks."

"Now go find Rylee."

CHAPTER SEVENTY

Finn's house didn't look much different in the light of day than it had last night. Rylee drove past three police cars, then pulled into the driveway, the gate wide open as they'd left it last night. What was different this morning was the crime scene tape that was up. The officers' bodies had obviously been taken, but their car was still there, doors open, several cops still milling around.

She stood inside Finn's living room, feeling the breeze hitting her as it blew in through the opening where the bay window once was. The morning was still cloudy, but the fog had disappeared.

"Ma'am…I'm sorry, but you shouldn't be in here. We're still processing."

She nodded at the officer. "Just picking up a few things. And a cat," she added, wondering how Smokey had fared. "Be out of here in a second."

She'd already gone by her apartment and showered and changed into clean clothes. Actually, she'd gone to her apartment and had a good cry. Another one.

She'd killed a man. A monster of a man, but nonetheless, she'd pulled the trigger. During the interviews last night, she'd been calm, collected. When the police had learned that Drake was the one who killed their two officers, they'd gone out of their way to make her as comfortable as possible. In fact, by the time it was all over with, she'd been treated more like a celebrity than anything else.

But then it hit her. She killed a man.

She'd gone to Finn…who else was she going to go to? But she didn't want to talk. Thankfully, Finn never questioned her. She opened her arms, and Rylee had buried herself there and cried.

She wasn't sure why she'd left this morning…left before Finn woke up. As she'd stood at the door, watching Finn, she had a recollection of that morning at the motel. It was much the same, wasn't it? Whatever she got from Finn that night, it wasn't just sex. She knew it then as she knew it now.

It was almost as if they were connected somehow, on another level. As if they'd known each other all their lives. Or as if they'd known each other in a previous life.

That thought made her smile and she finally moved down the hallway toward Finn's bedroom. A previous life? No, she wasn't one of those crazy people who believed things like that. No.

But…there was *something* between them that couldn't be explained. One hot summer night in June couldn't have bonded them like they were. And working together a month now, that surely wasn't enough time.

A month? She pulled her phone from her pocket, her brows drawn together. December 22. Already? Christmas was upon them and she hadn't even noticed. Christmas…and her birthday.

Yes, she supposed she had noticed. A few Christmas lights here and there, decorations in yards. It was different in Corpus, though. It was warm and tropical some days, cool and damp others. Not the Christmas weather she was used to.

Maybe that was it. Or maybe it had just snuck upon her. It wasn't like they'd had idle time the last few weeks.

She pushed open Finn's door, finding Smokey curled up against the pillows on the bed. She raised her head, startled.

"Hey, girl…just me." She sat down on the bed, rubbing Smokey's head, listening to the comforting purr. "How about we go back to the office, huh?"

She didn't know where else to go. They couldn't stay here. And her small apartment? No. They'd all be more comfortable at the office. It felt a little awkward to be rummaging through Finn's drawers and closet, but she knew Finn would need clean clothes. Two pairs of jeans, some T-shirts, two sweatshirts, a sweater. She found her drawers to be as neat as everything else in the house and hesitated only a second before grabbing undies and a couple of bras.

She had Finn's car. She supposed after she had Smokey settled at the office, she'd head back to the hospital. Surely they wouldn't keep Finn. She'd been surprised that they'd kept her last night, but it was probably more of a precaution than anything else.

She should have stayed. She should have asked Finn last night how she was. She shouldn't have run again.

She didn't really run, though. She just wasn't ready to talk.

Because she killed a man.

It hit her again like a ton of bricks...her chest tight, her heart aching. She sunk down onto Finn's bed, burying her head in her hands as her tears came again.

She killed someone.

CHAPTER SEVENTY-ONE

"I'm...I'm fine. I'm all cried out, I think."

Finn shoved her hands in her pockets, watching as Rylee unloaded the two grocery sacks, putting things into the fridge. Her hands moved in a nervous motion, but Finn didn't say anything.

"And I thought I'd cook. Something simple, but still...not takeout." She paused in her task. "Okay...I'm not fine. I...I can't shake it. I can't..." Rylee looked at her, wiping at a tear that escaped. "I feel...I feel...heavy," she said, touching her heart.

"I wish I had some words of wisdom for you, but I don't."

"You ever...you ever kill anyone?"

Finn shook her head. "I did shoot a suspect once. Third year on the force. He was eighteen, just a kid. I stayed at the hospital that whole first day, so afraid he'd die."

"What did he do?" Rylee asked in a whisper.

"Robbed a convenience store...had a gun." Finn moved to her and pulled her into a tight hug. "You did nothing wrong, Rylee. You did everything right." She closed her eyes, feeling Rylee cling to her, hearing her quiet tears. "I should have been the one to shoot him, not you. I lost my gun in the shuffle and I...damn, it happened so fast."

"He was going to kill me," Rylee murmured. "I didn't do anything wrong."

"No. You did everything right."

They stood there in Sammy's old kitchen, holding each other tightly. Finn let her mind go blank, keeping her eyes closed as Rylee moved deeper into her arms. Seconds passed...maybe minutes. Then Rylee loosened her grip on her, finally pulling out of her arms. "Thank you. That was nice." She wiped at her eyes. "Okay. I think I'm cried out now."

"Yes. That was really nice." Finn smiled. "So...you're going to cook, huh?"

"I am." Rylee touched her face. "You look...lovely."

"I have bruises under both eyes and my nose feels like it's twice as big as it should be. Not lovely."

Rylee tilted her head. "Do you think it's going to hurt when we kiss?"

"Are we going to kiss?"

Rylee leaned forward, touching her lips lightly with her own. "I want to kiss. I want to make love, Finn. I want to be with you. I *need* to be with you."

Finn met her gaze. "Okay...it won't hurt a bit."

* * *

It was different...yet it was almost the same. Different...it was noon, not midnight in some dark hotel room. The same, though, as she pulled Finn close, their skin touching...the act seeming more familiar than it should.

It had been six months. It could have been yesterday.

"I've thought about this so often," she whispered against Finn's lips. "So often."

And she had. At night, alone, when she closed her eyes...the woman from the bar—the woman who had taken her breath away—would haunt her dreams. Who would have thought that fate would throw them together again?

Finn rested her weight on top of her, nudging her legs apart as she settled between them. Rylee opened willingly, pulling Finn as close as possible. She closed her eyes, feeling Finn's tongue shyly meet her own.

Shy? No. There was no place for shy between them. Rylee let her tongue dance with Finn's and she heard the quiet moan that mingled with her own. This wasn't the time to be shy and it wasn't the time for words. The throbbing between her thighs begged for attention and she arched against Finn.

But Finn wouldn't be hurried. She left her mouth, her kisses trailing across her breasts, lips nibbling softly before capturing her nipple. Rylee moaned with pleasure, lying back, letting Finn take her time in loving her. But still…wishing she'd hurry.

Finn surprised her by leaving her breast, coming back to her mouth, kissing her almost tenderly.

"I feel like I'm dreaming."

"You're not dreaming." She smiled against Finn's lips. "Although I admit, this has been a dream of mine since June."

"I wish you hadn't left that morning."

"God…me too." She pulled Finn back to her mouth. "Stop talking."

It was Finn's turn to smile against her lips, but she said nothing else. Instead, her hand moved between them, sliding slowly across her skin. Rylee's hips rose, seeking that hand, those fingers.

Her head rolled back as Finn entered her, her eyes slammed shut. Yes, she could be dreaming, she thought. She'd pictured this moment so often—Finn inside her, her wetness spilling out. But no, she wasn't dreaming. She opened wider, hips arching, bringing Finn even deeper inside her.

She was panting now, her breath coming in short bursts, her hips rocking, her hands clutching Finn to her. Finn's mouth was nibbling at her neck, finally moving to her ear, her tongue delving inside. She moaned loudly, her body on fire as Finn pounded into her. She lay back, her mouth opened wide, her eyes closed, her body nearly convulsing when her orgasm hit. She squeezed her legs tight, holding Finn inside, her scream muffled as she buried her head against Finn's shoulder. Little by little, she relaxed…her legs opening, her arms loosening their grip, her hands falling away…

Was she dreaming?

Soft, light kisses on her skin, murmured words she couldn't decipher, eyes that refused to open.

Was she dreaming?

No. Her heart felt full…felt about to burst open. She tried to smile through the tears, but she couldn't. She tried to stop the tears…but she couldn't do that either.

It was simply too much.

CHAPTER SEVENTY-TWO

The crime scene tape had been removed, and from the outside, her house looked perfectly normal. The inside, however, was a different story.

"I didn't notice the bullet holes in the wall yesterday," Rylee said as she walked in ahead of her.

Finn had already called someone to repair the bay window. They would be there at one, they'd said. Now she supposed she'd have to hire someone to patch and paint the walls. Maybe now would be a good time to change colors. Maybe Rylee would like to have some input.

Her gaze went to the bar and she felt her heart clench, her breath nearly leaving her. Her father's glass lay on the top, shattered. She walked over to it, staring in disbelief. She didn't realize she had tears running down her face until Rylee touched her arm.

"The...the glass," she said stupidly.

Rylee rubbed her back soothingly. "I'm sorry, Finn. I know how much it meant to you."

Finn nodded and picked up a piece, her tears dripping on it.

Rylee said nothing, just kept a hand on her back as she cried. Finn tried to make the tears stop. She hadn't cried in forever. Not until

Sammy died. And now? It was ridiculous to cry over a damn broken scotch glass.

"You never cried when he died, did you?" Rylee guessed.

No. She wasn't really crying over the broken glass, was she?

"I was too angry to cry. Angry at her. Angry at him." She dropped the glass back on the bar and wiped at her tears. "He was never around. I didn't get to be with him much. This was going to be our chance. To work together...to be together...finally." She rubbed the corners of her eyes, then shook her head. "God...sorry."

"Nothing to be sorry for."

"Damn near twenty years ago. Too late for tears now." She cleared her throat. "I'm fine."

Rylee turned to face her. "Tears make us human, Finn. Tears can be cleansing, healing."

Finn met her gaze, remembering the tears in Rylee's eyes when they'd made love, remembering the nearly desperate hold she'd had on her. She hadn't questioned the tears then, hadn't even acknowledged them.

"And your tears last night?" she asked gently.

"Do you really want to know?"

"Yes."

Rylee nodded. "Not...not joy, exactly. Being with you, after everything that had happened...I had a sense of...of wholeness. A sense of being home. It was overwhelming." She looked away for a moment, then back at her. "I don't believe in previous lives and all that. I should say, I *didn't* believe, but there was such a feeling of...of relief almost. Like I'd lost you in a previous life and had been searching for you—my soul had been searching for you. That night at the bar...it was like I *knew* you. Inside, I knew you." She touched her heart. "I can't explain it other than that."

Was that how it had been? Finn had looked across the bar and the very breath had been sucked from her chest. Was that what it was? Had their souls reconnected somehow, as Rylee was suggesting? Or was it simply a matter of two lonely people finding each other and reaching out?

Rylee squeezed her arm and smiled. "I didn't mean to render you speechless with all that. I'm not asking you to marry me or anything, you know."

"Yesterday...yesterday was a good day. And last night...I feel close—connected—too. More so than our time together warrants." She touched Rylee's cheek, which had the barest trace of a bruise on it.

"I've always been alone. I've learned to embrace it. But now...I don't want to be alone anymore."

Rylee tilted her head, studying her. "So like...we can spend the night together sometime?"

"A lot of the time."

Rylee smiled. "And Smokey?"

"Yeah, I figure you're a package deal, right?"

"Right." Rylee's smiled faded, and she moved closer, hugging her. "I'm really sorry about the glass, Finn."

"Yeah...I'm going to miss it. It was like a friend," she admitted.

"Maybe you could go see your mother...maybe she's got another one that was his."

Finn took a deep breath. "I know what you're trying to do, Rylee... but I think it's too late to reconcile with my mother."

"It's not too late. As long as she's still here...it's not too late."

"I used to think that I hated her." She nodded. "I *did* hate her. I blamed her."

"I know. But as you said, it's been almost twenty years."

Finn shook her head. "I don't know if I can."

Rylee didn't push. "Well, think about it." She pointed toward the glass, ending the conversation. "I suppose we should clean this up."

Finn nodded, but her mind was still on her mother. Go see her? Talk to her? God...could she? After all these years...could she?

CHAPTER SEVENTY-THREE

Rylee laughed at the large pizza box sitting on Dee's serving tray. "Really? Pizza Jamboree?"

"It was a gift," she said. "I'll never be able to eat it all. Help yourself."

Rylee surprised her by leaning down and kissing her cheek. "How are you?"

"Better. One more day in here, then I get sprung, thank goodness."

"That's wonderful. We can pick you up."

"That'd be nice. Thanks."

"Who's the pizza from?" Finn asked as she plucked a slice out of the box.

"Duncan Frazier." She pointed to the vase beside the bed. "And these. He sent a very nice note too."

"I guess so. He was the only one to get out of there without a scratch."

"Did you ever find out what his involvement was?" Rylee asked.

Dee shook her head. "From what I gathered, I think Hernandez propositioned him, much like he did Daniel. The FBI's involved so I guess it'll all come out. The best thing he's got going for him is that this thing blew up before Hernandez started flooding him with cash." She raised her good arm up. "But I'm sick of talking about it. I had to sit through nearly two hours of questioning by the so-called detectives who think they broke the case."

"Your partner?" Finn asked around a bite of pizza.

"Ex-partner." Dee eyed her, seeing a relaxed look on her face that she'd not seen before. "So…how are things in your life?" As a blush crept up Finn's face, she laughed. "Good Lord! You're forty years old and you still blush?" She turned her attention to Rylee. "You must be working wonders with her. Look how calm…relaxed she is." She looked back at Finn. "Good sex will do that, if I remember. It's been a while."

This time it was Rylee who blushed. Dee laughed again. It felt good to laugh, she realized.

"Speaking of sex…my cute nurse asked me out."

"You're kidding? Isn't that a violation or something?"

"Just because you're having sex now, don't act all righteous with me. I told you she'd been flirting with me."

"How old is she?"

"Old enough."

"That's wonderful, Dee. We can't wait to meet her." Rylee laughed. "That is, if you trust Finn around her."

"That's debatable."

Finn wiped her hands on one of the napkins, then tossed it down. "So you'll still be here tomorrow? It's Christmas Day."

"Yes, I know. I'm surprised you know that, however. Do you even celebrate?"

"No."

"Figured as much." Dee looked at Rylee. "She didn't even know it was Thanksgiving when I showed up with a meal."

"We're not actually celebrating Christmas tomorrow," Rylee said. "It's my birthday. And I've never celebrated my birthday before. It was always Christmas and my birthday was an afterthought."

"So what are you going to do?"

"Fancy hotel. Jacuzzi. Room service," she said with a grin. "And a cake. No Christmas. Just birthday."

"I'm kinda jealous."

Finn closed the box on the two remaining pizza slices. "So how long will you be out of work?"

"Hard to say. I've got to suffer through physical therapy first."

"I guess the department is still reeling, huh? What with Mabanks and all."

She nodded. "I'm not sure if they're more shocked by his death or what he was mixed up in. He was always so straitlaced, by the book…family man. His image has been tarnished, that's for sure." She looked at Finn. "I do hate it. He had a good, honorable career…up until all of this."

Finn nodded. "Yeah, but he made the choice, Dee. They all did."

"And most of them paid the ultimate price. The Petersons were the only two of the group to survive, but their lives are probably in shambles. You can't turn on the news without them being mentioned. I won't be shocked if Lori files for divorce."

"I haven't watched the news. You get any good press?"

"A blurb as being injured in the raid, nothing more, thankfully. I keep expecting a damn reporter to come up here and demand an interview."

"Well, good thing you've got a cute nurse watching your back."

Dee grinned. "I hope she's watching more than my back."

CHAPTER SEVENTY-FOUR

Rylee laughed, then clapped her hands as Finn came to the end of the Happy Birthday song, all the while standing in nothing but her navy undies, holding a massive cake with, yes, thirty candles. By the time she finished singing and put the cake down, only twenty-eight were still burning.

Rylee didn't give her time to light them again. She took a deep breath, blowing out all of the others on the first try.

"Did you make a wish?"

"Of course." She walked around the table, hugging Finn tightly. "Most of it has already come true. Thank you for a wonderful birthday."

"You're welcome. It's been pretty fun for me too."

Rylee pulled away from her. "Get back in bed. I'll bring you some cake."

"I haven't opened the champagne yet."

"Let's save it for later," she said as she was already cutting into the cake.

They'd gotten to the hotel yesterday afternoon. They hadn't left the room yet...not that she expected them to. They'd made good use of the Jacuzzi tub and room service. Finn had surprised her with quite an elaborate breakfast this morning. Much more food than they could possibly eat; light and fluffy blueberry pancakes that she'd drowned in maple syrup, gourmet sausages on top of buttermilk biscuits that were smothered in cream gravy, scrambled eggs and crispy strips of bacon, a fruit bowl with the biggest strawberries she'd ever seen, orange juice, and a pot of rich, roasted coffee. They'd stuffed themselves silly, then had crawled back into bed, cuddling and kissing until they'd fallen asleep again.

Noon had brought the cake and champagne in an ice bucket, along with thick club sandwiches of ham and turkey. She'd eaten only half of hers, saving room for the cake. She cut a large piece now, smiling at Finn who was propped up against pillows.

"Just so you know, I've gained at least five pounds today alone."

Finn rubbed her flat stomach. "I think I did too."

"You could stand to." She paused. "It's nice to see you this way."

"What way?"

"Relaxed. Smiling. Content."

Finn nodded as she took the cake from her. "I feel good. You make me feel good."

Rylee got in beside her, then leaned over and kissed her. "Thank you. You make me feel good too." She wiggled her eyebrows. "Inside and out."

Finn bit into the chocolate cake, the icing getting caught at both corners of her mouth. "How come you didn't answer your phone earlier?"

"When Mom called? Well, we were kinda in the middle of something."

"Mmm. She called yesterday too."

Rylee sat up, crossing her legs, the cake forgotten. "She's upset with me. She's called a lot in the last week or so, but, well, you know, we were kinda busy chasing down bad guys."

"She leave messages?"

"She did. That's how I know she's upset with me. She wanted me to come home for Christmas. In fact, she *insisted* I come home for Christmas."

"You didn't call her back?"

"I texted her the other day, told her I was working and couldn't get away." Rylee held her hand up. "Which was the truth."

"And her message today?"

"Her message today was that she was disappointed in me and that my father was disappointed in me and she hoped I enjoyed spending Christmas alone."

"Wow. No mention of your birthday, huh?"

"No. Like I said, my birthday was always an afterthought." She leaned over and kissed Finn. "That's why this has been so special for me. It's my birthday. It's not Christmas. It's just my birthday."

Finn nodded. "Dee was right, you know. It hadn't really registered that it was Christmas time. I...well, I never celebrated. Didn't put a tree up or anything."

"What about when you were young? At home?"

"Yeah, we did everything, all the traditional stuff. Big tree, lots of presents. I didn't like it so much because it was Christmas...I liked it because my dad was there. He didn't have to run off to the office or leave early or come home late. He was there, all day." Finn looked past her, staring at the wall, going back in time, no doubt. "I've been thinking about what you said. About contacting my mother."

"And?"

Finn looked back at her. "I think maybe you're right. Maybe I should."

Rylee squeezed her leg, letting her hand linger there. "I think that would be good for you...good for her."

"I...I realize how selfish it was for me to disappear from her life. She lost her husband...she lost her daughter too. She had no one. I had no one either, but that was my choice. Being alone wasn't her choice."

Rylee touched her face, looking past the bruising and into her dark eyes. "It's Christmas. Why don't we go see her today?"

Finn shook her head. "Nope. It's not Christmas. It's your birthday."

"Well, we could make an exception, just this once."

"It's your day, Rylee. But...well, maybe I'll call her later. Take baby steps."

"Okay." She picked up her cake again, then paused. "I...I might fall in love with you." She put her cake down again. "Kind of a warning, you know. So you won't be all shocked and everything later."

Finn nodded, her expression serious. "I think I fell in love with you that night. It was like you were always there...with me, just below the surface, just...hanging around." She smiled then. "You don't know how many times I wanted to put my skills to use and try to track you down."

"Why didn't you?"

"Because you left. I didn't think you wanted to be found."

"If I had to do it over again..."

"You'd what?"

Rylee took their cake and set them aside. "Here…let me show you."

* * *

Rylee opened her eyes, wondering what time it was. She didn't remember falling asleep. She only remembered Finn's mouth ravishing her, she remembered her orgasm nearly blinding her, she remembered pulling Finn up to her. She smiled at the memory. Yeah…she'd pulled Finn up to kiss her. That was the last image in her mind.

Finn was leaning against the pillows, twisting something in her fingers. Rylee scooted up closer to her, watching her.

"I fell asleep," she said unnecessarily.

"I did too."

"Is that the key?"

Finn nodded. "It occurred to me that now that I've lost the glass… this is all I have. This key that he left me." She held it up to the light. "It must have been important or he wouldn't have left it." She folded her hand around it. "A key to something…I have no idea what. I suppose I'll never know."

Rylee leaned her head against Finn's shoulder. "Maybe your mother might know. Maybe it was something—a locked box or something—at the house."

Finn opened her hand, holding the key again with her fingers. "Maybe it's something else entirely," she said quietly.

"What do you mean?"

"Maybe it's for something I had all along…something I've never given to anyone."

Finn took her hand and opened it, placing the key on her palm. Rylee looked at her questioningly.

"Maybe it's the key to my heart."

Rylee felt her own heart melting. "Oh, Finn….that's…that's so sweet."

Finn smiled and looked a little embarrassed. "I'm fairly certain I've never been called sweet before."

"Sweet…romantic. Adorable." But she handed the key back to Finn. "I've already picked the lock so I don't really need a key." She kissed her softly. "Thank you. You keep it. Someday…you'll find what it opens."

They lay together…legs touching, shoulders touching, heads touching. Finn folded the key up again in her hand and let out a contented sigh.

Rylee closed her eyes…a smile on her face. "By the way, I lied earlier."

"Oh?"

"When I warned you that I might fall in love with you." She took a deep breath, the smile still on her face. "Too late."

Bella Books, Inc.

Women. Books. Even Better Together.

P.O. Box 10543
Tallahassee, FL 32302

Phone: 800-729-4992
www.bellabooks.com